Take Me There

Take Me There

P.F. KOZAK

APHRODISIA

KENSINGTON BOOKS

http://www.kensingtonbooks.com

APHRODISIA are published by

Kensington Publishing Corp.
850 Third Avenue
New York, NY 10022

ISBN-13: 978-0-7582-2271-8
ISBN-10: 0-7582-2271-8

First Kensington Trade Paperback Printing: November 2007

10 9 8 7 6 5 4 3 2 1

Printed in the United States of America

Acknowledgments

Thank you to my husband, whose constant love, infinite patience, and exceptional intelligence support me in my writing and in my life. From my heart and soul, thank you to IK. You're the inspiration that gets me from here to there. Keep dangling that carrot, it's working! And to my Burning Love, Hot to Trot team, *alla famiglia! Ti amo!*

Prologue

How do I know you are with me?
The same way I know
There are flowers in the room
Before I ever see them.
The same way I enjoy a cool breeze on my face
By closing my eyes.
Your scent is as familiar to me
As evergreen at Christmas
Or fresh mown grass on a warm summer's day.
Your essence aerates in my throat
As would coriander and ginger, with a hint of musk.
You come to me on my breath
And fill my senses with your presence.
You come into my blood
And flow through my heart like molten light.
How do I know you are with me?
I know just as surely as I know I am alive!

—*"How Do I Know"*
P. F. Kozak

Chapter One

Someone shouted, *Turn the wheel, NOW!* But there was no one with her. Presley opened her eyes and saw the sixteen-wheeler in her lane. Or was she in his lane? Sleep confused her thinking and slowed her reflexes. Suddenly, the steering wheel wrenched from her hands and turned sharply to the left. She lunged forward as shafts of wheat surrounded the car. Her head hit the hard plastic, and everything went dark.

Presley looked down. She saw her car in a wheat field, with a body slumped over inside. It took a moment before she realized the body was hers. The same voice that shouted at her earlier spoke again.

You must go back, it is not yet time.

Presley turned to look behind her. Instinctively, she tried to shield her eyes from the bright light, but her arms did not move. *Who are you? I can't see.*

Who I am does not matter. You must go back.

Presley knew he told her the truth. But she felt so peaceful, and free. *I want to stay here.*

You cannot! It is not time.

Who are you? Presley moved closer to him. With speed she did not understand, she rushed into the light that surrounded the disembodied voice. A feeling of euphoria engulfed her as she reached for him.

When they touched, her whole being shook with sensation, an orgasmic bliss like none she had ever known. She knew him! His essence flooded her soul just as his name formed in her mind. *Vadim!*

My Ninotchka, you cannot stay!

Searing heat ripped her heart when he spoke her name. But it wasn't her name, was it? She tried to tell him, *My name is Presley, Presley Knowles.* But the words stayed in her mind. With the dizzying sense of spinning out of control, she fell backward toward the wheat-covered car.

When Presley woke, her head throbbed. Gingerly touching her forehead, she felt a bandage. She slowly turned her head and realized she lay alone in a hospital room. Forcing her focus away from the pain, she closed her eyes and whispered, "Vadim?"

She heard his voice in her mind. *I am here, precious one. You must rest. Quiet yourself and sleep. I will help you.*

Even with the pain in her head and the need to sleep, she managed to ask, "Why wouldn't you let me stay?"

My Ninotchka, you cannot yet be in this place with me.

She whispered to him again, hoping he heard her. "Vadim, please, I need to be with you."

Ninotchka, you know not what you ask of me. Sweet Lord, by all that's holy, how can I refuse her?

Vadim comes to Presley, continue reading
Presley goes with Vadim, turn to page 10

Presley floated in a timeless void, as though drifting on a cloud. Even with her mind fogged with the haze of sleep, she thought someone must have opened a window. She could smell something. Just as the wind would carry the scent of lilacs into a room, so did this fragrance saturate the air around her bed.

But it was not sweet like flowers. It smelled more like a blend of coriander and ginger, with a hint of musk, a deeply rich, masculine odor. As the scent intensified, she began to taste it. The aroma welled up in the back of her throat and she aerated it, just as a cat aerates scent through its mouth.

She inhaled deeply, trying to draw in more of it, whatever it was.

She heard his voice again, this time from beside her bed. "Ninotchka . . ."

Presley fought the pain in her head and forced her eyes to open for a moment. She thought she glimpsed a large man with long hair and a beard standing beside the bed. Closing her eyes again, she muttered, "You aren't real."

Oh, but Ninotchka, I am. The bed shifted as Vadim lay down beside her.

Presley whimpered. "My head hurts so much! It's making my stomach sick. Get a nurse, I'm going to throw up!"

Ninotchka, be still. I will see to you. Presley heard him speak even though he made no sound. His voice cut through the pain inside her head.

She wanted to ask him what he would do, but couldn't make the thought congeal into words. She only managed a whispered, "Vadim."

Shhhh, my beautiful one. I do not have much time here with you. Allow me to help you while I can. Brushing her hair away, he placed his hand on the bandage and gently rubbed her forehead. As he did so, the throbbing in her head subsided and the nausea calmed.

"Whatever you're doing, it's helping. It doesn't hurt nearly as much now."

Quiet now. The injury is severe. Allow the healing to penetrate deep into your skull.

Vadim continued to stroke her head, lulling Presley into a

dreamy haze. When he threaded his fingers through her hair, her scalp tingled. Then he traced a line down her face. She felt him tremble as he touched her cheek. *You are even more beautiful now than you were before.*

Before what? She tried to say the words, but could only think them. He still answered her, speaking to her silently.

Before this time, in a different place.

I don't remember.

That is a good thing, Ninotchka. The memories would only cause you distress.

Who are you?

I am one who cares for you. Whatever else is of little consequence.

Says you!

Is that not obvious?

Shit, this can't be real! But, what the fuck? It's the best damned dream I've had in a long time. Presley shifted, moving closer to him. When her body touched his, euphoria washed away the remaining pain. *My God, this feels fantastic! These drugs are incredible!*

A deep rumble of laughter filled her, laughter that came from the man lying beside her. Imbedded in the sound came the thought, *I assure you, dear heart, what I have to give you is not an opiate.* As the ripples of amusement faded, she heard him say, *The centuries do not change some things. Even now, your expression delights me.*

Presley snuggled in closer. *You smell so fucking good. What cologne are you wearing?*

Do women of your time often use such language? It seems some habits have changed! And I correct your perception. I have no odor as you think of it, Ninotchka. What you perceive as fragrance is my energetic signature.

Your what?

Dear one, I must leave soon. The strain of holding manifestation is great. There are better uses of this time than reflecting on my scent.

Damn, this is a dream with attitude! The pain is gone and you're making me horny as hell! That means we'd better get to the fucking part.

I did not know how much your mouth has regressed as you have progressed!

Well, it is the twenty-first century. I don't know where you're from, but things have changed.

I know one universal law that has not changed. How a man takes a woman is still the same.

Presley smiled. Her complete comfort with this man surprised her. *Yes, Vadim, fucking is the same.*

Presley offered no resistance as Vadim's strong hands caressed her. Waves of sensation rolled through her body. He kissed her neck and her face, his whiskers tickling her skin. His long hair fell loosely around his shoulders, making the thinnest curtain around their bodies' growing hunger.

"Vadim . . ." Presley said his name aloud, the sound of her own voice startling her. Realizing this may not be a dream at all, she silently voiced her concern to him. *What if someone comes in?*

No one will know I am here. If I sense anyone close by, I will leave as I came.

Are you a ghost? Or am I hallucinating from the whack I took upside the head?

Again, a rumble of laughter filled her. *Some might call me a ghost. Others might call me an incubus. I am what I am.*

If you are an incubus, are you going to fuck me?

That does not frighten you?

You're kidding, right?

I sense you are inclined to my being on top of you?

Well, yeah!

I, too, am inclined. I have been alone too long.

I've never fucked a ghost before.

My Ninotchka, you have been with me before!

Before Presley could question the last thought she heard, Vadim's mouth covered hers. His breath had the ambrosial flavor of his scent, and his prana intensified her arousal. Somehow, she felt his caresses inside her body as well as outside. There seemed to be no separation between them as his ravenous desire became hers.

He kissed her, his large hands massaging her breasts. The most exquisite sensation moved between her legs as he tickled the sensitized flesh. Presley moaned.

You must mind yourself, Ninotchka. It appears you still vocalize your heat.

How do you know that?

There are some habits that do not die with the body!

Presley couldn't help but smile. *There have been a few complaints from neighbors about how loud I am. It's true.*

I suspected as much.

Presley flexed her fingers against his chest. *Did that habit begin with you?*

I have no doubt. You became vocal only after laying with me several times. As I am about to lay with you again, the sound may carry and cause concern.

Her hospital gown seemed to melt away. Presley had no sense of him rolling on top of her, but somehow he had. She felt his skin against hers, his body hard and solid. When his organ penetrated her, an incredible heat moved into her belly.

She clutched at his arms and murmured, "Vadim, love me again."

Dear God in heaven, I have never stopped loving you.

Fully imbedded inside Presley's body, Vadim did not move for a moment. Then, claiming her with a preternatural bellow, he lifted himself up and lunged back into her. She couldn't tell if the sound filled the room or if she'd heard it in her mind.

The intensity of Vadim's thrusts nearly split Presley in half. Never had she been fucked like this, with the ferocity of a wild animal. Her whole body burned with his fire. She clung to him as a montage of images from another time passed through her mind, pictures she did not recognize or understand. She knew they belonged to him.

His hunger and desire penetrated her body and soul. Losing herself in waves of pleasure, she lost any sense of herself as being separate from him. They had fused in rapturous reconnection.

When Vadim's climax hit, his orgasmic rapture merged with Presley's. As he emptied himself into her, he proclaimed to the heavens, *Sweet, merciful God, you have brought her back to me!*

Somehow she knew to just quietly hold him and wait. At first, he did not move or speak. Then, as the horizon does with the rising sun, Vadim's body began to glow. Presley realized the light seemed to be consuming his body. Light-filled tears mingled with her own when she pleaded, *Vadim, please, take me with you. Don't leave me!*

My Ninotchka, I cannot take you with me. It is not time.

I don't want to stay here without you. Not knowing why the thought came to her, she pleaded with him. *You left me then. Don't leave me again.*

The light that had been his body faded. As the fog of sleep closed in around her, Presley heard Vadim's disembodied voice: *Sleep now, and heal, my beautiful one. On my soul I promise, I will not leave you. I will find a way.*

Go to page 15

We can be together if you come with me. Will you come with me, Ninotchka?

Presley's *yes* formed in her mind. With it came a rush of movement, as though a trap door popped open on top of her head and she flew through it.

Ninotchka! Presley tried to stop but couldn't. Momentum propelled her forward. Vadim grabbed her, and her movement slowed. *Steady, dear one, you are new to this. Focus on me. I will help you to adjust.*

Presley regained her balance, and tried to focus. Vadim still held her. Not really knowing how to touch him, she stretched out her hand. He grasped it. Her focus now completely on the movement of her hand, she squeezed. He squeezed back.

What am I doing?

You are exercising your spirit body.

Why can't I see you?

You can see me. You have to look with your inner eyes.

I don't understand.

Dear one, if you force the focus, the image will elude you. Look gently with your mind's eye, as you would with peripheral vision. The subtle spirit body requires a delicate focus both to see it and to move in it.

There is nothing subtle about you! She couldn't stop the thought as it glared in her mind like a neon sign.

She heard a deep, masculine laugh. It rumbled through her like the feeling of riding in an old pickup truck on a dirt road. *My beautiful one, I never claimed to be delicate or subtle. I am, in fact, predisposed to bluntness.*

She smiled and squeezed his hand again. *No kidding!* She could not explain it, but she felt safe with him. His strength enveloped her. She thought of the movie *Bus Stop* when Marilyn Monroe's Cherie wrapped herself in Bo's leather coat at the end of the film. She felt herself snuggle into the feel of him around her the same way Cherie had into the lamb shearling lining of that coat.

However, Presley's vision remained blurred. She could only see a misty form hovering beside her. *I sure as shit can feel you, but I still can't see you.*

The resonance of Vadim's laughter again moved through her. *Your vision will improve as you become accustomed to a lighter body. I cannot say the same about your language!*

Am I dead?

No, dear one, you are not dead. I told you, it is not time. You will return to the physical form in due course. Your body sleeps now, and heals.

Vadim moved closer to Presley, his intention clear to her. She had no fear; in fact, quite the contrary. The sense of connection to him nearly overwhelmed her. But she still had her wits, and wryly acknowledged her understanding. *You know, I've never fucked a ghost before.*

Vadim's amusement created a luminescent glow around them. *I am not a ghost! I simply do not have a physical body!*

Excuse me, but where I come from, someone without a body is called a ghost! Sure as hell you're not an angel.

Here, my body is as real as yours.

Presley shook her head in confusion. *Where is here?*

Here is where we are.   .

Without thinking about the movement, Presley rubbed her head and muttered, *This is the weirdest fucking dream I've ever had!*

Vadim grabbed her hand and pressed her palm against his cheek. *Ninotchka, I am not a dream. It is a different reality, to be sure, but it is nonetheless real.*

You have a beard. Touching Vadim's face as she had seen blind people do, Presley traced a line up his jaw bone. *And you have long hair!*

I have both. I am the same as the last time you saw me.

Where? I don't remember.

Long ago, in a different time and place.

An image flashed in Presley's mind. She knew it belonged

to Vadim. She saw a young woman stoking a fire in a large stone fireplace. *Who is that?*

That is you, as you were then.

No shit!

Before she could comprehend the speed of his movement, she felt Vadim's body press against hers. *Do all women of your time have such foul mouths?*

Presley fought to keep her wits about her. *Do all male ghosts get hard-ons?*

If they believe they can, I expect they do.

You're really going to fuck me, aren't you?

I have waited a very long time to have you again, Ninotchka. I see your need as clearly as I know my own.

Do we have a bed? With this mist all around, I feel like I'm on the Yorkshire moors in Wuthering Heights.

If you imagine what you want, I will make it for you.

What? You're going to build a bed?

In a manner of speaking. Show me in your mind what you want.

Presley remembered a king-size bed covered with pillows she'd had in a Barcelona hotel. She had spent several hot nights in that bed with a Spanish bullfighter. She focused on visualizing the bed, without the bullfighter.

In utter amazement, she watched the mist clear beside them and the bed in her mind take shape.

How the bloody hell did you do that?

Molding astral matter is like shaping clay. Manifestation of objects is not difficult.

Says you!

Indeed I do!

Before Presley could say anything else, Vadim picked her up and effortlessly put her on the bed. She wanted Vadim. In the transparency of this place, desire could not be hidden.

With the whisper of a thought, the flimsy cloth of her hospital gown disappeared and she lay naked. She still could not see him clearly but could feel his skin against hers, and she could smell him.

Presley nuzzled Vadim's neck to take in more of his scent. *God almighty, you smell good! What is that?*

What you perceive as scent is my energetic signature.

Your what?

My Ninotchka, those questions are not for this moment. It is time for us to consummate our love once again.

Presley wanted to protest, to tell him she certainly didn't love him. She didn't even know him. But as his hands found her breasts and his mouth covered hers, her feelings belied her protestations. She did know him, and as he continued to caress and fondle her, the memory of a long forgotten love cleaved her heart.

My God, Vadim, love me again!

My beloved, I have never stopped loving you.

Vadim's hunger could no longer be contained. He knelt between Presley's legs and lowered himself on top of her. As he penetrated her, the rigidness of his organ sent shock waves through her body. His incorporeal body did have substance here, as did hers.

Never had she known such a soul-wrenching ache as the one that passed through her with his first thrust. The intensity of their connection melted any divisions between them. They shared the same searing heat, the same rapture, the same soul. His sensations became hers and hers became his.

She shuddered violently as her identity dissolved into his. The mist surrounding the bed glowed with light as they consummated their reunion. With Elysium bliss, Vadim proclaimed to the heavens, *She is mine again! Sweet merciful God, you have brought her back to me!*

Vadim stayed on top of her. For a fleeting moment, she wondered why his weight did not bother her. Then she realized, in this astral place, those things didn't matter, not at all. She stroked his hair. At times he appeared to sleep, but she

knew he only lay quietly. His need to remain in her penetrated every fiber of her being. She'd hold him as long as he
needed to be held.

When at last he rolled off of her, Presley felt as though
some part of her own soul had been torn loose. She suddenly
knew he meant to send her back.

Vadim, please, let me stay with you!

Ninotchka, you cannot.

I can't go back there without you, I just can't!

Presley could feel his pain as if it were her own. *My
Ninotchka, I cannot be with you as you are. I am in this
place. You have moved on.*

Vadim, I will not go! Presley understood staying would
mean her physical death. *I won't go back and leave you!*

*Ninotchka, this is not your decision to make. You must
finish the lifetime you have begun.* Presley could feel defiance
welling up inside of him. *You will go back, and I will find a
way to come to you.*

Vadim, you will promise me . . .

*On my soul, my Ninotchka, I will not leave you. I will find
a way.*

Presley could feel herself slipping back. She knew she
could not hold on to him here, in this astral plance. *Vadim,
please . . .* His presence faded as she once again merged with
her sleeping body.

As the heaviness of her body engulfed her, she heard him
say, *Sleep now, my precious one. When you wake, you will
be well.*

Chapter Two

Presley did sleep. She slept peacefully and deeply. When she woke, an attractive doctor stood by her bed, reading her chart.

"Well, hello, Ms. Knowles. You finally decided to come around."

Presley rubbed her head, more from trying to recall her amazing dream than from pain. She felt the bandage. "Where am I?"

"You are in Memorial Hospital. Suppose you tell me where."

Then she remembered. "Abilene, Kansas. I'm writing a story on Eisenhower." Her eyes opened wide. "My laptop! What happened to it? All my research is on it, and the article I wrote."

The doctor stopped her when she tried to sit up. "Everything you had in the car is in the closet with your clothes. I want you to be still until I look you over."

"Please, check if my computer is there. I have to turn in my Ike story. The deadline is next week."

"Calm down. I will look."

Presley settled herself. "I'm calm. Please check for me."

As the doctor went to the closet, Presley noticed a physique worth a second look. "What's your name?" Even in his clinical white coat, he looked good.

"Dr. Hanson." He reached up and pulled her laptop from the shelf. "Is this what you're worried about?"

"Thank God! Is my briefcase there, too?"

"Yes, ma'am. I also see your handbag and suitcase. Everything seems to be here."

"At least you Kansas folks are honest."

"We do our best." He came back over to the bed. Reaching into his pocket, he took out a small penlight. "Stare straight ahead." He pointed the light at her eyes. "Do you want to tell me what happened?"

"I must have fallen asleep driving to the airport. I remember seeing a truck coming at me and then . . . Well, you know the rest."

"I suppose you did fall asleep. The trucker said he would have hit you head on if you hadn't swerved into that wheat field. You are a very lucky lady to still be among the living."

Presley muttered, "It's not yet time."

"Time for what?"

Not really knowing why she'd said it, Presley laughed. "Not time to meet my maker. I have a deadline to make." Dr. Hanson took the bandage off of her forehead. "Ouch! Watch the hair!"

"Sorry." He smoothed her hair back. She thought his hand lingered a bit longer than necessary. "So, who wants a story about Ike?"

"*The New York Times Magazine.* They commissioned a 'What If Ike Were President Now?' story."

"Are you a reporter?"

"Sort of. I freelance and sell my work to news agencies, mostly. Lately, I've been doing more for newspapers and news magazines."

"Sounds interesting." He examined her forehead. "Do you know your body is one for the books?"

"Well, thank you, Dr. Hanson! I'm pleased you noticed."

"Ms. Knowles, I meant how your body has healed itself. I

checked you out when the ambulance brought you into the emergency room . . ."

Presley interrupted, "Again, thank you."

Dr. Hanson smirked. "Can I continue?"

"Certainly."

He rubbed his fingers over her forehead where the bandage had been. "You were in pretty bad shape. You had a gash here the length of my index finger, from where you hit the steering wheel. I stitched you up to stop the bleeding, and monitored you for signs of a concussion."

"I had a concussion?"

"You should have had one. But the CAT scan showed no injury to your brain."

"I don't remember having a CAT scan."

"You slept through it. You've been sleeping for two days."

"Excuse me? I've been in here for two days?"

"Sleeping like a baby."

"Did I have a coma?"

"Ms. Knowles, you have a baby—you can't 'have' a coma. You were never comatose. You weren't even unconscious. The EEG showed only normal, stage four sleep patterns. It seems you were very tired."

"I guess so. I haven't stopped since I flew back from England. Maybe I'm more jet-lagged than I'd thought."

"You might also like to know that the gash I stitched up has healed. There's only a thin red line left." Dr. Hanson picked up a small pair of surgical scissors from a tray by the bed. Presley winced as he removed the stitches. "What should have taken at least two weeks took two days. You've got astounding recuperative powers."

When he finished, Presley touched her forehead. "Then I'm going to live?"

"I would bet my reputation on it." He picked up her arm to take her pulse. "I'll make sure everything is normal. If everything checks out, I'll sign your discharge papers and you can leave."

"Amen!"

"You might want to let Vadim know you are all right."

Presley looked at Dr. Hanson like he had just grown two heads. "I don't know anyone named Vadim."

"The paramedic said you asked for him several times in the ambulance. Once I had you in the emergency room, you said 'Vadim, let me stay' over and over again. You even whispered his name in your sleep."

Presley closed her eyes and rubbed her forehead, trying to remember. "I must have been delirious, or dreaming. I don't know any Vadim."

"If you say so." Dr. Hanson sat down on the edge of the bed. "I'll discharge you this afternoon on one condition."

"And what would that be?"

"That you agree to have dinner with me, so I can keep an eye on you. You could have amnesia if you don't remember knowing Vadim."

"I do not have amnesia! I must have heard the name somewhere and it lodged in my brain." Changing the subject, Presley feigned concern. "Is this dinner with you medically necessary?"

"Of course it is! I want to make sure you don't have any more memory lapses, which could indicate a subdural hematoma."

Presley laughed. "Oh, I see. Tell me, Dr. Hanson, do you have a first name?"

"Yes, Presley, I do. It's Daniel."

"Daniel, isn't it unethical to ask me out before discharging me?"

Daniel picked up the clipboard with Presley's chart and leafed through the pages. He took a pen from his shirt pocket and signed a form. "I've now signed the discharge papers."

"But you haven't examined me yet."

"I can always re-admit you if I find anything."

"Before I say yes to dinner, I should ask if Mrs. Hanson will mind."

"My mother encourages me to get out and have some fun. She won't mind."

"No wife?"

"No wife. Since you have no memory of Vadim, I assume no husband?"

"None."

"Then are we good for dinner? I'll take you to one of Ike's old haunts, Mr. K's Farmhouse."

"I would like that." Suddenly, the closet door that had stood open banged shut. Both Daniel and Presley jumped.

"Well, that's weird." Daniel went to check the door. "I can't imagine how that could have happened."

Presley thought she heard faint laughter. "Dr. Hanson, did you hear that?"

"Hear what?"

Presley closed her eyes and took a deep breath. "Nothing. That door slamming shut spooked me."

"Understandable. We probably have a malfunctioning vent and a gust of air hit it just right. In fact, I could smell something odd by the closet, like someone's cologne. It has to be the vent."

"Of course. That's the most logical explanation." Even as she agreed, Presley felt uneasy. "Let's get on with the exam so I can get out of here."

Daniel wrapped the blood pressure cuff around her arm. "You know, of course, I'm breaking several rules so I can have dinner with you."

"You shouldn't tell me that when you're taking my blood pressure."

He didn't answer as he held the stethoscope against her arm and listened.

Presley teased him, "I bet you're really good at playing doctor."

He peeled the cuff off of her arm. "If you're a good girl and behave while I finish your exam, you might just get a lollipop to suck on when we're done."

"Oh, baby, good thing you already took my blood pressure! I think I might have blown out the gauge with that one!"

Daniel laughed as he pushed a thermometer into her mouth. "Here, Ms. Knowles, suck on this for a few minutes."

Presley sighed. Not being able to say anything, she settled back to enjoy the remainder of the exam. She closed her eyes as Daniel's hands explored her, hoping that more of the same would be on the menu for later that evening. On the heels of that thought, she heard, *Your desire is evident. It should be me, not him.*

As she pushed the thought away, Presley tensed and grimaced. Daniel immediately asked, "Presley, are you having pain?"

Presley gestured toward the thermometer, which Daniel removed. "No, Dr. Hanson. I'm not in pain, except for hunger pains, which I understand you will remedy."

"Are you sure? Ms. Knowles, it is true that I want to have dinner with you tonight. However, my first concern is your health. Lying to me to get out of here could prove dangerous, even life threatening."

Presley's face flushed as she once again heard laughter. This time, she mentally shoved the sound away in anger. Directing her irritation at Daniel, Presley snapped back, "Dr. Hanson, I am not lying to you! I have never felt better in my life. I have no head pain, and goddamn it, I am hungry. I haven't eaten in two days!"

"It seems the patient I'm treating is exhibiting symptoms of acute idiopathic reactive hypoglycemia. Translated, that means you are getting bitchy because you need to eat."

Presley was not amused. "May I please get dressed now?"

"Yes, Ms. Knowles. There is no reason that I can see to keep you here. My shift ends in fifteen minutes. I will come back to get you then."

"Thank you, Dr. Hanson." Softening her tone, she added, "Daniel, I am looking forward to dinner."

"Me, too." He took hold of her hand. "Let me help you stand up."

When Presley stood, she realized for the first time she had nothing on underneath her hospital gown, and that it gaped open in the back. "I guess the mystery is gone, considering you've already seen all there is to see."

Daniel smiled. "Quite the contrary. Why do you think I asked you out?"

"For a doctor, you're pretty sharp."

"For someone who fell asleep at the wheel, so are you."

"Don't you have to sign out or something?"

"Actually, I have one more patient to see before I leave. Do you need a nurse to help you dress?"

"No, I'm all right."

"Then I'll see you in a few minutes. Wait here for me."

"Yes, doctor."

Presley went to the closet and wheeled out her suitcase. Fortunately, she had one clean dress left from her trip to England. After she'd finished her research in Eisenhower's war room at Southwick House in Portsmouth, she'd flown straight to Kansas City.

She'd spent two days at the Eisenhower Library, and had worked on finishing her story for the better part of the last two nights. She had only slept a few hours in several days. No wonder she had fallen asleep at the wheel.

Considering she had wrecked the rental car she'd driven to Abilene from the airport, she had to figure out how to get back to Kansas City. Perhaps her sexy doctor friend would drive her there.

No doubt she would be in Abilene at least another day or two before she could catch a flight back to New York. Accidents always involved paperwork, and that meant time she didn't have. However, Dr. Hanson would be around. Staying in Abilene for a few more days, and nights, might not be so bad after all.

Going into the bathroom, Presley saw her reflection in the

mirror and groaned. Her hair looked as though she had been in bed for two days, and for all the wrong reasons! Presley gently touched the long, jagged line on her forehead and thought of Frankenstein.

Who is Frankenstein?

Presley shook her head and muttered. "Christ, now I'm hearing voices. Maybe I do have a concussion."

You do not have a concussion.

"Glad you think so!" Presley glanced into the room to make sure no one heard her talking to herself. "Either I'm really losing it or I do have brain damage!" Again, she thought she heard laughter.

Ignoring the unsettling thoughts, she quickly wet her hair and attempted to scrunch her auburn curls into submission. Putting on the dress and a little lipstick made her look presentable. She thought about trying to cover the red line on her forehead with makeup but decided against it. After all, Daniel had asked her to dinner after seeing her at her worst. The scar wouldn't matter to him.

Presley stacked her belongings on the bed and waited. Daniel came in a few minutes later carrying a tray.

"What's that?"

"It's a ham sandwich and a glass of orange juice."

"Aren't we going to dinner?"

"Yes, but I don't want you fainting on the way. Let's get your glucose level back on track before we leave."

"Fried chicken is actually what I had in mind."

"Where I'm taking you, they serve the best pan-fried chicken in Kansas. But I'm not letting you set foot outside this room until you eat that sandwich and drink the OJ."

"My, my, forceful, aren't you?"

"When I need to be, I am. My bedside manner depends on the patient."

"I'll keep that in mind."

"I hope you do!" Daniel gathered her luggage. "I'll load your stuff in my car while you eat."

The sandwich tasted better than Presley thought it would. The juice washed it down nicely. Even though she could have gone for seconds on both, she remembered dinner and an evening with her sexy doctor waited. When Daniel returned, she held up her empty plate and asked, "Satisfied?"

"Well, at least for now." The wink following that loaded remark gave her more than a small clue as to how the evening would progress.

A nurse followed Daniel into the room with a wheelchair. "What's that for?"

"That, Ms. Knowles, is for you."

"Dr. Hanson, this really isn't necessary!"

Daniel took the wheelchair and parked it beside Presley. "It's hospital policy, Ms. Knowles. Now, get in the chair and enjoy the ride."

"Oh, for crying out loud!" Presley plopped down in the chair and scowled.

"My mother used to warn me that my face could freeze with a puss on it. I'll pass her sage counsel on to you."

Presley flipped him the bird as he pushed her into the hallway.

Once they were outside, Daniel stopped. "All right, Presley, walk across the parking lot."

"Excuse me! I thought you were playing chauffeur."

"Now, I'm playing doctor. I want to make sure your balance and coordination are okay."

Presley muttered, "I thought playing doctor would happen later." She stood up and took a few steps. "Aren't you coming?"

"That will happen later, too. Right now, I'm watching you walk."

"You're a real comedian! All right, which way am I walking?"

"My car is parked over there, in the parking lot for hospital staff. The silver BMW."

"My, my! A BMW! You must have a successful practice."

Presley straightened her spine and walked toward the car, hoping the view of her behind appealed to him.

Once she reached the car, Presley turned and watched Daniel walking toward her. In a brown sports coat, a beige shirt and perfectly creased brown trousers, he could have stepped out of *GQ*.

He unlocked the car door and opened it for her. "Presley, I want you to know, it is a real kick in the ass finding someone like you in Abilene."

"What do you mean 'someone like me'? I've been sleeping for two days! We haven't even had a real conversation yet."

"Let me ask you something."

"All right, ask away."

"Do you give a shit that I'm a doctor?"

"What kind of question is that?"

"Just answer it. Do you give a shit that I'm a doctor?"

"No, not really. But I do give a shit that you're smart. You also have a nice butt and pecs to die for."

"Exactly!"

"Daniel, I don't know what the fuck you're talking about!"

"You're interested in me, not the M.D. after my name."

"That surprises you?"

"No, actually, it doesn't. You're obviously a lady that's been around. You've probably met some interesting men in your travels."

"A few."

"And I bet you usually let a man know when you're interested. Like this Vadim guy, whoever he is. You got me going when you had an orgasm in your sleep, moaning his name."

"What did you say?"

"You climaxed in your sleep. I thought it was one hell of an erotic dream, except you didn't have any rapid eye movement. Orgasmic dreams usually don't happen in non-REM sleep, but not for you! You rattled the bed you came so hard. Damn, I could write a paper on your libido, from what I witnessed." Daniel smiled and kissed her forehead. "Now you know why I'm interested. Get in the car. Let's go to Mr. K's, have some dinner, and talk."

Presley sat quietly in the car as Daniel drove down old US 40 toward Mr. K's Farmhouse. She did have a dream; she knew she did. Fragments of it flashed in her mind, images she didn't understand. Without meaning to, she muttered aloud, "It isn't time."

"What did you say?" Daniel slowed the car. "Presley, are you all right?"

"Dr. Hanson, I'm absolutely fine. And that's exactly what's wrong."

"I don't understand."

"I'm as fit as the proverbial fiddle, and I shouldn't be." She paused, knowing she had to ask him the question she couldn't get out of her mind. "Will you tell me something?"

"If I can. What do you want to know?"

"Did I die?"

"You're sitting here beside me. Obviously, you didn't die."

"Don't be glib, Daniel. I'm serious. At any point from the accident on, was I clinically dead?"

Daniel didn't say anything as he drove into the restaurant parking lot. He parked the car under a large oak tree. The sky glowed with a glorious Kansas sunset.

"There's nothing like the sun setting over the wheat fields. I have loved it for as long as I can remember."

"You didn't answer me."

"Presley, why are you asking me this?"

"Because I need to know. Did I die?"

Daniel tapped the steering wheel several times before turning to answer her. "This goes against my better judgment, but if you want to know, I'll tell you. The paramedics' report says that when they arrived at the car, you had no pulse. They observed no detectable heartbeat or respiration."

"Did they resuscitate me?"

"They didn't have to. They reported you gasped for air as they removed you from the car. You started breathing again on your own. The EMS crew stabilized you as much as they could until they could get you to the hospital."

Presley laid her head on the back of the seat and closed her eyes. "Then I did die."

"You had a gash on your head and you were in shock. If you had died, you wouldn't be about to have fried chicken for dinner."

Presley wanted to ask more questions, to tell Daniel what she remembered, to ask him what she'd said about Vadim. But, her handsome doctor would probably explain it all away as a hallucination. And she really did need to eat. So she simply agreed with him.

"Yes, of course, you're right. You're the doctor after all."

"That's better. Now, let's get some real Kansas food in you. Doctor's orders!"

Daniel helped her out of the car. Wrapping his arm around her waist, he supported Presley as she walked. Figuring she might as well get the evening moving in the right direction, she asked, "Do you work out? You seem to be in better shape than most doctors I've met."

"As a matter of fact, I do. I also play ball when I can. I went to college on a baseball scholarship."

"You were that good?"

"I was. Actually, I still am."

Presley smiled. "I'll keep that in mind." She felt his arm tighten around her waist as a result of her comment. "If you were that good, why aren't you playing pro ball?"

"I've wanted to be a doctor ever since I can remember. Playing ball paid for school. When the scouts approached me, I said thanks, but no thanks. Then I went to med school."

"My, you are dedicated, aren't you?"

"Yeah. I'm into saving sexy journalists' lives."

"Lucky for me." Even as she said it, Presley's eyes welled up. Squeezing her eyes tightly shut to hold in the tears, she again heard the words, *It is not yet time.*

"Presley . . ." Daniel stopped and turned her around to face him. "You have to tell me if you're having pain. You can't play around with this."

Presley felt the tears slide down her face. "Dr. Hanson, I am physically perfect. You said so yourself."

"Then what's wrong?"

"You wouldn't believe me if I told you."

"Try me."

"Can we please go in and sit down? I could use a glass of wine."

"Certainly. But, the strongest drink you'll get in here is a root beer float."

Presley wiped her tears and forced a smile. "Christ's sake, Dorothy, I am in Kansas, aren't I?"

"Once we see how your food settles, we can go to my place for a drink." Daniel brushed her hair back from her forehead and gently touched the healed wound. "We might even end up over the rainbow before the evening ends."

"As Dorothy said to the Tin Man, 'Where do you want to be oiled first?'"

"My mouth, of course. I understand that feels wonderful. The rest will follow."

Daniel's suggestive joke made Presley laugh, and helped her regain her composure. "Since we've already got this rapport going, Dr. Daniel Hanson, may I ask you something? Would you have a sofa I can borrow tonight? I've got no place to sleep, unless you know a motel with a vacancy."

"I have a guest room. And you're welcome to it. If you stay with me, I can keep an eye on you tonight."

"I was hoping you'd say that."

The waiter recognized Daniel immediately and found him a table in a private corner. Without bothering to look at a menu, Daniel ordered the pan-fried chicken with all the fixings and two root beer floats.

"Are you sure this is a family restaurant?"

"Of course it is. What made you ask that?"

"All the wooden paddles hanging on the wall. It reminds me of a few S&M clubs I've seen."

"Those paddles are a part of Abilene history. You see that one over there?"

"Yes."

"Ike had a paddling with that one for his seventy-fifth birthday, and then he signed it. It is a tradition here, to be paddled on your birthday. Not even the General escaped that one."

"No kidding!"

"No kidding." Daniel reached across the table and put his hand over Presley's. "I'll ask you about those S&M clubs you've seen later. Right now, I want to know why you were crying outside."

"I told you, you won't believe me."

"Christ, Presley, just tell me!"

"All right, you asked for it. I had a near-death experience after the accident. That's why I asked you if at any point they pronounced me clinically dead."

"Presley, I'm sure what happened seemed very real to you. Near-death visions are normal during a severe trauma."

"Excuse me! 'Seemed very real'? In other words, it wasn't real!"

"I didn't say that. To you, it had reality."

"And to you it obviously doesn't! You are dismissing it without even asking what happened."

"Then tell me what happened."

"No, thank you. I'll wait and find a gypsy somewhere who'll listen with an open mind."

"I hate to tell you this. Kansas doesn't have many gypsies."

"I'm sure I'll find some in New York. If not, I'll ask for an assignment in Romania."

"Whatever happened is obviously upsetting you. I'm willing to listen if you want to talk about it."

Ninotchka, you may tell him about me if you wish.

Presley forced herself not to react to Vadim's voice in her head. Convinced Daniel would slap her sweet ass back in the hospital if she sent up any more red flags, Presley changed the subject. "Wouldn't you rather hear about the S&M clubs I've seen?"

Daniel deferred the conversation. "Let's save that for later." Pointing to the table next to them where an elderly couple had just been seated, he whispered, "I don't want to have to perform CPR during dinner."

The waiter brought the root beer floats and the appetizers. Grateful for a distraction, Presley immediately sampled the food.

"These little yellow thingies are yummy. What are they?"

"Cheddar cheese poppers. I can eat a whole plate of them myself. I love them."

"Well, depending on how long the chicken takes, you may have to get more. I'm starving." Presley studied the paddles as she ate. "Do they happen to sell those paddles as souvenirs?"

"No, they are only decoration."

"Pity. I guess we'll have to improvise."

Daniel held up his hand. "I could use one of these, if needed." Then, he playfully picked up a cheese popper. "Open wide."

Presley opened her mouth and Daniel tossed the cheese ball onto her tongue. "Good reflexes, flexible tongue movement, wide oral cavity. Could be an interesting night."

Presley laughed and nearly choked on the cheese ball. She quickly sipped her root beer to wash it down. "I didn't know that was a test."

"You passed with flying colors."

"Have you done this cheese ball test before?"

"Nope, you're the first one."

"Daniel, why are you in Kansas? You aren't like anyone else I've met here."

"I grew up in Abilene. After I got my M.D., I decided I didn't want to be another white coat in a big city hospital. I wanted to come back home to practice."

"Don't you get bored? They roll up the sidewalks here at night."

"I pull three shifts a week in the emergency room. No way in hell am I bored."

"So, you plan on staying here?"

"I expect to. I take it you can't wait to leave."

"I tried to leave. It seems my guardian angel had other plans."

"Lucky for you, and for me. Shall we toast that angel who had other plans?' Daniel held up his root beer float and waited for Presley to do the same.

Presley stared at the foamy mound of ice cream floating in her glass. With images of an imposing man with long hair and a beard in her mind, she picked up her root beer. As she bumped Daniel's glass with her own, her toast could have been a prayer. "Thank you, Vadim, for saving my life."

With tears sliding down her face she sipped her root beer and set the glass down on the table. Dabbing at her cheeks with her napkin, she composed herself and ate another cheese popper.

"I thought you said you didn't know any Vadim."

"I don't, at least not in this lifetime. You wanted to toast my guardian angel. So I did."

"Presley, I don't understand."

"Neither do I. But damn straight, I will!"

Daniel put his hands over Presley's. "Don't take this the wrong way, but as your doctor, I think I have to say it. Once you get back to New York, you may want to consider getting some counseling. Have you ever heard of Post-Traumatic Stress Disorder?"

"Of course I have! I live in Manhattan. We've had an epidemic of it there."

"I think the trauma of the accident may be affecting you. I

can recommend a few doctors who specialize in treating the disorder."

"So, now you think I'm nuts?"

"You survived a serious accident. I'm suggesting you could need some help coping." Daniel lifted Presley's hands and brushed her knuckles against his lips, kissing them gently. "You're a quirky lady, but you are definitely not nuts."

Not wanting to derail the whole evening, Presley sat still and swallowed her annoyance. Sliding her foot against Daniel's calf, she blatantly flirted. "Does being quirky make me a good witch or a bad witch?"

Daniel caught her foot between his legs and squeezed his calves together. Presley's breath caught when she felt the muscular strength in his legs. "If my luck holds, you are a very beautiful, very bad witch," he murmured.

Presley glanced at the elderly couple at the next table, having the uneasy feeling that someone was listening. They seemed oblivious to everything except their food. Turning back to Daniel, she continued to come on to him shamelessly. "Perhaps you should reconsider the guest room offer."

"Are you getting cold feet?"

"My feet are quite warm, thank you. If you want to keep an eye on me tonight, shouldn't we be in the same room?"

"That is certainly an option. We'll talk about it later, over a glass of wine."

Daniel relaxed his grip on her foot just as the waiter brought their dinner. All thoughts of what would happen later became secondary to the mouth-watering fried chicken and mashed potatoes. Presley devoured the chicken, cleaning her plate well before Daniel finished. He offered her his chicken leg, which she accepted and greedily ate.

Along with coffee and homemade apple pie for dessert, Daniel asked for a double order of cheddar cheese poppers to go. By the time the waiter brought the check, Presley's hunger pains had finally quieted.

"Feeling better?"

"Absolutely! Thank you for bringing me here. The food is out of this world!"

"Well, if you're still hungry, we can stop for a Big Mac and fries on the way home."

"Smart ass." Pointing to the small shopping bag sitting on the table, she added, "Those cheese balls you got for me will do."

"What makes you think those are for you?"

"Do you mean to say you won't share your balls with me tonight?"

"It depends on how badly you want them!"

By the time they left, a crescent moon could be seen low in the sky. Daniel's car sat alone in the shadow of the oak tree. Before opening the door for Presley, Daniel turned her around to face him. "I don't want there to be any misunderstanding between us, Presley. You are an incredibly sexy lady, and I'm hoping we party all night. But my first concern is your health. If you don't want anything to happen, you can just crash at my place. It's okay if all you want to do is sleep."

"Now, don't you go getting all noble on me." Presley put her arms around Daniel's neck and pressed her pelvis against his. "I wouldn't have asked to stay with you if I didn't want something to happen."

Putting both hands on her ass, Daniel pulled her tightly against him. The hard ridge in his trousers rubbed against Presley's leg. Leaning in close to her ear, he whispered, "And what would you like to happen, Ms. Knowles?"

Without hesitation, Presley answered. "I want to know I'm still alive. I want to fuck as many times tonight as that jock body of yours can handle."

"I like a woman who isn't afraid to say she wants it." Then Daniel kissed her, a kiss so hot and deep Presley could barely breathe. She clutched the back of his coat as his tongue invaded her mouth. He squeezed her ass cheek with one hand and fondled her breast with the other. His fingers sunk deep into her soft flesh. Presley moaned into Daniel's open mouth.

He pulled his head away and muttered hoarsely, "I want to fuck you right here, against the car." He reached under her skirt and tried to pull her panties down.

Presley tried to think straight. They could be arrested if they got caught fucking in a public place! Putting both hands flat on his chest, she pushed as hard as she could and hissed, "We can't do it here! This is a restaurant parking lot, for fuck's sake. They know you!"

Daniel stumbled backward with the force of her push. When he got his balance, he turned away from Presley. Drawing in a deep breath, he exhaled audibly. "Jesus Christ, you're driving me crazy." Reaching into his coat pocket, he took out the remote and unlocked the car. "I'm sorry. I nearly lost it. You're right, we need to go home." He opened the car door for her.

Presley tried to ease the tension with a joke as she sat down. "Maybe you should find us a wheat field where we can fuck in the car. You have a great back seat."

Daniel leaned against the open door, the bulge in his trousers close to her face. Presley had the impulse to unzip his pants and blow him. Before she could act, he growled, "If you want to fuck in the car, that can be arranged." Then he slammed her door shut.

Once he settled into his seat, Presley spoke her mind. "Daniel, what the fuck is going on?"

"I don't know what you mean."

"You seem pissed off."

"You don't get it, do you?"

"Get what?"

"I wanted you so much I could have raped you. I don't know what the frigging hell happened to me!"

The disquieting answer to that question could not be spoken aloud. The thought that formed in Presley's mind scared her. *Vadim, let him alone! He's hasn't done anything to you.*

Oh, but he has, Ninotchka. He wants you in his bed. Presley nearly jumped when she heard the response, the clarity of

Vadim's voice in her mind shocking her. *It is only right that I share his body when he takes you.*

Forcing herself to stay calm, Presley tried to reassure Daniel. "If not for the restaurant being right here, we could have done it against the car. I wanted to as much as you did."

"Presley, I'm very attracted to you. And I'm not afraid to hit on someone as sexy as you are. But I have never come as close to forcing myself on a woman as I just did."

"I'm flattered!"

"Maybe I should drop you at a motel. I'll pay for the room."

"Not unless you intend to check in with me! You're not the only one who is hot and bothered!"

"You still want to come home with me after that?"

"Unless you want me to sit here and masturbate in front of you, you damn well better take me home with you!"

Daniel chuckled and appeared to relax. "You would diddle yourself in front of me, wouldn't you?"

"In a New York minute!"

"You are definitely a bad witch."

"Wait until you find out how bad."

Chapter Three

Daniel pulled into his driveway, next to a quaint red brick house. He used the remote on his dashboard to open the garage door. His was the last house on the tree-lined street.

"This is a cul de sac, isn't it?"

"Sure is. I like the privacy."

Presley poked him in the side. "Do you date a lot of screamers?"

"Quite the opposite. When I'm pulling a night shift, I need to sleep during the day. Here, I don't have traffic or neighbors bothering me. It's wonderfully quiet."

"You know what they say, all work and no play . . ."

"What do you think I'm doing tonight?"

"Why don't you open the door for me and we'll talk about it?"

Daniel hit the remote again to close the garage door. Another button turned on a light.

"That's a nifty little gadget. If it's also hooked up to a dimmer switch in your bedroom, you've really got something there."

"Maybe you should submit that idea to the remote folks. I'm sure they would get a kick out of it."

Daniel got out and came around the car to open Presley's door. Remembering her impulse in the restaurant parking lot, Presley waited for the right moment to follow through.

When Daniel opened her door, she swung her legs around, but remained seated. Sliding forward just a bit, she positioned herself in front of the ridge in his trousers. She reached up and lightly stroked his bulge.

"You are a bad witch, aren't you?"

"Yes, and your hourglass has run out. I'm going to start on you right here."

Before Daniel could react, Presley unzipped his trousers. Slipping her hand inside, she stroked his organ. Daniel moaned, "Fuck, yes!"

She rubbed him through his briefs until the veins in his cock thickened. Then she undid his belt and pulled his trousers and underwear halfway down his ass. His blood-engorged prick dangled in front of her face.

Before she took him in her mouth, she rubbed his hardness against her face. "I wanted to blow you in the parking lot. Now that we're really alone, I can give you head without getting arrested."

Daniel threaded his fingers through her auburn curls. "Oh, yes, pretty Presley, suck it good."

The musky scent of Daniel's genitals filled her nose as she licked the side of his prick. When her tongue touched him, pearls of pre-cum formed on his tip. She licked them off, and then covered the head with her mouth. Daniel shuddered.

Bracing himself on the hood of the car, he shoved his cock deeper into her mouth. Presley caught the base of his organ in her hand before he choked her. Holding him still, she sucked hard while she circled his glans with her tongue.

Daniel groaned. She let him slide his cock in and out of her mouth while she held the suction. "Sweet Jesus, Presley, no one has ever blown me like this. Do me, baby!"

Holding the base of his cock tightly, Presley continued to suck, licking his glans with every thrust. As she licked him, another odor mingled with Daniel's. The odd scent filled her mouth, overpowering the salty sulphur taste of Daniel's organ.

Sucking Daniel made her clitoris throb, making her hotter than she had ever been while blowing a man. As Daniel's orgasm closed in, the need for her own climax made her wild. She had the overwhelming urge to suck him harder than she had ever done before, just to make herself come. Suddenly she remembered. Vadim had called that odd, spicy odor his energetic signature!

She didn't have time to stop. Daniel grunted loudly and his cock exploded. When the spurts of Daniel's semen filled her mouth, the flavor of Vadim scalded her throat. As she swallowed Daniel's cum, she realized what Vadim had done. His laughter echoed in her mind.

Presley gently withdrew Daniel's now softening organ from her mouth. He still had his eyes closed, breathing like he had just run a hundred yard dash. Shaken, but unwilling to tell Daniel what she knew, she quietly asked, "Are you all right, Daniel?"

It took him a few moments to respond. His breath still ragged, he managed to say, "I'm okay, just flat out like a lizard drinkin'. Where the fucking hell did you learn to do that?"

"You're the one who mentioned I've been around. I've picked up a few tidbits along the way."

"I guess you have! I'm surprised my asshole didn't come out my dick!"

Her inner turmoil notwithstanding, Presley had to laugh. "Dr. Hanson, that may be the crudest comment I've ever heard in this particular situation!"

"Now that's saying something, isn't it? There are some napkins in the glove compartment. Could you give me a few? I need to clean up."

Presley found the napkins. "Allow me." She gently wiped the semen and spit from Daniel's shaft, and dabbed at his glans. Daniel winced. "I'm sorry, did I hurt you?"

"No. In fact, it felt damn good. I'm tingling down to my toes."

Presley could see how much he enjoyed it. His penis had thickened in her hand. "My, my doctor, I'm not the only one with phenomenal recuperative powers!"

"My dear Presley, our night together has only just begun."

The urge to tell Daniel about Vadim welled up in her. She quickly squelched the idea. Given his reaction to her dinner confession, he would surely dismiss anything she told him as a figment of her imagination.

"Hey, there." Daniel took Presley's hand and pulled her up. "You seem a million miles away." Wrapping his arm around her waist, he held her tightly. "Everything all right?"

Swallowing her unsettling thoughts as she had his semen a few minutes earlier, Presley managed a smile. Running her fingers through his thick brown hair, she reassured him, and even more so, herself. "Everything is fine." Wiggling her pelvis against his, she added, "You know your pants are still down?"

"I know that very well. Quite unseemly for a doctor, don't you think?"

"Perhaps you should pull them up?"

Daniel nuzzled her neck. Again fully erect, he rubbed against her skirt. "Were you serious when you said you wanted to fuck as many times tonight as my jock body can handle?"

Presley desperately needed to fuck. For as many times in her life as she had wanted to get laid, nothing could compare to this. The throbbing between her legs had moved into her temples.

"Oh, yes, Daniel, I meant it!" When she answered his question, her pulse pounded with arousal and with fear. Presley opened her mouth and took a deep breath. Vadim's scent had faded, but it had certainly not disappeared. "Do you smell something?"

"Just your perfume. It is fucking intoxicating."

Presley didn't tell him she never wore perfume. Instead, she reached between them and fondled his balls. "How many times can you screw in one night, doctor?"

"My record is three. I expect to break it tonight. You are

one hot lady!" Presley gasped when he reached under her skirt and squeezed her vulva. "Before we go inside, I want to fuck here, against the car. We aren't in the parking lot anymore!"

Daniel moved aside the crotch of her panties and slipped his fingers inside her swollen lips. Presley involuntarily rubbed against his hand and nearly whimpered, "Daniel, I need to come so bad!"

"Pretty lady, you are so fucking wet! Oh, yes, I'm going to make you come hard, just like you did in your dream."

Presley closed her eyes. Vadim could hear everything being said. *Vadim* . . . She knew he would answer if she silently called to him.

Vadim overshadows Daniel, continue reading
Presley challenges Vadim, turn to page 43

Ninotchka?
Don't hurt him!
Ninotchka, my presence will do him no harm. He will only know what it is to be with a woman as he has never been before.
You promise me . . .
On my soul, I swear to you, he will not be harmed.

Presley had the sudden impulse to strip naked. She suspected the impulse came from Vadim. The very idea of making love to both men at the same time inflamed her. "Daniel . . ."

"Yes, pretty Presley?"

"Let me take off my clothes. I want to get naked."

"Oh, baby! You really are a bad witch! Have at it, Elphaba!"

Not caring about being in a garage, Presley stepped to the side and pulled her dress over her head. Watching Daniel closely, she very slowly lowered her panties, just enough to expose the edge of her pubic hair. Then she stopped.

"Don't stop! Take them off!" Daniel growled at her, his voice deeper than before.

Not knowing where she got the courage, she brazenly answered, "I want you naked, too." Their eyes met. Presley saw a silver light in his, and remembered that the same glow had surrounded Vadim. His scent permeated the garage. Making sure Daniel still had control, she addressed him directly. "Daniel, I want to watch you strip, too."

"You are one kinky lady! Maybe I should have borrowed a paddle from Mr. K's."

Presley smiled. She knew that remark had certainly been Daniel's. "Maybe I should help you undress." She kicked off her sandals. With her panties balanced precariously on her hips, she walked the few steps to where Daniel stood, the cool cement soothing her hot skin.

Daniel took off his coat and handed it to her. "Have you ever thought about moving to Kansas?"

"Not once." She tossed his coat on top of her dress and proceeded to unbutton his shirt. Reassured that Vadim had not hurt Daniel, she asked a different question. "How long can you stay?"

Daniel's eyes glowed silver for a moment. "Not long." The voice that answered came from Daniel, but it wasn't Daniel that answered.

"I understand." Presley focused on Daniel and rubbed his bare chest with both hands. "Dr. Hanson, do you know you're a stud puppet?"

Daniel laughed. "Glad you think so. How about this? I'll show you mine if you show me yours."

"Deal." Presley waited until Daniel peeled off his shirt and kicked his pants across the floor before finishing her striptease.

"Christ, your tits are good." Daniel pinched her nipples and Presley moaned. "You like that, don't you?"

"I always have liked it a little rougher."

"You're my kind of lady." Squeezing harder, Daniel asked, "Just how rough do you like it?"

"Rough enough to make me squeal. Dr. Hanson, it's a good thing your neighbors aren't too close."

"Yes, I would say that's definitely a good thing." With no preamble, Daniel turned her around and bent her over the hood of the car. "Do you still want to come, pretty lady?"

"Cunting hell, yes. Fuck me and make me come."

"And do you want me to make you squeal?" Presley shuddered. The timbre in Daniel's voice belonged to Vadim.

Her heart raced as she answered, "Do you think you're man enough to make me squeal?"

"Why don't we find out? Spread your legs wider for me. Let me see your cunt."

Bracing herself against the car, Presley opened her legs and displayed herself lewdly. Knowing Vadim could see her through Daniel's eyes made her crazy. Without warning, Daniel slapped her ass with the flat of his hand. She yelped, both in surprise and in pain. "What the fuck are you doing?"

"You didn't know that in Kansas we spank bad witches before we fuck them? That's how we make them squeal!" His hand again connected with her ass. "I told you at the restaurant I would use my hand. You obviously didn't believe me!"

Daniel continued to smack her. Her cunt itched as her cream dripped down her legs. She groaned with each slap, her ass getting as hot as her pussy. Pleading with him, Presley wailed, "Jesus Christ, I need to come. Fuck me!" She didn't know if she should beg for mercy from Daniel or Vadim. They were both making her wild.

Leaning in close to her ear, one of them said, "Are you ready for it?"

She moaned in shameless agony, "Fuck me, you son of a bitch!"

"Now, let's hear you squeal!" A steel rod slammed into her, threatening to split her in half. She screamed with the shock of the unexpected penetration. With one thrust, Daniel had fully buried himself inside her.

Presley squirmed, being pinned between the hood of the car and the rock-hard body holding her there. Daniel gripped her hips with his hands. With no pretense of gentleness, he pistoned in and out of her, each thrust thumping her against the hood of the car.

The fucking went on and on. Having no idea how long Daniel's cock invaded her pussy, she relaxed into the sensations. Her focus shifted, becoming softer and less controlling. When she did so, something opened inside of her.

An alchemy she could not explain merged her sensations with Vadim's. In turn, Daniel's lust also became hers. When she felt their shared climax closing in, she cried out "Vadim!" in triumphant celebration. As celestial fire burned in her blood, Daniel's voice carried Vadim's hallelujah. He roared to the heavens, "Ninotchka!"

Go to page 47

Ninotchka?

Stay away from him!

You ask much of me, dear heart.

I'm not asking you, I'm telling you! Leave him alone! The thoughts flew from her mind like daggers.

I see your fire, my beautiful one. The man you are with sees it as well. It is having an effect on him.

As I want it to. This night belongs to him, not to you.

I disagree, Ninotchka.

I don't give a shit if you disagree! I'm telling you to fuck off!

Vadim's odor intensified as his laughter rang through her mind. With absolute clarity, she heard, *I will be present this night. If you deny me entry to him, then you must open to me yourself.*

This situation was unconscionable. Here she was with Daniel masturbating her against the car while Vadim looked on. Talk about being caught between a rock and a hard spot! Presley had to do something. *Give me a minute . . .*

As you wish, Ninotchka. But be aware, he has no defense against me save for your willingness to let me in.

I know that already! I'm working on it!

She had to distract Daniel so she could deal with Vadim. The only thing she could think of was to undress. "Daniel, I want to take off my dress so you can suck on my tits."

Daniel squeezed her breasts through her dress. "You read my mind, pretty lady."

Presley thought what she couldn't say. *I didn't read your mind, but someone else did!*

She pulled her dress over her head, and tossed it on the car seat. Daniel did the same with his coat. She also kicked off her sandals. In nothing but her panties, she leaned against the fender of the car, and waited.

"Oh, yeah, mama!" Daniel shamelessly ogled her.

His blatant lechery caught Presley unaware. "Dr. Hanson,

you saw me naked in the hospital. There should be no surprises."

"Dear lady, that was professional. This is personal." He caressed her breast with the back of his hand. "Very personal!" Presley felt his prick twitch against her bare leg.

"Shouldn't you take off your pants before they fall down?"

"Don't mind if I do."

While Daniel took off his clothes, Presley focused on Vadim. *What do I need to do?*

Only what you did before, Ninotchka. Relax, and allow.

You won't bother Daniel?

He will only feel me through you. Nothing more.

All right, I'm ready.

Presley jumped when Daniel palmed her breast. "Is everything all right? You drifted again."

"Everything is wonderful, now that you are naked." She trailed her hand down his chest to his stomach. "Dr. Hanson, you are ripped!"

"Thank you, Ms. Knowles. And you have great tits."

"Works out well for both of us, doesn't it?"

"Sure as hell does!" Daniel pushed her back onto the hood of the car and tugged at her panties. Presley stopped him.

"Not yet!" Quieting the urgency in her voice, she said as seductively as she could manage, "I want more appetizers before we get to the main course."

Daniel smiled. "How about this? After I eat your pussy, your tits will be dessert."

Presley visibly relaxed. "Oh, yes, that will work. Tongue fucking will definitely work."

"I know it works for me. Lie back and relax."

That is exactly what Presley needed to do. Daniel took off her panties. Spreading her legs wide, he kissed her inner thighs. Presley sighed. "That feels good."

"Slide forward a little." As she did so, Daniel slid his hands under her ass. He gently lifted her legs and put them on his shoulders. Lowering his head, he easily captured her pussy with his mouth.

The exquisite sensation between her legs gave Presley a single point of focus. She drifted with it, allowing the tingles to fill her mind. The tingles began to sparkle with a translucent light, bringing to mind sunshine glistening on water. Presley knew it had to be him.

Vadim?

You have done well, Ninotchka. I am quite comfortable here with you.

What now?

You need do nothing more than allow. We will share the intimacy of lovemaking. Your sensations will be mine as mine will be yours.

Cool!

No, dear one, it is hot, not cool.

Without meaning to, Presley laughed out loud. Daniel raised his head and smiled. "I'm glad you're enjoying yourself."

"Oh, doctor, I'm certainly enjoying myself. Please, continue your examination."

This time, when Daniel's tongue touched her, a laser beam of heat shot through her pelvis. Presley moaned and writhed against his face. He held her firmly against his mouth and continued to suck. Her clitoris ached with need as he lapped at it.

Presley scratched the hood of his car with her fingernails. "Daniel, please, I can't stand it. Fuck me."

"Not yet, pretty Presley. Remember dessert?"

With her legs still over his shoulders, he bent over, forcing her knees to her chest. He licked her breast, and then caught a nipple with his lips. Sucking the pink nub fully into his mouth, he pinched it between his teeth.

She tried to rub her pussy against his stomach. But Daniel had her pinned to the car, her legs splayed open. She struggled to get out from under him, to no avail. Still holding her down, he moved to the other breast, kissing and licking it before he suckled her nipple.

Desire like she had never known before seared her belly. Her cunt throbbed. She had to have his prick inside her; she had to have relief. She screamed at him, "Fuck me, you son of a bitch! I need to come!"

"You are so fucking hot!" Daniel lowered her legs and pulled her up. "Presley, I'm going to make you come like you've never come before! Turn around and bend over." She did as he told her. Unexpectedly, Daniel gave her ass a hard slap and barked, "Spread your legs wider."

Presley opened herself, body and soul. Daniel entered her roughly, even harshly. His thrusts were those of a man violating a woman, with no concern for gentleness. He held her hips and pounded her with a forcefulness she welcomed. She wanted to be taken, to feel his strength overpowering her. She wanted it to be Vadim.

With the feeling of Vadim all through her and his scent enveloping her, she lost herself in a place of sheer sensation. As her climax shook her body, her identity dissolved into a pool of light and feeling, a pool she shared with Vadim.

Chapter Four

Vadim had chosen this path. Now he had to endure the consequences. As the orgasmic plateau faded, so did his capacity to hold his presence in the physical world. The spontaneous release of his energy had weakened him. He drifted away like smoke, even before he could say good-bye.

He had understood he would have to leave her behind and had braced himself for it. But when it happened, and he found himself once again alone, he could not bear it. Looking around their shack that he had rebuilt in this astral place, he saw her everywhere. Terrified that he would forget, he had filled the room with memories.

Everything in it had a connection to her: the fireplace where she'd cooked, the table where they'd eaten, the bed where they'd slept. Now, those memories were heart-rending reminders that he had lost her again. He roared in agony as darkness filled his heart.

His rage could not be contained. He had created this room, and by God, he would destroy it! He picked up a chair and smashed it against the wall. With a sweep of his arm, he knocked to the floor all the earthenware dishes and jugs he had so carefully crafted. They shattered, the sharp shards more pieces of his heart than clay.

The pile of grain sacks and wool blankets that had been their bed morphed his fury into madness. He ripped the bed apart with his bare hands, shredding the ethereal material into bits. In his blind rage, he wanted to smash everything that had been part of her.

When he reached for the wooden trunk with the broken lock, he stopped. As much as he could not bear its existence, he could not bring himself to destroy it. That trunk held his most treasured remembrances, the things he most cherished about his life with her.

Staring at it, he felt a small crack open in his embittered heart. As the trunk always had, somehow it calmed him. He opened it and stared at what he had kept. All the things that had been hers were there. He sat on the floor and reached inside. He pulled out the first thing he touched.

The comb he held in his hand looked as clean and new as the day he'd given it to her. He had carved it himself out of bone. Her hair had been long and straight then, not the fiery curls she now had. Looking at it, he smiled, imagining her now trying to keep this small bit of business in her hair. No doubt, it would pop out faster than buttons on a fat man's shirt!

Reaching in again, he closed his hand on her dress. He didn't have to see it to know what he held, having long ago memorized the texture of the cloth. When he pulled it out of the trunk, as he had a thousand times before, his rage melted into a pool of grief so profound all sense left him. He hugged the dress to his chest and moaned, the pain slicing through his heart.

He had touched her again, and she knew him! She even remembered his name! The wail of his anguished prayer filled the room. "Oh, merciful God, how could you be so cruel, to bring her back to me and then take her away again?"

As he held the dress against his face and sobbed, he heard, "Where there is love, there is mercy."

He knew the voice. With an edge sharp as a razor, he shouted, "Get the living hell out of my home! This space belongs to me!" Leaving the dress on the floor, he stood. "I told you, I do not want your help."

"You would chase me away again, even in your pain?"

"My pain is my own and not your concern."

"The last time you told me to leave, I did. By your own choice, you remained alone. It is different now. You no longer wish to be alone."

Vadim looked at this ethereal being, a beautiful woman who had followed him through the centuries. He had no desire for her and, in fact, had never trusted her. "Why do you still plague me with your riddles, and haunt me as you do?"

"Because I promised your beloved I would help you."

"What sort of demon are you, that you would come here again? Take your lies back to Hades where they belong!"

"Love such as you have is a divine gift worthy of protection."

"I never asked for protection."

"No, but your beloved did."

"You lie! My Ninotchka does not remember our lifetime! She could not have called to you."

The etheric sylph glided past him to where he had left the dress on the floor. With a touch as delicate as a whisper, she picked it up and placed it back in the trunk.

"That is the dress she wore when her lifetime ended."

"Do not speak of that! You know nothing of it!"

"Oh, but I do. Her last thoughts were of you and your safety. She would not betray you, even if it meant her own death. She would not admit to knowing you, or having ever seen you."

The sharp pain in Vadim's heart nearly made him double over. "I cannot bear your torture! Leave me!"

Rather than leave, this guardian spirit moved closer to him. "It is time you know the truth of her last moments. Your beloved did not know you had returned. She did not know you witnessed what they did to her. She did not know you sacrificed your life trying to save her. As she flew to the light, her prayers were only for your protection."

As he remembered that day so long ago, something inside Vadim broke wide open. The pain in his heart exploded and he started to sob. The next thing he knew, the being he had tried to chase away held him.

He clung to her as he cried out, "God forgive me, I tried to save her!" Shaking with soul-shattering pain, he screamed, "They wanted me, not her. They slit her throat, and then set on me. I fought those sons of Satan to my last breath!"

Vadim had no sense of how long she held him. When he finally began to quiet, she carefully re-created the bed he had destroyed and led him to it. He did not fight her. He had no fight left. All he had was this self-made hell, a prison with walls he had built himself.

She sat on the bed beside him and stroked his hair. Her touch comforted him. Closing his eyes tightly against the sting of his tears, he continued to shake. He wanted to die. But he couldn't. He was already dead.

Almost like singing him a lullaby, she softly said, "Since that day, you have been alone. Your rage and grief have held you in this place. No one could convince you to leave; you had to walk out the door yourself. Now, the door stands wide open, for you to come and go as you please."

Vadim's mind drifted as she spoke, the gentleness of her words carrying him to a quiet space of rest. He murmured, "My Ninotchka is with another this night. I cannot be with her, just as I cannot be what she is."

"Your only limitations are those you place on yourself."

Had he not been so drained, her cryptic remark would have once again triggered his anger. Instead he remembered a phrase Presley had used, and he smiled. In response, he simply said, "Says you!"

As he thought of Presley and repeated her quip, a warm breeze moved though him. Her voice drifted in on that gentle wind. *Vadim?*

Ninotchka?

Where the fuck are you? You just disappeared!

The shock of hearing Presley speak to him so clearly left Vadim dumbstruck. He heard the one sitting beside him whisper, "Tell her you are resting and will return to her soon."

Gathering his wits, Vadim replied, *Ninotchka, I could not hold on. I am resting now. I will return when I am able.*

Don't take too damn long! Not having you close by hurts like hell!

He smiled and repeated, *Says you!*

Her voice faded, but the warmth remained. He whispered, "She heard me. God have mercy on my soul, she heard me!"

Opening his eyes, he bolted upright in his bed. The entire room glowed with mother-of-pearl light. Wisps of color floated in the luminescent whiteness. He held up his hand and stared at it. Hardly believing it possible, his skin shone with the same radiance.

"In the name of all that is holy, what is this?"

"It is divine grace raining down upon you. It is the door you have opened with your beloved."

"Merciful heaven!" He looked upon his companion with eyes that could finally see the truth. "You are not of the devil, are you?"

"Darkness is merely the lack of light. When a crack is wide enough to let in the light, miracles happen."

Now more amused than annoyed, Vadim chided his guest. "Do you ever speak in clear language? Your riddles are beyond my understanding."

She returned his gibe with one of her own. "Shall I speak to you as your beloved does? You appear to respond to her curses with considerable potency!"

"My Ninotchka has acquired a foul mouth in our time apart, and you correctly assess my response. However, I hardly think that expression suits you as it does her."

Her smile spread though his heart like jam on fresh-baked bread. "Perhaps not."

"Do you have a name?"

"I am known as Ezra."

"Ezra is a man's name. You are most certainly not a man!"

"The vibration of the name is to my liking. I will call myself whatever I choose."

"I am Vadim."

"It is a pleasure to at last meet you, Vadim. The introduction is long overdue."

Vadim stood and paced across the room. As he walked, ripples of light swirled around him. "You said you would help me. Will you help me return to Ninotchka?"

"You already have."

Struggling to control his impatience, he continued. "I could not sustain in her world. I did not have the strength."

"You do now." Ezra waved her hand through the sparkling light. A kaleidoscope of color rippled through the room.

"These pretty colors may make a woman happy, but they do not make a man strong!"

"Dear Vadim, what do you think created this light?"

"I do not know. I opened my eyes and it glowed like sunlight."

"It appeared while you had your eyes closed?"

"It did." Vadim considered the question. He'd had his eyes closed because Ninotchka had heard him. He muttered aloud, "She heard me and we spoke."

The realization of what had happened hit him like a lightning bolt. "I have called out to her from this room a thousand times. She never heard! Now, I merely thought of her. She recognized it to be me."

"You have rent the veil and consummated your love, even as you are spirit and she is incarnate. The energetic exchange has bound you one to the other. What is done cannot be undone."

Vadim tried to grasp the full import of Ezra's words. "We are tied together, as with a piece of rope?"

"Indeed! But that which binds you is much stronger than rope!"

"Lord have mercy! Can this be true?"

"The truth is in your heart."

"What do I have to do? How can I be as she is?"

"She can anchor you in her world if she so chooses."

"How?"

"The way is your choice and your creation. You will discover it with your beloved."

Remembering Daniel, Vadim tensed. "She is with another man. I sense he will soon stake his claim to her. There is already an attachment forming between them."

"Show me."

He did not want Presley to know he could see her with Daniel. "How do I view without her knowledge?"

"How does a mouse walk along the wall and not draw attention to itself?"

He focused on the image and thought about her meaning. "He does so with stealth and silence. His intention is to get from here to there without being seen." Vadim suddenly understood Ezra's riddles. "You speak as an oracle, with questions as answers."

"Your wisdom increases with your strength. Show me, Vadim, and prove to yourself that you can."

Vadim focused on Daniel's house. He could feel Presley's heat, even before he located her in the house. He knew they were together. Pausing for a moment to center himself, he scanned the house. The sight of Presley naked in Daniel's bed made him pull back.

"I cannot do this."

"You must do it, Vadim. It will test your skill and strengthen your resolve. Watch, and learn."

Vadim tried again, this time quietly focusing directly on the bed. He saw Daniel lying beside Presley, naked and erect. He knew he meant to mount her and that Presley wanted him on top of her. He held his focus steady and watched.

Presley did not sense him. Her focus remained solely on Daniel and their lovemaking. Daniel already touched her with a familiarity that went beyond a casual affair. Vadim easily tapped into Daniel's thought stream and picked out telling phrases. He heard, *she's so fucking hot, sweet pussy, oh yeah, baby,* and, the most telling thought of all, *I don't want her to leave.*

He watched as Daniel rubbed her womanhood and made her squirm. He watched as Presley kissed his chest and slowly trailed kisses down to his organ. She licked him and, again, took him in her mouth. Daniel allowed only a few minutes of her expert ministrations. Vadim steadied himself as Daniel rolled her over and lowered himself on top of her.

Presley gasped as Daniel penetrated her. He saw her cling to this man and rake her fingernails across his back. Daniel rode her with the passion of a man claiming a woman. Vadim gently listened. With no more presence than a mosquito on the bedpost, he tuned into Presley's mind.

Sorting through her jumbled thoughts, he heard only fragmented phrases of arousal and need. Focusing with all the concentration he possessed, he heard something that filled his heart with hope. As she balanced on the precipice of her climax, he heard her call to him, *Vadim, please, come back to me.*

He wanted to answer. Ezra's hand on him pulled him back. "Do not make yourself known to her."

"Why, when I know I can?"

"Doing so now would cause her distress. She is in the throes with another. Allow her the space to be with her companion, while you rest."

Vadim studied Ezra for a moment. What he felt in her both surprised and delighted him. "You are drawn to the one she is with! I can feel it all through you!"

Ezra appeared bemused. "This man is a healer, and his virility is evident. I am not beyond feeling desire for one such as he."

"Perhaps you should move closer to him."

The light around Ezra grew brighter. "Perhaps I already have."

"Will you make yourself known to him?"

"Perhaps in a dream. A seed planted in fertile ground will grow."

"With him, it will grow stiff."

"And his pleasure will be mine."

Vadim snorted sarcastically. "What would you know of a man's pleasure?"

"You do not believe I can share a man's pleasure? Have you not shared some of the same with your beloved?"

Vadim scanned Ezra for validation of her claim. What he saw caught him unaware. Images of Ezra with mortal men flooded his consciousness. Most were gaining release by their own hand, with Ezra clearly present. "Are you of the succubi?"

"No more than you are of the incubi. Now you see why the legends have their origins in truth."

"You have shared physical love as I have with Ninotchka?"

"In a manner, I have."

"But you say I have rent the veil. If you have known physical love, why is it not also true of you?"

"The fusion of your consciousness with your beloved has created an exceptionally rare bridge between our worlds. She carries awareness of you. Those I have known did not know of me."

"Who are you, Ezra?"

"A very old soul, Vadim. One who, like you, tires of being alone through the centuries."

"Have you ever walked the earth in mortal form?"

"So long ago it seems as though it never was."

Vadim moved closer to her. "Have you tried to manifest, as I wish to do?"

"It is not done among those such as I."

"Did you not tell me, 'Your only limitations are those you place on yourself'?"

"You have always been a renegade, Vadim. You've never learned that some laws exist for a reason."

"Such laws be damned! With or without your help, I will be with my Ninotchka again."

"And if I agree to help you, will you agree to help me?"

"How can I help you? I know nothing of these matters."

"The bridge you have created to the physical world, perhaps I want to walk there with you."

"To be with him?"

"We will see. I can do nothing that will violate his free will, just as you must honor the right of Presley Knowles to choose."

"She already has."

"Has she?" Ezra waved her hand and a vision of Daniel and Presley appeared. Presley held a baby in her arms.

"Dear God!" Vadim tried to read the circumstancees. He could not. "Please tell me that child is mine and not his!"

"It is not yet written. The scales could tip either way."

"He will not want my Ninotchka if he has you."

"Then you must be willing to help me to our mutual benefit."

"What would you have me do?"

"You must share with me the mortal seed you now carry."

"I do not understand."

Ezra moved closer to Vadim. He couldn't tell what dazzled him more, her beauty or the light around her. Placing her hand on his chest, she communicated her need. "I cannot become flesh and blood unless you share with me that which your beloved has shared with you."

Vadim looked into eyes as blue as the sky and saw in them his future. "You said my Ninotchka would anchor me. That is what you want?"

"She will anchor you, and you, Vadim, will anchor me."

Even though Vadim had never felt any desire for this being, he knew what she expected of him. Her aching need overwhelmed him. "Once we do this, what will happen?"

"Much like cement is created by adding water to powdered stone, so will a new way of being be created by our joining."

Vadim caressed Ezra's cheek. "Your skin is warm and smooth, and shines of polished alabaster. It already has the feel of living flesh."

"In this place, we are not mortal, but our bodies are real. We can love as they do, if we so choose."

"Why have you not told me this before?"

"Would you have believed me?"

Vadim leaned down and kissed her forehead. "I believe you now."

He effortlessly picked up Ezra and carried her to his bed. She trembled in his arms. "Are you afraid?"

"I have never known a man in this way. What I know of physical love is only what I have stolen as a thief in the night."

"There is no need for fear. I will not hurt you." As he gently laid her on his bed, again her beauty captivated him. "How could one as beautiful as you not know the love of a man?"

"While mortal, I had the body of a cripple. No man wanted me. I died young and untried."

Ezra had wrapped herself in a sheer sari veil, which hid her charms from Vadim. He signaled his intention, and Ezra nodded her assent. Like a snake following a charmer's flute, the sari slithered from her body. Then, with a wave of his hand, his own clothing vanished.

Vadim drank in her beauty, wondering how she'd conceived this body of a goddess. Her thought pierced his mind. *Watching the dreams of men, I have seen what they desire. I am that vision manifest.*

Vadim buried his face between her breasts, the compulsion to love her all consuming. He felt her hands in his hair, holding his head tightly against her breasts. As he knew would happen, her hunger became his. *What would you have me do?*

Spread my legs and enter me. Do not hold back.

He had never known such need. Without hesitation, he knelt between Ezra's legs. When his organ touched her outer lips, searing heat moved through his groin. He penetrated her with an iron rod, as hot as a blacksmith's fire.

Ezra screamed and clutched at his back. She'd said not to hold back. No force existed that could make him do so. The intensity of their passion transcended physical sex and entered the potent exchange of tantra. As Vadim initiated Ezra into the act of physical love, the joining of their bodies merged with the ecstatic union of spirit.

Their combined loneliness and need, all their dreams and prayers, and everything that defined their past and their future coalesced in that moment. With a climax that reverberated through time and space, Ezra and Vadim transmuted the word into flesh. Together, they touched the face of God, and He smiled.

Chapter Five

"Daniel, why are we leaving so early? My flight isn't until seven o'clock tonight. It's only ten A.M.!"

"Because we are taking the scenic route to Kansas City. What good is it knowing a Kansas farm boy if I can't show you why I love this place?" He loaded her luggage into the trunk. "That's why I got someone to cover for me today, so I could have the whole day with you."

"Still trying to convince me to stay?"

Daniel slammed the trunk lid shut. "I told you last night I didn't want you to leave. I don't think my showing you some farmland and lakes on the way to the airport will change your mind."

"I have to get back. I should have been on a plane five days ago."

Daniel grumbled, "Yeah, I know. Remember, I'm the one who stitched you up."

Presley poked him in the side. "You're just grumpy because you didn't sleep well last night. You tossed and turned all night."

"I had weird dreams. Sorry if I kept you awake."

"What did you dream?"

Daniel rubbed his head. Presley had the oddest sense of déjà vu; that was how she'd rubbed her head when trying to remember Vadim. "I dreamed about a woman."

"Well, that tells me plenty. Did she happen to have auburn hair?"

"No, actually she had blonde hair, and she was stacked like a brick shithouse! Jesus, was she built! Sort of a cross between Marilyn Monroe and Madonna."

"I could be jealous! Someone you know from the hospital?"

"No, never saw her before, at least that I remember." Daniel rubbed his head again. "Funny thing, I can still smell her perfume, sometimes so much I can almost taste it."

As she had many times in the last few days, Presley silently called for Vadim. *Damn it, where the hell are you? And what are you doing to him?* She heard no answer.

Daniel interrupted her concentration. "Presley?"

"Sorry, did you say something?"

"I asked if you are ready to go."

"Ready as I'll ever be. Where are we going?"

"I'm going to show you the Kansas version of Manhattan. We'll pick up some lunch there and then drive to Tuttle Creek Lake for a quick picnic, before heading to the airport."

"Sounds romantic. And it's a beautiful day. Let's hit the road, Jack!" She didn't feel nearly as cheerful as she tried to sound.

During the drive to Manhattan, Daniel kept the conversation going with a steady steam of his childhood memories. He pointed out his high school and stopped for a moment beside the ballfield where the college scout had seen him play. They passed the house where he'd grown up, now owned by a plumber. He drove past the Belle Springs Creamery where Ike and his father David had worked, and showed her the cemetery where Ida and David Eisenhower were buried.

He then took back roads to Junction City, driving past Milford Lake, where he often went fishing. By the time they reached Manhattan, Presley needed food. "Dr. Hanson, I need to eat."

"Wait until we get to the lake. I'll find a place to park, and unzip."

"Funny as a crutch, doctor. Maybe you should try doing stand-up."

"Uh-oh. She's getting bitchy. Low blood sugar alert!" Daniel found a Shop Quik convenience store and parked the car. "Wait here. I'll run in and get us some food."

While Presley waited for Daniel to return, she again called to Vadim. Closing her eyes, she focused on her memory of him. *Vadim, where are you? Why won't you answer me?* She waited and listened. Before she heard him, she smelled him. *Vadim?*

Ninotchka, I am here.

Where the mother fuck have you been? I heard you the other night and then nothing!

I have been resting. Reaching you as I did depleted me.

Well, it hasn't done a whole hell of a lot for me either! This whole thing has me so fucked up! And what the fuck are you doing to Daniel with this woman he dreamed about?

You curse too much.

Yes, and fuck you, too.

Presley felt the familiar ripple of his laughter move through her body. *Ninotchka, you are too much woman for this doctor. You need my strong hand to keep you in line.*

Yeah, you and what army? Look, Vadim, I don't have much time. Daniel will be back in a minute. Promise me, and I do mean swear on a stack of bibles, you won't do anything to hurt him.

I swear to you, Ninotchka, he will not be harmed.

Who is this woman in his dream?

That does not concern you.

To hell it doesn't! He could smell her perfume, like I smell you. Who is she, Vadim?

Before Presley could hear an answer, Daniel opened the car door and tossed something in her lap. She jumped. "What the hell is this?" She held up a package with two round pink balls covered with coconut.

"Those, sweetheart, are Hostess Sno Balls. Eat them."

"This cupcake is total junk food! What kind of doctor are you, anyway?"

"One who doesn't want to be in a confined space with a hypoglycemic bitch!"

"Fuck you!"

"On a blanket or in the back seat?" He put the bag of food on the back seat. "We'll decide after lunch."

"Ballsy bastard, aren't you?" Presley ripped open the package. Coconut fell all over her lap. "Shouldn't these things be illegal?"

"With your fondness for balls, cheese and otherwise, I thought you'd enjoy them."

"Just what I need, another smart ass."

"You've met a few, I take it?"

"Too damn many lately!" Presley bit into the marshmallow-covered pink ball, dropping even more coconut. "There's chocolate cake in this! It's good!"

"Wait until you hit the creamy filling. You should really get off on that!"

"When I get back to the city, I'll check out when open mike night is at a few comedy clubs, in case you're interested."

"Do you want me to come to New York?"

"Thinking of changing careers?"

"I'm serious. If you won't stay in Kansas, what if I come to New York?"

"Daniel, you told me you didn't want to be in a big city. That's why you came back to Abilene."

"My roommate from med school has a successful private practice in Manhattan. He's been after me to go into partnership with him. Maybe I should consider it."

"Can we slow down? This is too much to swallow with only a cupcake in my stomach."

Daniel started the car. "I thought I would throw it at the

wall and see if it sticks." As they backed out of the parking lot, Vadim's scent lingered.

They rode quietly for a few minutes. Presley tried to center herself and think before she spoke. "Daniel, we need a reality check. You're seriously considering turning your life upside down for someone you've only known for three days?"

"Five days, and yes, I am."

"For God's sake, why?"

"I told you, I don't want you to leave. That means, leave my life. I'm already comparing the women I know to you. I can't imagine anyone else stepping up to the plate the way you have."

Without knowing why she said it, Presley asked, "What about the woman in your dream?"

"That isn't a real person. I don't know her."

"Humor me. What if that woman were real? What then?"

"I'd say she should be on a billboard in Times Square, preferably modeling lingerie."

"Be serious."

"I am serious." Daniel stopped the car by the lake. Presley hadn't noticed they'd arrived. "We only have a few hours left before you leave. I don't want to go off on some imaginary tangent and piss away the time."

"And I don't want you to do anything rash without thinking this through. We both have careers to think about, and very different lifestyles. We can't just toss all that out the window because we've fucked like rabbits for three days."

"It's more than that."

"Daniel, don't go there."

"I have to say it, Presley. This is the only time in my life that I've felt like I'm falling in love."

"Can we please leave it at that for now? My stomach is doing flip flops. I need some real food."

"We can leave it for now, but this isn't going away. I plan to visit New York soon, to see you and to visit my friend. We'll see where things stand then. Agreed?"

"Agreed." Trying to lighten the mood, she added, "Of course, I'll expect a follow-up exam. Be sure to bring your stethoscope and thermometer."

"I'll also pack a few pairs of surgical gloves for that rectal exam we didn't get to this time."

"Should I pick up a sexy nurse costume, Dr. Hanson?"

"Couldn't hurt. A low-cut white number with a short skirt will do nicely. And don't forget the accessories. A garter belt, sheer white stockings, and spike heels are part of the uniform."

"What kind of nurse wears that uniform?"

"The kind this doctor dreams about! Let's eat. You grab the food. I'll get the blanket out of the trunk."

When Presley came around the car, Daniel stood staring into the open trunk. "Is something wrong?"

"Don't you smell it?"

"I smell honeysuckle, nothing else."

"No, it's not honeysuckle. I've never seen honeysuckle anywhere around here. That's the smell from my dream last night."

Not meaning a word of it, Presley tried to reassure him. "Daniel, I'm sure it's just some sweet flower growing close by. Your nose is playing tricks on you."

"Maybe you're right." He tucked the blanket under his arm and closed the trunk.

Daniel spread the blanket beside the car, in the shade of a large horse chestnut tree. Presley saw they were quite alone, not another living soul in sight. She chuckled when she thought *Yeah, but there are a couple dead ones hanging around.* Quickly covering her indiscreet laughter with a cough, she feigned choking.

"Are you all right?" Daniel took the bag of food from her.

"I just have a tickle. What do you have to drink in there?"

"Coffee and water."

"Could I have some water, please?" She took the bottle

Daniel offered. "This is a nice place. It's unbelievably beautiful."

"This is my favorite fishing spot. I can stand here for hours and not see anyone." After Presley had a drink, he took the open bottle from her and chugged some himself before putting the cap on. "I wanted a spot with some privacy for our bon voyage."

"Dr. Hanson, you have this thing about doing the nasty in a public place, don't you?"

"Never used to, until I met you."

"Nice to know I'm such an inspiration to you." Presley kicked off her sandals and sat down on the blanket. Her skirt slid up her thighs. "There's no way I can be modest and sit on the ground in this dress."

Daniel smiled. "I know."

They ate the ham sandwiches and chips, with more cupcakes for dessert. By the time Presley finished her coffee, she felt relaxed and refreshed.

Daniel glanced at his watch. "It's one-thirty. We should leave here by three to get you to the airport. So, what's it going to be?"

"Come again?"

"Exactly! Shall it be in the back seat or right here on the blanket?"

Presley chooses the blanket, continue reading
Presley chooses the backseat, turn to page 70

Presley stretched out on the blanket like a cat waking from a nap. Her skirt slid up even more. "Here will be just fine."

Daniel lay down beside her. "Yeah, mama." Fondling her breasts, he growled, "Who's your daddy?"

Presley stroked his hard-on. "You are, Dr. Hanson. You're my daddy."

"Then be a good girl and give me your panties. I want to see how wet your pussy is."

Presley lifted her bum and pushed her panties down to her knees. Sitting up, she peeled them off and handed them to Daniel. "Do you know, for a doctor, you're a kinky son of a gun!"

"I have my moments." He rubbed her underpants against his face. "They're damp. Last night, they were soaked. If you ask me nicely, I'll make you sopping wet."

Presley knew from their few nights together he liked to top her. She could go both ways, as could he. But being a bottom with him really sexed her up. No doubt he would soon have her begging him for it.

She knelt in front of him and raised her skirt. "Please, doctor, rub my pussy. I want you to make me soaking wet."

Daniel traced the folds of her labia with his finger. "Why do you want to be wet, Presley? Tell me why I should make you hotter."

"If you make me wet, your prick will slide in when you fuck me." He had teased her this way last night, making her answer questions while he played with her. It drove her nuts!

Parting her lips, Daniel diddled her clitoris. Presley moaned. "Do you like that, Presley?"

"Fuck, yes!" Presley squirmed, trying to rub against his fingers.

"Now, now, Miss Potty Mouth. I told you last night, you must answer sweetly and politely when I ask you if you like it. Let's try it again. Do you like it when I do this?" As he asked the question, he rammed two fingers into her cunt.

Presley bit her lower lip and groaned. Daniel pulled his fingers out and rammed them back in. "Presley, answer the question. Do you like it?"

Presley gasped and managed to say, "Yes, Dr. Hanson, I like it very much."

"That's good. That's very good." Daniel continued to finger fuck her. "What else do you like?"

"Daniel!"

His voice deep and controlled, Daniel repeated, "Presley, what else do you like?"

Presley licked her lips and tried to draw in enough air to speak. "I like it when you suck on my nipples."

"Then show me your tits."

Presley had enough presence of mind to ask, "What if someone sees us?"

With his fingers still deeply buried in her cunt, Daniel raised himself up and looked around. "There's no one here. We're alone, and we're hidden by the car. Now, take off your dress and show me your tits."

Presley hesitated. She couldn't allow herself to think too much about the consequences if they were seen. A gentle breeze off the water distracted her. It carried the odor of honeysuckle, sweet and strong. The scent made her giddy, replacing her indecision with capricious freedom. She wanted this.

Without inhibition, she pulled her dress over her head. She knelt in front of Daniel completely nude. "Please, Dr. Hanson, suck on my tits."

"Oh yes, Presley. That's what I wanted. I knew you would tell me what you like." Daniel knelt in front of Presley, unzipped his khakis, and exposed himself. "Jack me, baby, jack your daddy."

Presley gripped Daniel's rock-hard cock in her fist. He let her know when she jacked him with the rhythm he wanted. "That's right, mama, slow and steady. Oh, yeah, that's good." He still had two fingers inside her cunt, massaging the swollen flesh. Using his thumb, he pressed on her clit and rubbed.

The intensity of the sensation nearly made Presley topple over. Daniel steadied her with his free hand. He leaned forward and caught a nipple between his lips. Sucking it into his mouth, he circled the hard rosebud with his tongue before squeezing it between his teeth. She shuddered and moaned.

Leaning into him to support herself, she pushed her breast deeper into his mouth. He sucked her tit like a hungry calf. She bent over and kissed the top of his head. His hair smelled of honeysuckle.

Allowing herself to be carried by the fragrance and the feeling, she remembered Vadim's instruction: *Look gently with your mind's eye, as you would with peripheral vision.*

When she did, she glimpsed the lovely woman Daniel had described. Not wanting to lose the vision, she quietly thought, *Who are you?*

I am Ezra, as you are Presley.

Does Vadim know you?

Yes.

What do you want?

Love.

Nothing else needed to be said. Presley could feel the benevolence of this being and her overwhelming need. Her heart filled with compassion as she allowed her body to open. Honeysuckle aerated in her throat as Ezra came closer.

She spoke the only thought in her mind. "Daniel, I want you."

Daniel raised his head and looked into her eyes. "You are one hot lady, Presley Knowles." Looking up at the sky and again at her eyes, he added, "It must be the light here. Your eyes look blue. But they're brown, right?"

Presley smiled. "Of course they are."

Daniel held her close and kissed her neck. "Are you ready to fuck?"

In a sultry whisper, tinted with shades of desire she had never known before, Presley answered, "Yes, Dr. Hanson, I am ready to be loved by you."

"Oh yeah, mama. Tell me again, who's your daddy?"

"You are, Daniel. Please, I need you now."

"Get down on all fours, sweetheart. We're having it doggie style."

Presley obediently got down on her hands and knees. The smell of honeysuckle was now an aphrodisiac, and she voluntarily spread her legs wide open. Nothing mattered except having Daniel fill her and fuck her.

He gripped her hips in both hands and positioned himself behind her. With one thrust, he entered her fully. Presley's cunt gripped him like a vice, with strength exceeding her own. Daniel groaned. "Goddamn, Presley, you're so fucking tight!"

With growing intensity, he repeatedly pulled out and slammed back into her. Each thump of his groin against Presley's ass increased the joy in her heart. Suddenly, Daniel grunted loudly and his body convulsed. As his seed spurted inside her flesh, the joy in her heart exploded. She radiated light as the ecstatic bliss of her climax overtook her.

Go to page 74

"No contest. The backseat. I've never done it in a car."

"How could you have never fucked in a car? Screwing in the backseat is a teenager's rite of passage!"

"Maybe in Kansas it is. When you grow up in Manhattan like I did, you get a room in a hotel."

"Hell, that's no way to learn to fuck. Miss Knowles, it's time you had your initiation."

Daniel stood and grabbed Presley's hand. "Up you go." He pulled her to her feet and held her close. "There are a few ground rules you should know."

Presley wrapped her arms around his neck. "What sort of rules?"

"The reason for backseat sex is because horny teenagers have no place else to go. It's out of necessity rather than choice."

"Okay, that seems obvious."

"Look at the circumstances. Raging hormones, boy with a hard-on that won't go away, girl with her hand in her panties every chance she gets. Put that combo in a backseat on a dark night, what do you get?"

"Babies?"

"Nope." Daniel pulled his wallet out of his back pocket and took out a condom. "A horny male is always prepared."

"Interesting that this horny male should have a rubber in his wallet."

"That's just it. You never know when you might need one. A man learns early on to be ready, willing, and able."

"It seems *you* are ready and willing." Reaching between them, she found his stiff cock. "Mmmmm, yeah, and definitely able!" She continued to stroke him.

"You're a natural. You already discovered the most important rule."

"Which is?"

"The horny boy looking for some action goes parking with the easiest girl he knows. You know, the girl they talk about in the locker room."

"Dr. Hanson, are you suggesting I'm easy?" Presley slowly

unbuttoned Daniel's shirt. Slipping her hand inside, she squeezed his pecs.

"Easy and hot as hell. You were made to get laid, sweetheart."

"Is that a fact?"

Daniel opened the door to the backseat. "That is indeed a fact. After you, my dear."

Presley crawled into the backseat, with Daniel following. "We need some air in here." He closed the door and opened the windows. A cool breeze blew in from the water.

Presley cuddled in closer. "This is cozy, but there isn't much space to move."

Daniel opened his belt and unzipped his pants. "You're getting the idea. The trick is to make the most of the space you have." He pulled his stiff cock through the opening in his underwear. "The first thing that happens is French kissing and feeling each other up."

Presley wasted no time. She gripped his prick and started jerking him off. Licking his neck, she whispered, "I want to do more than this."

Daniel reached under her skirt. He pushed the crotch of her panties aside and found her clit. "Sweetheart, we're only getting started."

He wrapped his free hand around her neck and turned her face to his. He kissed her with such hunger it took Presley's breath away. When he exhaled into her mouth, she realized he tasted of Vadim. But she also smelled something else. The breeze blowing across the water carried with it the scent of honeysuckle.

Realizing they were not as alone as Daniel thought, she pulled back. Looking into Daniel's eyes, she saw an iridescent glow. With the taste of honeysuckle rising in her throat, she quietly asked, "Daniel, what color are my eyes?"

"They look blue today. Last night, I thought they were brown."

"I thought yours were brown, too. Today, they look silver."

"Must be the reflection from the water."

"That must be it. What else could it be?" She couldn't tell him what she knew, so she decided to roll with it. Feeling sexy, and even more daring than usual, Presley moved to the other side of the seat.

"What are you doing?"

"Getting naked." She reached for the hem of her dress. "Or isn't that allowed?"

"Oh, baby, that is definitely allowed." While Presley pulled her dress over her head, Daniel took off his pants and underwear. Before she had a chance to peel off her panties, Daniel pinned her to the seat and lavished her breasts with kisses.

He sucked a nipple into his mouth and nibbled. Presley sighed, abandoning herself to the tingles moving through her body. When she closed her eyes she saw sparkles. The smell of honeysuckle filled the car, and flowed into her.

She focused on the odor and the presence she felt with her. *You aren't Vadim! Who are you?*

I am known as Ezra.

Where is Vadim?

He is here, with me.

What do you want?

To know love as you do, and to know this man.

Presley fought to stay calm. Her concern was now more for Daniel than for herself. She lifted his head from her breast. "Daniel, how are you feeling?"

"Like I'm ready to get laid. How about you?"

In the split second it took to make her decision, her purpose increased tenfold. "Oh, yes, doctor, you are going to get laid." With strength that startled her, she shoved Daniel backward. He fell against the seat, muttering, "What the fuck?"

"Dr. Daniel Hanson, welcome to my world." With that, Presley took off her panties and straddled him. Taking hold of his engorged prick, she rubbed it against her clitoris. Daniel reacted so violently he lifted her with an upward thrust.

"Christ, Presley, don't torture me. Put it in. Ride me!"

Without saying a word, Presley did as he asked. She mounted him, pushing his prick into her swollen hole. Lowering herself onto his shaft, she sat on his lap, and waited.

Their eyes met. Daniel's glowed silver and she knew hers radiated blue. With an unspoken acknowledgement of this preternatural coupling, Presley raised and lowered herself on his cock. Daniel groaned, and grabbed her ass. "Christ, yes. Ride me hard, Presley. I want to watch your tits bounce when you come."

And Presley did ride him, using his prick as she would a dildo, with nothing in her mind except her own pleasure. Without warning, Daniel held her still and pushed his index finger up her ass. Gritting her teeth to stifle a scream, she shook uncontrollably as her orgasm claimed her.

Daniel's growl cut into her consciousness as he signaled the onset of his climax. Honeysuckle perfume filled her nose as Daniel's semen filled her yoni. His open wallet, with the condom still in the package, lay on the seat beside them.

Chapter Six

By the time Presley had claimed her luggage at JFK and hailed a cab, it was after midnight. She'd managed to nap on the plane; hopefully it was enough to keep her going until she got home. Sitting in the taxi, she stared out the window at the lights flashing by.

Daniel hadn't said much during the two hour trip to Kansas City, and she hadn't been able to think of anything to fill the silence. So, she'd turned on the radio and listened to the news. She'd also had no sense of their invisible companions. Once again her awareness of Vadim, and now Ezra, had faded with her orgasm.

The good-bye at the airport had been more difficult than she'd anticipated. Presley cringed when she thought about how she'd cried when Daniel had kissed her. He'd wiped the tears from her cheeks and promised he would come to New York as soon as he could. She wasn't sorry about that.

Closing her eyes, she thought of Vadim. Had something really happened to her head in the accident? Could she have some weird brain injury that caused delusions and hallucinations? She shook her head, negating her own doubts. Daniel had noticed Vadim's scent and had smelled Ezra even before she did. They both couldn't be crazy.

Ninotchka, you are not crazy.

Presley's eyes popped open as Vadim's scent welled up in her throat. "Fuck, here we go again!"

The cabbie glanced over his shoulder, "Are you all right, miss?"

She hadn't meant to say that out loud. "Yes, of course." Wanting to somehow justify having talked to herself, she added, "I just got a message on my cell. Don't want to deal with it tonight."

"Don't blame you. Where you going again?"

"I'm going to the Village. You can drop me at the corner of Barrow and Hudson."

"No problem."

Settling back into the welcome silence of the ride, Presley let her anger fly. *What the hell gives you the right to show up and then disappear without any explanation? You're playing with me like I'm some sort of fucking party doll! I don't like this, Vadim, not one bit. And my name isn't Ninotchka. It's Presley! Got that? PRESLEY!*

What sort of name is that for a woman? I have never known the name Presley.

It's the name my parents gave me. I can't help it if they were card carrying Elvis fans. At least they didn't call me Elvis!

Who is this Elvis you speak of?

Christ, you are out of touch, aren't you?

I am not of this time.

No shit!

I will learn.

Presley's stomach rolled. The lurching of the cab in traffic was only partly responsible. *What do you mean, you'll learn?*

You have already taught me much. I will observe and study. I will learn.

That implies you intend to hang around.

That and more.

The fine line between motion sickness and butterflies in

her stomach had definitely been crossed. She opened the window to get some air. The cabbie made an unnecessarily fast approach to the Triborough Bridge ramp. She really thought she would throw up.

Ninotchka? She didn't respond. *Presley?*

Vadim, I can't, I'm sick.

Settle yourself, and let me help you.

As he had in the hospital, Vadim somehow quieted her nausea. She took a deep breath of the cool night air. *How do you do that?*

The same way I come to you, by having the intention to do so.

Says you!

On the heels of the ripple of laughter, an exquisite warmth wrapped around her, an invisible embrace that made her melt into the seat. *My dear Presley, indeed I do!*

Recanting her outburst, she softened her tone. *You can call me Ninotchka once in a while, if it makes you happy.*

It does. But if it pleases you to be known as Presley Knowles, I will make every effort to adjust.

As the cabbie flew across the bridge, Presley remembered to look at the amazing canvas of Manhattan. The magical lights of the city always welcomed her home. *Aren't they beautiful?* The question crossed her mind conversationally, as though Vadim sat next to her in the taxi.

Through your eyes, they are indeed quite beautiful. This is the place you call home?

Yup. The city is where I belong.

There is much to learn.

Vadim, I will be at my corner soon. I have to pay the driver and get my stuff upstairs. I can't talk to you and do that.

Understood.

Are you going to disappear again?

No, Presley, I am not. The firm determination she heard both excited and frightened her.

While rummaging in her purse to find her wallet, she found

a piece of paper Daniel had given her. On it, he had written the name and phone number of a doctor who specialized in Post-Traumatic Stress Disorder. She crumpled it up and threw it on the floor of the taxi.

At the corner of Hudson and Barrow, she paid the driver and collected her luggage. After hooking her briefcase onto her suitcase, she hefted her laptop and purse onto her shoulder. She took her time walking the half block to her building, enjoying the feel of being back in her neighborhood.

When she got to the door, her doorman immediately came to help her. "Welcome home, Ms. Knowles. You were gone quite a while this time." Taking the handle of her suitcase, he pulled it into the lobby.

"Ah, Carlton, thank you. I'm beat."

"Not too tired to give me grief. You know my name isn't Carlton. It's Carl, just plain Carl."

"You look like a Carlton."

"And you look like you've been hurt! What happened to your head?"

Presley had forgotten about the red line on her forehead. "That's my Frankenstein scar. I had a car accident in Kansas. Spent a couple of days in the hospital and met the sexiest doctor on earth, a Dr. Daniel Hanson! Let's just say we hit it off."

"Leave it to you to have an accident and get yourself a doctor out of the deal. Are you all right?"

Presley didn't quite know how to answer that, considering everything. So she made a joke. "You should know by now I have a hard head! Right now, what I need to be all right is some food. The TV dinner they served on the plane didn't do it."

"It's too late for take-out. I have to order before midnight when I want something delivered."

"If you'll watch my stuff for a few minutes, I'll run around the corner to the all-night deli and grab a few things. I've been away for nearly three weeks. My cupboards are bare!"

"No problem, Ms. Knowles. I'm here till six. Take your time."

Presley handed her laptop to Carl, who took it and her suitcase into the mailroom. "I'll be right back."

Walking back to Hudson Street, Presley reached for Vadim. *Are you still here?*

She heard his answer clearly. *I am.*

Cool. He didn't have to tell her; she felt his confusion. *It is a modern expression, Vadim. It means something is good or agreeable.*

Then you are pleased I am still here?

Yes, Mr. Ghost, I am.

I am not a ghost.

Yes, you are! She stood outside the deli. *I have to do some shopping. We'll discuss your situation later.*

Indeed we will! Someone patted her ass, and she jumped. When she turned around, she saw no one on the street.

That was you! How did you do that?

We will discuss it later, as you suggested. Do your shopping, Ninotchka.

My name is Presley! She didn't wait for an answer. Going into the store, she muttered, "Smart-ass ghost!"

Presley bought only what she needed for a sandwich now and for some breakfast in the morning. Surprised that they had her favorite cereal, she ignored the price-gouged sticker on the Honey Nut Cheerios and threw the box in her basket.

On the way to the cash register, she spotted some Utz Cheese Balls on the snack rack, stuck between the potato chips and pretzels. Her eyes misted as she threw them in with the Cheerios. The thought she voiced sounded like a prayer. *Vadim, don't let anything happen to him. Don't let her hurt him. Promise me.*

Ninotchka, I swear to you, no harm will come to the doctor. Come, let us pay for your goods and leave this place.

The walk back to her building somehow seemed longer. She didn't reach for Vadim. She thought about Daniel, and how she missed him already. For as many times as she had traveled, she had never sustained an emotional connection with her lovers. This time, she couldn't seem to stop it.

Carl carried her luggage to the elevator. On her floor, it took two trips from the elevator to her door to get everything inside. By the time she locked up for the night, it was nearly two A.M.

She left her luggage in the living room. Once she had all the groceries in the kitchen, she made a quick ham and cheese sandwich. After she refrigerated the milk, eggs, meat, and cheese, she took her sandwich, a can of ginger ale, and the cheese balls to her bedroom. The rest of the groceries could sit in the bag until morning.

Forgetting she had an invisible companion, she took a bite of her sandwich and went to draw a bath. She wondered how long it would be before Daniel could come to New York. Vadim startled her when she heard, *Ninotchka, your thoughts are full of this other man. You fail to remember I am here.*

How the hell could I forget you are here? You keep reminding me!

I understood you to be pleased that I am here.

I am, but not every fucking second! I'm exhausted. I want to soak in a hot tub and go to bed. I'm not feeling chatty at the moment.

We do not have to talk. Words often interfere with true communication.

So what are you going to do, watch me take a bath?

Perhaps, if it pleases me to do so.

You're a ghost and a voyeur?

I am not a ghost.

Yeah, I know. You told me. I see you aren't denying being a voyeur.

If that is the enjoyment of watching a woman in her bath, I would not deny that.

Presley mumbled, "I didn't think you would."

Too tired to continue this internal dialogue, she focused on undressing and taking her bath. The hot water immediately soothed and relaxed her. She finished her sandwich and drank her ginger ale. The cheese balls remained unopened. They reminded her too much of Daniel.

Presley closed her eyes and drifted. Soaking in a hot tub always helped her to sleep. She pushed aside memories of Daniel and the last few days with him. It hurt too much to think of him. She didn't want to be involved with any man, especially not with a doctor in Kansas, of all places!

Instead, she distracted herself. Her fingers explored the crevice between her legs. Brushing against the tight curls with her hand, she felt familiar tingles spread through her pelvis. She thought of Vadim. Even if he remained silent, she could feel him close by.

Her finger found the hardened nub of her clitoris. Gently caressing the sensitive flesh, she envisioned him watching her. The tantalizing idea that he could somehow see her in the tub while she excited herself heated her more than the hot bath.

As she rubbed and probed her body, her hips rolled in the water. At first, erotic images floated in her mind, visions of being spanked and fucked by shadowy, nameless men. Soon, the sensation between her legs became her only reality, the need to come overshadowing all her thoughts.

As her orgasm swelled in her groin, Vadim's voice cut through her mind. *Ninotchka, let me in! Hold me!*

Not knowing how or why, her instincts kicked in. *Vadim, come to me. I will hold you!* Water covered the bathroom floor as she thrashed in the tub, her orgasm obliterating all sense and reason.

Exhausted and dazed, Presley patted herself with a towel. She pulled a night shirt over her head and put on fresh panties before falling into bed.

She slept deeply, not rousing until a siren from the street woke her. Glancing at the clock, she groaned when she saw the time. Ten o'clock. "Damn it, I forgot to set the alarm." She'd wanted to be up by eight to organize her notes.

Remembering she had left her suitcase by the sofa, she went to get it. She heard paper rustling in the kitchen, just the slightest crinkling sound. "Great, I leave for a few weeks and mice move in."

Going back to the bathroom, she grabbed the broom. Inching her way back toward the kitchen, she chastised herself for being such a pussy. Bolstering her courage, she whispered, "Okay, they're only mice. They're more afraid of me than I am of them."

She lunged at the kitchen door, waving the broom and shouting loudly, "All right you little motherfuckers, get the hell out of here!" Immediately after her forceful proclamation of territorial rights, she heard a pop and the sound of pebbles hitting the floor. Then she heard a man's voice cursing.

Stopping cold inside the kitchen door, she stood in complete shock. Cheerios covered the floor. A tall bearded man with long hair stood in the middle of them. He wore wide blue trousers, leather boots and a baggy white shirt. The shirt gaped open to the waist, revealing a chest covered with dark hair. Looking at her with silver eyes, he said simply, "Hello, Ninotchka."

She managed to say, "Holy shit!" before she fainted.

When she came around, she found herself on her bed. Truly believing she'd had a nightmare, she sat up and rubbed the scar on her forehead. "Maybe I should have another CAT scan."

"You do not need any more doctors."

Slowly turning her head, she saw the blue pants, then the open shirt. Her eyes stopped at the arms crossed over his chest. She looked away. "You aren't real! You can't be real."

"Oh, but I am real, just as you are."

Looking again, this time she allowed herself to see his face. Presley stared at him. "Vadim?"

"That is my name. We know one another well, Presley Knowles."

Presley fell backward onto her pillow and closed her eyes. "This can't be happening. It is fucking unbelievable!"

"You curse too much."

"You've already told me that." She opened her eyes and again stared at this man towering over her. "If you were shaved and had a scalp lock, you'd look like Yul Brynner playing Taras Bulba!"

"You must explain these names. I do not understand."

Not believing she could actually be having this conversation, she still answered. "Taras Bulba was a Cossack in a movie. You look like you stepped off of the back lot."

"I rode with the Cossacks, before I knew you."

Presley looked at him again. "Your clothes, they are Cossack clothes, aren't they?"

"In my time, it is what we wore."

"When exactly was that, Vadim?"

"I do not know the year. I lived during the time of the Zaporozhian host, when Sahaidachny was hetman."

"You're Russian?"

"We made our home on the Ukrainian steppe."

"We?"

"Ninotchka, you were my woman."

Presley rubbed her head again. "My brain must really be damaged. This is nuts!"

Vadim knelt beside the bed and placed his hand on hers. Closing his eyes, he took a deep breath. A moment later he said, "Your body is perfect. There is no remaining injury."

"Glad you think so." Presley slid her hand out from under his and touched the top of it. "You're solid!"

"I am flesh and blood, just as you are."

"How is that possible? You're a ghost, aren't you?"

"I have told you repeatedly, I am not a ghost."

"Then what the hell are you?"

"Those of us on the other side shed the incarnate body as a snake does its skin. Our essence self continues."

"Says you!" For the first time, Presley heard him laugh. It

gave her a chill to realize it was the same sound she had heard in her mind. Once again, it rippled through her body.

"Presley Knowles, your expression is why I am here."

"Excuse me?"

"My memory of your words was the bridge between us after I drifted away."

"You mean when I heard you the other night?"

"Yes, indeed."

"Well, I'll be damned!" She felt his hand again. "You're actually real, aren't you?"

"I am."

She sat up and touched his beard with her fingertips. "You saved my life." Quickly putting her hand down when she saw it shaking, she quietly added, "Thank you."

"Presley Knowles, I am pleased I could be of service."

"Just call me Presley."

"As you wish, Presley."

"You didn't answer my question. How can you be physical? You're a dead guy."

"It is because of you."

"Now I don't understand."

"You agreed to hold me. I asked and you agreed."

"I did?"

"You certainly did." Vadim stood and pointed to the bathroom. "Last night in your bath, you agreed."

Presley tried to remember. Then it all flooded in. "Oh, my God, when I came, I heard you say, 'Hold me' and I said I would!"

Vadim smiled broadly. "You did indeed. While you slept, I anchored to you and allowed my etheric body to thicken into denser matter. It is what you now see in the flesh."

"But you're dead!"

"It seems death is relative to the observer." Vadim took her hand and pressed it to his chest. She felt his heart beating against her palm. "It also seems I am now very much alive."

Rivulets of fire streamed through her body as she flexed

her fingers against Vadim's chest. "That means you are here to stay?"

"That is unknown. It is not yet written."

She pulled her hand away. "What the hell does that mean? Are you going to disappear like you did the other night? Poof, up in smoke?" An intense emotion she didn't understand overwhelmed her. She couldn't stop the choking sob that welled up in her throat. "Get the hell out of here with that shit! I don't want any part of it!"

She sat up, intending to get out of bed. Vadim caught her. "Ninotchka, I did not say I would leave."

"No, you said it is not yet written." She tried to pull away from him, but he held her firmly. Looking into his eyes, she remembered the accident. A flood of memories she had held back for nearly a week broke free.

"I wanted to stay with you over there. But you sent me back. Now you're here and you may not stay? Fuck that! Losing you again would be worse than death, worse than what they did to me. Vadim, if you go, this time I am going with you! I don't know how, but by God, I will!"

The silver in Vadim's eyes deepened. She could feel him probing her mind. In barely a whisper, she heard him say, "God in heaven, you remember!"

Like watching a movie in her head, Presley saw the men who'd attacked and killed her so long ago. She knew Vadim saw it, too. His pain shot through her, as did his memory of what they had done to her, and how he tried to save her.

"They killed you, too, didn't they?"

"Yes." He said nothing more.

She wiped her nose on the sheet. "This is like being in a fucking Roger Corman movie." She tried to get up and, again, he stopped her. "Jesus Christ, Vadim, I have to pee! If I wet the bed, I'll rub your nose in it like a damn dog!"

"Even in my time, the bitch that wet had her nose rubbed in it, not the one watching her do it!" He released her arm. "Go, do your business."

"Thank you!" Presley scrambled from the bed and nearly ran to the bathroom. She really did have to go. Turning around to close the door, she nearly hit Vadim with it. "Do you mind?"

"I am interested in how you do this. Soon, I will need to manage myself."

"Ghosts pee?"

Vadim walked into the bathroom and looked in the toilet bowl. "This is the chamber pot?"

"Yeah, sort of." Presley followed him in. "You didn't answer me. Do you pee?"

"Once I have some food and water, I expect I will need the pot."

"The Cheerios! You were trying to eat, weren't you?"

"My stomach is functioning again and I am hungry."

"I bet you are!" Presley watched him studying the commode. "All right, Vadim, you want to see how this thing works? I'll show you." She stepped in front of him, lifted her nightshirt, lowered her panties, and sat on the toilet.

Not caring that he could hear her, she sighed with relief as her bladder emptied. Once finished, she pulled a wad of toilet paper off the roll, cleaned herself, stood, and pulled her panties up. Then, she instructed him. "See this handle?" Presley pushed the silver lever. "This flushes the toilet. Everything goes down the pipe and into the ground under the city."

Vadim smiled. "You do not have to empty it?"

"Nope. It empties itself."

Vadim pushed the handle himself and watched the water swirl in the bowl. "There is much for me to learn."

Wandering around the bathroom, he examined the tub and looked out the window before stopping at the sink. He tried to push the silver handle down, as he had to flush the toilet. Presley put her hand over his, saying, "No, like this." Together, they pulled the handle forward. Cold water flowed from the faucet.

Vadim cupped his hand and filled his palm with water.

Bending over, he sipped a few drops. Presley took the glass she kept on the sink and filled it. Handing it to Vadim, she said quietly, "Drink slowly, Vadim, until you get used to it. It could make you sick if you drink too fast."

Closing his eyes, he took a drink, and held the water in his mouth. When he swallowed, he winced as someone would with a sore throat. He drank again. This time, he swallowed more naturally.

He put the glass back on the sink and took her hand. "Will you teach me about these things that are so strange to me? I know nothing of your world, but I want to learn."

Presley stepped closer. "You're serious, aren't you?"

"Oh, yes, my Ninotchka, I am serious." Wrapping his arm around her waist, he pulled her against him. "I am not leaving you. Whatever it takes, I will do."

Vadim's manhood pressed into Presley's pelvis. She squirmed against him. "Whatever it takes?"

"Yes, Ninotchka, whatever it takes."

Presley knew this man; she knew him well. Touching him brought her closer to the memories of a life she'd lived centuries ago. She pressed into him more forcefully. "Do you still remember how to use it?"

"Some things are not erased by time or space. Not even death can make a man forget how to love a woman." Effortlessly, Vadim picked her up. "You will accept me into your bed and lie with me again?"

Presley caressed his whiskers and nuzzled his neck. Opening her mouth, she inhaled. His delectable scent filled her mouth and permeated her lungs. She whispered into his ear, "Does your whole body smell like this?"

"Yes."

"Then put me on the bed and take off your clothes. I want to sniff you and make sure you are really my mate, like wolves do."

The rumble of Vadim's laughter vibrated against her. "Presley, it is the male wolf who sniffs the female." With confidence worthy of a Cossack, he strode back into the bedroom. Still holding her, he smelled her hair and then whispered to her, "You will teach me your ways and I will teach you mine."

"Vadim, I have so many questions . . ."

"Questions will come later. Now, we will know each other again as man and woman." He put her on the bed and whispered, "Most gracious Lord in heaven, thank you for bringing her back to me."

Having the eerie sense of lying on an altar, Presley continued to watch him. Vadim's eyes glowed silver. His clothing shimmered with the same iridescence she saw in his eyes. His pants, shirt, and boots faded in the light, and then disappeared, leaving him standing naked beside the bed.

"Fuck! How did you do that?"

"Concentration, and the intention to do so. Shall I manage yours as well?"

"Hell, yeah. Do me, baby!" Vadim passed his hand over Presley. She had the oddest sensation of her nightshirt and panties vibrating, and then they were gone. Her skin tingled where they had been. "That is so cool!"

Vadim smiled. "I remember. 'Cool' is finding something agreeable."

Presley licked her lips and stared at his thick organ. "Oh, yes, I find it very agreeable. You're really hung. I mean, for a ghost."

"You persist in this notion that I am a ghost. It is time you understood how real I am!" Vadim crawled on the bed beside Presley. "Woman, open your legs for me."

Presley swatted his arm. "You could at least say please!"

"You forget, Ninotchka, I know what is in your heart. You cannot hide what you want from me."

"You think I want you?"

"I know you want me." Vadim positioned himself over Presley, his hair hanging around his face.

Presley brushed his hair away so she could see his amazing eyes. "You could use a haircut and a shave!"

"My appearance is of little concern to me. I am what I am."

Vadim's hypnotic eyes held her own as she replied, "Well, Mr. Ghost! That will have to change!"

Before she could make a GQ joke about doing a piece for *Ghost's Quarterly*, Vadim lunged forward and buried his solid-flesh, blood-engorged prick inside of her.

Presley gasped and clutched his back. Not only did his scent fill her mouth, the heat of it scorched her throat. She thought she would choke on it. She heard his voice in her mind, as she had before. *Ninotchka, do not resist. Simply allow the energy to fill your body as it does your soul.*

Vadim, I can't breathe!

Shhhh, now. Yes you can. Quiet yourself and inhale.

With his cock throbbing inside of her, Presley took a breath through her nose. Her throat still felt constricted, but she could breathe. The odor from Vadim's skin filled her lungs. She took another breath, this time relaxing under him.

She pinched his arm and smiled. "Do you think you could tone down that smell? It choked me like the time my uncle wore too much Old Spice aftershave."

Vadim slowly lifted his pelvis and slid back into her. "You will adjust to it as you acclimate to my energy."

Presley met his gentle thrust with her pelvis. "Is that a fact?"

"Indeed it is." Vadim again lifted his pelvis, this time entering her more forcefully. Presley moaned.

"Fuck, that's good!"

You are experiencing pleasure?

His voice in her mind sounded as natural as his voice in her ears. She answered in kind. *Oh, yes, Vadim, I am.* She hesitated for only a moment before she added, *I want to feel more, I want to feel you. Fuck me hard.*

The luminescence in Vadim's eyes grew brighter. His skin shimmered with it, as if a silver spotlight lit the room. Presley realized the light around him also surrounded her. Each thrust made the sparkles brighter, transporting Presley into a space of theistic sensation.

Vadim rode her as would a stag rutting a doe. The force of his thrusts pinned her to the bed, her grunts blending with his as they soared in mystical union. Presley had no sense of time or place. Her only reality became the heat and the light of Vadim.

His climax exploded inside her belly and filled the room with a kaleidoscope of colored light. It rained down on them like confetti. As if he willed it, her climax hit without warning, joining with his. In an electrifying spiral of incorporeal energy, the fusion between them completed.

Chapter Seven

Daniel woke up with a headache. After he'd left Presley at the Kansas City airport, he'd bought a bottle of Kentucky bourbon. Once he'd gotten home, he'd put away enough of it to give himself one hell of a hangover.

Fortunately, his shift at the Memorial didn't start until two o'clock. He had enough time to get himself together before going to work. When he looked at himself in the bathroom mirror, he muttered, "Christ, I look like shit!"

Running his fingers through his hair, he thought of Presley. She had really gotten under his skin. Not only was she hot as hell, she had brains. And damn it all, he hadn't wanted her to leave.

Waking up next to her three days running had made him realize how much he wanted a partner, someone to share his life. Now that she had gone back to her own life in New York, he not only felt alone, he felt lonely.

Taking off his underwear to piss and then shower, he noticed dried semen on them. He didn't recall having a wet dream, but he must have had one. Then he remembered. He'd had another dream about the blonde.

"I am in bad shape. I'm dreaming about a chick I don't know." He threw his shorts in the hamper. "And I'm talking to myself! I really need to get a life!"

He got in the shower and stood under the steaming water. As he rubbed his body with a bar of soap, the blonde from his dream again popped into his head. She had more curves than Route 66, and tits, Christ, those tits were right out of *Playboy*.

Lathering up his hands with plenty of soap, he slicked up his cock. He couldn't remember much of the dream but remembered enough to make him hard. The blonde had motioned for him to come closer. As he had, her clothes had disappeared and she'd stood naked in front of him.

Daniel wrapped one hand around his erect penis and leaned against the tile wall with the other. As the hot water pelted him, he imagined her there with him in the shower. His fist became her pussy as he jerked off. Thrusting into his hand, he saw her clearly, this naked blonde he didn't know.

Forgetting Presley, forgetting the hospital, even forgetting his own name, he felt sensation overwhelm his consciousness. The pressure in his groin became unbearable just before the red heat of his lust exploded. He roughly pumped his cock as semen splattered against the wet tile.

Winded, he leaned against the wall until he caught his breath. It occurred to him Presley must have left her soap in the shower. The steam smelled sweet, like honeysuckle and strawberries.

Once he'd showered, dressed and had some food and coffee, Daniel felt almost normal. Wondering if Presley had arrived safely in New York, he took out his wallet to find her business card. When he dialed her cell, he got her voice mail.

"Hey, Presley. It's Daniel. I wanted to make sure you made it home all right last night, and . . ." He paused, not knowing how to tell her he missed her. "And I wanted you to know I really enjoyed your company the last few days. I hope to come to New York soon. Give me a call when you get this message. Bye."

Daniel sees Ezra on the street, continue reading
Ezra appears at the hospital, turn to page 97

Trying to shake himself out of the deep blue funk that threatened to color his day, Daniel decided to run some errands before starting his shift at Memorial. He still had a couple of hours before he had to see any patients.

The round trip to Kansas City had nearly left his gas tank empty, so he stopped to fill up before going to the bank. After he got more cash, he picked up his dry cleaning and then went to get more postage stamps.

He had trouble finding a parking space close to the post office and finally opted to park illegally by the railroad tracks, next to a closed factory. He didn't see anyone else around. But the NO TRESPASSING sign still glared at him as he walked past it.

Fortunately, there was no line. He bought a supply of stamps and quickly headed back to his car. As he rounded the corner to walk along the railroad tracks, it surprised him to see a woman standing next to his BMW.

She had her back to him, but the hourglass figure in a short white dress seemed vaguely familiar. When he got close enough to see her blonde hair, his heart thumped in his chest. As he picked up his pace, he whispered, "Dear God, it can't be!"

Trying to be cool about this unnerving encounter, he came up behind her. "Excuse me, miss, you shouldn't be on this street alone. Do you need help?"

She turned around. The shock of seeing her face to face left Daniel speechless. "Hello, Dr. Daniel Hanson. It is a pleasure to meet you." She held out her hand to shake his.

Daniel didn't react. He couldn't. The woman from his dream stood there, in a dress that did little to hide her voluptuous body. "Who are you?"

"My name is Ezra." She reached for his hand and held it in hers. "I am hoping we can come to know one another."

Daniel shook his head, trying to think straight. "Have we ever met?"

"In a manner of speaking. You may not remember." Ezra put her other hand on top of Daniel's. "None of that is important. What has been is already gone. Our focus must be now."

Looking into her sky-blue eyes, Daniel wondered if a drowning man had this vision of the sky before going under for the last time. "Ezra, let's go someplace to talk."

Ezra squeezed his hand as she tensed with some unseen threat. "I cannot. My time here is short."

Daniel could see the near panic rising in her. "Ezra, are you in trouble? If you are, maybe I can help. I'm a doctor."

"I know well you are a healer. I, too, am a healer." Ezra moved closer to Daniel and gently caressed his cheek. "There is a way you can help me, if you have a mind to do so."

The faint odor of honeysuckle filled his nose. The uncanny déjà vu of this meeting had his mind reeling. He couldn't remember enough of his dream to know if this had been part of it. The honeysuckle: he'd smelled it yesterday and again this morning. Presley had smelled it, too. And the dress—he'd joked with Presley about getting a sexy nurse's uniform. The connection couldn't be a coincidence.

"Do you know Presley Knowles? Did she arrange for you to be here?"

"I have awareness of Presley Knowles. But I assure you, she did not arrange this, nor does she know I am here."

"Have you talked to her?"

"We have not spoken."

"Then how do you know her?"

"The answers to your questions will come, but not now. We must do what needs to be done while there is time."

"Ezra, you aren't making sense. What are you talking about?"

"You did say you would help me."

"Of course I'll help you. But you have to help me understand."

"I promise you I will. But it cannot be now."

"Ezra, why are you so anxious? At least sit in the car with me for a few minutes."

Now close to tears, Ezra clearly communicated her urgency to him. "Daniel, please, will you hold me?"

"Of course I'll hold you." Daniel put his arms around her and held her close. He couldn't resist the compulsion to kiss her hair. Holding this dream woman and having her glorious tits pressed into his chest gave him a hard-on. He couldn't control it. Ezra had to feel it, the ridge wedged against her belly. "I'm sorry about this. You are a very beautiful woman."

"Do not apologize, Daniel. Your arousal calms me. It is a declaration that I please you."

"Ezra, a man would have to be dead for you not to please him!"

Ezra's smile made her eyes sparkle. "Even then, perhaps I could find a way."

Daniel lightly brushed Ezra's back with the palm of his hand. "I bet you could at that." Still holding her tightly, he tried to get more information. "Will you tell me what's wrong?"

"Only that I need something that only you can give."

Resting his hand on the soft curve at the top of her ass, Daniel urged her to continue. "What would that be, beautiful lady?"

Ezra did not reply. Daniel felt her thigh muscles gently clench and release. With the contraction of her pelvis against his, he had the compulsion to pull up her skirt. She repeated the motion and the compulsion became stronger.

Daniel glanced down the street. He saw no one. Struggling to keep his wits, he again asked her to come with him. "Ezra, my house isn't far. Let's go there and we will have some privacy."

"Daniel, I cannot, not yet. You must agree to hold me and we must seal the promise."

"Ezra, I don't understand."

"Daniel, please, we must do it now. Over there, take me there." Ezra pointed to a secluded alley beside the factory.

"We can't do that." Even as he said it, Daniel knew he could not walk away from her.

"Daniel, please!"

The impulse to do as she asked overwhelmed him. "C'mon, before somebody comes by."

He took her hand and practically dragged her toward the alley. She almost fell. "Wait, please." She stopped and kicked off her white stiletto heels. After tossing them by the car door, she again took his hand. "I am ready."

"Yeah, so am I. Let's go." Daniel took Ezra deep into the narrow alley. "It's dirty in here. Your dress will be ruined."

"I will get another. That is not important."

"If you say so." Daniel squeezed her breasts. "I've been dreaming about your tits all week. I must have seen you somewhere. I couldn't make up tits like this."

"Lift my dress."

"Yes, ma'am! I'm pleased to oblige." Daniel pulled Ezra's skirt up around her waist. She had nothing on under it. "Shit, Ezra. You really want this bad!"

"I want you, Daniel. Do it now."

Daniel unzipped his khakis and extracted his cock from his undershorts. The intoxicating odor of honeysuckle and strawberries filled the small space of the alley, making him feel stoned. While flying high as a kite, Daniel forgot any concerns he had about being seen. "Oh, yeah, baby, I'm going to fuck you real good."

He pushed Ezra's legs wide apart with his knees. Sliding his prick against her clit, he made her moan. "Tell me how much you want this, Ezra. You went to all the trouble to track me down. I want to hear you tell me why."

"I want you inside of me, Daniel. I want you to hold me."

"I'll hold you, Ezra. You can take that to the bank." Daniel lunged forward, burying the full length of his cock inside her cunt. Grabbing hold of her wrists, he pinned both arms over her head and lunged again. Ezra muffled a scream with the force of the impact. "I'm going to make you come, beautiful Ezra. That's what you want, isn't it?"

"Sweet heaven above, yes, I want to share an orgasm with you."

Daniel continued to pound himself into her. Each thrust brought him closer to the edge, and seemed to do the same for her. The intensity of the sex escalated into mutual delirium. She writhed against him in frenzied heat as her climax overtook her.

Suddenly, his own orgasm seized him. In a blinding flash of light, he ejaculated. Sensation surged through him with the jolt of a lightning strike. All sensibility left him, for how long he couldn't be sure. When he finally came down from the feeling of electrical shock, he leaned against the wall, suddenly alone.

He shoved his softening prick back into his pants, and then ran out of the alley. "Ezra, where are you? Ezra?" He looked up and down the street. She wasn't there. Running back into the alley, he saw there was still no sign of her.

Staggering out of the alley, he leaned against the car to steady himself. Looking down, he saw her shoes lying next to the car. With undeniable relief he picked them up and tossed them onto the seat. He wasn't crazy; she did exist. She had been there, and then she had vanished.

Go to page 104

No sooner had Daniel hung up from his message to Presley than his cell phone rang. Hoping Presley had called him back, he answered without looking at the number.

"Hello."

"Yes, hello, Dr. Hanson? This is Mrs. Parsons. I'm working the emergency room today. We've just been notified that a three-car accident has occurred, with several people seriously injured. Dr. Richards asked me to call you to come in. We may need help."

Daniel's professionalism barely covered his disappointment that the call wasn't from Presley. "Yes, of course, Mrs. Parsons. I'm on my way."

Grabbing his keys, Daniel ran to his car. He needed gas, but couldn't take the time now to fill the tank. Hoping he had enough left to get by, he backed out of his garage. The odd sweet floral scent that had followed him since yesterday still lingered.

As he rolled down the window to air out the car, he muttered, "That has to be Presley's damn perfume!"

When Daniel arrived at the hospital, he saw several ambulances and knew it must be a bad one. The paramedics were shifting the victims onto gurneys and wheeling them inside. His trauma training kicked in, and he immediately began helping with the triage process. Out of the five people brought in, three of them sustained life-threatening injuries.

Dr. Richards, the elder statesman of the medical staff, shouted at him, "Hanson, I'll take this one. You get the others." The patient with severe bleeding and shock had gone into cardiac arrest. A trauma team already had him in the resuscitation area.

The nurses managed the two with minor injuries and Daniel treated the other two, one with blunt force trauma from being thrown from the car and the other with a head injury similar to Presley's. Forcing the distracting memory of Presley out of his mind, he focused on doing his job.

Once the golden hour had passed, the emergency room had quieted to its usual routine. The accident victims had been stabilized and admitted. The trauma team had succeeded in resuscitating the bleeder and had taken him to surgery. The other two critically injured patients had been taken to intensive care.

Daniel found Dr. Richards in the doctor's lounge having a quick cup of coffee before seeing his next patient.

"Nice work in there, Eric. When you called the code blue, I thought we had lost that one."

"We almost did. The oddest thing happened. He flatlined. We intubated him and used the defibrillator. Nothing. I pumped adrenaline into him and sparked again, figuring if that didn't do it, I would have to pronounce him. All of a sudden, his eyes popped open and seemed to glow blue for a split second. Startled the living shit out of me. He coughed a couple of times and then started breathing again."

"Jesus, that sounds like one for the books!"

"I've been doing this since you were in diapers, my friend. I've never seen anything like it."

"There seems to be an epidemic of it lately. I had an odd one about a week ago."

"You mean that Knowles woman, the reporter?"

"Yeah, her."

"I heard about that. I also heard she left with you when you discharged her."

"Unless you still need me in emergency, I'm going back to my regular shift."

"No comment?"

"None."

"Well, if you ever feel the need to unburden your soul, I'm always good for some tasty dish."

"You're a gossip whore, do you know that?"

"Helps keep me going." Dr. Richards checked his watch. "I need to get back out there. See you later."

Daniel also checked the time. He still had forty-five minutes before his shift started at two o'clock. If he hid in the lounge, maybe he could relax for a few minutes before making his rounds. After pouring a cup of coffee, he sat on the sofa and closed his eyes.

He must have dozed for a few minutes because he started awake when he heard a female voice say his name. "Dr. Daniel Hanson?"

It took him a moment to get his bearings and remember he sat in the doctor's lounge. Figuring they needed him again and a nurse had come to get him, he answered without looking up. "Yes, what is it?"

"I hope you remember me, even though we have never met face to face."

Daniel did not recognize the voice. When he turned to see who spoke to him, he was struck dumb. There, next to the closed door, stood the blonde woman from his dream. She wore a short white dress, with a neckline revealing cleavage worthy of a classic pin-up girl. The white stiletto heels had to be at least four inches high, making her already long legs appear even longer.

Trying to convince himself that he wasn't still asleep and dreaming, Daniel got up and walked over to where she stood. "Who are you?"

"My name is Ezra. I am pleased we are finally able to speak."

"How did you get in here? This is a restricted area of the hospital."

"No one saw me come in. I am here only to introduce myself to you."

Daniel rubbed his temple. "I don't remember how I know you, but I must have met you somewhere. I've been dreaming about you."

Ezra smiled, making her blue eyes sparkle. "Have they been pleasant dreams?"

Daniel glanced at her cleavage. "Oh, yes, I'd say they were good dreams."

Ezra came closer, narrowing the short distance between them. Reaching up, she lightly brushed his lips with her fingertips. "That pleases me that you enjoyed them."

Being so close to this mystery woman not only excited Daniel, it also intrigued him. "Where are you from, Ezra? You sure as hell don't look like you're from Kansas."

"I have lived in many places. Perhaps soon, I will live in Abilene."

Forcing himself to remember the hospital rules, Daniel knew he had to get her out of the doctor's lounge. "Ezra, you can't stay here. This lounge is only for hospital staff. I'm a doctor, but you're not allowed in here. If someone should come in, there could be a problem."

"I am also a healer, even if I am not recognized as such in this place." Ezra smiled. "Do not worry. No one will come in while I am here."

"We can't be sure of that. Why don't we go to the cafeteria and talk? I'll buy you a cup of coffee."

"I do not want coffee. I want you." Ezra put her arms around Daniel's neck. "Will you hold me, Daniel?"

Ezra's breasts pressed into his chest. Daniel could not control his reaction and his hard-on pushed into her soft belly. The urge to kiss this beautiful woman overwhelmed him. Wrapping his arms around her waist, he spoke the words into her mouth. "Oh, yes, Ezra, I will hold you."

The moment his mouth covered hers, the odor of fresh honeysuckle and strawberries enveloped him like a cloud. It made him high, the way smoking dope in college had made him feel. He licked the inside of her mouth, the sweetness of her fragrance coating his tongue.

Pulling away from the kiss, he tried again to persuade her to leave. "Ezra, we have to go somewhere else. I am about to break enough rules to get my ass thrown out of here."

"Daniel, they will not throw you out. No one will know."
Ezra reached between them and gently stroked his erection.
"I do not have much time. You must be satisfied before I
leave."

Gritting his teeth in a fruitless attempt to sustain control,
Daniel realized he had to have her, no matter what the consequences. "Jesus Christ, Ezra. I don't know who the hell you
are, but you're driving me fucking crazy!"

Daniel grabbed her hand and pulled her toward an over-
stuffed armchair in the corner. Ezra caught her heel on the
carpet and nearly tripped. "Daniel, wait." She quickly kicked
off her shoes, leaving them on the floor. "Now, where shall
we go?"

"Over here." He led her behind the chair. "Ezra, this will
have to be a quickie. Are you sure you want to do this?"

"Oh, yes, Daniel Hanson, I need you inside me. It will anchor the connection."

Not really registering what she said, Daniel bent her over
the chair. "If you say so. God, your tits are unbelievable." He
reached around Ezra and filled his hands with the perfect
mounds of flesh. "I've been dreaming about them all damn
week!"

"You must raise my skirt!"

"Sweetheart, you read my mind." Daniel pulled up her skirt.
Ezra wore nothing underneath. "Do you always want it this
badly?" Daniel unzipped his pants and untangled his cock from
his underwear.

"Dr. Daniel Hanson, I want you."

"Well, pretty lady, you are about to receive what you came
here to get." Forcing her legs apart with his knees, Daniel
wasted no time positioning himself behind her. With one
hard thrust, he penetrated Ezra, not stopping until his balls
brushed her inner thighs. Ezra stifled a scream, the sound
being more of a gasp.

With no hesitation, Daniel pulled out and slammed back into her. His urgency increased with each thrust, his pelvis thumping against her rounded ass. No longer caring where they were or who might walk in, Daniel fucked Ezra with mindless lust.

With a force Daniel had never before experienced with a woman, Ezra's cunt squeezed his prick. When her orgasm hit, the intensity of the spasms shot through his groin, triggering his climax. Semen erupted from his cock with unexpected power. He lunged forward with the force of it, losing awareness of everything but the sensation, and then, suddenly the sensation stopped.

When Daniel regained consciousness, he found himself slumped over the armchair, with his softened prick still exposed. He was alone in the room.

"Ezra, where are you? Ezra!" Quickly arranging himself and zipping his pants, he ran to the washroom. He knocked and shouted, "Ezra!" Opening the door, he found the toilet empty. Running out to the hallway, he nearly hit Mrs. Parsons with the door.

"Dr. Hanson, are you all right?"

Realizing he must look frantic, Daniel made an effort to calm himself. "I'm sorry, Mrs. Parsons. I'm looking for someone. Did you by any chance see a blonde woman in a short white dress in the hall?"

"No, doctor. No one has walked past the nurse's station since Dr. Richards returned to emergency. Are you sure you are all right?"

"Yes, thank you, Mrs. Parsons. I'm fine. I suppose I fell asleep in there and had a nightmare."

"It's no wonder, considering that accident. It's a blessing no one died from it."

"Yeah, it is. If you'll excuse me, I need to wash up before my shift starts."

Daniel went back into the lounge and leaned against the

door, his sense of reality shaken to the core. Had he been sleepwalking and thought he fucked his dream woman?

Then he looked down. Lying on the floor were her white stiletto heels. Not knowing if he should laugh or cry, he picked them up. She had been here, and then she had disappeared.

Chapter Eight

"Eat this slowly. I don't want you making yourself sick." Presley set the plate of scrambled eggs in front of Vadim. "Where is the bread?"

"I made you toast. It's on the plate with the eggs."

"That is not bread."

"Yes it is."

"Bread is dark, and torn from a loaf."

"If you mean pumpernickel, I don't have any."

"You would bake me fresh bread, made of dark rye and beer. It is what I ate with eggs." Vadim pushed the thin slices of toast from his plate. "Have you forgotten everything?"

"You have a serious attitude problem, Mr. Ghost." Presley picked up a slice of the rejected toast and took a bite. "I have never baked bread and never will. That's why God made bakeries." Before Vadim could correct her, Presley added, "Yeah, I know, you're not a ghost."

Using his knife as a shovel, Vadim scooped eggs onto his spoon. He studied them before putting them into his mouth. "It seems eggs have not changed." After he chewed them, he tried to swallow and instantly gagged.

Presley grabbed a wad of paper towels. She ran to him and covered his mouth with the towels as he retched again. "Damn it, Vadim, I told you to take it slow. Your stomach doesn't know from food. You haven't eaten anything in hundreds of years."

Vadim pushed her hand away. "You will not wipe my face like a spitting child! I will eat!" This time, he picked up a bit of egg in his fingers. Putting it in his mouth, he chewed slowly and then carefully swallowed. Even though it obviously caused him pain, he managed it.

"Do you have milk in this time?"

"Of course we have milk. Do you want some?"

"Warmed milk always settled my belly."

Presley quickly poured some milk in a mug and microwaved it for a minute. After she handed Vadim the warmed cup, he asked, "Is there a fire in that box?"

"Not exactly. It's called a microwave. We use it to heat food."

"You will teach me how it works?"

"I can show you how to use it. I don't know how it works."

Vadim sipped the warm milk and easily swallowed. Obviously finding it soothing, he smiled. "Perhaps I am once again as a child suckling from his mama's teat."

Presley pushed back his long hair and curled her arm around his neck. Pulling his face close to her breasts, she teased, "If you are into suckling, I have some teats right here you can suck."

The silver sparkles in Vadim's eyes brightened. "I see my Ninotchka still lives inside Presley Knowles. Your whoring ways have survived." He slipped his hand under Presley's shirt and squeezed her breast.

"Excuse me!" Presley yanked his hair. "What do you mean, 'whoring ways'?"

"You sold yourself before I took you as my woman."

"I did what?"

"Ninotchka, you do not remember? You earned your keep at an inn by selling yourself to men. I took you from there to be my woman, so you belonged only to me."

"Are you telling me I became your personal whore?"

"You became my woman and shared my bed. No other man dared touch you. I would have killed him."

Vadim's large hand massaging her bare breast took some of the edge from his words, but not all of it. "Would you still kill another man who touched me?"

"Your doctor still lives, does he not?"

Vadim calmly sipped his milk while he continued to rub her breast. Presley pushed his hand away. "Vadim, you gave me your word! You told me Daniel would not be hurt!"

"The doctor is well and being closely guarded."

"By the blonde, I suppose?"

"Yes."

"Vadim, what the hell is going on? In some weird way, I know you. When I had my accident, I recognized you and wanted to stay with you. Daniel doesn't even believe I had a near death experience. He sure as hell can't handle a run-in with some stupid blonde bimbo ghost!"

"Ezra is not a ghost, nor is she stupid."

"You know her, don't you?"

"I do. She is a highly evolved soul who wishes to know the love of a man."

"Fucking shit! She's after Daniel, isn't she?" Presley leaned on the table, gripping the edges until her knuckles turned white. "Vadim, I'm telling you, if Daniel is hurt in any way because of this, I will rip you apart with my bare hands." She meant every word she said.

Vadim again sipped his milk, further infuriating Presley. "Ninotchka, you will be hearing from the doctor soon. You can ask him yourself if he is well."

"What do you know that you aren't telling me?"

"I know many things that I cannot tell you. It is part of who I am."

"You mean a ghost."

"If that continues to be your chosen frame of reference, then yes, Presley, it is part of being a ghost."

"I need to call Daniel. And Vadim, he better be all right."

"He is."

Presley left Vadim in the kitchen and went to find her purse. Retrieving her cell phone, she saw she had a message from Daniel. The relief she felt when she heard his voice made her knees rubbery. He sounded fine, with no hint of anything out of the ordinary having happened. The message had come in about two hours ago.

She pressed the callback button and got his voice mail. "Hello, Daniel? This is Presley. I just got your message. It seems we're playing phone tag. I don't know what your schedule is like today, but call me back when you can. I'm fine, and hope you are, too. Talk to you later. Bye."

When she turned around, she saw that Vadim stood in the kitchen door watching her. "It is obvious you care for this man."

"Let me see, we've established you are not a ghost—you are a voyeur and it seems you also get off on eavesdropping."

"I am not familiar with the word."

"It means listening to private conversations."

"You were not having a conversation. He did not answer."

Presley threw her cell phone at him. "You are a fucking piece of work!"

Vadim caught the cell phone, moving so quickly Presley didn't see him lift his arm. "And you are still the passionate one who left me so long ago."

"I didn't leave you; you left me."

"It seems we left each other." Vadim walked over and gave her back the phone. He stood in front of her, as intimidating and fierce looking as she expected he had been four hundred years ago. After they'd made love, he'd somehow retrieved his clothes that had disappeared. He again wore the baggy blue trousers, open white shirt, and leather boots.

Presley took the phone, her fingers lightly brushing his hand. Her whole arm tingled from the contact. "We have to get you some other clothes. You also need a haircut and a shave. Even if this is New York, you can't go out looking like that. You'll scare the bejesus out of people."

"You are already trying to change me? My clothes, hair, and whiskers have served me well for several centuries. I do not need to change."

Presley closed her hand around Vadim's. "Everyone needs to change, Vadim. It is the only way we grow."

"Now you speak to me as Ezra would."

"Ezra talks to you?"

"She has haunted my existence since those sons of dogs slit my throat."

"Ezra has been with you that long?"

"No. I would not permit her to stay with me. Every time she would come, I would force her to leave."

"Why?"

"Because I did not trust her. I did not understand she wanted to help; I thought her to be a demon harvesting my soul."

Presley almost made a joke, but saw the seriousness of Vadim's conviction. "Who did stay with you?"

"No one."

"Vadim, there had to be others. You couldn't have been alone all this time."

"It was my choice to remain alone. I had my space, and the memories of our life. I needed nothing more."

Still holding his hand, Presley led him to the sofa. "Let's sit."

"If you wish."

Presley had to find out more about Ezra. Daniel's life should not be impacted by any of this. She felt responsible for bringing him into it. "Vadim, you know I wanted to stay with you after my accident. But Daniel shouldn't have to suffer the consequences of what happened to me. He is a doctor and he did his job. That's all."

Vadim's penetrating stare rocked her to her toes. "He did

more than that, Ninotchka. He took you into his bed, and is on the brink of claiming you as his own."

"No one can claim me, Vadim. Neither Daniel nor you has any claim on me."

"Men have always claimed women, dear one. You may not care to call it that, but it is what animals do."

"We are not animals; we are human beings."

Much to her surprise, Vadim laughed raucously. "Presley Knowles, human beings are animals, and mate as such! For all the years that stretch between us, it seems some things have yet to be fully understood."

"Is that why you are letting Ezra chase Daniel? So he doesn't claim me?"

"I cannot control what Ezra does. She is an old soul with wisdom and strength reaching far beyond what I have acquired."

"What does she want with him?"

"When she saw him with you, Ezra experienced desire. She was drawn to him as a man and as a healer."

"Jesus Christ! She watched us fuck?"

"We both watched."

"I can't believe this shit! She watched us fuck and now she wants some for herself?"

"You are jealous."

"And you and your ghost girlfriend both need a lesson in privacy!"

"In the spirit world, nothing is hidden. The transparency of thought is a way of life."

"Well, this is the world of flesh and blood. Here, privacy and boundaries mean something!"

"It does not seem to trouble you that I can hear your thoughts. We have been communicating as such since your accident."

"Talking to you in my head isn't the same as you and Blondie watching Daniel fuck me!"

"Your memory is short, Ninotchka. Of your own volition, you permitted both Ezra and myself to share the loving with you."

"And that's another thing! Exactly what did I agree to with this 'hold me' business?"

"You have agreed to share your silver cord."

"My what?"

"It is the thread that connects spirit to matter. Your essence self could not remain in a physical body without it. At death, it severs. The spirit is released and the body grows cold."

"You don't have one, do you?"

"No, I do not. Only incarnates do. I cannot sustain physical substance without it."

"Is that why you kept disappearing?"

"Indeed, it is. Now, I am using your cord. You agreed, and we consummated the pact."

"Does that mean I am tied to you?"

"Yes."

"Can it be untied?"

"At the moment of your death, we are both released."

"So I have to die to get rid of you?"

"That is how we separated centuries ago."

Her attraction to this brawny man could not be denied. Sitting this close to him, she had trouble thinking clearly. But the independence she had fought so hard to retain hung in the balance. "Vadim, I don't plan on dying anytime soon. If we are joined at the hip, what happens when I see other men? If you can read my mind, you know I'm not into monogamy."

"And what would you say if the doctor asks you to be his woman?"

"I slept with him. I didn't say I would marry him."

"It is in his mind as a possibility. Therefore, it could become reality."

"I'm not talking about Daniel. I'm talking about you! It sounds like you intend to stay here."

"I do."

"Here, with me?"

"Of course."

"For crying out loud, Vadim, you can't just move in!"

"I already have. It is what you wanted."

"There has to be an out clause! I didn't know what I agreed to do!"

"You understood and agreed on a soul level. Otherwise, the fusion between us would not have happened."

"It's like you made up the game and didn't bother telling me the rules! This is so fucked up, I can't even wrap my mind around it!"

"Given time, you will adjust."

Presley jumped when the cell phone in her hand rang. Flipping the unit open, she saw Daniel's number. "It's him."

"I know." Vadim quietly stood and went back to the kitchen.

"Hello, Daniel."

"Presley, thank God you answered. I really need to talk."

"Daniel, you sound upset. Is everything all right?"

"She's real!"

"What?"

"She's fucking real! Her name is Ezra."

Presley's heart filled her throat. "Daniel, what happened?"

"The woman from my dream, she showed up today and told me her name. The damnedest thing is, she's disappeared! The only way I know I'm not delusional is that I have her shoes!"

"You have her what?"

"Her shoes! She kicked them off before we . . ."

Daniel's voice trailed off. He didn't have to say it. Presley knew. "You fucked her, didn't you?"

"Yeah, I fucked her, and then she fucked me! She vanished into thin air! I have no idea who she is, where she is . . ."

Presley breathed into the phone, "Or what she is."

"What did you say? I couldn't hear you."

"Daniel, did she ask you to hold her?"

"How do you know that?"

"Did she?"

"Yes."

"And did you tell her you would?"

"A couple of times."

"Oh, God!"

"Presley, you know something about this, don't you? Did you set me up like some freaking pigeon?"

"Fuck, no! No way in hell did I set you up."

"But you know who she is, don't you?"

"Daniel . . ." Presley wanted to tell him, but she couldn't bring herself to do it. "You would think I'm crazy if I tried to explain this."

"Goddamn it, Presley! I've just had a woman disappear while my frigging cock was in her cunt! And you know one hell of a lot more than you're telling me. That's it! I'm coming to New York!"

"Daniel, wait! Hello, Daniel?" Looking at the phone, she saw the display had returned to the number pad. "Shit, he hung up!" Presley pressed the call back button and got Daniel's voice mail. "Daniel, call me back, please!" She hung up and waited. The phone didn't ring.

After several minutes, she tried again. This time the call forwarded to an answering service. "Dr. Hanson's line, may I help you?"

"Yes, please. I'm trying to reach Dr. Daniel Hanson. Is he available?"

"I'm sorry, Dr. Hanson has been called away on a personal matter. You may leave a message, or if this is an emergency, you will be directed to another staff doctor."

"No, thank you, that's all right. I'll try his home number."

After leaving another message on Daniel's home answering machine and sending him a text message, Presley gave up. Going back to the kitchen, Presley found Vadim fussing with the microwave. "What are you doing?"

"I want more warm milk. I cannot light the flame." He

continued to push the buttons, making the oven beep and the time flash.

"Watch me. This is how to do it." Presley put the cup of milk inside and closed the oven door. Pressing the one-minute button, she explained, "One minute is enough time to warm a cup of milk. For now, use only this button." The oven beeped. "That means it's finished." She opened the door and handed him the warm cup.

"I have never seen such things!"

"Glad you're enjoying yourself. Wish I were."

"You are troubled by the doctor?"

"He told Ezra he would hold her, and then he fucked her. Now, I think he is on his way to New York. Yeah, you could say I'm troubled." Presley noticed Vadim's eyes glowing. "You already knew about Ezra, didn't you?"

"Yes."

"Why didn't you tell me?'

"The doctor can surely speak for himself. I knew he would."

"You want Ezra to nail him, don't you?"

"It's a far better outcome than if he would challenge me for you."

"And if he did?"

"I would fight for you."

"You mean that, don't you?"

"Yes."

As Presley watched, the silver glow in Vadim's eyes deepened to the color of liquid mercury. "What makes your eyes glow like that?"

"Energetic changes in my auric field."

"They just got darker. What changed?"

Vadim set his cup on the table and walked behind her. Pulling her tightly against him, he pressed his erection into her ass. "This changed."

The fusion between them became a reality for Presley as Vadim allowed her to feel his desire. "My God, Vadim! You're on fire!"

"I am, and you are the flame in my soul."

"Can you feel me the same way?"

"I can."

"Fucking hell, this is definitely better than drugs!"

"You do not need opiates when you are with me. What I have to give is beyond anything you have known."

"When you said you would fight for me, is this what you meant?"

"There is no longer any need to fight as I did before. Now, my weapons are not of this world. The doctor cannot be to you what I am."

Vadim raised her shirt, exposing her breasts. He roughly fondled her tits and pinched her nipples. Presley heard him, even though he didn't speak aloud. *I felt your need. You wanted me to touch you like this. It ignites your fire.*

Presley leaned back against his chest and softly moaned. *Vadim, can you hear my thoughts now?*

I can.

Your cock feels like a steel rod against me. Please, put it in me.

Are you not concerned we might conceive?

I wear a birth control patch. I can't get pregnant unless I stop wearing it.

Then, you could not conceive with the doctor?

Presley answered, speaking her thought as easily as thinking it. "No, because of this." She lowered her panties and put Vadim's hand on a small circle stuck to her right hip. "It's called a contraceptive. It protects women from having a baby unless they really want one."

Vadim slid his hand farther inside Presley's panties and gripped her vulva in his palm. She saw a picture in her mind of Vadim bending a woman over a table and pulling up her skirt. *That's me, isn't it?*

Yes, Ninotchka, it is. It is the first time I had you, at the inn. His hand flexed inside her panties. *You left with me that night. You never wanted another man once I spread your legs.*

If you were hung then like you are now, I can see why.

My organ is the same. My ability to satisfy you is more.

Then do it!

Vadim pulled Presley's shirt over her head. Then he knelt on the floor behind her and took off her panties. She stood naked in front of him. Leaning forward, he rubbed his whiskers against her bare ass, and then he put his open mouth against her cheek. Clenching the flesh between his teeth, he sucked and licked her ass cheek.

Presley braced herself against the table. Vadim sent another picture into her mind, this time showing her what he intended to do. *I see you have always wanted this.*

Oh my God! You would do that to me?

We are animals, dear heart. All animals want to be licked.

Before Presley had a chance to prepare herself, Vadim spread her ass cheeks and licked the sensitive skin around her anus. When he inserted his tongue into her hole, she involuntarily clenched her rectum. Without stopping what he was doing, Vadim directed her. *Ninotchka, you must relax and allow the pleasure to carry you.*

This is new to me, Vadim. I'm working on it. Presley focused on relaxing. While he continued to lick her, Vadim sent another wave of his arousal through her body. Presley moaned. *You're so fucking hot! You're going to come in your pants.*

I will not release my seed until I am inside you. We will climax together.

Says you!

Vadim's hot breath blasted inside her when he laughed. *Presley, your expression comes at a most inappropriate time.*

Vadim, it isn't every day I get rimmed by a ghost. I'm creaming down my legs!

Vadim forced her legs farther apart. He licked the insides

of her thighs, and then nuzzled her pussy. *You told me you enjoy my scent. As you are now aware, I also enjoy yours. A man does not forget the scent of his mate.*

Presley shuddered. The intensity of Vadim's emotion coupled with their combined arousal brought her right to the edge. She held on, wanting him inside of her when she came.

Understanding her need, Vadim immediately stood. This time, he took off his shirt and dropped his pants rather than making them disappear. Presley bent farther over the table, in the same position she had seen in her mind.

When Vadim drove his rock-hard cock into her, their arousal merged in a heated frenzy so intense Presley nearly fainted. She felt his arms supporting her as he gently caressed her mind with his. *Ninotchka, allow my strength to become your own. Everything I am is now yours. Draw on it and be lifted into the heavens.*

Presley floated in a void of sensation. With a primal instinct as ancient as time, she released herself to Vadim. Her identity merged with his. They became one body and one mind. The cock in her vagina became part of her. His sensations belonged to her as hers belonged to him.

Vadim held her tightly. Her orgasm joined with his as electrical current pulsed through their bodies. Rays of sparkling light surrounded them as they soared in boundless bliss. He claimed her body and her soul.

Chapter Nine

Presley left Vadim alone while she ran out for more groceries. Stopping at a small bakery on the way to the market, she bought him several varieties of rye and pumpernickel bread.

When she got back, she found him where she had left him, staring out the window at the street below. He did not turn around when she came in.

"You know I'm back."

"I am aware. Thank you for the dark bread."

"How did you know I got you dark bread?"

When he turned around, his eyes again glowed silver. "I watched you as you shopped. I know everything you purchased and how you carefully selected items you thought I could eat."

"Geez, Louise! If the CIA ever finds out about you, we're in deep shit!" His eyes briefly glowed brighter as she felt him probing her mind for the meaning of CIA. "You know, that eye thing you do is freaky. Can you turn off those night-lights?"

"I have never tried. I expect I could dim them, if that would please you."

"It's not about pleasing me, it's about not drawing attention to yourself. You can't do that in front of people on the street."

"I am satisfied being here with you. I do not need to go out among others."

"What are you, an agoraphobic ghost? If you are determined to be incarnate again, then you have to learn how to live in this city."

"If you will teach me, I will learn."

Presley glanced at the clock. The afternoon had slipped by without her getting any work done. She still needed to proof her article and get it ready to turn in tomorrow. "We will get to it, but I have to work on my story. I have a deadline tomorrow."

"It is the work you do for money?"

"Yeah. It's how I can afford to keep you in black bread and milk, and maybe throw in a pair of jeans and a shirt or two."

"Whatever I need, I can manifest."

"Excuse me? What did you say?"

"I can manifest that which I need to sustain myself."

"Vadim, New York City isn't la la land. Things don't magically appear when you need them. You have to buy what you need."

"It is not magic, Presley Knowles. It is the ability to manipulate matter. If there is a genuine need, one such as I am can manifest what is needed."

Not believing a word of it, Presley challenged him. "All right then, you see these jeans I'm wearing?"

"I prefer a dress. Trousers are for men."

"Don't change the subject. Do you see that what I am wearing is different than what you are wearing?"

"I do."

"Then, let me see you manifest a pair of these that fit you, since you need new clothes."

Vadim hunkered down beside Presley. Trying not to be distracted by his hand on her leg, she watched as he examined the material. He paid particular attention to the zipper, tracing it with his finger. As much as she wanted him to pull it down, she kept still and allowed him time to study the metal.

With his hand still on her thigh, he looked at the back of a chair. Following his lead, she also turned her attention to the chair. She could hardly believe it when she saw a misty silver shadow form. It slowly coalesced into a wispy shape, similar to a tailor's pattern for a pair of pants.

Vadim stood. Without taking his eyes off of the outline on the chair, he held his hands over the garment. As she continued to watch, the shape gradually became solid. When Vadim finally lowered his hands, a new pair of jeans lay draped over the back of the chair.

"Well, I'll be damned!" She picked up the pants and brushed the material against her face. "They're real!"

"Just as I am, Presley. Reality extends far beyond what can be known with the physical senses."

"Can you teach me how to do this?"

"Perhaps. It depends on your willingness to go beyond what you know, to a place of greater truth." Vadim took the jeans. "Shall I put them on?"

"Go for it!"

Vadim laid the jeans on the chair. He then untied the string holding up his baggy trousers and let them drop to the floor. He had on nothing underneath. Presley stared with unabashed admiration at his genitals hanging heavily from his groin. "It is gratifying that you appreciate my manhood."

"You know what I'm thinking, don't you?"

"I do. You want to take me in your mouth." Vadim stepped out of his trousers and left them in a crumpled heap on the floor. "I understand men of this time hold the experience in high regard."

Presley had to laugh at Vadim's matter-of-fact observation. "Yeah, I suppose you could say most guys appreciate being blown."

"I prefer being inside the flesh of a woman, but am open to 'being blown' as you say."

Even though Vadim appeared calm and controlled on the outside, Presley could see his cock thickening. Their eyes met for a moment, and she spontaneously probed him. *I'm catching on to this.*

Vadim's eyes sparkled, his amusement evident. *Your attempt to read me is admirable.*

She continued to look at him, her concentration creasing her forehead. *Okay, maybe I'm not as good at it as you are, but I'm learning.*

Ninotchka, remember what I told you, do not strain. Reach lightly and what you wish to know will come.

Presley closed her eyes and took a deep breath. When she again looked at Vadim, she remained relaxed and quiet. Rather than seeing anything in her mind, she felt it in her body. The turbulence of Vadim's arousal rolled through her like a dust cloud. *Oh yeah, you're hot again. That's what I wanted to know.*

And now that you know, what will you do?

Show you why men will pay big coin to get a blow job.

Presley sent Vadim a clear image of a hooker kneeling in front of a man with his zipper down and his cock in her mouth. *You are still inclined to such activities. That pleases me.*

Let's see if this pleases you. Presley knelt on Vadim's trousers. The contact with his clothing made her legs tingle, sending tremors up her thighs and into her pelvis. Her clitoris throbbed with the vibration. *What the hell are these pants made of? It's like they're alive!*

They have absorbed my energy. You are reacting to the concentration of my essence in the cloth.

Presley grasped Vadim's prick in her hand. *Let's see how much energy is concentrated in this!*

Vadim shuddered as her tongue connected with his erection. *Ninotchka, I am not used to these sensations. Have mercy!*

Presley slowly licked the sides of his prick before she took his uncut head into her mouth. *Vadim, it is time you know what you have gotten yourself into!*

Not knowing where she'd gotten the nerve, Presley sucked him like she had never sucked before. She held the base of his prick tightly in her hand and used her tongue to caress the flesh she held in her mouth.

Vadim's voice in her mind stopped, and instead she heard the grunts and groans of a man in the throes of arousal. The sounds drove her on as she lapped at him. Her own spit dribbled down her hand and ran down her arm. She didn't care. All she wanted was to bring Vadim to his knees and make him scream her name.

She felt his large hands in her hair and braced herself as he leaned against her. Even supporting his weight, she didn't waver. Lapping and licking, sucking and pulling, she brought him to the edge. Then she stopped, and released him from her mouth.

Vadim pushed forward, trying to lodge his prick back in her mouth. She turned her face to the side, so his cock bumped against her cheek. He bellowed, "Woman, what are you doing? Why do you torture me?"

Presley looked at him, her mind clearer and her vision sharper than they had ever been before. With clarity and conviction, she answered him. "Power, Vadim. It is who I am now. I am not your personal whore anymore. I am your equal."

She could feel her eyes glowing as Vadim's did, as if someone had screwed two tiny silver lightbulbs in them. With a new sense of herself, she again took his tormented cock into her mouth. She sucked as an infant would at her mama's nipple, her singular goal to pull the cream into her mouth.

"Ninotchka!" Vadim roared with defeat as Presley claimed her prize and swallowed every drop of her victory.

Neither Vadim nor Presley had the breath to speak. She leaned against his legs, feeling his fingers still tangled in her hair. *Ninotchka, I need to sit.*

So do I. Presley slowly stood. She picked up Vadim's newly created jeans, then took him by the hand and led him to the sofa in the living room. "Here. Take these and put them on. I'll get you some bread and warm milk."

"Ninotchka, you have become a woman of both strength and courage. You are well able to walk at my side."

"Glad you think so. Put on your pants and sit down already."

Presley went back to the kitchen. When she returned a few minutes later, Vadim had pulled on the jeans. Amazed at what a difference seeing him in regular clothes made, Presley asked, "Can you make a shirt the same way you did the pants?"

"I can. But I have to have a sense of the garment before I do. I do not know how a shirt of this time is fashioned."

Presley handed him the cup of milk and bread. "Here, take this. I have something to show you." She picked up the remote control to the television and turned it on.

"What is that?"

"Television."

"How does it work?"

"It's like when we talk to each other in our minds, except this is with pictures of people and stories about them."

"You hear me when our thoughts vibrate on the same frequency. There are frequencies with this television?"

"Yes, there are frequencies. The radio waves travel through the air. The television can hear the signal just like your brain can hear my thoughts." Presley focused on Vadim. She brought to mind an image of Vadim in bed with her. "You see what I see, don't you?"

"I do. Your appetite is evident."

"Hold that thought until I finish! Instead of seeing pictures in my mind, you can see pictures on the television." Presley sat down on the sofa beside Vadim and showed him the remote. "This little gadget lets you change channels. I suppose you could say it lets you change to many different frequencies and watch the pictures on each one, until you find one that interests you."

"I am familiar with the concept of transmitting thought. This television receives the signal from another source?"

"Yup. We have people who spend their lives doing nothing but making the pictures for television and broadcasting the signals." Presley handed Vadim the remote. "Take this. Push the channel button to change signals."

Vadim took the remote and pressed the button a few times. He stopped on the local news showing a story about a warehouse fire in Brooklyn. "What is this?"

"That's the news. Some things on television are real and some aren't. Most stories aren't real, and are just people acting. But news shows are about real things happening to real people." Presley pointed toward the window. "That's a real building burning in that direction. It's another part of the city called Brooklyn."

Vadim sipped his milk and settled back against the sofa. He flipped through a few more channels. "I will learn about your world with this television."

"That's the idea." Presley watched his rapid-fire remote technique for a few minutes. "I swear to God, using a remote has to be in male DNA. You've never seen one before and you're doing what every man I've ever met does. You might want to slow down and actually watch something for a few minutes."

"When I find something that holds my attention, I will."

"I've heard that before!" Presley went to retrieve her laptop. After plugging it in at her desk, she checked on Vadim again before settling down to work. He had switched back to the news. She watched him dunk a slab of dark rye into his cup of milk and bite off a mouthful. "Take it slow with that bread, Vadim. I don't want you puking on my sofa."

"Woman, your worry is unnecessary. My belly is quiet."

"While you're watching, check out the clothes the men are

wearing. You need a shirt to go with those jeans. Your boots will hold you for a while, unless you want to try your hand at a new pair of shoes, too."

"I will take note of the clothes. What I need will come."

Presley smiled. "Put me on that list for later." Vadim ignored her innuendo, his focus solely on the television. Presley muttered, "Shit, it really is in your DNA." She left him to his educational viewing, and went to work on her story.

Throughout the evening, Presley forced herself to concentrate on finishing the article. It had started to rain. She found the sound calming, which helped her concentrate. Vadim sat quietly on the sofa, absorbing television shows. She got up only once, when she heard him laugh. Wondering what on earth would be funny enough to make a four-hundred-year-old Cossack laugh, she had to have a look.

"What's so funny, Vadim?"

"These women stomping grapes!" He laughed again. "Do you see, Ninotchka? They are making wine, and fighting in the barrel. Their skin is turning dark from the stain!"

Vadim continued to chuckle at the *I Love Lucy* he had stumbled upon. Presley hadn't considered how his view of the modern world could be skewed by what he watched. "You do understand this is a show to make you laugh. It isn't real."

"What is real and what is not real has little meaning to me, Presley Knowles. My reality is my creation."

"Can't argue with that." She noticed his empty cup on the floor. "I'm going to make a sandwich. Do you want more milk?"

"Yes, and more bread as well."

"Did you see any shirts you can make for yourself?"

"There is one over there." He pointed to the recliner in the corner. A perfectly tailored white dress shirt lay across the chair. "That will serve me."

Presley went over and picked it up. Vadim had materialized another piece of clothing, made with similar material to the blousy shirt he wore, but cut with accurate precision to look like a designer shirt. "How did you do this?"

"I modeled it after one I saw on the television. It came easily once I understood the fashion."

"Yeah, right! Easy as pie."

"No, Presley. Pie would be considerably more difficult."

"On that note, I need a sandwich!"

By the time Presley had finished editing her article, it was almost midnight. She attached it to an e-mail. After checking the e-mail address and the read receipt request one last time, she clicked the send button.

Vadim still sat on the sofa, totally engrossed in his current channel. Presley sat down on the sofa beside him. "What are you watching now?"

"Be still and watch with me. You will see."

Presley glanced at the cable box and saw the Cinemax channel number. It didn't take long for her to know why he'd stopped on this channel. "Oh God, you're watching Skinamax!"

"Is it not a crime in this time to do such things where one can be seen?"

"Well, yes and no. It's not a crime for television, but it is a crime if we did it where other people could see us naked."

"Seeing a bare woman made my organ hard. It matters not that it is television."

Vadim's matter-of-fact pronouncement about getting an erection watching soft-core porn made Presley laugh. "So, you like to look at bare women?"

"I would not be a man if I did not." Presley refrained from explaining that in the Village, many men preferred naked men to naked women.

Not caring that she felt shit-faced tired, Presley still wanted to fool around. She lifted Vadim's hair and whispered in his ear, "Should I take off my clothes?"

Vadim turned his head, his face so close to hers their noses nearly touched. "Your fatigue is evident, Ninotchka. It is too much for us to couple. Your body must rest."

Vadim's breath still had his scent, now mixed with a hint of rye. Presley moved in closer and rubbed her cheek against his whiskers. "But I want to touch you."

"Perhaps you might allow me to touch you." Vadim put his arm around her waist. "I have learned much today from your television."

"What have you learned?" Presley's heart thumped in her chest. Vadim's erection pressed against her leg and she could feel his heat rising

"I have learned modern women enjoy being kissed, and they respond to being held and touched."

"Damn, that's the truth!" Presley lightly touched the bulge in Vadim's jeans. "What else have you learned?"

Vadim cupped Presley's breast in his hand. "I learned that women want physical love as much as men. Many women told Oprah they are dissatisfied with how their men make love."

Presley didn't want to disrupt the mood, but couldn't help laughing. "Fuck, Vadim! You watched Oprah?"

"She is an attractive, sensible woman. You could learn from her as I did!"

"Maybe so. But right now, I'm more interested in what you've learned."

"Take off your shirt for me, Ninotchka."

Presley lifted her T-shirt over her head and peeled it off, leaving her naked from the waist up. "You, too. Take off your shirt."

Vadim opened his shirt and let it slide down his arms and onto the sofa. Presley picked it up and smelled it. "It pleases me that you find my scent stimulating," he said.

"Oh, baby, you should bottle this and sell it at Saks." Presley wrapped his shirt around her neck like a scarf. "I think

I'll keep your shirt and put it over my pillow tonight. You have another one now."

"Yes. Is it satisfactory?"

"I haven't seen it on you yet, but it looks like you did one hell of a job. You even gave it French cuffs. I'll have to get you some cufflinks."

"I will fashion some once I understand the mechanism. I could not see how Mr. Bond made them work."

"Mr. Bond?"

"James Bond. He took them off before bedding a large-breasted woman."

"For Christ's sake, did you watch anything other than sex today?"

"I watched the woman in the grapes. She made me laugh. But the lovemaking interested me more."

"Yeah, it interests me, too." Presley leaned forward and rubbed her breasts against Vadim's bare chest. "I am tired, but can't we get each other off before I fall over?"

"You wish to climax by my hand?"

"You read my mind." Presley stood to take off her jeans. She still had Vadim's shirt wrapped around her neck. "Can I put this on?"

"If you wish, you certainly may."

Presley put on Vadim's shirt, leaving it open. She saw Vadim fumbling with his zipper. "Stand up. I'll do it." Vadim stood. Presley carefully pulled down his zipper, being careful not to snag him in the teeth. Sliding her hands inside the waistband, she squeezed his ass cheeks before lowering his pants.

Vadim's cock rubbed against her belly. He moaned. "Ninotchka, my organ threatens to break, it is so hard."

"Sit down." Vadim started at the commanding tone in Presley's voice, but did not contradict her. He sat on the sofa. Presley pulled off his jeans, leaving him nude. "Vadim, there is no way in hell I'm going to pass up the opportunity to have that piece of meat inside me. You're hung like a frigging horse!"

Not giving him a chance to object, Presley straddled him. Grasping his prick in her hand, she positioned the head so she could mount him. Sliding it closer, she felt his flesh make contact with hers. When she lowered herself onto his cock, a vivid image of a blacksmith heating a metal rod came to her, a picture she knew came from Vadim.

"You have climbed onto the horse, Presley Knowles, now you must ride!"

With strength Presley had never before witnessed, Vadim slid his hands under her ass and lifted her up until his cock nearly popped out. Then he dropped her back on his lap, the scalding rod of his prick piercing her flesh.

The sensation caused Presley to scream. "Vadim, my God, Vadim!"

Showing no mercy, he did it again, this time pushing upward as she fell. Presley felt his cock fill her belly and push against her womb. He held her there, his arm wrapped around her waist. He reached between them with his other hand and forced his fingers into the folds of skin. Rubbing her clitoris with speed that rivaled her favorite vibrator, Vadim followed her into the timeless space of orgasm.

They sat together for several minutes, Vadim's cock still deeply buried inside her. Presley leaned against his chest and rested her head on his shoulder. Nuzzling her hair, Vadim whispered, "Ninotchka, you must sleep."

The haze of drowsiness already claiming her, Presley muttered, "Yeah, I know." She made no attempt to get up. Vadim pulled his shirt tightly around her as she drifted in his scent and fell asleep.

Presley started awake. She thought she heard banging and someone calling her name. Disoriented, she looked around. She lay on the sofa, still wearing Vadim's shirt. The light from the TV flickered on the walls, and rain splattered against the window.

"Vadim, where are you?" He didn't answer.

"Presley, open the fucking door!" Presley bolted upright on the sofa.

"Daniel?"

Daniel pounded on the door again. "Presley, wake up. I know you're in there. Your doorman told me so. Presley!"

Presley jumped up and ran to the door, holding Vadim's shirt closed with her hand. "I'm coming! Be quiet, you'll wake up the whole fucking building!"

She unlatched the door and opened it. Daniel stood in the hallway, dripping wet and looking angry as hell. "It's about goddamn time you opened the door!"

"What are you doing here? Fucking hell, you're soaked!"

Daniel came in and dropped his overnight bag on the floor. "In case you haven't noticed, it's pissing rain, a frigging cloudburst! The fucking cab driver, who couldn't speak English, dropped me five blocks away at Houston and Varick instead of Hudson and Barrow. I couldn't get another cab in the rain, so I walked here."

Presley closed and bolted the door. "Why didn't you call me? I've been here all night."

"I tried to call you. I've been trying to call since I got off the plane. I kept getting your voice mail."

"My cell didn't ring. Shit! I forgot to recharge it today. The battery is probably dead."

"No kidding, Jackson! You apparently also forgot I told you I was coming to New York!"

"I know you told me, but I didn't think it would be tonight! And why didn't Carl buzz me? He's supposed to let me know when people are coming up."

"I told him my name and that you were expecting me, which I thought you were. He said you told him about me. He let me come right up."

"I'll make sure I thank him for that."

"Do you always sleep in a man's shirt, obviously soaked in aftershave?"

"No. I usually sleep buck naked! But when someone is pounding on my door at three o'clock in the morning, I grab whatever is close by!"

After unbuttoning his shirt, Daniel took it off and dropped it on the floor. "I don't suppose you could offer me a towel, Miss Hostess?" Then he pulled off his shoes and socks. Kicking his cloth tote bag with his bare foot, he growled, "Whatever I have in there is probably just as wet as what I have on."

"You're a surly son of a bitch tonight, aren't you?"

"Sweetheart, you ain't seen nothing yet!"

Presley remembered the shirt Vadim had made and thought she could give that to Daniel to put on. But it had disappeared, just as Vadim had. She ran to the bathroom to grab a towel, quickly swapping Vadim's shirt for her robe. Coming back into the living room, she handed him the towel and the shirt.

"Here. Dry off and put this on."

Daniel tossed the shirt back at her. "No, thank you. I don't want your boyfriend's shirt. Tell him he needs to tone down the aftershave."

Presley had to smile, even with Daniel's sarcastic sniping. "He doesn't wear aftershave."

"Is that so? Is he some European pretty boy who drenches himself with cologne?"

"He's not European, he's Ukrainian."

"Who gives a shit!" Daniel picked up his wet shirt from the floor and tossed it at Presley. "Here's another one for your collection. I should have known you didn't take what happened between us seriously. You seem to collect men the way you do shirts."

"You need to calm the fuck down!" Presley dropped the wet shirt on top of his bag. "And don't sit on my furniture in those wet pants! Take them off. I'll get you a blanket."

Presley left Daniel standing in the living room. Going back

into the bedroom, she pulled a blanket off of the bed. Taking a moment to compose herself, she reached for Vadim. Like a switch clicking on in her head, she suddenly felt him. *Where the fuck are you?*

I am close by.

You haven't left me again, have you? Presley braced herself for the answer.

I have not left, Ninotchka. I have merely suspended my physical form.

Are you coming back?

Yes.

"Presley, what are you doing?" Daniel stood in the bedroom door.

"Getting you a blanket."

Daniel came closer. "What the fuck is going on? Who is Ezra?"

"We can't talk about this while you're so pissed off."

"Oh, I think we can!" Daniel yanked the blanket from Presley's hands and threw it back on the bed. "I'm asking you again. Who the fuck is Ezra?"

"All right, you want the truth? She's a ghost!"

Daniel's hands rolled into fists. "Is this some kind of motherfucking shakedown, Presley? Are you and Ezra setting me up in some con game? Do you want money, or is this just how you get your kicks?"

"You son of a bitch! How dare you! How fucking dare you say that to me! You didn't believe me about my near-death experience, and now you don't believe me about Ezra."

"Presley, I want the truth! Who the fuck is she?"

Without warning, the room filled with brilliant blue light. Presley grabbed Daniel's arm. "Oh, my God, she's coming. I can feel her."

"What are you talking about? Presley, what is this?"

"It's Ezra. She's coming."

As Presley and Daniel watched, the soft blue light coalesced into a human form. The shape began to solidify and within a few seconds, a blonde woman in a short white dress stood in front of them. A moment later, a silver light followed. Vadim wore his jeans and new white shirt, his silver cuff links shimmering even after his mercurial light had become flesh.

Chapter Ten

"Presley, what the fuck is this? How did you get them in here?"

"I have Penn and Teller hidden in my closet! Give it up already! They're ghosts!"

"Bullshit!"

"Vadim, tell him!"

"Our essence is of spirit, it is true."

"So, you're Vadim." Daniel walked over to where Vadim and Ezra stood. "You actually do exist. I'm Dr. Daniel Hanson. Ms. Knowles spoke of you repeatedly in the hospital, then couldn't make up her mind if she knew you or not."

"I am aware."

"You're one big dude, pretty damned solid from what I can see. Not too shabby for a ghost." Turning to Ezra, Daniel looked down at her bare feet. "Still no shoes. Nice touch."

"Daniel, I would shut the fuck up if I were you! You don't want to piss him off."

"Why, Presley? Afraid I'm catching on to this little scam of yours?"

"Hell, what's the point of denying it? I'm sure you've already figured out we do it all with mirrors!"

"This is one slick operation, I'll give you that much." Turning to Ezra, he added, "You should play Vegas. Disappearing while fucking! I doubt Harry Houdini could have pulled that one off!" He brushed her face with the back of his hand. "I brought your shoes back. No need to get another pair for the next sucker."

Ezra reached up and took his hand. "Daniel, Presley Knowles speaks the truth about who we are." Daniel tried to pull his hand away, but Ezra held it tightly, wrapping her fingers around his the same way he held a baseball bat. "Perhaps this will convince you."

Without letting go of Daniel's hand, Ezra's body began to fade. She became transparent before once again becoming blue mist. The mist enveloped Daniel.

"My God! Ezra?" Not comprehending how it could be possible, Daniel could hear Ezra's voice in his mind.

Daniel, I am as Presley described. My physical body is transient just as my spirit is eternal.

The fragrance of honeysuckle filled his nose, the cloying odor so intense he could hardly breathe. "Where the fuck are you, Ezra? I can hear you, but I can't see you."

I am here Daniel, all around you. My thoughts intertwine with yours in a spiral of light.

The misty blue light floated upward toward the ceiling, then drifted across the room to where Presley stood. Congealing once again into human form, Ezra appeared beside Presley.

"Holy shit!" Presley jumped backward, tripped on the carpet, and fell. Before she hit the floor, Vadim caught her. Daniel hadn't seen him move.

"Ninotchka, you must be careful. You do not want another head injury."

"Well, if I do fall and whack my head again, at least we have a doctor in the house, not to mention a couple of ghosts to close the crack in my head."

"Christ, Presley, how can you make jokes in the middle of this insanity?"

"It's what Abbott and Costello did in *Time of Their Lives.*

I figure if it worked with their ghosts, it will work with our ghosts, too."

She paused. No one responded. "Geez, you're a tough crowd! I'm one of the funniest people I know, and not even a smile. Oh, well. Anybody want a drink?" Presley took Vadim's hand and pulled him toward the living room. "C'mon, Vadim, I'll warm you up some milk. I don't think you can deal with vodka yet. By the way, nice job on the cuff links."

Vadim and Presley disappeared into the living room, leaving Daniel alone with Ezra. "What you did just now, I still want to think you faked it, but I don't think you did."

"Daniel, I am sorry this has caused you so much distress. There was no other way."

"Yeah, right! I feel like a damn marionette and you're pulling the strings. "

"I had one small chance to open the door to this world. I could not explain it to you. I had no time."

"So you appeared, seduced me, and then disappeared! Do you have any idea what that did to me? I thought I had lost my mind!"

"I meant to come back to you once the connection between us had fused and I regained my strength. But you left to come to Presley Knowles. I followed you."

"Back up. What do you mean, the connection between us had to fuse?"

"She means she hooked into you the same way Vadim hooked into me." Presley stood in the door with a glass in her hand. As she shook it, the ice cubes clinked against the sides. "Here, I brought you some vodka. You look like you could use a drink."

"Presley, I don't understand any of this. It's fucking with my head!"

Presley handed him the glass. "We all need to get a grip. But you still have to take off those wet pants before you sit on my furniture." She picked up the blanket from the bed and handed it to Ezra. "Here, you got his pants off once. See if you can do it again."

Presley's catty comment further irritated Daniel. "Your graciousness is only exceeded by your bitchiness, Ms. Knowles." Presley flipped him the bird and left.

"Here. Hold this." Ezra bunched the blanket under her arm and took the glass. Daniel opened his belt, unzipped his pants, and took them off. He tossed them over the top of the bathroom door.

"Do not be angry with Presley, Daniel. She is not responsible for my coming to you."

"Why did you come to me?"

"Because I am attracted to you."

"You have one hell of a way of showing it!"

"It is the only way I know to show it. I have not been incarnate for many centuries and have never known the love of a man."

"You really expect me to believe that horse shit?"

"I cannot make you believe anything. I can only tell you my truth and hope that you can accept me for what I am."

"Truth? That's an interesting word, now, isn't it, considering you conned me into screwing you."

"Daniel, I did not create the alchemy between us. It exists of its own volition, a dynamic of our souls that we cannot consciously control."

"You know, that's exactly what I thought when you left me with my prick hanging out of my pants." He grabbed the blanket from under Ezra's arm, bumping her breast with his knuckles as he did so. "I'm sorry. I didn't mean to do that."

Being this close to her affected him; he couldn't control it. Daniel suddenly became acutely aware that Ezra could see his erection, as he had on nothing except his underwear. He quickly wrapped the blanket around his waist.

"I do not mind that you touched me. And your desire pleases me."

She still wore the white dress. He knew she had nothing on under it. The vivid memory of lifting her skirt and taking her nearly made him do it again. He resisted the impulse.

"Ezra, I think we should join Presley in the living room."

"Perhaps so." Ezra lightly touched his arm. "Daniel, I am grateful to have known you as I did. If it never happens again, I have that memory to sustain me."

Daniel looked into eyes that glowed as blue as the Kansas sky. The depth he saw in them threatened to overwhelm his judgment and compel him to do things he didn't understand or want to do. Yet, he could not deny how much he wanted to be with her, no matter what the consequences.

"Look, Ezra, you have to give me a chance to come to terms with all of this. I don't pretend to know what you are or where you came from. But I do know you are incredibly beautiful, and I am attracted to you."

Ezra gave him back his vodka and smiled. "The spirits in this glass may help you with the shock of having spirits in your life."

"I sure as hell hope so." Daniel took a sip. "Let's go talk to Presley and Vadim. I want to find out what Presley knows about all of this."

When Daniel and Ezra came into the living room, Presley and Vadim were sitting together on the floor. Vadim had his arm draped around Presley's shoulders, the silver cuff link sparkling on his wrist.

Presley gestured toward the sofa. "Make yourselves comfortable. We're fine on the floor."

"Thank you, Presley." Ezra sat down and scrutinized Presley for a moment. "I see you are beginning to understand."

"Some of it. Vadim told me you are a heavyweight."

Daniel sat beside Ezra on the sofa. "Would you mind explaining what you're talking about? You know more than you're telling me. I want the truth, Presley, and I want it now!"

Presley continued to speak to Ezra. "Have you convinced him that I'm not a liar and a con artist?"

"Daniel is challenged by this, Presley. He needs time to integrate what he has witnessed."

"Integrate my ass! The eight-hundred-pound gorilla is tap dancing in a tutu and he still doesn't believe it." Presley turned toward Daniel. "You didn't believe me when I told you I had a near-death experience, you didn't believe me when I said Vadim saved my life, and now, even with the grandstanding she did, you still don't believe they are ghosts. And you want me to tell you what I know? I don't think so!"

Vadim interrupted. "Ninotchka, your fire is showing."

"Yeah, and so is her pussy! You're too damn late, Ezra. Sharon Stone already did it in *Basic Instinct*!" Presley stood. "I'm not sitting here staring at her cunt. Have at it, Vadim." She moved to the recliner.

The sound of Vadim's laughter echoed in the room. Daniel glared at him. "What's so damn funny, Vadim? She's being a bitch!"

"Do you not understand, Dr. Daniel Hanson? Presley is jealous! She does not want to see the womanhood of another you have known. It means you have found pleasure with someone else."

"Well, big dude, maybe I don't want you to see either." Daniel unwrapped the blanket from around his waist and tossed it over Ezra's lap.

"Daniel, I do not understand. Have I done something wrong?" Ezra tucked the blanket tightly around herself.

Daniel put his arm around Ezra. "Don't worry about it. Presley needs to get over herself."

From the corner, Presley shot back, "Well, isn't that the pot calling the kettle black!"

"Original, Presley. With wit like that, you should be a writer!" Having completely lost any sense of decorum he might have had, Daniel leaned back, his erection barely covered by his underwear. He looked at Vadim, and then pointed to the television. "I like your taste in movies. This one looks like a winner." He sipped his vodka and watched as two teenagers went at it in the back seat of a car.

"Jesus Christ!" Presley found the remote and turned off the television.

"Party pooper!" Daniel pulled Ezra closer. "So, have you slept with Vadim?"

Without hesitation, Ezra answered. "I have had intimacy with Vadim."

"Well, now, let's mark up the score card. I've had you and Presley. Obviously, Vadim has had both of you, too. Since we seem to be one big dysfunctional family, maybe you and Presley should be the next up to bat. What do you say, Presley?"

"Fuck off, Daniel!"

"I would love to." Daniel bolted back the rest of his vodka. "Seeing as how this hard-on is killing me, watching you two ladies go at it would be just what the doctor ordered."

"Ninotchka, mind yourself. He is goading you."

"Am I? I still don't know what the fuck is going on, I have a woody that's about to explode and it's almost dawn. Don't you two have to find coffins or something?"

Presley smirked. "You fucking asshole! They're ghosts, not vampires."

"Oh, excuse me. I got my undead myths confused."

Daniel, do not punish Presley. This is not her doing.

"What did you say?" Daniel rubbed his temple. Ezra's voice seemed to be inside his head.

Presley leaned forward in her chair. "Daniel, look at her eyes!"

Daniel turned and looked at Ezra. Her eyes glowed like blue Christmas tree lights. "What the hell is that?"

"She's reading you. Vadim's eyes glow silver when he does it to me. You can hear her in your head, can't you?"

"Hell, no!"

You can hear me, Daniel. Do not deny it. Daniel again rubbed his temple as he heard Ezra speak. *Presley Knowles can help you to adjust as she has, if you will let her.*

In an instinctive response to Ezra's voice in his mind, Daniel answered in kind. *I don't trust her. I don't know if she's telling me the truth. I don't even know what's real and what isn't anymore.*

Presley Knowles has never lied to you. Her honesty is without question. You can trust her.

Daniel saw Presley watching him. "Okay, you're right. I do hear Ezra in my head. She says I should trust you, that you can help me adjust."

"Smart lady. You should listen to her."

Daniel shook his head like a dog shaking off water. "I've had enough of this for tonight. Christ, I'm tired."

"Yeah, me too." Presley stood and went to the window. "The sun is coming up. We should try to sleep for a few hours. Of course, I don't know if Vadim and Ezra need to sleep."

"Ninotchka, our bodies need to rest the same as yours do."

"Then, Daniel, you and Ezra take the bedroom. Vadim and I will stay out here on the sofa bed. You can get to the bathroom from the bedroom. There's another door for it in the kitchen that we can use."

"Are you sure about this?" As much as Daniel wanted Ezra, his feelings for Presley had not diminished.

"I'm sure. We aren't going to know if this works unless we go for the gusto. Are you game?"

"Do I have a choice?"

"I don't think either of us do. So, why don't we relax and enjoy the ride?"

"Maybe you're right." Daniel stood and helped Ezra to her feet. "Ezra, are you okay with what Presley is suggesting?"

"I am." Much to Daniel's surprise, Ezra went to Presley and hugged her. "It is most generous of you to offer us your bed. I understand what you are feeling."

"Do you?"

"I know you are torn between these two men. There is an ache in your heart because of it."

Presley nodded toward Daniel. "Ezra, this is not the time or the place to discuss this."

"Vadim has told you, among our kind, there are no secrets. Our thoughts and feelings are known. That is the way of truth."

Presley quickly brushed her face as a tear slipped down her cheek. "Christ, you sound like Stuart Smiley doing Louise Hay."

Daniel asked Vadim, "Does she always talk like this?"

"Which one?"

"Good point!" Daniel took Ezra's hand. "Let's go to bed, pretty lady."

"Ezra . . ."

"Yes, Presley?"

"Help yourself to any of the clothes you find in the closet. I usually sleep in a T-shirt. I have plenty, from all over the world. Oh, and FYI, the panties are in the bottom dresser drawer."

Before Presley had a chance to take another shot, Daniel hustled Ezra into the bedroom and closed the door.

*Follow Daniel and Ezra to the bedroom, continue reading
Stay with Presley and Vadim, turn to page 148*

"Daniel, if you do not wish to be with me this night, I will leave."

"And go where, Ezra?"

"Back from whence I came."

"You're using antiquated language, just like Vadim does. What's that about?"

"It is how we interpret the thought impressions of your language. I am sorry if it offends you." Ezra quietly walked over to the dresser and opened the bottom drawer. "It seems I have caused offense more than once this evening." She picked out a pair of panties. "These were not in your vision. I did not understand they were expected."

"Run that by me again. My vision? What vision?"

"You created a thought form of the costume you desired. I clearly saw the white dress and shoes. But I did not understand the garments underneath the dress." She held up the panties. "You did not visualize these."

"No one knows I said that, except Presley. She had to have told you!"

"Presley Knowles did not tell me, Daniel. I saw the image you created." Ezra went to the closed bedroom door. "Come here and listen."

Daniel retraced Ezra's steps to the door. He heard Presley crying. "Is she all right?" He put his hand on the doorknob, meaning to go back to the living room. Ezra stopped him.

"Vadim is seeing to her needs. She needs him now more than she needs you."

"Really! And how did you come to that conclusion?"

"Because I feel her pain. You have hurt her deeply by mistrusting her."

"The only logical explanation is that she is lying. If she isn't . . ."

"Then, Daniel, it is all true. If I am as Presley says, it flies in the face of everything you believe."

"You got that right, sweetheart! I'm a doctor. I see death every day. I'm sorry, but dead is dead. I've had to tell too many families they've lost someone to not understand the finality of death."

"What about your grandfather?"

"I don't know what you're talking about."

"Yes, you do. You were sixteen. He had taken you fishing." The blue in Ezra's eyes deepened as she spoke. "I see you always loved to go fishing with him. On this day, he complained his breakfast had not settled well, and suggested you should perhaps go home early."

"Ezra, don't do this."

"You must see the truth of who I am. Perhaps this will finally convince you. Be still and listen!" The authority in Ezra's voice startled him into silence. "As you walked the path away from the lake, your grandfather fell to the ground. You knelt beside him and cushioned his head in your lap. His heart stopped as you held him. He died in your arms."

"How could you know that? I've never told anyone I held him."

"You also never told anyone he spoke to you as he left."

"I imagined that."

"Did you? Your grandfather has watched over you all these years. He says to tell you it's about damn time he set the record straight. He told you not to cry. He wanted you to smile as he left, so he recited his favorite bit of poetry in your ear.

Me and Tim a-fishin' went.
Met three whores with an old pup tent.
They was three and we was two
So I bucked one and Tim bucked two."

Daniel leaned against the bedroom door, stunned by Ezra's words. "Granddad would sneak a six-pack into the car when we went fishing together. Every time he would crack one for me, he'd recite that damn poem."

Daniel struggled to retain his composure as he vividly remembered his grandfather's death. "I held his head. I didn't know what else to do. His eyelids fluttered, and then his breathing stopped. I started to cry. I was absolutely terrified. I heard his voice in my head, telling me to stop crying, and then he recited that damn poem. It calmed me down enough to run and find someone to help. But it was too late."

"You have never acknowledged what happened, Daniel, not even to yourself."

"I know it had to be my mind playing tricks on me. Shock does that."

"You did not imagine it, Daniel. He wanted you to know he continued to live and would not forget your time together."

"The ornery old buzzard loved telling me his jokes. My mother would've had a fit if she'd known he gave me beer and told me dirty jokes." Daniel took a deep breath. "I suppose you know he's why I became a doctor."

"I know."

"I told Granddad I wanted to be a doctor. My father wanted me to play ball, but Granddad told me to stick to my guns. Then, watching him die and not being able to help him sealed it. I knew I had to be a doctor, no matter what it took."

"He helped you win the scholarship. He believed in you and helped you to believe in yourself."

"Funny, isn't it? Now, he's asking me to believe in him, and I guess, in you."

"Do you believe, Daniel?"

"Ezra, I don't know. But I can't deny what I've seen and heard." Daniel could still hear Presley crying and finally understood what he had done to her. "She's not lying, is she?"

"No, she certainly is not."

He put his hand back on the doorknob, but did not turn it. "Are you sure she is all right?"

"I am sure. Vadim is caring for her."

"She loves him, doesn't she?"

"They are revisiting a love that has endured many centuries."

"But we haven't known each other for centuries, have we?"

"No."

"Then, Ezra, why me? Why are you here because of me?"

"The attraction is strong, Daniel. I know you feel it as I do."

"Let's see if we can find you a shirt to wear to bed."

"You do not want me to leave?"

"Pretty lady, I'll be in bad shape if you leave. I don't think the big dude wants me hitting on Presley while he's around."

"You called Presley Knowles pretty lady. It hurt her to hear you say that to me."

"She doesn't give a shit about me. She has Vadim."

"You are wrong. She does care for you, more than you realize."

"I don't want to talk about Presley right now. I want to know about you."

"You are avoiding this tender place in your heart."

"If you can read my mind, then you know what I want to do."

"You would enjoy touching me?"

"All those dreams I had about you, they were all about touching you." Ezra still held a pair of panties. Daniel took them from her hand and tossed them back into the open drawer. "You won't be needing these tonight."

"Your clothes are in the other room. You also have nothing to wear. Might we sleep skin to skin this night?"

Daniel wrapped his arms around her waist and pulled her close. "Would you like that, Ezra?"

"The touch of a man is new to me. I want to feel your body against me."

"What else do you want to feel?"

"Your desire, and your masculine heat."

Daniel kissed Ezra's neck, and then whispered into her ear, "What about your feminine heat? Do I get to feel the heat of a woman?"

Ezra leaned into him, her breasts crushed against his bare

chest. "Daniel, there is so much inside of me that has never had a voice. My passions are untried. I do not know of such heat."

Even with his exhaustion, Daniel felt an extraordinary surge of lust. His already stiff cock turned to stone. "Oh, I think you're feeling it now, pretty lady." Grabbing the hem of her dress, he pulled it up and off of her. She stood naked in front of him. "You are incredible!"

"Teach me, Daniel. Show me how to love a man."

Daniel peeled off his undershorts. "Do you know what I want?"

In the same instant Daniel saw Ezra's eyes change, something also changed in his. His eyes felt warm, and his vision sharpened. "You want me to kneel and take you in my mouth," she replied.

"And you want to know how I taste." He stared at her in disbelief. "Ezra, I can see inside your mind."

"As I can see inside of yours." Ezra knelt in front of Daniel and grasped his cock in her hand. As she did, Daniel could smell himself as Ezra did. He felt the intensity of her reaction.

How is this possible? I know what you are feeling.

We are connected, Daniel. We share the same desire.

Before he could respond, her mouth covered his cock. The sensation obliterated any attempt at understanding what was happening. Intense heat moved though his groin and he choked back the urge to cry out, for fear of being heard by Presley.

The scalding heat from Ezra's tongue increased. In his mind, he saw a candle flame lapping at his prick, an image he knew came from Ezra. Suddenly afraid she would actually burn him, he stopped her.

With a force of will he didn't know he possessed, he bent over and grabbed her arms. Ezra gasped as he pulled her to her feet. "Sweetheart, I won't let you eat me alive!"

Daniel pushed her onto the bed. Ezra pushed back with her mind, but Daniel held his own. He heard his grandfather's voice, *Son, she's strong but you're stronger. Show her she can't control you. You have free will. Use it!*

In an incredible battle of wills, Daniel challenged Ezra's strength. He could feel her conflict. She burned with wanting him but did not want him to control her. She wanted to control him.

He pinned her arms over her head and held her. Looking into her eyes, he pushed the words into her mind. *Ezra, I won't let you or anyone else control me! I swear to God Almighty, I am my own man and intend to stay that way.*

Without listening for a response or even caring if she had one, he shoved his granite prick into her cunt. She writhed underneath him in a sexual frenzy he had never felt before. When he felt his balls boil over with scalding liquid, he put his hand over her mouth to stifle the scream that filled his mind.

Go to page 154

Presley went back to the window. "The rain has finally stopped."

Vadim came up behind her and put his hands on her shoulders. "At least on the outside."

Reaching into the pocket of her robe, Presley pulled out a crumpled wad of tissues. She wiped her eyes, and then blew her nose. "I'm sorry, Vadim. I shouldn't be reacting this way."

"There is no shame in caring for someone, Ninotchka."

"It isn't just that and you know it!"

"You are angry at Dr. Daniel Hanson."

"You bet your sweet ass I am! I can't even count how many times during the last week he called me his 'pretty lady'! Sounds like he rolls it off like toilet paper."

"When he saw you wearing my shirt, he also felt anger."

"Yeah, right! I didn't call him a liar and a con artist! I can't fucking help it that a couple of ghosts followed me home like two stray dogs." Presley leaned against Vadim's chest as a sob escaped. "Oh, God, Vadim, I'm sorry. I didn't mean that."

"Do not ever forget, Presley, I know what is in your heart. I feel the ache that is there."

Presley turned around and sobbed into Vadim's chest. Unable to speak, she shouted at him in her mind. *Damn it, Vadim, what the hell am I supposed to do? You're here and I want you to be here. But Daniel made me feel special. When he called me his "pretty lady," I thought he meant it. I really did.*

He did mean it, Presley. I told you he is considering asking you to be his woman. That has not changed.

Which is even fucking worse! That means I have to choose between you two.

It does. Unless Ezra wins his heart.

And if she does, then what?

Then, she will be his woman, and you will be mine.

Presley raised her head and wiped her nose. "You mean that, don't you?"

"I certainly do."

Presley had been too distraught to notice when she'd leaned against Vadim, but she noticed now. "You're hard again. Jesus, you have the stamina of a bull moose!"

"I have many years of catching up to do. I expect my organ will stiffen frequently."

"Well, yeah. That's one for our team."

"I did not know this to be a contest."

"It's shaping up to be a doozy. Don't ask! It means one of a kind, or even bizarre. In this case, definitely bizarre."

"Am I competing with Dr. Daniel Hanson?"

"Considering he's probably already fucking Ezra in my bed, who knows? And what the hell did she mean when she said she's been intimate with you? You never told me that!"

"You never asked."

"Have you fucked her?

"In a manner of speaking."

"Son of a bitch! I didn't know ghosts could get laid!"

"She had never known physical love. I shared with her what I could."

"You mean she's a virgin?"

"Your doctor is her first within incarnation."

"Well, I'll be damned. I didn't know that! And here I'm thinking she's a tramp!"

"No, Presley. That term better suits you."

"Says you!"

Vadim chuckled. "Shall we transform the sofa into a bed and I will demonstrate the truth of my words?"

Presley went to the sofa and tossed the cushions onto the floor. "Can you grab that handle and pull out the mattress?" Vadim opened the bed. "I keep sheets on it, so it's ready when I need it. Ezra left the blanket, and we can use the sofa cushions for pillows."

"I have never slept on a mattress, only grain sacks and rags."

In Vadim's tone, Presley heard an uncharacteristic vulnerability. "You've had a tough time, haven't you?"

"It is not my way to whine."

"You told me there is no shame in caring for someone. There is also no shame in admitting you've been through hell and come out the other side."

Vadim untied the belt of her robe and opened it. "I do not wish to dwell on that time. I would rather enjoy being with you again."

Presley's robe fell to the floor. "I want you naked, too." She unbuttoned his shirt, and then remembered the cuff links. "How did you manage these? I thought you didn't know how they worked."

"You did. While you slept, I suggested you have a dream about them. I saw the mechanism in your dream."

"How totally cool is that! They are beautiful."

"As are you, my beautiful one."

"That's even better than pretty lady. And I know you mean it."

"I certainly do."

Presley carefully opened the clips on the cuff links and removed them from Vadim's shirt. They sparkled in her hand. "How did you make these?"

"They are molded from the silver cord that sustains us both."

"I don't understand."

"I did it like this." Vadim reached over her head and closed his hand. Presley felt a slight tugging at her scalp, and then Vadim lowered his arm. When he opened his hand, a mass of sparkling light filled his palm. "This substance is from your cord. It flows like a stream from your crown, and now from mine. It is possible to dip into the stream and fill a cup, without diminishing the flow."

Presley looked at the cuff links, and then took off her pearl earrings. "Can you make me earrings to match these?"

Vadim studied them. Then he closed his hand. When he opened it again, the sparkling substance had changed into a pair of earrings.

"Damn, you're good!" Presley put the cuff links and pearls on the end table so she could put on the new earrings. "That's another one for our team."

"It seems I am tipping the scales in my favor?"

"It seems you might be. Take off your pants and let's find out how much."

"You are not too tired?"

"I just got my second wind." Presley opened Vadim's jeans and slid her hand inside. She watched his face as she rubbed his cock. He grimaced and ground his teeth together. "Do you like that?"

"Oh, yes, Ninotchka, it is a good feeling."

"I smell you. When you are hot, that odor is so strong. I love it!"

"And I smell you. Your musk tells me you are ready for me."

Vadim picked Presley up and put her on the bed. He took off his clothes and joined her on the mattress. Presley cupped his balls in her hand and fondled him. "Tell me what you want, Vadim. Do you want me to blow you again?"

"I want to touch you Presley, and then feel my organ inside you." Vadim placed the flat of his hand on her belly. She felt a slight tingling.

"What are you doing?"

"Sensing if there is life in your womb. As yet, there is no child."

"I told you, I'm not pregnant." Presley rolled over and kissed his chest. "What do you mean, as yet?"

"If there is to be a child, I want it to be mine."

"Who said anything about having a baby?"

"I glimpsed what is to come. I saw you holding an infant. I know nothing of the circumstances around the child's birth."

"How do you even know it's mine?"

"You looked upon the child with deep love. It is my belief that it is yours."

"And you can't tell who the father is?"

"No. It is not yet written."

Presley patted the patch on her side. "As long as I'm wear-ing this, it won't be written. I would be a terrible mother! I can't even remember to water my plants."

"There may come a time when you change your mind."

"Not likely!" Presley tugged his whiskers. "How about using these for something more than keeping your face warm?"

Vadim chuckled. "I see the image in your mind. Is there a modern word for that behavior?"

"The word is kinky. If you plan on staying here, you will learn the interesting nuances of that word."

"It seems I already am." Presley's breath caught as Vadim buried his face between her breasts and brushed her skin with his beard. Presley shivered from the sensation.

"Oh, yes, that's right, slow and easy. Take it slow and easy."

Vadim took her instructions seriously. With maddening slowness, he used his whiskers as a painter would a brush on canvas. He stroked each breast with precision and purpose, drawing a portrait of his longing for her on her skin.

He sucked her nipple into his mouth, his beard scratching her like a thistle. Rather than pulling back, she arched her back to push her tit more deeply into the bramble of his beard. The wiry pinpricks did not hurt. In her heightened space of arousal, the pain became pleasure.

As the morning sun streamed in the window, Vadim con-tinued his unhurried exploration of Presley's body. He trailed kisses down her bare belly, being sure to drag his beard as he moved. Presley abandoned herself to the exquisite sensations of being loved by this anachronistic man.

He seemed to understand exactly how she wanted to be touched. Remembering he could hear her thoughts, she asked, *Are you enjoying this as much as I am?*

Reach inside and see for yourself.

Presley opened herself to Vadim, smiling as she sensed his

pleasure. She also saw what he intended to do to her. *Vadim, don't! That will make me scream, and I can't with our guests in the other room!*

Oh, but Ninotchka, perhaps I want them to hear you scream.

Presley braced herself as Vadim moved lower. She shuddered when she felt his fingers part her lips. The first scrape of his beard against her clitoris made her grunt, which she managed to control. Then he deliberately scoured her tender flesh with his facial hair. She grabbed a sofa pillow and bit into it to muffle the sound that erupted from her throat.

She tried to roll over to break the contact, but he held her fast, torturing her with his tongue as well as his beard. Her climax closed in, but he backed off as it did, not letting her finish.

Unable to scream with her voice, she cried out in her mind, *Vadim, fuck me! I need to come!*

We will climax together, Ninotchka. Vadim rolled on top of her. This time, when his eyes glowed silver, Presley knew hers did as well. As Vadim drove his cock deep into her womb, Presley burned with his fire as he did with hers.

He fucked her hard, as a man does when claiming a woman. When her climax exploded in her belly, she knew he had triggered it with his own. In an exquisite cosmic dance, she abandoned herself to the orgasmic quasar she shared with Vadim.

Chapter Eleven

When Presley woke up, she really had to pee. She quietly got up and found her robe, not wanting to wake Vadim. Remembering Daniel and Ezra were in the bedroom, she went through the kitchen to use that door into the bathroom. She went in, not even thinking about knocking. Daniel stood at the sink with a towel around his waist, combing his hair.

"Oh, shit! Daniel, I'm sorry." She quickly retreated back into the kitchen.

"Presley, wait!" He grabbed her hand and pulled her back into the bathroom, then closed the door. "We have to talk."

"Where's Ezra?"

"She's still asleep. And Vadim?"

"He's out like a light." Presley couldn't stop the flash of memory from Abilene, when she'd first seen Daniel in a towel. The urge to cry welled up again. She masked it with a wisecrack. "Do you know he's never slept on a mattress before? He may sleep all day!"

"Ezra, too. She might look like Marilyn Monroe, but she snores like a truck driver."

"Ezra snores?"

"She woke me up. That's why I got out of bed and showered. I helped myself to your towels and soap. I hope you don't mind."

"Of course not. Glad to return your hospitality." Her eyes misted over. She couldn't help it.

"Presley . . ."

She didn't let him finish. "Daniel, I have to pee. May I use the bathroom? After all, you're a doctor! You've seen it all, haven't you?" Without waiting for a response, she lifted her robe and sat on the toilet. As she had the day before in front of Vadim, she audibly sighed as she relieved herself.

"Feel better?"

"Yes, thank you." After using the paper, she stood and flushed. "You can have the bathroom back now." She turned to leave.

He grabbed her arm again and stopped her. "Presley, I'm sorry. I know you're pissed and I don't blame you."

"If that's all you think I am, then you're more clueless than I thought you were."

"I know I hurt you. I heard you crying last night. I wanted to go to you, but Ezra stopped me."

"I bet she did! What did you think she would do?"

"She said you needed Vadim more than me. Is she right?"

"Why do you give a shit what I need? You think I'm a liar and a con artist."

"What I said isn't the truth, Presley. I know you aren't lying about this. I don't pretend to understand who or what Ezra and Vadim are, but I do know they aren't human."

"They are now! Haven't you been listening? They are anchored to us, Ezra to you and Vadim to me. We are Siamese twins, sharing our silver cord."

"Our what?"

Presley gestured over her head. "Our fucking silver cord! It's this stream thing we need to stay alive. Other than that, I don't know what the hell it is. But Vadim made my earrings out of it."

Daniel lifted Presley's hair. "They're glowing silver, like his cuff links and his eyes."

"Yeah, I know. He can make things out of nothing."

"Presley, this is all nuts!"

"Tell me about it."

"Do you want to be with Vadim? Is Ezra right? Do you need him more than me?"

"Why are you asking me this, Daniel? What difference does it make now?"

"Fucking shit, Presley, do I have to write it on the wall with your lipstick? I'm in love with you!"

"Daniel, don't do this!" A sob broke from Presley's throat. "I can't handle it."

When Presley sobbed, a glow appeared in front of the door to the kitchen. The silver light congealed into the shape of a man. A moment later, Vadim stood beside her, once again wearing his wide blue trousers and baggy shirt. "Ninotchka, are you all right?" Vadim's eyes continued to glow silver. "I heard you cry out."

Presley stood between the two men. Her heart cleaved in that moment, not knowing which one she wanted more. Before she could gather her wits and compose herself, Daniel stepped in.

"She's fine, Vadim. We're having a private conversation. Do you mind?"

"Yes, Dr. Daniel Hanson, I do mind."

Sensing the buildup of hostility between Daniel and Vadim, Presley forcefully called to Ezra in her mind. *Ezra, wake the fuck up and get in here, before Vadim takes Daniel out!*

Presley heard clearly, *Stay calm, my sister. I am coming.*

Vadim barked at her, "Ninotchka! That was not necessary!"

"The hell it wasn't, Vadim! I'm not going to stand here and watch you nuke him!"

Daniel protectively put his arm around Presley's shoulders. "What's he talking about?"

"I called for Ezra." The door from the bedroom opened.

Ezra came in with a sheet wrapped around her like a sari. "Like I said, I called for Ezra."

"Why the hell did you do that?"

"Because Vadim is pissed. He told me what he's done to anyone who has touched me before. I don't want a repeat performance." Presley stepped away from Daniel and moved closer to Vadim. "Ezra, Vadim told me you are an old soul. How about making like Solomon before they split me in half?"

"Presley Knowles, if I am to imitate Solomon, then I would suggest to the two men they should split you in half. That is the wisdom of Solomon."

"Shit, Ezra! You're not helping!"

"If it is my help you want, then allow me to speak the truth as I see it."

Vadim moved behind Presley and put his hands on her shoulders. "Ninotchka, I warn you, this one speaks in riddles, with questions as answers. She is not easy to understand."

"What fucking woman is?" In the same way Vadim had moved closer to Presley, Daniel now moved closer to Ezra. Presley bristled when he said, "So, pretty lady, what truth do you see?"

"The air ripples with strong emotion. There is tremendous love, and there is the pain of love lost. What has been hidden is now revealed, and what is done cannot be undone. We are all connected, one to the other. We share the same love, and the same pain. It is the word made flesh."

Vadim squeezed Presley's shoulders with his large hands. "I told you, dear heart! Her words are always riddles."

"Well, it's dense, I'll give you that." Presley could feel the meaning of Ezra's words more than she could articulate it. "Ezra, are you saying we are all hooked into each other? I mean, like we are all tuned in to the same radio station?"

"In a manner of speaking, yes, Presley Knowles, that is accurate."

"Holy shit!"

Daniel rubbed his temple. "Presley, how about a translation?"

"Daniel, don't you get it? I yelled for Ezra in my head and she heard me. I heard her answer. What she's saying is we are all hot wired now, all four of us. Which means, Dr. Hanson, I am as wired to you as she is! Hot fucking damn! Is that cool or what!"

"Do you mean you can get into my head like Ezra can?" Vadim's laughter filled the bathroom. "What the fuck are you laughing at?"

"You do not find it amusing that two women will be cleaning your house? Consider what you hide from them. In the world of spirit, nothing is hidden." Vadim continued to chuckle.

"Ezra, is he right? I don't want the two of you poking around inside my head."

"It is possible to block access. When someone knocks, simply refuse to open the door."

Presley sent a particularly vivid picture of making love with Vadim to Daniel, and aimed it right between his eyes. Her eyes grew warm and her vision sharper as she focused. Daniel glared at her.

"Testing the waters, Presley?"

"Just seeing if I could do it. I guess I can."

"Your eyes are glowing like his."

"I know. I can feel it. Yours will probably glow blue, like hers."

As Daniel stared at her, the color in his eyes deepened to a vibrant blue. The thought formed in Presley's mind. *Come back to Abilene with me. We can have a normal life together there.*

"It's too damn late for that, Dr. Hanson. My normal life ended with my accident."

No one said anything for a moment. Then, Ezra broke the silence.

"Is it customary to have extended personal conversations

in such a confined space? The energy becomes rather oppressive, does it not?"

"Ezra, it sure as hell does." Presley turned and pushed Vadim toward the door. "I need some coffee. How about some warm milk and black bread?"

"I would like to try some eggs again as well."

"You got it, Mr. Ghost. Should I open the door or are you going to walk through it?" Vadim opened the door and escorted Presley into the kitchen.

Ezra and Daniel did not immediately follow. Presley could feel Vadim scanning her as she busied herself making coffee and putting food on the table. She tried to block him, as Ezra had suggested, but felt him push back. She turned to face him, angry at the intrusion. "Damn it, Vadim! What do you want to know? Ask me, for God's sake. I'll tell you."

With infuriating calmness, he asked simply, "Do you want me to leave so you can be with Dr. Daniel Hanson?"

Presley answered as honestly as she could. "I don't know, Vadim, and that's the truth." She felt more tears stinging her eyes. "You know what's in my heart, at least that's what you told me. Look there now! You'll see what the two of you are doing to me."

"I see your conflict. Ezra is correct that there is great love, and the pain of separation from either of us is evident. It is true we are all connected, but it is also true that neither Dr. Daniel Hanson nor myself care to share our woman with another."

Presley brushed the tears from her cheeks. "So, where the fuck does that leave me?"

"In the middle, it seems."

Needing a distraction, Presley pointed to his trousers. "Where are your jeans?"

"They are in the other room. When I heard your distress and came to you, I clothed myself as I am accustomed. I did not take the time to put on my new clothes. I shall do so now if it would please you."

"It would." Vadim went to the living room to change clothes.

Grateful for a moment to regroup, Presley leaned against the counter by the sink and closed her eyes. Her moment alone was short lived. "Are you not well, my sister?"

Ezra stood behind her, still wrapped in the sheet. "I'm fine, Ezra, just overwhelmed. Where's Daniel?"

"He went to retrieve his bag. He said he left it by the door."

"Oh, God, that means he's in the living room alone with Vadim!"

Presley ran to the living room, expecting to find the two men at each other's throats. Instead, the sight shocked her into silence. There stood both men, stark naked, with Daniel rummaging through his bag and Vadim scooping his jeans off of the floor.

Daniel saw the shocked look on her face before Vadim did. "Welcome to the men's locker room. My clothes are still wet. I don't suppose you have a dryer in this place?"

Ezra had followed Presley into the room. Before Presley could say anything, Ezra matter-of-factly remarked, "Both men are incredibly virile and pleasing, are they not, Presley Knowles?"

"No shit, Sherlock!" Immediately, Presley felt both Vadim and Ezra probe her for the meaning of her words. Daniel apparently felt it, too, because he looked at Presley with a questioning look.

Saying nothing aloud, Presley brought to mind images of Basil Rathbone playing the famed detective in *Hound of the Baskervilles,* and underscored the images with words to explain solving mysteries.

Ezra smiled first, having understood the impressions she received. She quietly repeated the phrase, emphasizing the context.

"No shit, Sherlock Holmes!"

Presley glanced at Vadim, and gently pushed the thought *Do you get it?* at him.

Yes, Ninotchka, I do. It is another of your modern expressions.

That's right.

Presley saw Daniel listening intently, his eyes shining pale blue. Directing the next thought at him, she asked, *Did you hear all that?*

Daniel didn't bother with silence. "Hell, yes! They both went into your head to understand what you said, and you told them!"

"That, Dr. Hanson, is what they do. That's what they've always done, except now we can see them and talk to them the same way."

"Holy shit!"

"Exactly!"

Ezra went to where Vadim stood, gliding more than walking across the room. With the authority of a teacher, she elaborated. "Those of us who have gone across often tap into the thought streams of the ones we watch. We read the energetic patterns, which, to you, are words. When it serves the incarnate, we can interject a thought stream, which is interpreted as an idea."

Vadim stepped into his jeans and zipped them up. "Ezra speaks the truth, Ninotchka. It is as you are thinking, a lightbulb appearing over your head." Vadim tossed his blue trousers at Daniel. "Here, Dr. Daniel Hanson, you can put these on until your own clothes are dry."

"Thanks, but no thanks." Daniel handed the trousers to Presley. "They reek of his aftershave."

"That isn't aftershave. That's how he smells. Ezra has a scent, too."

Daniel looked at Ezra. "The honeysuckle smell? Sometimes I also smell strawberries."

"That's Ezra's odor. Vadim calls it their energetic signature."

"I thought it was your perfume in Abilene."

"Nope. It was Ezra following you."

"That shirt you had on last night, it's his, isn't it?"

"Give that man a cigar!"

Vadim smiled knowingly and said to Ezra, "That is a prize given at a carnival. I saw that on the television last night."

Daniel took the blue trousers back. "What happens if I put these on?"

"Got me! Are you feeling lucky, stud?"

Presley knew she had thrown down the gauntlet. She waited to see if Daniel would pick it up. As she thought he might, he carefully stepped into Vadim's trousers, and tied the drawstring that held them up. "Christ!"

"What, Daniel?" Presley saw his startled look. "What's happening?"

"They're fucking vibrating!"

"Vadim said they've absorbed his frequency. They made my skin tingle."

"Well, they're doing more than that to me!"

Vadim laughed. "Ninotchka, your doctor's organ is hardening."

"How the hell do you know that?"

"Because I can feel it as well, Dr. Daniel Hanson. I find it quite pleasurable."

Daniel started to untie the trousers. Presley stopped him. "Daniel, wait."

"Presley, I'm taking the fucking things off."

"Daniel, I can feel it, too. It feels wonderful."

"You can feel what?"

Presley's eyesight sharpened. She knew her eyes must be glowing. "I can feel your erection. It's like you are inside of me."

"It's his energy, Presley, not mine!"

Ezra interrupted. "That is incorrect, Daniel. Vadim's energy amplifies your frequency, but it is still yours. I, too, can feel it."

"Christ almighty, all three of you can feel my hard-on?

How perverted is that?" Daniel picked up his bag and went back to the bedroom, slamming the door behind him.

Presley followed him. Before opening the bedroom door, she turned to Vadim and Ezra. "I'm telling you both, I want some time alone with Daniel. Do you hear me?" Her eyes grew hot as she shot the thought at them like a laser. *Don't either of you dare come in here without being invited!* She slammed the door behind her as Daniel had.

Vadim's blue trousers were in a crumpled heap on floor. Daniel had flopped on the bed naked. He lay there with his arm under his head, staring at the ceiling. Presley had seen him hard many times during the last week, but nothing compared to the erection that rested on his belly. Both the length and the width of his penis exceeded anything he had achieved with her. The blood vessels bulged under the skin, seemingly about to burst.

"That looks painful."

"It is."

"Are you all right?"

"No, Presley, I'm not all right."

Presley lay down on the bed beside him. "I'm sorry I got you into this."

"It's not your fault. All you did was have a car accident. If anything, it's my fault. I'm the one who saved your life."

"Daniel, you stitched me up. Vadim saved my life."

"And now, he owns your soul."

"No, he doesn't. And neither do you."

"I never said I did."

"Vadim told me you want me to be your woman, and that you want to marry me."

"I told you I didn't want you to leave Abilene."

"And I told you I'm not ready to settle down. That is true with you and with Vadim."

Daniel turned his head and looked at her. "What do you want, Presley?"

"Right now, I want to jerk you off."

Daniel's cock twitched even as he said, "No, thank you."

"Daniel, I really can feel it. It's making my clit go crazy! I swear to God, it's swollen twice its normal size." Presley gingerly reached out and touched Daniel's penis. He groaned and grabbed her hand.

"Jesus Christ, Presley, stop it! Just leave it alone!"

"Daniel, please! Let me touch you! Let me feel this with you."

Daniel's grip on her hand relaxed as the throbbing between her legs increased. She heard Daniel's *yes* even though he didn't speak. Slowly and gently, she caressed him. As she did, her clit reacted. She had the oddest sense of masturbating herself as she masturbated him. The touching excited her but belonged to him.

Daniel gasped as she tickled the tip of his cock like she would her own clit. She increased the rhythm as she had always done with herself, rubbing faster and harder as orgasm neared. But she had never known arousal like this before. She needed relief, the ache between her legs quickly becoming unendurable.

She had the sudden urge to forcefully pump Daniel's cock, and realized the impulse had come from Daniel. Having lost herself in her own sensibilities, she forgot she had to masturbate Daniel like he would masturbate himself.

"Daniel, show me how you want it."

"Like this." He took her hand and wrapped it around his prick. He changed the rhythm, using a steady up and down stroke. "That's right, pretty lady, do it just like that."

As much as she wanted to finish with him, Presley stopped and pulled her hand away. "Fucking shit, Daniel! Is any woman that plays with your dick your 'pretty lady'?"

Presley tried to get off the bed. Daniel caught her. "Presley, what's wrong with you? We aren't stopping now! We're too damn close!"

"Let Ezra get you off! She doesn't seem to mind your fucking bullshit line."

"Oh, no, pretty Presley, I'm getting off with you!" Daniel yanked her robe open and pinned her to the bed. As he crawled on top of her, Presley clearly heard Vadim in her mind. *Ninotchka! Let me come in and stop him!*

With all the willpower she possessed, she shouted at Vadim in her mind. *No, Vadim! You will not interfere! I want Daniel to fuck me.*

Presley clearly saw an image in her mind of a door closing. She knew Daniel had pushed it shut. As she felt him penetrate her, he whispered in her ear, "I'm going to fuck you so good!"

Daniel's singleminded intention of fucking obliterated any other thought in her mind. His need overwhelmed her. Opening her legs as wide as she could, she willingly accepted him into her body. In that moment, nothing existed for her except the need, and the compulsion to satisfy the need.

With intensity rivaling Vadim's, Daniel drove himself into her. The crescendo of their lovemaking went far beyond anything they had previously experienced together. Their combined arousal lifted them into an ethereal zone of sensation, and as had happened with Vadim and with Ezra, their identities dissolved. They became one point of consciousness with a singular focus.

They fell over the cliff together, their climax coming in a flash of blinding light. Presley's scream blended with Daniel's groan, a cacophony of sexual sound that filled the room. For what seemed like forever, the sense of union continued.

When Daniel finally rolled off her onto the bed, Presley saw his eyes still glowed sky blue. "Daniel, are my eyes glowing like yours are?"

"They're silver, like a guy I saw on *Star Trek* once." Daniel chuckled. "How damn ironic. The episode was 'Where No Man Has Gone Before.'"

"You're into *Star Trek*? I didn't know that. I used to watch it all the time."

"Do you remember that episode?"

"Is that the one where the two crew members mutate?"

"That's the one."

"Christ, Daniel, is that what's happening to us?"

"I don't know Presley, I really don't." Daniel got up and pulled Presley up beside him. "Let's get dressed and go talk to our friends."

"I need to shower first."

Daniel kicked Vadim's blue trousers to the side. "I need to dry some pants. Do you have a hairdryer?"

Presley picked up Vadim's trousers. "I have one in the bathroom. I'll get it after I hang these up." She went to the closet and put Vadim's trousers on a hanger. She hesitated for a moment before hanging them in the closet beside her clothes. As she held the blue piece of cloth, the sense of Vadim filled her. The incredible rush of energy made her flush.

After hanging Vadim's trousers, Presley looked around in the closet for anything Daniel could wear. She didn't have any pants that would fit, but she had her collection of T-shirts from all the places she'd traveled. When she came out, she mentioned them. "I have plenty of big T-shirts. Help yourself to one if you want."

"I felt what those pants did to you."

"I know you did." Presley went to get the hairdryer.

After she had showered, she scrunched her curls, and then came back into the bedroom to get dressed. When she saw the shirt Daniel had chosen, she snorted.

"That's an unbelievably feminine sound you just made!"

Presley smirked. "Well, what did you expect? You're wearing 'Who's your mommy'! Couldn't you find a shirt from the Super Bowl or something?"

Daniel looked down at the logo on his shirt. "I thought it appropriate, considering the circumstances."

"Nice to see your humor is coming back."

"It's certainly better than crying in our beer about it. We have to get a handle on what's happening. Our guests don't seem in any hurry to leave."

Presley went to the closet to get some clothes, and came back with a pair of jeans and a shirt. "You have to know I'm completely fucked up. I don't want Vadim to leave."

Daniel went to her dresser, retrieved a sexy pair of panties from the bottom drawer, and tossed them at Presley. "Yeah, I know. I don't want Ezra to leave, either."

"Are you falling in love with her?"

"I don't think I'm in love with her; I think I'm bewitched by her."

"The way Samantha 'Bewitched' the two Darrens for eight seasons?"

"You watch a lot of television, don't you?"

"Hey, it's how I chill! I love old movies and old TV series."

Daniel smiled. "I've picked up on that. You've already initiated Vadim."

"Daniel, talk to him. He's amazing. I don't want you to hate each other because of me."

"Ezra, too. She really is new to all of this. Do you know why she didn't wear panties last night?"

"Please, tell me. I can't wait to hear this."

"She read my mind and didn't see them. She wore what she thought was acceptable to me, not having any idea that nurse's costume came from a porn movie."

"The one you told me to get?"

"That's why I thought you two had cooked up a scam. You're the only one that knew about it. I thought you had told her."

"That would be pretty fucking stupid, wouldn't it? As Lina Lamont would say, 'What do you think I am, dumb or something'?"

"That's a decent impression."

"It should be. I've seen *Singin' in the Rain* at least a dozen times."

"I have no doubt." Presley pulled on her T-shirt and Daniel chuckled as he read it. "'Warning! I have an attitude and know how to use it!' That's the damn truth!"

Presley went back to the closet. "Here's one for Ezra." She tossed another shirt at Daniel.

He held up a black T-shirt with rhinestone lettering. "You have a warped sense of humor. 'Dead Sexy' isn't exactly subtle."

"Neither is Ezra."

"Go easy on her Presley. There is a naiveté there that is real . . ."

"And . . ."

". . . and I'm beginning to feel how honest and sincere she is."

"Even with the big tits and blonde hair?"

"Even with all of that." Daniel went to open the bedroom door. Before he opened it, he added, "And don't forget the rock-hard ass. She has that, too." Presley swatted him as she went through the door into the living room.

Chapter Twelve

Vadim and Ezra sat on the sofa watching television, each holding a cup. Presley smiled when she saw Vadim dunking black bread in his. She said softly to Daniel, "I taught him how to use the microwave yesterday. He loves warm milk and black bread."

As Ezra gingerly lifted her cup to her mouth and took a small sip, Daniel whispered, "Looks like he made Ezra some, too."

"She'll have to take it slow. Vadim barfed when he first tried to eat solid food."

"You know, if I could put my personal feelings aside and study what is happening here, I could win a Nobel."

"I want to see you put your personal feelings aside. I'll write an article about it and win a Pulitzer."

As Presley walked over to Vadim, she nodded toward Ezra. Daniel took his cue and went to her. "Presley told me you should take it slow with that. You don't want to get sick."

"Thank you, Daniel. Vadim already explained the sensitivities of introducing food into our physical bodies. He said his belly hurt the first day. He is better now."

Presley put her arms around Vadim's neck. "That's true. He is doing better today. So, what are you watching, Mr. Ghost?"

Vadim gestured toward the television. "Ninotchka, there were others!"

"What are you talking about? Others what?"

"Others like me! Look, and you will understand."

Presley studied the screen for a few seconds before it registered what they were watching. "Oh, for crying out loud! Of all things for you to come across!"

"What is it?" Daniel watched for a moment. "That's Rex Harrison, isn't it?"

"Of course it is! And that's Gene Tierney. They're watching *The Ghost and Mrs. Muir!*"

Daniel laughed. "Damn, that's rich!"

Vadim frowned. "Dr. Daniel Hanson, why is that amusing?"

"Vadim, stop calling me Dr. Daniel Hanson. Just call me Daniel. Presley can explain why it's amusing, can't you, Presley?" Daniel glanced at her. "And why does he always call you Ninotchka?"

"That was my name four hundred years ago, when I was his main squeeze."

"Oh, well! That explains it!" Daniel shook his head and muttered, "Jesus Christ, what else?"

Presley ignored Daniel's irritation. "Vadim, this is a movie called *The Ghost and Mrs. Muir.*"

Vadim didn't let her finish. "Yes, indeed! Mrs. Muir is living in Captain Gregg's house. He is most displeased with her presence there."

Daniel interjected, "Go ahead, Presley, explain it to him. I want to hear this."

"Shut the fuck up, Daniel. I'm working on it." Turning back to Vadim, she softened her tone. "Vadim, remember last night, when I explained the difference between the news and a story with actors?"

"I do remember, Ninotchka." He again gestured toward the television. "But this one, he is like me!"

Daniel chuckled. Presley glared at him with an accompanying *Fuck you!*

Rather than shushing him, that made him laugh louder. He shot the thought back at her, *Nicely done, pretty lady.*

On the heels of that thought came Vadim's. *Ignore him, Ninotchka. He's goading you again. Watch the television and listen to what Captain Gregg is saying.*

Totally exasperated, Presley took a deep breath and tried to be patient. "Vadim, listen to me. This is a movie, a made-up story. Captain Gregg is an actor. So is Mrs. Muir. It isn't real."

"The Captain came to Mrs. Muir in this story just as I came to you. Perhaps the person who wrote this story knew someone like me."

Daniel chimed in, "He could be right about that."

"Indeed I could be. A woman named Josephine Aimee Leslie wrote the story, hiding behind the name of a man. Perhaps she wanted to protect the one who came to her."

"How the hell do you know that?"

"Ezra told me."

Both Presley and Daniel turned to Ezra, who sat quietly sipping her milk. Daniel knelt beside the sofa, the question forming in his mind just as it had in Presley's. "Ezra, how do you know this?"

"I accessed it, as it is written in the Akashic."

"Presley, do you know what she's talking about?"

"I think so. It's a sort of cosmic library."

"Is she right, Ezra?"

"Presley Knowles is correct. The Akashic is a library of all events. The records can be read as one would read a book."

Daniel ran his fingers through his hair and muttered, "Yeah, if you know the language."

"Obviously she does." Presley massaged Vadim's shoulders as she asked, "Can you do what Ezra did? Can you read the Akashic?"

"I expect I can. I have never tried." He took another bite of bread, chewed, and easily swallowed. "But I will not try now, sweet thing. I am watching the movie."

"Of course you are." Presley leaned over and whispered in his ear. "I want to ask you one more thing, and then I'll leave you alone to watch the movie."

"What is it, Ninotchka?"

"Why aren't you pissed off that I just fucked Daniel?"

"I am. However, if it is your wish and your will, I have no choice but to allow it. So, I move on."

"How very Dr. Phil of you."

"Oprah respects Dr. Phil. He is a wise man."

"Oh, for Christ's sake!" Presley threw her hands up in the air and went to the kitchen to get some coffee and some food.

Daniel followed Presley to the kitchen, and helped himself to a cup of coffee after Presley poured hers. "It's mind-boggling, but they're real, aren't they?"

"At least you believe me now."

"Do you love him, Presley?"

"I don't know how to answer that. It's like asking me if I love the oxygen that I breathe or the blood in my veins. There's a connection to him that is so deep inside me I don't know what to call it."

"I think they call it your soul."

"What does that make him, my soul mate? How fucking trite is that!"

"Well, maybe it's true."

"Whose side are you on, anyway?"

"I'm just pointing out there may be a deeper vein to all of this."

"Well, then, what about Ezra? She's hot after you!"

"She told me she's a healer. In some weird way, I know she's got the same burning inside of her to help people as I do. She's benevolent, Presley. I'm just beginning to get how really compassionate she is."

"Daniel, what is happening to us?"

"I don't know, and that's the truth. With this empathy thing that is happening, I'm sensing they don't mean us any harm.

In fact, far from it. There's this innocence and naiveté there that can't be questioned."

"Even in Vadim?"

"Especially in Vadim. He doesn't seem to know how to do anything other than be what he is."

"Shit, you've hit a bull's eye there! He's honest to a fault. Ask him any question, he'll tell you the truth, whether you want to hear it or not."

"You know, we're both in this up to our ass cheeks, you by design, me by accident. I don't think we have any choice but to go along for the ride until we see where it's all going."

They didn't hear Ezra come into the kitchen. Presley jumped when she spoke. "Could I have some more milk, please? Vadim is correct. It quiets the sick feeling in my stomach."

"Do you feel ill, Ezra?" The concern in Daniel's voice went beyond what a doctor would ask a patient. He went to her and put his arm around her shoulders. "Are you going to vomit?"

"I do not think so, Daniel. It is not comfortable, but there is not a strong urge to heave."

"The milk helps?"

"It does."

Daniel took her cup. "Presley, could you fill it up again?"

Presley poured more milk and heated it in the microwave. During the minute it took for the milk to warm, she watched Daniel with Ezra. For the first time, she saw something she hadn't noticed before. She saw tenderness in Daniel toward Ezra, and a depth of feeling that went far beyond a casual sexual attraction.

Using her newfound ability, she gently probed Daniel. She wanted to know more about his attraction toward Ezra. Daniel didn't notice her scrutiny, but Ezra did. She looked directly at Presley, the blue-eyed stare piercing Presley like an arrow. Even though the intensity of the eye contact made Presley shiver, she did not look away.

The microwave beeped. Presley did not turn to get the milk. She continued to study Ezra, as Ezra did her. Daniel interrupted the staredown. "You two look like two cats about to have one hell of a fight. Not that I would mind seeing the two of you in a cat fight, but how about if we play nice for now?"

Presley retrieved the cup from the microwave. "We aren't going to fight, Daniel. I think we might be on the verge of an interesting friendship."

Ezra smiled as she took the cup from Presley. "I am grateful you are beginning to understand, Presley. We do not have to be rivals. The pool of love we share is infinite."

Imbedding the connection with Vadim into the phrase, Presley softly answered, "Says you."

Ezra's eyes glowed blue for a moment and Presley saw the picture in her mind of the moment Vadim broke the barrier between them using that phrase. Along with it came a wave of heartrending grief which transmuted into euphoria as Vadim reconnected with her.

Presley's eyes filled with tears. "My God, Ezra, you were with him, weren't you?"

"I was."

"He told me he heard me after he said, 'Says you,' but I had no idea he had such pain before it happened."

Daniel's concern shifted to Presley. "What are you talking about? What did Ezra just tell you?"

"She is showing Ninotchka that which I did not want shown." Vadim stood in the doorway, visibly angry. Approaching Ezra, his eyes glowed. "Why do you do this?"

Daniel moved to place himself between Ezra and Vadim. Ezra stopped him. "It is all right, Daniel. This is not the first time I have felt Vadim's anger." Ezra stood directly in front of Vadim. Both in height and bulk, he overshadowed her.

As Presley and Daniel looked on, Ezra transformed. The bed sheet she had wrapped around herself like a sari changed into a garment of beauty, shimmering with mother-of-pearl light. That seemed to enrage Vadim even more. "Do not think that taking on your spirit colors will dissuade my temper! You have no right to show my weakness to my beloved!"

Ezra's voice also changed, taking on a vibrato of authority that surprised Presley. Speaking calmly and firmly, Ezra chastised Vadim. "There is no shame in grieving a love lost. It softens the hard shell around the heart and allows light into the darkened soul."

"My pain is my own! Ninotchka need not know of my suffering."

Presley couldn't tell if Ezra walked or floated over to her, the line between corporal and ethereal now being blurred. In the same authoritative voice, Ezra spoke to her. "Presley Knowles, do you not wish to know of Vadim's journey back to you?"

Presley's stomach jumped like she had just been called to the principal's office. She could feel Vadim and Daniel watching her closely, waiting for her response, both to Ezra's question and to her intimidating presence. Taking a deep breath, she collected herself before answering.

"Of course I want to know what he went through, but I would prefer hearing it from him." Presley walked past Ezra and went to Vadim. Lightly brushing his whiskers, she joked with him, "Mr. Ghost, do you know you still need to shave and get a haircut? It would be nice to see what you look like under all that hair."

"Ninotchka, I will trim my beard and hair. I will also tell you whatever you care to know about my life."

"You will answer my questions?"

"I certainly will."

Sensing she had successfully diffused Vadim's anger, Presley focused again on Ezra. The bed sheet continued to glow. "You know, Ezra, I thought we could go shopping today, and get you some clothes. But, hell, if you can do that to a sheet, maybe I don't need to bother."

Daniel chuckled. "Do you know you have more balls than most men?"

"Dr. Hanson, in New York the word is chutzpah!"

Ezra closed her eyes, and took a breath. "Chutzpah is insolence, shameless audacity, and utter nerve." Ezra smiled. "Yes, Presley, that is the correct word."

"Then you won't mind my asking, why did you flash Vadim's past at me?"

"My sister, the path he has walked has been a difficult one. Without some prodding, he would not have been inclined to share it with you. You will not fully know him until he shares his experience with you. The seeds just planted will bring a rich harvest."

"Okay, I think I get that. Then tell me this, why the grandstanding with the clothes?"

"You do not know of our kind and how we clothe ourselves." Ezra waved her hand in the air. The sheet she wore completely dissolved and she suddenly seemed to be clothed only in colorful swirls. "In the world of spirit, our garments are color. The color that surrounds each of us is not a matter of adornment but of our nature. Whether there is brilliance or sobriety is a matter of advancement, not of ego. One wears what one is."

"Well, that little number you're wearing now is pretty fucking spectacular! What does it mean?"

Vadim answered her question. "It means, Ninotchka, that Ezra has assumed her light, and her garment has evolved to be what she is."

"Well, what am I supposed to do with that? Light some candles and start a new religion?"

Daniel had been listening quietly to the entire exchange. What he interjected caught her off guard. "Presley, if you could stop being snarky for a few minutes and listen to what they're saying, you might learn something."

"And what, pray tell, have you learned?"

"That this is part of our evolution we never dreamed of."

"Woo-hoo! How totally scientific of you! That will certainly help me to cope with all of this."

Daniel continued in spite of Presley's sarcasm. "Instead of our standing around here like a flock of frigging sheep, why don't you take Ezra out for a shopping spree and I'll take Vadim to get a shave and a haircut?"

"You're joking, right?"

"Dr. Daniel Hanson is not joking, Ninotchka. He wishes to spend time alone with me."

"And Vadim, how the fuck do I know you won't smite him, or do some other biblical fire and brimstone thing?"

"I give you my word, Ninotchka, I will not smite him."

Daniel chuckled. "And if he shall smite me on my right cheek, I shall turn to him the left."

Presley rolled her eyes and then patted her left ass cheek.

"I don't know if I would smite that cheek, but I sure as hell would bite it!" Daniel laughed.

Presley ignored Daniel's crack. "Ezra, if we're going out, you have to wear something other than your coat of many colors. My clothes won't fit you. They're not right for your body type. You've got more T&A than I've ever had."

"I have my white dress, if I might borrow some panties. I could manifest something else, but until I see the fashion of your time, I will not know what is appropriate."

"Daniel, what do you think? Vadim will be fine in his jeans and white shirt. Can she get away with that dress?"

"This is New York. She may give a few guys a hard-on, but she won't get arrested. I think she's right. Even if she can make something out of nothing, she won't know what's right until you take her to a few stores."

"All right, we'll do it. But I don't think we should go too far away. This is their first field trip. I'll take Ezra to a few stores in the Village that are close by. The place where I get my hair cut is only a few blocks from here. You can walk in without an appointment. I'll give you the address."

"Will they also trim his beard?"

"There's a guy there I use. Ask for Devon. I know he trims beards."

"Devon?"

"Hey, that's his name. He cuts my hair all the time and he does a good job. Don't go getting homophobic on me."

"I'm not the one you should worry about." Daniel nodded toward Vadim. "Vadim, would you have a problem if a homosexual man cut your hair and trimmed your beard?"

"As long as the only hair he touches is the hair on my head, I do not have a problem."

"Interesting way to put it. Hopefully, we won't end up on the front page of the *Post* tomorrow."

"Let's have some food, or in Ezra's case, some milk. I definitely need to eat something before we go out. Then we'll get ourselves together and tackle our first field trip."

While Presley and Daniel ate, Vadim went back to watch the end of the movie. Ezra took her milk and went to the bedroom to dress. Presley sat quietly and ate her cereal.

"I still have Ezra's shoes in my bag, but I don't know if she'll be able to walk very far in them. The heels are at least four inches high."

"I have a pair of Birkenstocks with adjustable straps that will probably fit her. They won't go with her dress, but I doubt anyone will be looking at her feet."

"You're right about that." Daniel stared into his coffee cup. "You know, in a weird way, they've become our wards. They might be ghosts, but they don't know jack shit about taking care of themselves here."

"I know. We're going to have to watch them on the street. Christ, what happens if one of them gets hit by a bus?"

"Well, they can't get killed. They're already dead." Daniel pushed his chair back and stood. "Let's get this show on the road. I'll need a key to get back into your apartment."

"There's an extra set on the desk in the living room. The hair salon is on Christopher Street, between Greenwich and

Washington. That's half a block west to Greenwich, and then one block south to Christopher. It's not far."

"What's it called?"

"*Hair Today, Gone Tomorrow.*"

"I'm taking Vadim to Christopher Street, to a place called *Hair Today, Gone Tomorrow*, to get a haircut and a beard trim from a gay stylist named Devon?"

"That's what you're doing, and remember, this was your idea."

"We really may be on the front page of the *Post* tomorrow."

Follow Daniel and Vadim, continue reading
Follow Presley and Ezra, turn to page 194

Chapter Thirteen

Daniel left Presley cleaning up the dishes in the kitchen. When he went into the living room, Vadim sat channel surfing. "Is the movie over?"

"Yes, Dr. Daniel Hanson, it is over. I missed some of it, but I saw Captain Gregg return for Mrs. Muir at the end. It was most satisfying to see."

"Glad you enjoyed it. And I will say it again, please stop calling me Dr. Daniel Hanson. Just call me Daniel."

"I will make every effort to comply with your wish, Daniel."

"Thank you, Vadim. By the way, do you have a last name?"

"I am known as Vadim. I have no surname."

"Maybe you should be a rock star, like Cher or Madonna."

"I am more suited to the music of Prince."

"Don't tell me, you accessed that from the Akashic?"

"No, I saw him on MTV television, singing at the Super Bowl."

"Yeah, I saw that game. He did a hell of a job, didn't he?"

"Indeed he did! And in the pouring rain! They say he worked the crowd. Do you believe so as well?"

"He did more than that. He was fucking amazing! Best half-time show they've ever done, sure as hell better than a wardrobe malfunction."

"In the retrospective, they reviewed that performance as well. A buxom woman bared her breast in the public arena."

"You're getting quite an education from television, aren't you?"

"It is helpful, to be sure. I have absorbed much information about your culture. As I told Ninotchka, I will learn."

"Her name is Presley." Daniel picked up the keys from the desk and put on his damp shoes. "These are still wet. Maybe I'll see if we can find a shoe store. This is the only pair I brought." Daniel checked to make sure Vadim had on shoes and saw his boots. "Those are nice."

"They are from another time, but Presley says they will service me for now."

"They're fine. Let's go."

Vadim hesitated when the elevator door opened. "What is this box, Daniel?"

"It is an elevator, Vadim. It will carry us downstairs to the lobby."

Daniel watched Vadim closely in the elevator. Vadim noticed. "You are probing me, Daniel."

"I want to make sure you are all right."

"Your curiosity about me is evident, both as a doctor and as a man."

"That sounds fair."

On the way out, Daniel spoke to the doorman. He didn't want a problem getting back into the building. "I don't know if the night man told you, we're guests of Presley Knowles."

"You're Dr. Hanson, right?"

"That's me. This is Vadim."

The doorman checked out Vadim. "He mentioned you. He didn't tell me about him."

"Vadim and Ezra arrived last night. I don't know how the night man could have missed them. You can see Vadim's a big dude, and Ezra, well, you'll see what I mean when she goes shopping later with Presley."

"Aw, hell, Carl was probably taking a piss."

"Yeah, that's probably it. Presley gave me keys in case we get back before the ladies do. We'll see you later."

Let's get the hell out of here. I don't want him asking any more questions.

It startled Daniel to hear Vadim reply, *Thank you for explaining our presence here. I know I appear strange to this man.*

You look like a pro wrestler. That might be a good career for you.

I would prefer singing like Prince.

Wouldn't we all?

They took their time walking to the hair salon, Daniel giving Vadim a chance to absorb all of the sights and sounds around him. When they reached the salon, Daniel coached Vadim before they went in.

"Vadim, be careful what you say in there. You don't want to draw attention to yourself."

"Understood, Daniel. They need not know my personal business."

"That's a frigging understatement."

There weren't many customers in the salon. When Daniel asked for Devon, the receptionist said he would be available in a few minutes and directed them to the waiting area.

Vadim scanned the shop. *The young man at the last chair is Devon.* Daniel followed Vadim's thought, and saw the tall, thin man with dark, spiky hair using a blow dryer on a woman. *I do not want hair like that!*

Not to worry, Vadim. We'll have it cut the way you want it.

When the receptionist directed them to an empty chair, she asked if they both wanted a haircut.

Vadim answered before Daniel had a chance. "I am the one who needs a haircut. My lady told me I also need to have my beard trimmed."

Feeling he had to somehow explain why he'd tagged along,

Daniel added, "I'm just here for moral support, and to buy him a drink when we're done."

"If you're into it, there's a karaoke bar across the street. I go there for lunch sometimes. There's always someone with a microphone. The American Idol wannabes are always good for a laugh."

"Thanks for the tip."

"You're welcome. Devon will be right with you."

Vadim watched her go back to the reception area. *She's an attractive young woman.*

Daniel smiled as he got the strong impression of Vadim studying the girl's ass. *I wouldn't let Presley catch you doing that.*

It would be stimulating to experience her reaction. Jealousy increases her fire.

I know that! She's jealous as hell of Ezra sleeping with me. Daniel felt a flare of something in his stomach. It felt hot, and the heat spread to his groin. His cock responded to the surge and started to harden. He realized it had come from Vadim. *It seems Presley isn't the only one who reacts to jealousy. Chill, big dude, here comes Devon.*

"Well, hello there! And what can I do for you two today?"

"My friend here needs a haircut and a beard trim. Presley Knowles said to ask for you, that you cut hair and trim beards."

"I certainly do beards." Devon fluffed Vadim's hair with his fingers. "It figures you're both friends of Presley's. She always gets the hottest men."

Vadim shifted in his chair to look directly at Devon. Daniel held his breath, hoping Vadim's eyes weren't glowing. The slight sparkle Daniel saw could easily be a reflection of the light. Daniel still warned him. *Vadim, watch the eyes.* Vadim blinked. When Daniel again looked, Vadim's eyes appeared normal.

"You have known Presley Knowles a long time?"

"She's been coming here since we opened, about two years now. I love her. She's a kicky bitch! She'll say anything, twice.

I told her one of these days someone will wash her mouth out with soap. Maybe you're the one to do it."

Vadim laughed, which eased the tension with Daniel. "I would agree with you, young man. If anyone can take Presley Knowles in hand, I am the one to do it."

"Oh, my, I am soooo jealous! I would trade places with her in a New York minute!"

Even with Vadim's claim on Presley, Daniel chuckled. *This guy is such a queen!*

If that means more woman than man, you are correct. He is trying to decide if he wants your organ in his ass, or mine.

Vadim's blunt assessment of the young man's proclivities proved too much for Daniel. He turned around and coughed, trying to cover his urge to laugh.

Devon yelled to the receptionist, "Cissy, could you get these gentlemen a glass of iced herbal tea, please?" Still fluffing Vadim's hair, he giggled. "I know you would probably prefer a beer, but we don't serve alcohol here."

Daniel muttered, "Got milk?" His comment blew past Devon.

"So, Presley's friend, what's your name?"

"I am Vadim. This is Dr. Daniel Hanson."

"Vadim, how much do you want me to take off?"

"I do not know. I want to please Presley. What do you think she would like?"

Daniel interceded. "Devon, do you have some pictures we could look at?"

"Coming right up!" Devon giggled again. "The pictures, I mean."

He took a binder off a shelf under the counter. "These are samples of celebrity haircuts. Take a look and see if anything catches your eye."

Vadim leafed through the book, not reacting to any of the hairstyles. He suddenly stopped on a page. "This one. I want my hair to look like this."

"Excellent choice! What do you think, Daniel?"

Daniel looked over Vadim's shoulder. He had the book open to a picture of Antonio Banderas, with long, wavy hair down to his shoulders. "It fits him, doesn't it?"

"It absolutely does! He has just enough wave in his hair to pull it off, too. And to go with it, how about this?" He flipped through the book to a page with Sean Connery. "This goatee would be fabulous with that haircut!" He leaned over and whispered in Vadim's ear. "Presley will love it!"

"Make it so!"

"Yes, Captain Picard!"

Daniel made himself comfortable in an empty chair beside Vadim's, and drank his herbal tea. While Daniel watched, Devon transformed Vadim from an anachronism to a stylish, well-groomed man of the 21st century. When he'd finished, Daniel couldn't believe the change.

Devon brushed the loose hair from Vadim's shoulders and took off the apron. "Well, Dr. Hanson, what do you think?"

"Devon, you've earned yourself one hell of a tip! He looks great!"

"Do you like it, Vadim?"

"If Presley Knowles likes it, then I like it."

"Of course she'll like it! You're a stud muffin with that 'do. Oh, and by the way, that cologne you're wearing has to be loaded with pheromones! It's heavenly! And those cuff links! Did you buy them around here?"

"I do not wear cologne, and the cuff links were not purchased. They were hand crafted."

Daniel jumped in. "I told him that herbal soap Presley got him is wicked stuff. Presley also got him the cuff links. She had them specially made. They are a one-of-a-kind item."

"Too bad. My boyfriend would go insane over a pair of those."

"Well, we'd better head out. I'll leave the tip up front, Devon. Thanks again."

Vadim stood and glanced in the mirror. "Yes, indeed, Devon. Presley Knowles was correct to send me to you."

"Well, now you know where I am. Don't be a stranger!"

Daniel paid Vadim's bill with his American Express card and, as promised, tipped Devon well. Cissy, the receptionist, gushed about Vadim's new look. "Oh, my God, I can't believe the difference! You look so good!"

Vadim smiled. "Your appreciation is well taken. I am pleased you find me appealing."

"Oh, yeah, you're definitely appealing! And if you ever want to have a drink, well, it would be really cool."

"Thank you. It is most kind of you to offer me the invitation. However, Presley Knowles is my woman."

"Lucky for Presley." As they turned to leave, Cissy winked at Vadim. "I'm here every day if you change your mind. You have a good day, now. Come back again soon!"

Once they were out on the street, Daniel had to poke some fun. "Christ, Vadim, that girl came on to you big time! You're not interested in testing the waters?"

"I do not need another woman, Daniel. I have Presley Knowles. No other woman could be to me what she is."

"Well, I guess I asked for that, didn't I?" Fortunately, he spotted the karaoke bar across the street, which provided a way out of the conversation. "Can your stomach handle a drink?"

"I believe so. I have had no trouble today."

It being the middle of the afternoon, there weren't many people in the bar. A couple of guys had the microphone and were singing a duet of "It's Raining Men." Otherwise, the place was quiet.

"What do you drink, Vadim?"

"Vodka. It has always been my favorite. I have not had any in a very long time."

"I don't suppose you have." Daniel ordered them each a double on the rocks. They watched a few others take the microphone and sing.

"Do you like music, Daniel?"

"Sure I do. Who doesn't?"

"Do you sing?"

"No. I couldn't carry a tune if my life depended on it."

"I sing."

"You do?"

"In my time, we sang for entertainment, and we sang on campaign."

"A campaign for what?"

"That is what we called a long march to do battle. Before I left with Ninotchka, I rode with the Zaporog." Vadim took a small sip of his drink, and savored the swallow.

"You were a Cossack?"

"I was. But the Zaporozhian Host turned to dust, as I did."

"Where have you been all this time?"

"Grieving for a life lost, and waiting for another to begin."

"Your life with Presley?"

"Yes."

"If you were a Cossack, how did you get involved with a woman?"

"I found her at an inn, and paid to be with her."

"I don't understand."

"Ninotchka was a whore."

"You're not serious!"

"Dr. Daniel Hanson, I am absolutely serious. She serviced me well and I took her to be my woman."

"Just like that, she went with you?"

"I offered her a better life than she had. She found me pleasing enough, and agreed to leave with me."

"How long were you two together?"

"Our life together ended in our seventh year."

"What happened?"

"I do not care to discuss it."

"Must've been bad, if you've spent all this time grieving." Vadim drank his vodka and didn't respond. Daniel considered trying to read what had happened, but thought better of it. "So, if you can sing, get the microphone and sing a song."

"I do not know any songs of your time."

"You heard Prince do 'Purple Rain.' Surely someone like you should be able to remember a song after hearing it once."

For some reason, challenging Vadim appealed to Daniel. The last person who'd sang had left the mike on the bar. Daniel got up to grab the microphone, and told the karaoke DJ to play "Purple Rain."

Daniel came back to the table and laid the mike in front of Vadim. When he sat down, he noticed Vadim's eyes glowing and sensed Vadim concentrating. Daniel drank his vodka and waited. The DJ cued the song. Fully expecting Vadim to do nothing while "Purple Rain" played, it surprised Daniel when he stood and picked up the microphone.

Dr. Daniel Hanson, you do not think I can do this. I will prove you wrong. The thought rang in Daniel's mind as Vadim started singing. The quality of his voice startled Daniel, rich baritone resonating from deep within his chest. Not only did Vadim know all the words to the song, his pitch-perfect voice rang throughout the bar.

With each line of the song, impressions of Presley saturated Daniel's mind. He knew Vadim sang for his Ninotchka, lamenting his loss, yet at the same time staking his claim on her once again.

The final chorus gave way to a soul-felt wail that made Daniel's breath catch. The sound was of a lone wolf howling at the moon, mourning the loss of his mate. Without question, this man would not easily let Presley go.

When Vadim finished, an eerie silence filled the space. Then the bartender started to clap, followed by the clapping and whistles of the few other patrons. Vadim stoically returned the microphone to the bar and took his seat at their table.

Vadim said nothing to Daniel. He sat quietly and finished his vodka.

"You did a hell of a job with that song."

"I would not say I could sing if I had no voice."

"In this day and age, you could be a rock star."

"I have no inclination to such things."

"Well, if you ever do, you've got the chops for it, not to mention a name that would sell." Daniel ordered another round. "Your stomach still all right?"

"I can drink vodka. To me, it is as mother's milk."

"Presley has a bottle. We'll finish these and then pick up at her place."

"Agreed." Vadim bolted back his double. "We must find you some shoes before returning to Presley's home."

Daniel finished his drink in one swallow. "To hell with the shoes. By tomorrow, these will be dry. If they aren't, you can make me a pair. Let's go." Daniel paid the tab and they left.

When they returned to Presley's building, the doorman did a double take as Vadim walked by. "Damn, you look different!"

Daniel followed Vadim. "He decided to get a haircut while we were out."

"I guess so! Looks good!"

Vadim smiled. "I hope Presley thinks so as well."

They rode the elevator to Presley's floor. Daniel opened the door, and immediately sensed the apartment was empty. "Looks like they're not back yet."

Vadim's eyes glowed for a moment. "They are not yet ready to return. They are having food now."

"Maybe that's a good thing. Gives us some time to drink."

Daniel went to the kitchen and rummaged through Presley's cabinets until he found the liquor. He brought a bottle and two glasses into the living room. Vadim had already turned on the television. Daniel poured the vodka and handed him a glass. "See what's on Pay-Per-View."

"I do not know what that is."

"Presley's slipping if she didn't explain Pay-Per-View." Daniel took the remote. "Here, let me show you."

Daniel found the pay channels and flipped though the titles. "Here we go. *Busty Babes Take Manhattan*. Sounds like a classic. And it's only $4.95 for 24-hour viewing. Such a deal!" He pressed the "Buy Now" button and the movie started. He settled in beside Vadim on the sofa.

The very first scene made both men pay attention. A blonde and a redhead were kissing and rubbing their bare breasts together. When one whispered "Lick me" to the other, Daniel's organ hardened. "Fuck yeah, some lesbo action right off the top."

Vadim watched, and quietly drank his vodka. When he picked up the bottle to pour himself some more, he also poured more for Daniel. They continued to watch the movie.

Daniel became aware of intense tingling moving into his groin, similar to what he'd felt earlier when he'd put on Vadim's trousers. He glanced at Vadim, a question forming in his mind. Vadim answered before the question translated into words.

"We have much in common, Daniel. We both enjoy vodka, we both get hard when we see a naked woman, and we both love Presley Knowles."

Daniel ground his teeth together. The surge in his groin increased. The throbbing became intense. "Leave Presley out of this, Vadim."

"I think not, Daniel. She is sitting here between us. You are thinking of her as you watch these buxom women excite one another, and you are thinking of having both Ezra and Presley in your bed."

"Shut the fuck up, Vadim! You have no right to invade my private thoughts!"

"I do when Presley Knowles is the object of your desire, for she is also the object of mine. She is my woman, not yours."

"You son of a bitch! You have no right to her! You should be fucking dead!" Daniel wrapped his arm around Vadim's neck in an attempt to choke him. Vadim rolled over on top of Daniel and tried to pin him down. Daniel shoved Vadim with both hands and knocked him onto the floor. Then he jumped on top of him.

Daniel rolled his fist into a ball. With the same force he used to swing a baseball bat, he connected with Vadim's jaw. Vadim roared, his rage moving through Daniel like a tidal wave.

Vadim rolled onto his side, throwing Daniel off balance. Daniel fell. Immediately seizing the advantage, Vadim straddled Daniel. He grabbed Daniel's wrists and held them tightly, preventing Daniel from taking another swing at him.

Vadim said nothing. He stared down at Daniel, the silver in his eyes darkening to the color of a storm cloud. Daniel felt Vadim's hard cock against his leg, and had the humiliating reaction of having his own cock twitch with the pressure.

Perhaps you would like from me what the young man wanted.

Daniel barely had time to register the thought before Vadim stretched out on top of him, still holding Daniel's wrists against the floor. Daniel struggled but could not break Vadim's hold. *What the fuck do you think you're doing?*

I am giving you what you will not admit you want. Daniel could do nothing to stop Vadim's violation of his body. The hard ridge of Vadim's cock pressed into Daniel's groin and Vadim slowly rubbed against him. The friction against his cock tortured Daniel, and he ground his teeth together trying not to respond. When Vadim's mouth covered his, an intense herbal odor filled Daniel's throat and nose. He thought he would gag.

Vadim kissed him, forcing his tongue inside Daniel's mouth. Daniel tried to turn his head away, but Vadim bit his lip and forced him to keep his head still. Vadim's whiskers scraped his face and spit ran down his cheek.

Daniel resisted his growing need to respond as the dry hump became more insistent. Again, he tried to break free, this time managing to shift Vadim slightly to the side. Vadim released Daniel's mouth as he attempted to regain his position. Using all the strength he had, Daniel sharply arched his back and twisted his arms. Vadim tumbled off of him.

Wasting no time, Daniel balled his hand into a fist and swung at Vadim. In a blinding flash of movement, Vadim grabbed his wrist and stopped his swing in mid-air. With strength Daniel had never witnessed in another human being, Vadim lifted him and threw him onto the sofa. Before Daniel could get his balance, he felt Vadim against him, pinning him to the sofa from behind.

The preternatural hiss Daniel heard in his ear sounded like a pit of snakes. "In my past, I slit the throat of any man who dared attack me, or dared touch my woman. But, Dr. Daniel Hanson, I swore an oath to Presley Knowles I would not harm you. I will not break that oath. But I will show you what it is to be me."

Vadim reached under Daniel and grabbed his cock. The unexpected sensation surprised Daniel. He pushed backward, trying to throw Vadim off of his back. Instead, he only managed to push his ass tightly against Vadim's rock-hard prick. With the contact came a rush of searing heat that moved through his ass into his genitals.

He tried again to push Vadim off. But his strength could not match Vadim's. The vice-like grip Vadim had on his cock limited his movement. He had no choice but to endure whatever Vadim did.

Like a gust of wind blowing though his mind, Vadim's voice rang out. *You will know, Dr. Daniel Hanson, what it is not to have a woman for centuries. You will know who I am, and what I have endured!*

A series of pictures flashed in Daniel's mind, as if he were looking through Vadim's eyes. He saw her: a thin, dark-haired woman with Mongolian features. There was no doubt she looked different, but the woman he saw was Presley.

The intense arousal Daniel felt focused on this woman, the woman that Presley had been. It seemed as though his desire for her would incinerate him. Then she disappeared, the image shattering like glass in his mind. He still burned for her, but could not reach her.

Vadim humped Daniel's ass. It did not matter that layers of clothing separated their skin. The burning need for release, and for this woman, filled Daniel, as it did Vadim. They shared the same sensations, the same ache, and the same lust. The heartbeat that throbbed in one cock also throbbed in the other.

At the moment of his climax, Vadim pumped Daniel's prick. Daniel undulated against Vadim's cock, as they both ejaculated in a single stream of light.

Then they both passed out.

Go to page 215

Chapter Fourteen

Presley heard the apartment door close. Vadim and Daniel had left. She hoped Vadim would be all right with Daniel. She also hoped they wouldn't get into a fight while they were alone.

After finishing the breakfast dishes, she cut through the bathroom to the bedroom. She found Ezra inside her closet.

"See anything you like?"

"Oh, yes, Presley, many things. Your clothes are like your spirit, bold and colorful."

"Thank you, I think."

"That is said in admiration, Presley. You are fearless and confident. Even with Vadim, you have proven yourself to be unafraid of what he is, and well able to handle his brash nature."

"He has a good heart."

"He always has, Presley. In a time when men had to kill or be killed, he found gentleness and love with you."

"Why did he get so upset when you showed me what happened?"

"The separation from you has caused him unimaginable suffering. The shame that has tormented him because he could not save you, and the grief he has endured because he lost you, have been his only companions for too long. He does not want you to think him less of a man because of it."

"But I don't! Hell, if anything, it makes me love him more!" Presley silenced herself, not believing she'd had said what she said.

"You surprise yourself, Presley Knowles. By your own admission, you love Vadim."

"I'm surprised I blurted it out like that! Ever since he fell out of the sky on the day of my accident, I've been trying to understand everything he makes me feel." Presley noticed Ezra's bare feet, which gave her the chance to change the subject. "Let me find you some shoes. We'd better get going. The men will be back before we ever get out of here."

Presley dug in the closet and found an old pair of leather sandals. "Here, Ezra. Try these. They're beat up but damned comfortable. You'll be able to walk in them."

"Thank you, Presley." Ezra sat on the bed and studied the straps. After unbuckling one, she slipped her foot in. When she lifted her leg to fasten the strap, Presley saw her bare pussy.

"Ezra, you have to put on some underwear under that dress! You'll get us frigging arrested if you bend over in a store!"

"Presley Knowles, please do not be distressed by my oversight. I had difficulty finding a pair that would stay in place."

"You mean they were too small?"

"That is correct."

"Let me see." Presley went to her dresser and rummaged in her underwear drawer. "Here, try these." She tossed a pair of oversized white cotton briefs at Ezra. "These are my granny panties. My grandmother gave me a package of them. I could never bring myself to throw them out."

"Thank you, Presley." Ezra slipped them on and smiled. "Yes, indeed! They are quite comfortable. I trust they properly cover my genitals?"

Presley smiled in spite of herself. "I'm sure they do. We'll get you some sexy ones that fit you."

"If you purchase a few things for me, I will be able to reproduce what I need by mimicking the example."

"Between you and Vadim, we could start our own business."

"No, Presley Knowles, it does not work that way. If there is genuine need, manifestation occurs. The intention of profit is not genuine need."

"It's the loaves and fishes routine, isn't it?"

"In a manner of speaking, yes."

"Okay, then, let's go get you some samples you can knock off."

Ezra finished putting on her borrowed shoes. As they left the building, Presley greeted the doorman. "Hey, Joe, how's it hanging?"

"Long and strong, Ms. Knowles. Haven't seen you for a while."

"Been traveling again."

"This must be Ezra."

"How do you know about Ezra?"

"Dr. Hanson told me you have more guests that arrived last night. Looks like you have a full house up there."

"It creates meaningful relationships, doesn't it, Ezra?"

"It certainly does, Presley."

"I can see why." Joe glanced at Ezra's cleavage.

Without missing a beat, Presley quipped, "Keep it in your pants, Joe. I'm taking Ezra shopping to get her some clothes that don't cause traffic accidents."

Ezra smiled sweetly and added, "Presley does not need any more accidents."

"Yeah, Carl told me you got yourself hurt pretty badly in one. You all right now?"

"Better than ever." Presley took Ezra's hand. "We're outta here. See you later."

Once outside on the sidewalk, Presley realized she still held Ezra's hand. She quickly let go. "If we walk down the street holding hands, people will get the wrong idea."

"You are concerned men will think we are lovers?"

"Well, yeah! This is the Village. Gay couples are every-where. Next to you, they'd think I'm the bull dyke."

Ezra looked down the block. "It is interesting that this is called a village. It is within a city."

"New York is a quirky place. C'mon, let's take a walk and I'll show you."

There were several small boutiques on Christopher Street Presley knew, as well as some shops on Bleecker, where they could find some decent clothes. There was also a new Victoria's Secret close by. As they quietly walked down the street, she smiled, thinking of Daniel seeing Ezra in sexy lingerie.

"You would do that for him, wouldn't you, Presley? You would make me attractive for Daniel?"

Totally unnerved by Ezra's ability to know her thoughts, Presley flushed. "Christ, Ezra! Do you and Vadim know every damn thought in my head?"

"Thoughts to us are like spoken words to you. We hear them as you do conversation."

But you do it as naturally as talking, don't you?

Yes. It is how we communicate with each other in the astral, and how we communicate with incarnates when necessary.

I'm getting better at it. But you and Vadim are amazing! You fucking hear everything!

It is a skill. You will improve with practice.

"Listening to what's in someone else's head isn't something I want to do often."

"Perhaps not. But you have probed both Daniel and Vadim."

"That's different."

"Why so, Presley?"

"Because I have an intimate connection to both of them. It happens when you fuck someone." Presley couldn't stop the surge of jealousy that pushed up into her throat. "But you know that, don't you?"

"Yes, I do."

"Fuck, Ezra! I can't compete with you! You're goddamn Mother Theresa in Marilyn Monroe's body! And guess what! Compared to your Aphrodite look, I come up short, in more ways than one!"

Ezra stopped in the middle of the sidewalk. Presley had no choice but to stop with her. "Presley, you have no reason to view me as a rival. It is not me either of them wants; it is you they both love."

Presley shook her head in absolute disbelief as blue tears slid down Ezra's cheeks. She quickly pulled a wad of Kleenex out of her jeans pocket and handed it to Ezra. "Shit, Ezra! It probably isn't the best time to bring this to your attention, but you're crying blue! Catch those before they stain your dress!"

"Thank you, Presley." Ezra wiped her face. Presley could still see the blue liquid glistening in Ezra's eyes.

"I know I upset you, and I'm sorry."

"If you have Vadim, why do you still want Daniel?"

"Why do you want Daniel, Ezra? Why do you think you have a right to step in and claim him?"

"I am not claiming him, Presley. I hope to earn his affection, and his love. But he compares me to you, and I cannot be what you are."

"No, you are more than I am." Presley looked down the block and saw a shop specializing in leather clothes. That gave her a way to change the subject. "How would you feel about a leather skirt, or maybe some leather pants?"

"They are clothes Daniel will like?"

"Oh, yes, I'm sure Daniel will like them."

Ezra forced a smile. "Then, please show me."

As they walked, Presley considered the situation. The attachment to Daniel had happened without her really meaning for it to happen. No matter what, they would always be close, she knew that. Sharing this encounter with Vadim and Ezra had bonded them in a way nothing else ever could. When she made the effort to be objective, she could see Daniel being happy with Ezra, just as she could see herself being happy with Vadim.

"Ezra, tell me something."

"What, Presley?"

"If you were to have a relationship with Daniel, how would you feel if he continued a relationship with me, too?"

"I am not sure I understand."

"I mean, what if I'm still close to Daniel and want to spend time alone with him once in awhile?"

"You mean as you did this morning when you had sexual relations with him?"

"Yeah, if you want to spell it out, that's what I mean."

"Where there is love and genuine connection, intimacy naturally follows."

"Maybe I can get you a job writing for Hallmark! Ezra, for Christ's sake! Would you be pissed off if I fuck Daniel? Yes or no?"

"No, Presley, I would not. I celebrate the bond between you. I would not deny it in any way."

"Well, do you want to sleep with Vadim again?"

"Perhaps, if he would have me. He is different than Daniel. The two men do not express physical love in the same manner."

"Damn straight they don't! That's why I want my Sno Balls and want to eat them, too." Presley lightly probed Ezra to see if she understood the reference. She did.

"Presley Knowles, do you think we are able to find the middle ground in this, a place where the pain stops and love endures?"

"Ezra, I'm beginning to think that is just what we have to do."

"The men will have to be convinced. They are territorial by nature and do not want to share what they consider to be their own."

"Well, Ezra, I don't give a shit if it's Daniel or Vadim! Neither of them owns me, and neither of them ever will!"

"Presley, I feel your resolve and determination. Your independence is an inspiration."

"Comes from years of holding my own in a man's world." Presley held the door open for Ezra. "We're here. Are you ready to shop?"

This time, Ezra smiled with genuine excitement. "Oh, yes, Presley, I am ready."

Presley expected Ezra to be timid entering a shop for the first time. Much to her surprise, the exact opposite happened. A young woman with short tar-black hair and a pierced lip approached them and asked if they needed help. Before Presley could answer, Ezra jumped in.

"Yes, please. I want to impress a particular man with some new clothes. My friend Presley thought he might like to see me in leather."

"Damn, girl! Just about every woman I know would like to see you in leather, too."

"Then you will help me find some things that will be attractive?"

"Sure. Come over here." The clerk led them to a rack of leather skirts. "What size do you wear?"

This time, Presley did jump in. "She's lost some weight, so we're not sure. Ezra, why don't we take a couple of different sizes and try them?"

"I will do that, Presley." Just like she had been shopping hundreds of times before, Ezra began sifting through the rack of skirts. She pulled out one and held it up to her waist.

"Too small, Ezra." Presley went up a couple of sizes. "Here, try this one."

Ezra held up the skirt. "Yes, I can see, this is better. May I look to see what else is there?"

"Have at it."

Ezra took a few moments to look, and then actually cooed. "Oh, Presley! Look at this one!" Ezra held up a dark brown leather skirt with a large link gold belt. She held it up to her waist and it looked like it would fit.

"Do you like that one?"

"Very much! Do you think Daniel will like it?"

"Ezra, he'll cream in his shorts when he sees it." Turning back to the clerk, Presley asked, "Do you have a top that would go with this?"

"We have a Marilyn sweater that is to die for!" She went to a rack along the wall and came back with a lightweight burgundy sweater with a collar big enough to be worn off the shoulder. "This is a large. They tend to run small. Try it with the skirt. It'll be hot!"

Presley took the sweater. "Where's the fitting room?"

"In the back, to the left."

Presley led Ezra to the fitting room. "Are you all right in there alone, or do you want me to come in with you?"

"I would like some help, if you could."

Presley followed Ezra into the small room. "Do you need help getting out of that dress to try on these things?"

"That would be appreciated. Thank you."

Ezra put her arms high in the air and Presley pulled her dress over her head. When Ezra's bare breasts tumbled free, they pressed against Presley's for a moment. A peculiar heat filled Presley's chest and her nipples became instantly hard.

Trying to ignore the sensation, Presley took the skirt off the hanger and handed it to Ezra. "Put this on while I get the sweater."

Still trying to ignore the warmth creeping into her belly, Presley busied herself taking the sweater off the hanger and straightening the collar. When she turned around, Ezra had just zipped up the skirt and was struggling with the belt.

"Presley, could you help me with this? I don't know how it works."

Presley tucked the sweater under her arm while she adjusted the belt around Ezra's waist and clipped it. Never in her life had she wanted to squeeze a woman's breasts. But being this close to Ezra's topless body, she actually had to squelch the impulse.

She held the sweater up and Ezra threaded her arms through the sleeves. Presley pulled it over her head and adjusted the collar. "Well, what do you think?"

Ezra turned around and looked in the mirror. Presley saw her eyes glow bright blue as she looked at her own reflection. "Oh, my goodness, Presley! It is wonderful!"

Presley had to admit the combination of the leather skirt with the sweater couldn't be more perfect. "How peculiar is it that at the first store we went into you found a perfectly matched outfit with a Marilyn sweater?"

"It is as it should be, Presley. I will be guided to that which suits me best."

"What do you say we pay for this and go find you some jeans?"

"May I wear these new clothes out of the store?"

"Wait here and I'll ask." Presley went to find the clerk. She came back a few minutes later. "You can wear the clothes. She just has to scan the tags to get the prices."

Presley picked up Ezra's white dress and went to check out. After ringing up the clothes, the clerk snipped off the tags. "You look great in that! I knew you would."

After charging the clothes, Presley got a shopping bag for Ezra's dress. When they left the store, Ezra practically glowed with happiness.

Presley took Ezra to several more stores and bought an assortment of shirts, skirts, slacks, and jeans, all of which could be mixed and matched. It seemed no matter what Ezra put on, she looked sexy as hell. If Ezra noticed Presley's uncharacteristic attraction to her, she didn't mention it.

When they got to Victoria's Secret, Presley saw a diner across the street. "Let's get you a few things here to ring Daniel's chimes, and then go get some food."

"I do not yet know if I can digest food, Presley."

"Then, we'll get you some milk. I need to eat."

Once inside the lingerie palace, Ezra became like a child in a candy store. She dropped all of her shopping bags on the floor beside Presley and practically ran to the closest rack of lingerie. Presley gathered the bags and went after her.

"Ezra! For crying out loud! What the hell are you doing?"

"I am sorry, Presley, but I had to see this." She held a black chiffon baby doll nightie, with matching sheer panties. "After I first visited Daniel in Abilene, he dreamed of seeing me wear a garment like this."

"Yeah, I bet he did."

"You said you would help me be attractive for him. He would adore this."

Presley closed her eyes and took a deep breath. She realized that by helping Ezra, she would be pushing Daniel into Ezra's waiting arms. Before she could stop it, she felt tears slide down her face. Her face felt warm where the tears ran. *Oh, my God, Ezra, are they silver?*

Yes, Presley, they are. You share Vadim's soul, as Daniel does mine.

Presley pulled the remnants of her last tissue out of her pocket and wiped her face. *Did I get them all?*

Yes, your face is clean. But your heart is still full.

I can't fucking help it that I'm in love with two men! I didn't plan this, it just happened!

Then let us work together to give the love that is there a voice. I have cared for Vadim for several centuries. An attachment has grown, and I have come to care deeply for him. Perhaps we can help each other.

Maybe we can.

Just then, a young clerk came up to them. "Excuse me, do you intend to purchase that lingerie?"

"We don't know yet." Presley knew the clerks in this store had a tendency to be snotty. She cued Ezra. *I want time to shop in here without being harassed by these clerks. Play along with me.* "This is Ezra. I'm sure you must have heard of her?"

The question obviously caught the girl off guard. "No, I'm sorry, I haven't. Who is she?"

"She is a favorite in the European cinema, here in the city

to do a location shoot. We had a break in the filming schedule, and she specifically asked to see a Victoria's Secret. I brought her here rather than the bigger one in midtown, to avoid the paparazzi."

"Oh, I didn't know."

Much to Presley's delight, Ezra picked up the ball. "My dear young lady, if you would be so kind as to allow us to shop quietly for a time, I would be grateful. I do not wish to draw attention to my presence here. And, yes, indeed, if you have this garment in my size, I would like to purchase it, as well as some other dainties that I fancy." Ezra's formal way of speaking lent substance to the European actress ruse. She sounded foreign.

"Yes, of course." The clerk looked at the tag on the lingerie. "This is a medium. With your body type, I believe a large would be more comfortable."

The young lady went back to the rack and found the same baby doll set in a large. "I hope this is to your liking, Ezra?"

Ezra held the sheer material up to her chest. "Yes, this will be fine. The man who shares my bed will find it quite attractive, I am sure."

The clerk, now practically fawning over Ezra, agreed. "The way you're built, with that on, he'll be all over you."

Ezra smiled a smile that could have won her a spot in a toothpaste commercial. "That is the intention, my dear. Now, if I might finish my shopping." In true diva style, she handed Presley the negligeé, and then strolled over to the panties. Presley shot the thought at her back, *Let's not overdo it, Ez.*

They will not bother us now, Presley. She is presently telling everyone not to draw attention to the actress in their midst. As she looked at the panties, she added, *It is quite pleasing to hear you call me Ez.*

It works. Glad to hear you don't mind.

Ezra selected a few pairs of panties. Presley talked her into getting a bra. Ezra only agreed to try it, but saw little need to use the garment.

Fortunately, Presley had enough money left over from her trip to Abilene to pay for Ezra's items in cash. She really didn't want this store to have her real name. When Ezra saw her taking the bills out of her wallet, Presley could feel her concern about the cost of their shopping trip.

She reassured her. *Don't worry about it, Ezra. Daniel doesn't know it yet, but he's picking up half the bill for today.*

Even though Ezra stood behind her out of her line of vision, Presley nonetheless felt her smile.

They left the store and Presley immediately led them across the street to the diner. She found a booth in the corner that gave them a bit of privacy.

The hostess brought them each a glass of water and menus. Presley looked at the beverage list and noticed milkshakes were on it.

"Ez, have you ever had ice cream?"

"No. It is not anything I have ever tried."

"Then, how about a vanilla milkshake? It is milk and sweet cream mixed together. I think you'll like it."

"I would be pleased to try, Presley. Thank you."

When the waitress came to take their order, it amused Presley to see she had on glitter makeup and a large gold nameplate necklace that said Tammy.

"So, what do you want?"

Tammy's abrupt delivery almost made Presley laugh out loud. Struggling to control herself, Presley asked, "What kind of soup do you have today?"

"Well, I don't know!"

"How can you not know what kind of soup you have?"

"Hey, my shift just started. I don't know what they got today."

"All right, then, can you tell me what kind of ice cream they use in the milkshakes? Is it all natural?"

"I don't know. It's in a big brown tub in the freezer. It's ice cream. What does it matter?"

"My friend has a sensitive stomach. I don't want her to get sick."

"Does she have a disease or something?"

"No, she doesn't have a disease. Look, just bring my friend a vanilla milkshake. I'll have a cheeseburger and a cup of coffee. You do have coffee, don't you?"

"Yeah, we got lots of coffee. You want fries?"

"No, just the burger, cooked medium, if you please."

"Yeah, sure. I'll tell 'em in the kitchen, but you'll probably get it well done anyway."

As Tammy walked away, Presley chuckled. "Ez, you just got a taste of classic New York. It's not only the city that never sleeps, it's also the city with the classiest people. That one is a real gem."

"I enjoy your humor, Presley. It is as eccentric as you are."

"I believe the more accurate word is idiosyncratic."

"You have made Vadim laugh. He has not known laughter in hundreds of years."

"I know. I've only had a glimpse of what he went through. I don't know how he survived it."

"There is no choice but to endure once the physical body dies. We make our own heaven, or our own hell."

"He really sat in that one room for hundreds of years?"

"He did, by his own choice."

"But you kept him company, didn't you?"

"No, Presley. He would not let me. I tried, but he would chase me away."

"Why, Ezra? It makes no sense to me."

"Presley, few have known grief as profound as Vadim's. You gave him the single point of light in his life. When he couldn't save you, the light went out."

"Not completely, Ezra. He saved my life. I still don't understand how he knew."

"Your soul spoke to his, and he heard. In a heartbeat, he

saw and responded. The karmic scales are now balanced. He did in this lifetime what he could not do before."

Tammy brought the milkshake and coffee. Ezra tasted the milkshake, leaving a white moustache on her upper lip, which she licked off. "Presley, this is sweet nectar! It is wonderful!"

"I thought you'd like it." Presley opened the straw and dipped it in the glass. "Drink it with this. Suck the liquid up through it. It will keep the ice cream off of your face."

Ezra tried it, and happily settled in to drink her shake. Tammy brought the burger a few minutes later.

"Could we have the check now, please? We're in a bit of a hurry."

"No problem." After quickly scribbling some numbers on her pad, Tammy slapped the check facedown on the table.

"Ezra, the one thing we haven't found yet is shoes. Maybe we can find a shoe store on the way home."

"That would be fine, Presley. But I think I can fashion a pair by copying yours. I understand better now how the shoes should match the clothes."

"Well, we'll see. If we pass a store that has shoes, we can always run in for a minute to see what they have."

Presley had eaten most of her burger when suddenly blinding pain shot through her jaw. For a moment, she thought she had broken a tooth. Then she felt Vadim's rage. She dropped the hamburger back on her plate. "Ezra?" Ezra's eyes were glowing as blue as the sky.

With searing pain still radiating through her jaw, she hissed, "Fucking shit, Ezra. We have to get home. Vadim will kill him!"

Ezra focused her shining blue eyes on Presley. The pain in Presley's jaw eased. *Vadim will not hurt Daniel, Presley. He will keep his promise to you.*

Presley fumbled for her wallet and threw her last twenty dollar bill on the table. *Daniel must have lost his mind, Ezra! He hit Vadim!*

They have both been drinking alcohol.

Shit! They're drunk? I knew we shouldn't have left them

alone! She pulled a pair of sunglasses out of her purse. *Put these on. Your eyes are shining like fucking headlights!*

Hoping she had all their bags, Presley bolted from the booth and almost ran into Tammy.

"Sorry, Tammy. There's money on the table. Keep the change."

"Yeah, right."

Ezra, do we have all our stuff?

Yes, we have everything.

Are Daniel and Vadim all right?

They are fighting.

How can you be so fucking calm? Vadim told me he could easily kill Daniel.

Trust, Presley. Vadim will do nothing to jeopardize his new life with you. His love for you will protect Daniel.

I hope to hell you're right.

Presley wanted to hail a cab, but didn't have enough money left to pay for it. She practically ran the three long blocks to her building. Just before they went inside, Ezra stopped her.

"Presley, catch your breath and calm yourself. You do not want to raise suspicion from your friend Joe."

"Okay, you're right. We've just had a wonderful shopping trip. All smiles, right?"

"Correct."

Forcing herself to walk through the lobby, Presley tried to pass before Joe noticed them. No such luck. "How was the shopping?"

Ezra answered. "We had a wonderful shopping trip. I would love to show you everything, but I really have to use the toilet."

"Not a problem, Ezra. I like the new outfit you have on. And those shades are hot!"

"Thank you, Joe. Come, Presley, we must go up now."

Presley yelled over her shoulder, "Later, Joe."

"Later, Ms. Knowles."

In the elevator, Presley's heart thumped in her chest. She wanted to thank Ezra for taking charge in the lobby, but couldn't bring herself to speak. She dropped all the bags in the hallway outside her apartment door so she could dig in her purse for her keys. The silence from inside sickened her, and she struggled not to throw up.

Her hands shaking, she unlocked and opened the door. A sob escaped from her throat when she saw Daniel sprawled on the sofa and Vadim lying on the floor. Ezra took off the sunglasses and walked past her to where the two men lay.

Ezra, is Daniel dead?

No, dear Presley. He is quite alive. The liquor and Vadim's energy have caused him to be unconscious. He will be fine when he awakes.

Presley's knees gave way and she crumpled to the floor. Ezra hurried to her and helped her to stand. Presley leaned against the wall while Ezra brought the shopping bags in and closed the door.

"You're sure they're all right?"

"Yes, Presley. You might like to know they shared a climax."

"They did what?"

"Vadim energetically raped Daniel."

"What the fuck does that mean?"

"That means Vadim forced Daniel into a submissive posture and then caused him to ejaculate."

"Vadim fucked Daniel?"

"In a manner of speaking, yes. They both remained clothed, but they climaxed together."

"Well, I'll be damned! That's why they passed out, isn't it?"

"It is. The alcohol and the overload of energy proved too much for both of them."

"And the pain in my jaw?"

"Daniel provoked the incident. He attacked Vadim, and punched him in the face. You felt Vadim's pain, and his anger at being assaulted."

"Jesus Christ! Daniel's lucky he's still alive! From what Vadim showed me, anyone that ever picked a fight with him didn't live long enough to talk about it."

"As I told you he would, Vadim honored his promise to you. He did not hurt Daniel."

Presley felt about to heave. "Ezra, I don't feel well."

"Come to the bedroom, Presley, and rest. You simply need to quiet yourself." Ezra helped Presley walk to the bedroom. "Sit on the bed and allow me to see to you." Presley didn't argue. She hated to throw up. Vadim had stopped it before. Maybe Ezra could help her now.

Ezra gently took off Presley's shoes. As Presley lay back, she remembered Ezra and Daniel had made love in her bed the night before. She tried to push the images back, but they came flooding in.

"You are sensing the energetic imprinting we left in your bed, Presley. I am sorry. I should have cleared it this morning. I will do so now."

"No, Ezra. I want to see what happened."

"As you wish."

Presley closed her eyes and let the pictures form. She saw Daniel and Ezra together. While she watched the ethereal slide show, Ezra massaged her stomach. Just as it had with Vadim, her stomach settled as Ezra calmed her.

The images in her mind should have upset her, but they didn't. Instead, the visualization took on an element of erotic fantasy. As she watched Daniel fuck Ezra, her body responded as if she were fantasizing.

Ezra must have sensed the shift in Presley's energy. When she slipped her hand under Presley's shirt and rubbed her bare stomach, Presley didn't protest. Then, Ezra's hand went higher and she gently caressed Presley's breast.

She heard Ezra's voice in her head. *Have you ever loved a woman, Presley Knowles?*

No. I prefer men. Always have.

But women better understand how a female body responds. I can feel your arousal when I touch your breasts.

It feels good, Ez.

Is your stomach quiet now?

It's fine. Thank you.

You are quite welcome.

Ezra continued to massage Presley's breasts. The heat in her chest from earlier in the day came back.

Presley opened her eyes. Ezra sat beside her in her new outfit. "I can see why Daniel is so attracted to you. You are a beautiful woman, Ezra."

"As are you, Presley Knowles. I can also see why Daniel is attracted to you."

"I know we are both feeling this. Are we going to do anything about it?"

"I am inclined to love you, if that is what you are asking."

"Yeah, I guess that's what I'm asking. Hell's bells, if Vadim humped Daniel's ass and they came together, then why shouldn't we do something together, too?"

"Presley Knowles, I am in complete agreement."

"You know, this afternoon when I helped you take off your dress, I wanted to touch your tits so bad!"

"I am flattered, Presley. I know you are not usually inclined to such things."

"You got that right. I know my way around a cock and balls. But tits, no, I don't usually want to cop a feel. But yours, Christ, Ezra, they're spectacular!"

Ezra pulled her hand out from under Presley's T-shirt. With no modesty or hesitation, she grabbed the bottom of her sweater and pulled it over her head. Her generous breasts tumbled free.

Presley could feel the fire burning in Ezra. She felt it, too.

She sat up and pulled her T-shirt off. The two women sat facing one another, topless, neither of them knowing what to do next.

"Well, hell, Ezra! If we're going to do this, let's just fucking do it!" Presley reached out and pinched Ezra's nipple, and then fondled her breast. "I'm no expert on being a lesbian, but I know what I like."

"Please show me what you like. I do not yet know what I like, or what is possible."

"The first thing is a whole lot of touching, everything and everywhere." Presley got up on her knees and rubbed Ezra's chest with both hands. "Jesus Christ, your tits are amazing!"

Ezra put her arm around Presley's waist and pulled her close. "I want yours to touch mine, the way they did this afternoon."

"You felt it too, didn't you?"

"Yes, it felt wonderful."

"You didn't let on to me that you felt anything. I know I sure as hell did."

"I knew it embarrassed you to desire me. I did not wish to make you more uncomfortable."

"Well, the cat's out of the bag now." Presley leaned into Ezra, and pressed her breasts against Ezra's chest. When their bare skin touched, flecks of sparkling sapphire floated in the air around them.

Ezra kissed Presley's cheek, and then kissed her neck. Presley moaned as Ezra's mouth covered hers. She recognized the kiss as Daniel's, Ezra having learned the fine art from him. Presley returned the kiss in kind, their breasts now fused in a passionate embrace.

Their shared fever intensified as they kissed, as did the blue light around them. Presley had the sense of floating inside a cloud. Suddenly she remembered why she had the intoxicating high. *Fuck, Ezra, I forgot! You're a ghost!*

I am not of this world, Presley Knowles, but I have never been more human than I am in this moment.

Have you ever masturbated?
I have never self pleasured.
Let's get naked and have at it.

Presley scrambled off the bed and took off her jeans, while Ezra took off her leather skirt. They both peeled off their panties and then lay down on the bed together.

"Too bad the guys are out cold. They would really get off on this. Did you see the movie they had on the TV?"

"I saw beautiful women loving each other as we are. Perhaps we will allow them to watch us?"

"Oh, yeah, mama! Now you're talking my language. That would be a fuck fest to end all fuck fests."

"I do not understand the words, but I do feel your inclination to entertaining the men with our loving."

"Ezra, you do have a way of putting things in perspective." Presley casually brushed the blonde curls between Ezra's legs. Ezra opened her legs wider. "You see how your body expects a man? It is instinctual that we want something pushed inside of us."

Presley pulled her nightstand drawer open and took out her favorite vibrator, shaped like a cock.

"What is that, Presley?"

"This little beauty, Ez, takes care of me when I sleep alone. Do you want to see how it works?"

"Oh, yes, I truly do!"

Presley snapped on the switch and the vibrator hummed in her hand. "Just relax, Ez. Let me show you how it's done."

Presley pushed the tip of the vibrator between Ezra's legs. As Presley suspected would happen, she felt the same sensation as Ezra did. Since she had more practice at sustaining control before her orgasm, she hoped she could make Ezra climax and manage her own orgasm at the same time.

As Presley massaged Ezra's clit, Ezra squirmed on the bed. Presley could hardly believe how erotic it could be to control another woman's arousal and watch her heat build. The visual stimulation coupled with the throbbing of her own clit made Presley burn for a cock in her pussy.

Without thinking about it, she did to Ezra what she wanted for herself. She rammed the vibrator into Ezra's cunt. Presley's pussy clenched, as if it had been penetrated rather than Ezra's.

She fucked Ezra hard, the blonde beauty moaning and writhing on the bed. Each thrust inside Ezra sent ripples of pleasure through Presley's genitals. Presley's pelvis undulated as if a cock had entered her from behind.

Presley couldn't be sure which one of them triggered the other's climax. She only knew they were coming, together. Ezra screamed as her body convulsed on the bed. With all the willpower Presley possessed, she continued to ram the vibrator into Ezra's cunt as they both shook with sensation.

When Presley collapsed beside Ezra on the bed, they could both barely breathe. She turned off the vibrator and dropped it on Ezra's stomach. They lay there together, letting the waves of pleasure they shared carry them into a wonderful, drowsy haze.

They must have drifted off to sleep, because the next thing Presley heard was Vadim's voice saying, "Ninotchka!"

Then Presley heard Daniel say, "Holy fucking shit!"

Ezra was asleep beside her, and Presley had her hand on Ezra's bare breast. The vibrator still lay in the curve of Ezra's belly.

Chapter Fifteen

"Ezra, wake up. We've been busted." Ezra rolled over in her sleep and put her arm around Presley's waist. The vibrator rolled off her stomach and wedged between them, the tip of it poking Presley's pussy.

Presley reached between them to pull it out and accidentally turned it on. It hummed in her hand until she found the switch to turn it off. Still holding it, she shook Ezra again. "Ez, wake the fuck up! Vadim and Daniel are in here."

Ezra opened her eyes and blinked. When she saw Vadim and Daniel standing beside the bed, she whispered, "Oh, my soul!"

"Well, ladies! It looks like you've worked things out, now, doesn't it?" Daniel put his arm around Vadim's shoulder. "Did you hear that, Vadim? It's Ez now."

"I did indeed hear it, Daniel. It is a surprise to witness such familiarity."

"Not to mention seeing it in the flesh, so to speak."

"Shut the fuck up, both of you!" Using the vibrator like a long finger, Presley shook it at them. "The two of you have more than a little explaining to do!" Presley glared at Daniel. "When you hit Vadim, you nearly busted my jaw! It hurt like frigging hell! I thought I'd snapped a tooth eating my burger. I'm surprised Vadim didn't kill you on the spot!"

"He wanted to, didn't you, Vadim?"

"I surely did. But I promised you I would not hurt him."

"Oh, so in lieu of killing him, you raped him! Nice to know how civilized you've become."

"Presley, I know I'm taking my life into my hands for the second time today by mentioning this, but it's hard to take you seriously when you're waving a dildo at us."

"Fuck you, Daniel! I sure as hell don't want the police stuffing you in a body bag. But instead of killing you, maybe Vadim should have shoved his cock down your throat. As least it would have shut your smart-ass mouth for a while."

"Vadim, remember earlier you mentioned how her fire gets going?"

"I remember, Daniel."

"Hot damn! Should we draw straws to see who gets to take her on?"

"If either one of you comes near me, you'll regret it!"

Ezra cuddled up behind Presley and stroked her hair. "She means it. Presley will severely injure your genitals if you touch her."

"Damn straight I will. I'll take the sons of bitches out!"

"Vadim, I think Devon might've been onto something when he suggested you wash her mouth out with soap."

"Yeah, and you've got cum stains on your pants, wise guy!" Presley snapped.

Daniel looked down at the fly on his pants. "So, I do. And my other clothes are probably mildewed in my bag. Vadim, do you think you can knock me out a pair of jeans like yours?"

"I do believe that could be managed, Daniel."

"While you're at it, you might want to get yourself another pair. You have cum stains too. I wonder how that happened?"

"It would seem something sexual occurred between us."

"Just like it did with the ladies. Is this kick-ass synchronicity, or what? C'mon, big dude, show me how you can make a pair of pants out of nothing."

Before leaving the bedroom, Daniel turned back to Presley and Ezra. "Once you ladies get some clothes on, you might want to join us. I don't know about you, but I'm hungry."

Daniel and Vadim retreated to the living room. Presley still had a head of steam up. "Can you fucking believe those two? They had a fistfight, and instead of killing Daniel, Vadim dry humped his ass. Now, they're best buddies. What the fuck is that all about?"

"In their own masculine way, Presley, they have bonded, just as we have."

"Ezra, I'm sorry. I don't get it. I thought Vadim had hurt Daniel, I really did." Presley couldn't stop the tears that welled up. "The possibility that he might have killed him nearly killed me too."

Ezra gently rubbed Presley's neck. "I know you feared Vadim had harmed Daniel. But he didn't, dear girl, because he loves you more than his own pride."

Presley relaxed as Ezra massaged her neck. "Ez, when you called me 'dear girl,' it felt like you were my older sister."

"I once was that."

"What did you say?"

"You do not remember, just as you do not remember your lifetime with Vadim. In a time long past, we were sisters."

Even though in her heart Presley knew Ezra told her the truth, she still couldn't accept it. "You're kidding, aren't you?"

"No, Presley. You are the reason I stayed with Vadim and protected him as much as I could."

"Dear God, Ezra! Why?" Presley shook her head, trying to make sense of it all. "How could I be the reason you stayed with Vadim?"

"The last breath you took so long ago carried a prayer for his protection. I have done what I could to honor your request."

"But why would you do such a thing? He has been isolated for hundreds of years. How could you stay with him all that time?"

"Because I made a promise that I would care for you and yours as you had cared for me." Ezra turned Presley around to face her. "This body you see is not the one I had when we were sisters. I could not walk then. My legs failed to grow properly, and my spine twisted, bending my body into a grotesque posture. You cared for me, and loved me, when all others thought me of the devil."

"Sweet Jesus, Ezra." Presley began to tremble. She shut her eyes as the memory, buried for centuries, rose to the surface. "I'm either totally psychotic or I really remember what you said to me."

"What did I say, Presley? I will tell you if it is true."

"You had a high fever, and I wrapped you in wet cloths, trying to bring the fever down. You stopped me, begging me to let you go." Presley stopped, overcome with emotion. She took a deep breath and tried to continue. "You said you wanted to run in the fields and pick flowers, and that you didn't want to hurt anymore."

"That is all true. What else, Presley? How did it end?"

"Your breathing—you couldn't breathe. I held you, and begged you not to leave me. You whispered to me, telling me not to be sad, and you promised you would always watch over me from heaven. You died in my arms."

Memories of how Ezra had looked so long ago and the humiliation she'd endured because of it saturated Presley's consciousness, the emotions real and immediate. Presley put her head on Ezra's shoulder and sobbed, her sense of love and loss so profound she couldn't contain it. Ezra stroked her hair and murmured soft words, so soft Presley couldn't hear what she said. When she'd quieted enough to speak, Presley wanted to know what she'd said.

"Ez, I couldn't hear you. What did you whisper in my ear?"

"I told you love is eternal. Where there is love, there is God."

"Geez, you really should be writing for Hallmark." Presley wiped the tears from her face and saw the silver glistening on her hand. "Holy balls, Ezra, I'll never be able to cry in public again. Look at this. My tears are silver."

"Mine are blue. They are harder to hide than yours."

"I suppose we can blame it on cheap eye makeup if anyone ever sees it."

Just then, Daniel lightly knocked on the door. "Everything all right in here? I heard you crying, Presley. Vadim told me to give you more time with Ezra, but I couldn't wait any longer to come in."

"We are fine, Daniel. Presley just had another shock. She is adjusting."

"What kind of shock? Presley, are you all right?"

"I will be, once I catch my breath. I just found out Ezra was my sister once upon a time."

"This is unbelievable! We're just one big happy family, aren't we?"

Presley smiled. "We could get an act together and call it 'The Aristocrats.'"

As she'd hoped she would, Presley made Daniel laugh. "Well, we're sure as hell dysfunctional enough to take it on the road. Vadim can do the singing, and become a rock star." Without explaining his offhand remark, he went back to the living room.

Pulling herself together, Presley gathered their clothes off the floor and pulled on her shirt. She tossed Ezra's new skirt and sweater at her. "Your sexy panties are still in the shopping bag. Do you want to put these back on, or do you want your new ones?"

Ezra grinned as she put her skirt on. "I want the ones that will cause Daniel to have an erection."

"Ez, I think all Daniel has to do is look at you to get an erection. I don't think it matters what you're wearing."

"Do you really think so?"

"You've been watching Daniel since I met him. You know as well as I do that when he's attracted to a woman, he doesn't hide it. Ezra, I know he's hot after you. Seeing him look at you the way he's looked at me is what's so damn hard for me."

"But Presley, he still looks at you that way. He did just a few minutes ago."

"So how do I stop being so frigging jealous of you? I don't want to resent you, Ezra, especially not now that I remember what went down between us. Being a possessive bitch is not my style, but I can't seem to help it."

"Allow the feelings to flow, Presley. Step back and observe without judgment. Be open to the truth, whatever it is."

"Says you!"

Presley felt the vibrato of Vadim's laughter ripple through her body. She shouted at the door, "Vadim, stop fucking eavesdropping!"

Ninotchka, I am interested in what is happening between you and Ezra. I see no reason why I should not listen.

Well, I do! Make yourself useful and bring the shopping bags in here, so we can finish getting dressed.

Your wish is my command, dear heart.

Says you! With the comment, Presley sent her amusement and affection. She knew Vadim would get it.

Ezra had finished dressing and Presley had put on her panties under her shirt when Vadim showed up at the door with the bags. "Here are all your parcels, Ninotchka. It appears you had a successful trip." He put the bags on the bed, and Ezra immediately grabbed the one from Victoria's Secret.

"Don't lose the receipt, Ez. I'll need it."

"I will be careful, Presley. I only wish to find a pair of panties to put on."

"I spent a ton of money, which you might tell your best buddy Daniel he's splitting with me. Considering that most of the things we got are meant to make him hot, it's only fair."

"I will be sure to tell him." Vadim turned to leave.

"Wait, Vadim. Let me look at you."

He turned around and stood at attention, as though being reviewed in a military inspection. Presley had been so upset earlier she hadn't noticed the haircut. Making a full circle, she walked around Vadim and stopped directly in front of him. She touched his whiskers, her hand lingering on his face. "Goddamn, you look good!"

Vadim's smile said it all. "I am pleased you find my appearance acceptable, Ninotchka."

"Devon did it, didn't he?"

"Yes. Your friend Devon made me look like a modern man."

"He sure as hell did!" Presley felt the now-familiar burning in her belly. She looked up at Vadim, and deliberately allowed the heat in her belly to warm her eyes. She knew the warmth meant they sparkled with silver. As if completing a circuit, Vadim's eyes also began to glow.

Ezra quietly left the bedroom and closed the door behind her. *Are you still angry, Ninotchka?*

You bet I am! But somehow that doesn't matter right now. Presley wrapped her arms around Vadim's neck, and squirmed against his pelvis. *How about a quickie?*

You are inclined to it, I see.

You could say that. Are you?

Oh, yes, Presley Knowles, I am most certainly inclined to it. Vadim grabbed the hem of Presley's shirt and pulled it over her head, leaving her only in her panties. *How shall I have you?*

Presley stepped back and took off her panties. She waited, giving Vadim a chance to look at her. She watched his eyes. As he scanned her naked body, the color changed. The bright silver turned smoky as he smoldered with his arousal. *Open your shirt.*

Vadim unbuttoned his shirt. When Presley saw his bare chest, the heat in her belly flared. *You did not answer me, Presley Knowles. How shall I have you?*

Open your jeans and I'll tell you.

Vadim unzipped his fly and exposed himself. Presley stared at his organ, amazed at the beauty of it. She loved men; she always had. But Vadim did something to her no other man had ever done. He made her ache with need. She had never known such raw throbbing as he made her feel.

Assuming an uncharacteristically submissive posture, Presley turned around and bent over. She put her hands on the bed to support herself and spread her legs wide open. *I want it from behind, Vadim. Push your cock in me as deep as it will go.*

Presley felt Vadim's hands on her hips. A cloud of his scent filled the room as he positioned himself behind her. He grunted when he penetrated her, his cock sliding into her body easily and comfortably. The gentleness of his entry then gave way to what simmered underneath the surface.

Vadim held her hips and forcefully banged against her ass, savagely claiming her in some feral mating ritual. As he thumped against her, the sense of being possessed by Vadim overwhelmed Presley. Rather than being a source of distress, it drove her higher. She wanted to be overwhelmed by him, to feel his strength and his power, to immerse her identity in his.

Presley wanted the sex to go on forever, to always be in this place of shared identity with Vadim. When the tingles signaled the onset of her orgasm, she tried to push them back, not wanting the exquisite sense of union to end. But Vadim drove himself into her in his own orgasmic frenzy. Together they went to the edge of the clouds, and together they plummeted into the eye of the storm.

Vadim did not immediately pull himself out of Presley's body. They floated back to earth and remained fused, body and soul, for several minutes.

During that time, Presley savored the extraordinary sense of connection they shared. Inhaling deeply, she breathed Vadim into her lungs, the infusion of his scent permeating every cell in her body. In a mystical transference of Qi, Vadim's life force continued to blend with Presley's. She could feel her body changing, but she didn't understand how.

Her hands had numbed, the circulation constricted from leaning on them for so long. *Vadim, I have to stand up. My hands are asleep.*

Of course, Ninotchka. My apologies for not considering your comfort.

Vadim withdrew and Presley stood, wobbling a bit as she got her balance. Vadim caught her around the waist and pulled her against him. He wrapped his arms around her. The hands that had once killed in order to survive now massaged her fingers and wrists. He kissed her neck, his breath giving her chills.

Vadim, I'm scared.

There is no need to be frightened, Ninotchka. No harm will come to you. I will see to it.

But I don't understand what is happening to me, and I'm scared shitless something will happen to you that will make you leave.

I am not leaving, Presley. On my soul, I will not leave you.

But if you stay, then what? How do we live the way we are? And what about Daniel and Ezra? What happens to them? If not for me, Daniel wouldn't be involved in any of this.

Dr. Daniel Hanson is a strong man, Presley. He will find his way in this new life, as will Ezra. For us, it is only a matter of riding the wave of our love.

Says you!

The vibration of Vadim's chuckle tickled her inside and outside. *Presley Knowles, you do have a way about you.*

Just then, Daniel knocked loudly on the bedroom door.

"Hey, you two, Ezra says you're finished copulating. I called out for pizza and beer, and ordered some ice cream for Ezra and Vadim, if you're interested."

Presley shouted back, "We'll be out in a few minutes. Thanks for getting us some food."

"Considering your tendency for hypoglycemic bitchiness, I thought it might be a good idea."

"Thank you, Dr. Hanson!"

"You're welcome."

Presley turned around to face Vadim. "You need to tuck your business back in your pants and button your shirt, and I need to put on some clothes."

"Ninotchka, we will make our way with this, and we will do it together. There is nothing to fear."

"I suppose when you've been through hell, and come out the other side, you're not afraid of anything. But that doesn't stop it from rattling my cage. I guess I'm on this roller coaster now. All I can do is hang on for the ride."

"Everything is as it should be. You will see."

"Now you sound like Ezra."

"Perhaps that is a good thing."

Presley kissed his cheek and then gathered her clothes. "I got Ez a shitload of clothes today. She looks great in everything."

"I expect she does. She is a beautiful woman."

"You know about her, about why she stayed with you?"

"I do. She only recently told me."

"Isn't it something? I mean, that we were sisters?"

"We stay connected to those we truly love. Neither time nor space can undo that which is connected by love."

"Well, before these last couple of weeks, I would have said that is New Age mumbo jumbo. I can't say that now, under the circumstances."

"You cannot deny what is obviously true."

"Yeah, that would be like saying the elephant in the polka-dot pajamas isn't in the living room."

"Daniel and Ezra are in the living room. There is no elephant, Presley."

"Vadim, that is a way of saying an obvious truth is being ignored."

"I have much to learn."

"You're doing just fine. You've only been here two days, for crying out loud."

"It will take time, I understand. But I am impatient to learn all there is to know."

"You'll get there. C'mon, let's get some food."

Once they had themselves together, Presley and Vadim joined Ezra and Daniel in the living room. They were sitting on the sofa watching television. Presley noticed they were holding hands.

"Is the food here yet?"

"Not yet. I didn't know if Vadim was ready to try pizza or if he would prefer ice cream, so I ordered enough to go either way. By the way, getting Ezra a milkshake for lunch was an inspired idea."

"I thought so. We may have to go back there. You have to meet Tammy."

"Who's Tammy?"

"Our waitress. Ez, tell him about Tammy."

"The young woman who served us had an unusual way of expressing herself. She didn't seem to know much about doing her job properly."

"Ezra's being polite. Let me put it this way, if Robert Altman and Martin Scorsese made a movie together, Tammy would be in it."

Daniel chuckled. "I get the picture. You and Ezra had a good shopping trip?"

"Yeah, until you punched Vadim, everything was hunky dory."

"At the time, it felt like the right thing to do."

"I'll say it again, you're lucky you're here to talk about it."

"Vadim already explained that to me. I know I fucked up. Vadim, tell her we kissed and made up."

"Dr. Daniel Hanson is correct. We did kiss."

Presley looked from one man to the other. Neither of them offered an explanation. "Ezra, tell me the truth, did they kiss?"

Ezra's eyes brightened for a moment before she answered. "Yes, Presley, Vadim forcibly kissed Daniel while they were fighting."

"No shit! I would have paid big coin to see that happen!"

A knock on the door signaled the pizza delivery. Daniel got up to answer the door. Before he did, he had the last word. "I expect I would pay a hell of a lot more to see what happened between you and Ezra." Then, he went to pay for the food.

They all went to the kitchen to eat. Daniel had ordered one plain and one pepperoni pizza, a six-pack of beer, and a couple of quarts of vanilla ice cream. Ezra wanted only ice cream, while Vadim wanted to try the pizza and also have some ice cream.

While they ate, Daniel broached the subject that also had Presley worried. "We have to figure out what the hell to do now. I hope everyone understands that."

Presley shook her head. "I don't know what to do now. This is like hiding two illegal aliens, except they can't be deported. I don't think saying they're ghosts will fly, do you?"

"No, it won't. If they're staying here, somehow we have to get them some sort of papers. I'm completely out of my league with this. I don't suppose you have any connections that could help?"

"I might. I did a story once on forged documents. I made some contacts then. Don't know if they can help, but it's all I've got."

Daniel turned to Ezra, who sat quietly eating her bowl of ice cream. "Ezra, you seem to have access to more information than we do. Do you understand the problem enough to offer any ideas about what we should do?'

"Where there is need, spirit will provide."

Presley could see Daniel becoming impatient, so she took over. "Ez, if you and Vadim intend to stay here, you have to have identities. That means you need papers that show you're legally here. Do you have any way of getting that?"

"If you show me what we need, I will see what is possible."

Daniel finished his slice of pizza and reached for another. "There is one other approach to take with this."

"Which is?"

"Let's say Ezra can make some sort of papers that appear legitimate. She looks Scandinavian, so let's assume for the moment that she is from Norway and Vadim is from the Ukraine. We are both United States citizens. If we marry them, then they are legal."

"Are you fucking crazy? I don't want to get married!"

"And why not? You are obviously crazy about Vadim, and I know firsthand what he feels for you."

"Which would be?"

"Presley, I know what happened to you, and to him. After we woke up, it's like I had his memory. I went looking around and saw more than I expected to see."

"The same thing happened with Ezra. I remembered her memories." Presley paused, trying to decide if she should ask what was really on her mind. "Daniel, you're a doctor, a really good one. Something is happening to me, I mean, to my body. Do you know what is going on?"

"No, but I know what you're talking about. Ezra and I had a talk while you were in the bedroom with Vadim. There is something happening that I can't explain, but I sure as hell can feel it. She said we are becoming light. Any idea what that means?"

"Kind of sounds like we're becoming ghosts too."

Vadim reached for a second slice of plain pizza. "Ninotchka, it is your choice to call us ghosts. I have told you many times that is not what we are."

"Then, please, explain to me what the hell you are."

"Perhaps Ezra could do so. She has more knowledge about energy fields than what I've acquired."

Both Presley and Daniel looked to Ezra for an explanation. She said nothing.

Totally exasperated, Presley couldn't contain her frustration. "Ezra, for fuck's sake! What is happening to Daniel and me?"

"I see little point in explaining what you will refuse to believe."

Daniel tried a more conciliatory tone. "Ezra, please, we will listen with an open mind, won't we, Presley?" He shot a thought like an arrow into Presley's mind. *Keep your mouth shut and just listen!*

Ezra scraped the last of her ice cream out of the bowl, and then stood. "Allow me to show you what is possible."

As Daniel and Presley watched, Ezra's new clothes faded and were replaced by the sari she had worn for many centuries. The garment sparkled like a kaleidoscope filled with blue and mother of pearl.

"Presley, come here."

Not knowing what Ezra had in mind, Presley nevertheless cooperated. Ezra held out her hand for Presley to grasp. Presley took Ezra's hand and immediately something akin to an electrical shock moved up her arm. Her instinctive response was to pull away, but Ezra held her hand firmly.

With the commanding tone of authority, Ezra barked, "Presley, be still!" Surprised into acquiescence, Presley stopped. "You will adjust to the sensation. It is time you understand what we are."

Daniel pushed his chair back, meaning to intervene. Vadim grabbed his arm. "Allow Ezra to do this. Presley is ready.

Your frequency is not yet high enough to make the transition."

"Transition to what? Vadim, I swear to God, if anything happens to Presley, I will fucking rip your throat out!"

Vadim calmly responded. "I would not allow any harm to come to my Ninotchka. You know that to be true. If you sit and watch, you will learn much."

Daniel sat back down, but Presley could see the tension in his body. "It's all right, Daniel. We want to know what's happening. So, let Ezra show us."

"Are you all right? Is she hurting you?"

"No, it doesn't hurt. It just feels really weird, like a mega vibrator is moving through my body. It went up my arm, and now I'm feeling it all over."

Ezra turned Presley to face her, and took hold of her other hand. "It is a correct assessment, Presley. You are now able to sustain a higher vibration. If you relax, and allow, you will know the I AM from which we all come and to which we all return."

Presley focused on Ezra. Ezra's eyes glowed brighter as the vibration increased. Presley heard Ezra's voice in her mind. *Be calm, my beautiful sister. Allow me to show you the wonders of spirit. I will keep you safe.*

Presley recognized the peacefulness and freedom that moved into her. *This is what I felt when I left my body in the accident. Am I dying?*

No, Presley, you are changing. You are becoming light.

The last thing Presley heard was Daniel's chair falling over as he shouted, "Jesus Christ! Where did they go?"

Chapter Sixteen

Presley floated like a helium balloon. Then, the exhilaration of soaring like a bird overwhelmed her consciousness. As she slowed, the sense of drifting like a piece of wood on a lake filled her.

Presley, can you hear me?

Ezra?

Dear sister, you must focus on me. I do not want you to go too far.

Where are we?

In a timeless space between our worlds.

Where are Daniel and Vadim?

They are in your kitchen. I have told Vadim we will return momentarily.

I don't want to go back yet. This is the best high I've ever had.

You must return shortly, Presley. Your physical body is in suspension. We must reconstitute it while the magnetic field remains strong.

That sounds like adding water to frozen orange juice.

As your vibration increased, the physical matter melted away, releasing your spirit body. Now, we must slow the vibration, and allow the physical matter to reattach to the spirit body.

What happens if I wait too long?

You are not strong enough yet to hold the patterning of your body. The subatomic structure of your physical self would no doubt dissipate.

You mean I would die?

I mean your physical body would cease to exist.

I don't want that, Ezra. Not now, not when Vadim is waiting for me. Take me back!

As gently as a bird landing on the limb of a tree, Presley returned and felt the solid floor of her kitchen under her feet. Ezra had her arm around her waist, supporting her.

Daniel pushed past Vadim and put his arm around Presley's shoulders. "For Christ's sake, what the hell happened? Are you all right?"

"I'm a little dizzy and queasy, but other than that, I'm fine, unless I lost some fingers and toes in transit."

"I assure you, dear sister, all of your body parts have returned with you."

Presley reached up and squeezed her own breasts. "Well, both tits are here, that's reassuring."

"What the fuck happened?"

"I'll let Ezra explain it to you. I need to sit down."

Vadim held the chair as Presley slowly lowered herself into it. He hunkered down beside the chair and held her hand. "Presley, do you now understand how we are no different than you?"

"Well, I know I was no different without my body than I am with it."

"Damn it, Presley! Everyone seems to know what the hell happened but me! I don't want to hear it from Ezra. I want you to tell me what happened. How the hell did you vanish in a puff of gray smoke?"

"It wasn't gray smoke, it was silver mist, just like Ezra's is blue mist."

Daniel leaned against the table. Presley could see his knuckles turn white as he gripped the sides, and she knew he was about to lose it again. Presley gave Ezra a nod, hoping she would intervene.

Ezra quietly approached Daniel. In the time it took her to take the few steps to where he stood, her clothes changed back to her new leather skirt and sweater. "Daniel?" She put her hand over his. "Please sit and allow me the opportunity to explain."

When Daniel turned his head to look at Ezra, Presley saw that his eyes had turned the color of dark blue topaz. "Do you know that since I started dreaming about you, I've been living in a Kafka play? What's next? Are you going to turn into a cockroach?"

"No, Daniel. The metamorphosis that is happening is not a story invented by Franz Kafka. It is a transformation of spirit, born of your soul's desire."

"Are you saying I wanted this absurdity in my life? I'm a frigging doctor! Medicine is my life! I made that choice years ago. If I had wanted la la land, I would have shaved my head and become a frigging monk!"

"Daniel, you are more than a doctor. You are a healer. You became a healer the day your grandfather died in your arms."

"Don't do this, Ezra! I'm telling you, don't do this!"

Presley saw Daniel's eyes turn from dark blue to deep purple. She could feel an explosion building inside of him. "Ezra, maybe you should back off and let him cool down."

"No, Presley. Daniel must accept what is his soul's choice. He must understand, he agreed to this, or it would not be happening."

"Who the fuck do you think you are? You don't control me, or my life! I swear to God, Ezra, I can walk away from all of this, and I will!"

Daniel pushed Ezra aside. Presley tried to go after him, but Vadim stopped her. "Let him go, Ninotchka. There is no reasoning with him while he is in this state." Then Presley heard the apartment door slam.

"Ezra! Stop him!"

"Vadim is correct, Presley. Daniel needs time to calm himself, and to integrate all that has happened."

Close to tears, Presley had to know. "Ezra, is he going back to Abilene?"

"That is unclear. His intentions are confused."

"Ninotchka, Dr. Daniel Hanson took his bag of clothing but is now finding his way back to the place where we drank this afternoon."

"So, he hasn't left for the airport?"

"Not as yet. He is considering his options."

"Thank God. Maybe he will decide to stay."

"We will give him a short time alone. If Ezra agrees that it is the appropriate action, perhaps we will join Daniel before he drinks too much."

Ezra and Vadim appeared to have an exchange that Presley couldn't hear. "Fuck this, you two! Don't you shut me out! I want to know what you just said."

Ezra nodded at Vadim, clearly indicating he should be the one to tell Presley what they'd said. "Ninotchka, Ezra is of the mind that you should go to Daniel now, before he has a chance to get drunk. Given his violent outburst this afternoon, it would not be advisable for him to consume too much alcohol."

Presley could feel Vadim's resistance to the idea. "And what do you think, Vadim? Will you let me do it?"

"I will abide by your decision. If it is what you wish to do, I will make no attempt to stop you."

"Then I'm going! Where is he?"

"It is a small tavern across from where you sent me for my haircut. They play music and people sing."

"You mean the karaoke bar?"

"That is the place."

"Ezra, one more time, you're sure I'm all here? I'm feeling okay now, but tell me again that nothing got lost or put back in the wrong place?"

"I am quite sure, Presley. You are as you were before."

"All right, then I'm out of here. What are you two going to do?"

"Ezra and I will wait and listen. If you need us, in any way, we will be there instantly."

"Will you join us later, once he's calmed down?"

"We will see, Ninotchka. It is possible you will bring him back yourself."

"I hope so. I need my purse so I have my cards and keys. Shit, Ezra, I don't have any cash. I spent it all today."

"Check in your bag, Presley. There is money."

"Ezra, you can't be making money! I'll get arrested for counterfeiting!"

"I merely replaced what you spent today for my clothes. The money is real. That is not a concern. As I told you, where there is need, spirit provides."

"We'll talk more about that later. Right now, I have to get out of here and catch up with Daniel."

Presley found her purse on the desk in the living room. She checked her wallet, which had been empty when they'd left the diner. In it, she found nearly three hundred dollars, which is what she had spent on Ezra that afternoon. She muttered, "Un-fucking believable!" Then she left to find Daniel.

She ran most of the way to the bar, only slowing down to catch her breath the last half block. When she got there, she hoped Vadim had had his story straight. She couldn't imagine Daniel wanting to go inside. The place was packed. She made her way past the clusters of people standing outside smoking, and stood in the doorway trying to spot him in the crowd.

Then she heard his voice in her head. *I'm over here, at the end of the bar.*

She zeroed in on his voice and saw him at the far corner of the bar, nursing a beer. *Stay right there! I'm coming.*

And how many times would that be today, Presley?

Smart ass!

She knew if he could snap one off at her like that, he wasn't too far gone. Edging her way through the crowd, Presley had to get past three men singing "I Will Survive" while several others danced to their off-key rendition. When she finally got to Daniel's corner of the bar, the first thing out of her mouth wasn't what she'd intended to say.

"What the fuck do you think you're doing?"

"I'm having a beer. Want one?"

"Hell, no!"

In an obnoxiously loud voice, Daniel yelled, "Hey, bartender, we need a ginger ale down here. The redhead isn't drinking tonight."

"That wasn't necessary."

"Sure it was. I have to let Ezra and Vadim know you're here with me. I expect they heard me, don't you?"

"People probably heard you at the Brooklyn Bridge!"

"Yup, I expect they did."

"Can we go someplace quiet to talk?"

We can talk here. We can have a private conversation a continent apart, as I understand it.

Daniel, stop being so pissy!

Is that what I'm being? Hell, I thought I was being civilized. Unlike Vadim, I can't remember the last time I slit someone's throat.

Presley chose to ignore that remark, and changed the subject. "Are you going back to Abilene?"

"Probably."

"Can you wait a few more days?"

"Why should I wait? I've seen enough parlor tricks to last me a lifetime."

"They aren't tricks, and you know it." The bartender

brought her a glass of ginger ale. "Could we have the check, please?" She took out her wallet and tossed a ten dollar bill on the bar. "This one's on Ezra."

"I'm not ready to go."

"I hope you aren't ready to go. That's why I'm here."

"That's not what I meant."

"So, we'll finish our drinks and then leave. Do you have your suitcase?"

"It's on the floor."

"There's a laundromat around the corner. Let's go wash your clothes."

"You can't be serious! In the middle of all of this, you're suggesting we do laundry?"

"You need clean clothes. You've been bitching about your wet clothes since you got here. It will be quiet there, and we can talk."

"Presley, there isn't anything to talk about. I need to get back to Abilene and to my own life."

Like you said, we can have a private conversation a continent apart. Abilene is just a drop in the bucket. And, who do you suppose will be on your doorstep waiting for you when you get to your house?

You think she'll follow me?

She followed you here, didn't she?

"Shit!"

"Daniel, finish your beer. Let's get the hell out of here."

Presley sipped her ginger ale while Daniel finished his beer. After he drained his glass, he picked up his bag and headed for the door. She followed.

Not knowing what to expect when they got out on the street, Presley tried to prepare herself for whatever might happen. She fully expected Daniel to hail a cab and go to the airport. Much to her surprise, he didn't.

"Which way is the laundromat?"

Presley couldn't hide her relief. A smile bubbled up from

her toes. "It's around the corner. Go right, and then take another right onto Washington."

"I've never seen anyone so damn happy about doing laundry."

"Hey, you need clean clothes. I guess no one ever told you it isn't sexy to smell like mildew."

"Maybe that's my scent, the way Vadim smells like herbal soap."

"No, you have a different smell."

"What do I smell like?"

"It isn't as strong as Vadim's, but you smell like woody musk, with a hint of sage. It's delicious!"

"Is it on my skin, or is it more than that?"

"It's more than just your skin. I can smell you when you talk to me in my head, like I do Vadim."

"I can smell you the same way."

"You can? What do you smell?"

"Cherries. But not like ripe cherries. You smell like the homemade cherry wine my grandfather would make for Christmas. It had the same sweet, heady aroma you have."

"Can you taste it?"

"It welled up in the back of my throat before you came into the bar. I knew you were outside."

"You understand, don't you, that we can't go back to how we were?"

"I know."

"Then why are you trying to run away from it?"

"Why does anyone run away? I can't handle it."

"Let me help you handle it."

"How, Presley? This is as new to you as it is to me."

Presley stopped. "We're here."

"What? Oh, the laundry. I forgot."

"Let's get the washers going before I answer your question."

They had the laundromat to themselves, except for one woman taking her clothes out of a dryer. They found an empty table and unpacked Daniel's bag.

"Damn, Daniel. This stuff really does smell bad!"

"I know. Can we get detergent here?"

"There's a vending machine over there, beside the machine that gives change."

Presley noticed Daniel's jeans. "Why don't those stink like the rest of your clothes?"

"Vadim made these for me. Remember? I asked him if he could after we found you and Ezra in the bedroom."

"I just remember how pissed off I was. But I do remember the stains. Interesting how that happened."

"How much do you know?"

"Just what Ezra told me. I haven't tried looking for myself to get more details."

"Don't bother. It isn't pretty."

"Oh, I don't know. You wouldn't mind seeing what Ezra and I did. I could get off watching you and Vadim."

Daniel scooped up all of his clothes in his arms and threw them into the closest washing machine. Presley knew she had set him off again. She followed him to the washing machine. "You might want to sort those. If your jeans fade, you'll look like a tie-dyed Dead Head."

"Have at it." He went to the vending machines to get detergent and change.

Presley pulled out his jeans and dark clothes and threw them into another washer. When he came back, she had just fished out his dark socks. She took the detergent and put it in the cup while Daniel filled the slots with quarters. Once the machine started, Presley knew she had just bought herself at least half an hour. The woman finished folding her clothes, and then left. They were alone.

"So, why are you pissed off at me now? I didn't say you had to fuck Vadim. I just said I wouldn't mind watching if you did."

"You really don't get it, do you?"

"No, I guess I don't. What am I supposed to be getting?"

"Ever since the day you woke up in the hospital, I've been attracted to you. You are the hottest and the brightest woman I've ever met. You're honest to a fault, and your mouth should be condemned by the board of health. I knew before you left Abilene I wanted to spend my life with you. I still feel that way."

"Now you're the one who doesn't get it."

"I get what I'm not getting. Vadim has what I want."

"You're not very good at thinking outside the box, are you?"

"I am a trained diagnostician. I have to think outside the box to do my job."

"Then, Dr. Hanson, stop being pissed off long enough to look at the facts. Vadim and Ezra are really dead heads. They both left this planet a long time ago. But they've come back, and they've brought something with them that is changing us."

"I know all of that. What am I not getting?"

"Goddamn it, Daniel, we're mutating! It's like the four of us are glasses of water poured from the same pitcher. We know each other's memories and can hear each other's thoughts. You might go back to Abilene, but I'm in your head forever. We can't go back to what we were before. Don't you see?"

"Everything in me rejects this, Presley."

"You may want to reject it, Daniel, but you can't deny it. It's happening to me just like it's happening to you."

"What happened to you with Ezra?"

"Somehow, she suspended my body so I wasn't trapped in it anymore. I was still me, with all my memories and dreams, but a bigger me, if that makes any sense. I could still think and feel, but I knew a hell of a lot more than I do here."

"Why did she take you out, and not me? Isn't it me she's after?"

"You aren't ready yet. I'm changing faster than you are because of my near-death experience. That's when I started morphing. That's why I said I could help you handle it. I'm a few lessons ahead of you."

"All right, Presley. I'm with you so far. You're actually making sense. But all of this doesn't change the fact that Vadim is here. From his point of view, you are his woman. If I made a serious play for you, I think he would kill me."

"No, he wouldn't. He promised me he wouldn't hurt you. If he didn't kill you today, he isn't going to kill you."

"Then, I'm shit out of luck, aren't I? Even if he doesn't kill me, you won't choose me over him."

"I don't have to."

"Why not?"

"Because we really are one big dysfunctional family. I realized today talking to Ez that I can fuck you any time I want to fuck you, and you can do the same with me."

"You really think Vadim will allow that?"

"He already has. He did this morning, and he will again, if he knows it's what I really want."

"Is it what you really want?"

"You aren't the only one that fell hard in Abilene. With all the men I've known in my life, I still can't believe I fell in love with a doctor."

"You've never said that before."

"I couldn't, until now. What do you feel for Ezra?"

"She drives me crazy! I don't know what I feel for her. I can't get past her tits long enough to find out."

"Have you really talked to her yet? I never knew what the phrase 'old soul' meant until today. She doesn't say very much, but she has incredible depth. Daniel, she is amazing."

"For you to say that, she must be. Did you two really fuck?"

"Your clothes are done." Presley got up to put the clothes in the dryer. Daniel followed her.

"Nice evasion."

"Thanks. Get the clothes from the other washer. I think they'll dry faster if we use two dryers."

After starting the dryers, Daniel asked again. "Are you going to tell me what happened? Did you and Ezra fuck?"

"Yes and no."

"What the hell does that mean?"

"That means yes and no. I fucked her with my vibrating dildo. She didn't do anything to me, really, but I felt what she felt. When she came, so did I. It was an unbelievable orgasm."

"So, the two of you passed out. Like I did with Vadim."

"You two passed out. We fell asleep."

"Subtle difference."

"Yes, but an important one. Ezra said you and Vadim came together too."

"I didn't want to, but I couldn't stop it. When it happened, I thought my balls would explode. Christ, Presley, he's an animal!"

Presley poked Daniel in the side with her elbow and winked. "I know. Why do you think I picked him over you?"

"So, that's what you want, a wild animal in your bed?"

"Don't knock it if you haven't tried it. So, if you and Vadim get to watch me and Ez, do we get to watch the two of you?"

"I never said I wanted any more of him. I'm into women, not men."

"Yeah, and you're also a jock. Everyone knows about the closet butt slapping that goes on in the locker room."

"Give him a message for me. If he ever wants to blow me, I might consider it. I'd love to hear his answer. Now, let's get back to what you and Ezra did. Did you suck her tits?"

Presley laughed. "You horny son of bitch! What kind of a question is that?"

"One I wouldn't mind hearing the answer to."

"No, not this time. I felt her up, but there was no oral action."

"Are you planning another time?"

"Maybe. When Ezra saw the movie you two were watching, with the blonde and the redhead getting it on, she thought you might be entertained by watching us."

"Ezra suggested that?"

"Absolutely! She could end up being the ultimate Stepford wife. All she wants to do is make you happy."

"Yeah, and she's also a cross between Morgan le Fay and Aphrodite. I can feel the power in her. When she turns it on, I wouldn't want to get in her way."

"Makes you nuts, doesn't it?"

"Okay, I'm only human, a mere mortal. She has gone to a lot of trouble to latch onto me. I'm not beyond being swayed by that."

"I know. I've seen it. I'm trying not to be jealous about the attention you give her."

"And I've seen you with Vadim. It's like the two of you have known each other forever."

"It feels like we have."

"What's he going to do when you fly to Abilene to fuck me?"

"He'll let me, if I want to go." Presley closed her eyes. She could feel them getting warm, and knew Vadim's eyes were glowing as he connected with her. She tilted her head to the side and listened.

"He's talking to you, isn't he?"

"They want to show us something."

"What now?"

"Ezra and Vadim heard what you said about flying to Abilene and want to show you what is possible. Before they demonstrate, they wanted to make sure we are alone in here."

"What did you say?"

"I told them to be quick, before someone comes in."

Within a few seconds, the laundry room seemed to get smoky as a blue-gray mist floated down from the ceiling. The colors separated into two clouds, which then took the shape of two willowy people. The wispy figures solidified, and Ezra and Vadim stood in front of them.

"Big f'ing deal, Presley. I know they can do this. So, what's the point?"

Ezra sat down beside Daniel and threaded her fingers through his. "The point is, Daniel, it will not be long before you and Presley can travel in the same manner. In the world of spirit, physical space is not an obstacle."

"But we're not spirit, Ezra, we're mortal. Without our bodies, we're dead."

Presley stood and put her arm through Vadim's. "That's what you're not getting, Daniel. We aren't mortal anymore, and we're not spirit either. I don't know what the hell we are, but the four of us are doing it together. Maybe we're creating a new species. You're the doctor. You tell me."

"Unless we volunteer to become lab rats, I don't know how we would find out. If our molecular structure is changing, we'd only know for sure by a molecular biologist studying our DNA."

"No, thank you! I'll live with the changes. I'm not becoming some specimen to be studied, ending up in the tabloids as the latest mutant."

"I'd agree with you. But, if we ever need medical treatment for any reason, like if one of you ladies has a baby, we could find ourselves in deep shit."

"Ninotchka, if you recall, I did see you holding a child, and could not read the circumstances."

"Yeah, I know." Presley felt the scar on her forehead. "When I had my accident, did anything weird show up on my blood tests?"

"No. But I don't know what's happened since then."

"Could you call your old roommate, the one that has the private practice here? If you trust him, maybe he can order some blood work for me, just to see if anything out of the ordinary turns up. At least then we'd know if we have to go underground with this."

"Let me think about it. If I decide it's a good idea, I'll give him a call tomorrow."

"Then you're not leaving yet?"

"No, not yet."

"Amen!" Presley pulled Vadim toward the dryers. "Let's see if these clothes are dry so we can go home."

Chapter Seventeen

Daniel found Presley's laptop sitting beside her desk. He managed to retrieve it without waking Presley and Vadim. Even in the living room, he could still hear Ezra snoring. He knew he hadn't woken her up.

He took the laptop and his cell phone to the kitchen. While the computer booted, he put on a pot of coffee. If he couldn't sleep, he might as well do some research. Dealing with the lack of sleep actually wasn't that different than keeping his hospital schedule. He'd gotten used to having sleepless nights and pushing through the next day.

Presley had wireless Internet access, but he didn't know her password. It took a few minutes to find an unprotected connection, but in New York, there were plenty of choices. Once he saw Google pop up, he knew he'd hit the bull's-eye.

He searched for Dr. Scott Brewer first. They had been roommates all through med school and had interned together. They'd gone different directions with their careers, but had remained close. Only a couple of months before, Scott had e-mailed Daniel to say he was moving into a bigger office space on the upper west side, and again offered him a partnership. The e-mail with Scott's new contact information sat on Daniel's computer in Abilene.

Daniel found Scott's phone number and new address in a Manhattan physicians' directory. While lying in bed listening to Ezra snore, he'd decided a medical evaluation for Presley would be a good idea. Her accident provided an explanation for any anomalies, and would give him an idea of what to expect for himself. If he did end up staying with Ezra, which seemed inevitable at this point, they would have to do something about her snoring.

He entered Scott's information into his cell phone address book, and then tucked the phone into his pocket. He would wait until after nine to call. Even though the information from Presley's exam could change his life, it wasn't a true emergency. That would also give him some time to make a list of the tests he wanted Presley to have. Along with a complete blood work-up, he definitely wanted another EEG.

After pouring a cup of coffee and making himself some toast, he settled in to do more homework. When they'd gotten home the night before, everyone had just wanted to go to sleep. But now they had to get moving on getting Vadim and Ezra's papers.

Ezra had said if she had some samples, she could create what they needed. So Daniel set about searching for passports, driver's licenses, green cards, and any other official paperwork that came to mind.

What he found startled him. He discovered Web sites that trafficked in black market identification and, for a price, they could deliver fake IDs to anyone, anywhere. He also found samples of international passports, comparing forgeries to the real thing. The samples of the real thing would be perfect for Ezra. He bookmarked the site and downloaded pictures of relevant passports.

He had just found a site with green card information when Presley came into the kitchen.

"What are you doing? Why aren't you still in bed?"

"I'm researching papers for Ezra and Vadim on the Internet. Go into the bedroom. You'll know why I'm not asleep."

Presley went through the bathroom to the bedroom. A few

seconds later, she came back into the kitchen. "Shit, Daniel! She snores like a boxer with a broken nose."

"There is definitely something going on there. She also has sleep apnea."

"What's that?"

"That's when a person stops breathing repeatedly while they sleep. I think that's why she snores. She's trying to breathe."

Presley got herself some coffee and sat down beside Daniel. "I think I know what's going on."

"What do you mean?"

"I have a hunch about Ezra and her breathing."

"I'm listening."

"Do you know about her last life, that the body she has now isn't the one she had then?"

"No. She didn't tell me that."

"That's probably because she doesn't want you to know what she looked like. Yesterday, when I remembered about her having been my sister, I saw everything. She had a twisted spine and withered legs. When she died, she had a high fever, and she couldn't breathe. She probably had pneumonia."

"Which may account for her breathing problems now?"

"That's how it feels to me. What do you think?"

"Makes sense. Do you know how she got this body?"

"No. Vadim might, but I don't."

"I'm going to call my roommate later, and make an appointment for you. Are you all right with that?"

"I am if you trust him."

"He's the closest thing I've ever had to a brother. I trust him."

"Even with this?"

"I'm not going to tell him about Ezra and Vadim, if that's what you're asking. This is just a follow-up to your accident. We'll get the information we need without full disclosure."

"Won't he wonder about your being in New York with me? It's not every doctor that comes home with the patient."

"When he meets you, he'll understand."

"Oh, really! What exactly will he understand?"

"That I'm here to get laid. What else is there to know?"

"It must be a guy thing. Getting laid can justify any questionable behavior."

"It's what men do, Presley. You, of all people, should know that. Scott is cool. He'll keep our visit confidential."

"What about Ezra? Shouldn't he look at her too? Her breathing problems could be serious."

"She may not need medical attention, considering her situation. Maybe if we tell her what we think is happening, she'll be able to do something about it herself. If this is residual past-life stuff, aren't there ways to clear such things?"

"You're asking me? Other than having slept with a guy a while back who burned sage to clear his space, I know nothing."

"Speaking of your checkered past, you never did tell me about those S&M clubs you visited."

"I'll get around to it. It'll give you something to look forward to."

"That and watching you and Ezra go at each other."

"Tell me the truth, that's really the reason you didn't leave last night, isn't it?"

"Hey, a man's gotta do what a man's gotta do. Right?"

"Yeah, right."

"Admit it, Presley. You're kinky enough to want it as much as I do. You're a natural exhibitionist."

"You'd better put a lid on it or you're going to get us both worked up."

"I love a woman who wears her nymphomania on her sleeve."

"Not that you're oversexed or anything! Christ, Daniel, Vadim hasn't had any for four hundred years. I can understand his libido being in overdrive. But, I swear to God, I don't know that I've ever met a man that has as much stamina as you do. And that's saying something!"

"And you're the only woman I've ever met who can keep up with me. That says something too, doesn't it?"

"I wouldn't underestimate Ezra. We were sisters, remember?"

"She's hot, there's no question about that."

"Well, Vadim told me she had never known physical love. Whatever they did together wasn't fucking like we do it. He told me you were her first."

"You mean, I fucked a virgin?"

"You sure as hell did."

"I'll be damned! And she picked me to do it!"

"That's what happened."

"No wonder she's so open to everything."

"I am open to everything that is part of you, Daniel." Ezra stood in the bathroom door, wearing only her new baby doll nightie.

"Ezra! Good morning! I hope we didn't wake you." Daniel didn't know what else to say. It embarrassed him to think he had been overheard. Fortunately, Presley picked up the ball.

"Ez, how much of this did you hear?"

"My sister, I do not need to listen through walls to hear. I know of your conversation."

"Are you pissed at me for telling Daniel about you?"

"No, Presley, I am not angry. I am relieved. You only told the truth. The truth should never be hidden."

"You have blue streaks on your face. You've been crying."

Daniel went to Ezra and kissed her forehead. "I'm sorry if I said anything that hurt you."

"You have not hurt me, Daniel."

"I didn't know your tears were blue." Daniel wiped away more tears as they slid down her face. "Why are you crying?"

"Because even in this new body that men desire, I carry the scars of a cripple. How can I hope to be with you when you cannot rest lying beside me?"

Daniel held Ezra as she cried, the pain of her previous life becoming a reality to him for the first time. "Ezra, we will manage this. Whatever is causing your breathing problems, we will find a way to fix it."

"Guys, I'm going to check on Vadim. If he's not awake yet, he should be." Presley graciously left them alone.

Daniel led Ezra into the bathroom and wet a washcloth with warm water. "Let me wipe your face." As gently as if he were caring for a small child, Daniel cleaned the blue stains from Ezra's face. He saw that the streaks ran into her cleavage. "Maybe you should clean your chest."

"I would like you to do it, Daniel. It is wonderful when you touch me."

Daniel tried to maintain his professional composure, but found it impossible to do while wiping Ezra's breasts with the cloth. "Ezra, do you know you drive me crazy?"

"I know you are attracted to me. I also understand it is difficult for you to feel the companionship with me that you do with Presley."

"Presley is an unusual person, Ezra. You shouldn't compare yourself to her."

"I have to, Daniel. She is the one you would choose if Vadim hadn't already done so. Perhaps if I become like Presley, you will feel for me what you do for her."

Daniel couldn't say anything for a few seconds. Ezra's sincerity and honesty left him speechless. When he found his voice, he tried to be equally honest. "Ezra, it's true I have feelings for Presley. It happened without either Presley or me meaning for it to happen. But it's also true that I haven't been able to get you out of my mind since the first dream I had about you."

"I came to you in your dreams. You did not initiate them, I did."

"Yes, but you didn't make me jerk off thinking about you."

"No, you self-pleasured by your own hand and with your own thoughts."

"Yes, you're right. My feelings for you are different than for Presley. If you and Vadim hadn't come along, I would have probably tried to get Presley to marry me. I don't know if she would've said yes to a proposal, since her career has always been her life."

"My sense is she would have agreed to be your long-term lover, but would have been reluctant to marry."

"Yeah, that's my sense too. What I really wanted was for her to live in Abilene with me. Can you see Presley living in Abilene?"

"No, Daniel. She is not meant to be in Abilene."

"When I said my feelings for you are different than for Presley, there is more to it than just the sex. You intrigue me, Ezra. The more I get to know you, the more I realize you've got this awareness and sensitivity that I've never seen in anyone else, especially not in Presley."

"But you love Presley Knowles."

"With Presley, what you see is what you get, and I like that about her. But with you, what you see, as beautiful as it is, doesn't even come close to what you get. You are an exquisitely wrapped package with a rare jewel inside."

"Daniel, your words are lovely. They give me hope."

"There is hope, Ezra. I know I've been an asshole about a lot of this, but I'm coming on board now. Maybe it's this metamorphosis thing kicking in. I don't know. But things look different to me today. I know it will take some time for us to get to know one another, but I am getting a handle on what we have to do. We can manage it if we work together."

"You mean all of us?"

"I mean all of us. It looks like we are in this together, doesn't it?"

"We are, Daniel. There is a fusion of soul energy that cannot be undone. We are truly in this together."

"I have to call Scott and make an appointment for Presley. But before I do that, I have one really important question to ask you."

"Anything, Daniel. I will answer honestly."

"Did you really say to Presley that you would let Vadim and I watch you be with her, I mean like you were yesterday?"

"The intimacy we share naturally extends to the physical. It would please me to have intimacy with Presley and share it with you and Vadim."

"It would please me too. Do you think you can get Presley to agree to it?"

"She said it would be 'a fuck fest to end all fuck fests.' I did not understand all the words, but I did understand she is inclined to entertaining both of you with our loving."

"Let me make this call, and then we'll go to the living room and discuss it with Presley and Vadim." Daniel took his cell phone out of his pocket. "Oh, and don't change clothes just yet. Keep that sexy little number on until we talk."

Daniel dialed Scott's number and got his receptionist. He introduced himself as Dr. Daniel Hanson, and said he needed to speak to Dr. Brewer about a personal matter. The receptionist put him on hold.

A few minutes later, he heard Scott's familiar voice. "Hey, Dan! This is a surprise!

"Scott! How the hell are you?"

"Doing good. Don't think I told you. The wife's pregnant with number three."

"Always figured you'd be a fertile son of a bitch. Congratulations."

"Thanks. So, what's this important personal matter?"

"I have a patient from New York City, Presley Knowles. She had a car accident in Abilene, a bad one. The head injury almost bought her the farm. She's all right now and back in New York. I'm here with her."

"You're in New York with her? Professionally or personally?"

"Both, but more personal than professional."

"Don't tell me this one finally nailed you! It's about god-damn time!"

"Well, let's just say I'm definitely involved. That's why I'm calling. I've got a favor to ask."

"Name it."

"Would you have time today to see Presley and check her out? I want her to have a complete blood work-up and, more importantly, an EEG. There may be a few other tests indicated, but those are the main ones. Are you equipped to do an EEG in your office? I don't want her to have to go to the hospital for this."

"I have a full-scale machine, and a portable one that's hooked up to a laptop. What's going on? Is she having problems?"

"Don't know. She's had a few odd neurological events since the accident. I want to know if the test shows anything."

"I see my last patient at four. I'll have time then to wire her up and have a look. Tell her not to have any caffeine this afternoon and to eat a light lunch. And make sure she understands she'll be hooked up for at least an hour."

"Yeah, I know the drill. Thanks, buddy. I knew you'd come through."

"Any chance you'll be moving to New York with this lady? I can use a good partner."

"At this point, my future plans are up in the air. If things change, and I end up moving to New York, I might take you up on that."

"I make a good living, Dan. You could too, and without the crazy hours you're keeping now. You're a damn fine doctor; you sure as hell outclassed me all through school. I would be honored to share an office with you."

"Thanks, Scott. It's good to know I've got that offer on the back burner, if I need it."

"I have a patient waiting. I've got to go. I'll see you around four."

"See you then. Later, buddy."

Daniel tucked his cell phone back in his pocket. When he'd told Scott his future plans were up in the air, he'd failed to mention how high up in the air they were.

Ezra sat on the bed waiting for him. Seeing her sitting there wearing that sexy lingerie made him remember his plan. "Are Presley and Vadim doing anything right now?"

"If you mean are they making love, no, they are not. They are in their bed, watching television together."

"Let's go out and have a little chat with them."

"Are you sure it is permissible for me to wear this garment? It is quite revealing."

"That's exactly why I want you to wear it, Ezra. Your body is beautiful. I want to see it."

"And you want Presley Knowles to love me in it."

"That too."

Daniel went to the living room. Ezra followed. Presley and Vadim were lying on the sofa bed, eating Cheerios out of the box and watching television. A thin blanket covered them. Presley still had on the T-shirt she'd slept in, and Vadim appeared to be nude under the blanket.

"You two look comfortable. What are you watching.?"

"The movie you bought. It's been playing non-stop since yesterday. I gotta tell you, it's a classic. No plot whatsoever, just women doing it in every conceivable position."

"Are you taking notes?"

"Funny guy."

"Seriously, you should be. I have a proposition for you."

"And, Dr. Hanson, I have one for you."

"You don't suppose we're thinking the same thing, do you?"

"I doubt it. What do you think, Vadim?"

"I am sure Dr. Daniel Hanson is not thinking what you are thinking, Ninotchka."

"There you have it, right from the horse's mouth."

"Before we exchange ideas, I should tell you I got a hold of Scott. His last patient is at four. We'll meet him at his office then. Don't have any more caffeine today and have a light lunch. Oh, and don't use anything oily on your hair. Your scalp will be wired."

"You'll be there too, won't you?"

"Yes. But Ezra and Vadim won't be."

"I explained to Vadim what we're doing. He understands. What about you, Ez? Are you okay with my getting an examination?"

Ezra stepped out from behind Daniel. "Yes, Presley. It is the correct course of action."

"Well, we seem to be on the same page with this. So, what's your proposition?"

Go with Daniel's proposition, continue reading
Go with Presley's proposition, turn to page 264

Chapter Eighteen

Daniel pointed to the television. "You're watching my proposition. You've seen enough of the movie by now to know what I want. You and Ezra are hotter than they are. I want a live sex show from you two."

"I figured that's what you had in mind, especially since Ez still has on her baby doll nightie."

"Ezra is all right with it, aren't you, 'Ez'?"

"I enjoy touching Presley. I would not object to touching her while you watch. I know it would give you pleasure."

"It would give me pleasure, all right. What about you, Vadim? Are you in?"

"Not as yet. But I expect to be after watching the women together."

"Yeah, me too."

"What's your idea, Presley? Should we toss a coin to see who has dibs?"

"No, we'll save mine for later. Promise me, no peeking. I want it to be a surprise."

"If you and Ezra distract me enough, I won't even think to peek."

Presley crawled off the sofa bed and went over to Ezra. She took hold of her hand. "Ez, are you sure you're all right with this? I don't want you to do it just because Daniel is pushing you to."

"Presley, Daniel is not pushing me. I want to touch you again, as I want you to touch me. I would enjoy sharing our love and our intimacy with the men."

"Do you know something? So would I."

Daniel picked up a pillow that had fallen on the floor and threw it at Vadim. "Get your ass out of bed, Vadim, and let the ladies have it. You take the recliner, and I'll get the rocking chair from the bedroom."

Daniel went to get the rocking chair. He discovered Presley had piled Ezra's new clothes on it. He scooped them up and tossed them on the bed. When he came back with the chair, Presley wasn't in the room. "Where did Presley go?"

"She went to get a cup of warm milk for me. I haven't eaten anything today," Ezra said.

"Are you feeling all right?"

"Yes, just a bit hungry."

"You might want to try some solid food later. Vadim seems to be handling it all right."

"I will. But now, I only want a little milk."

Daniel put his chair down next to Vadim. Vadim sat in the recliner, buck naked, with a full erection. "Jesus Christ, Vadim, you could put on some pants!"

"I see no reason to do so. I will be more comfortable if my organ is not confined."

"Point well taken. I'll probably have to unzip in a few minutes too."

Daniel made himself comfortable in the rocking chair. Ezra had already stretched out on the bed. He had seen pictures of Marilyn Monroe in a 1953 collector's copy of *Playboy* his father had. Ezra's likeness to her was uncanny. Seeing Ezra in this sex kitten pose brought back a forgotten memory. The centerfold in that issue had featured Marilyn in the nude, lying on red velvet. He had jerked off more than once while looking at that picture.

Presley jarred Daniel out of his private reverie when she came back with two cups of warm milk. She gave one to Vadim and one to Ezra.

"Don't I get one?"

"You don't need any. You'll be making your own cream in a few minutes."

"Do you always say every crude remark that comes to mind?"

"Yes. Twice, if necessary."

Daniel's cock twitched in his pants. Presley wouldn't be a shrinking violet with this. He knew she would deliver the goods. He'd wanted to watch two women together ever since he'd had his first wet dream. The two sexiest women he had ever known were about to give him the show of a lifetime. He couldn't believe it had taken this weird situation to finally get him here.

Presley sat down on the sofa bed and waited for Ezra to drink her milk. The anticipation of what they would do together nearly sent Daniel over the edge. He had to calm down, or he wouldn't make it past seeing their tits. He jumped when he heard Vadim's voice in his head.

Allow me to help, Daniel.

Vadim, don't fucking do that! I don't want you messing around in my head!

I only wish to prolong this experience for you. I know how excited you are. It is evident you are struggling to hold back your climax.

Shit, Vadim! I've wanted this all my life, and I feel like I'll shoot off like some teenager seeing a naked woman for the first time.

I can help you sustain control.

How?

If we share the experience, I will manage our arousal. I

can hold us both back until we are ready to finish inside the women.

You can do that?

Yes.

Can Ezra and Presley hear this?

No. They are anticipating each other. They are not listening to us.

Good! I don't want them to know I can't control myself.

Then you will allow me in?

What do I have to do?

Simply allow. I will do the rest.

Daniel relaxed and closed his eyes. When Vadim overshadowed him, he pushed back with momentary resistance. He focused on relaxing, knowing he couldn't hold on without help. As he relaxed, he felt stronger and more alive than he'd ever felt before.

You're in, aren't you?

I am.

I still feel like me. A ripple moved through Daniel, which he recognized as Vadim's laughter. *What's so damn funny?*

I am not possessing you, Dr. Daniel Hanson. I only wish to prevent your ejaculation until you are ready for it.

Daniel's ambivalence about allowing Vadim into his body evaporated when he noticed Presley taking the cup from Ezra and setting it on the table beside the sofa.

Looks like the curtain's rising. Let's rock and roll!

Presley's fire is up. She is focused on Ezra, but is well aware we are watching.

What about Ezra?

She is simmering, and remembering yesterday. She wants to press her breasts against Presley's, and kiss her again, as she did before.

Hot damn! Vadim, your running commentary is right on! Keep it up!

That is certainly my intention, Daniel.

Sharp, big dude. Presley is rubbing off on you.
That would also be most pleasurable.
Daniel chuckled. *You're pretty smart, for a four-hundred-year-old Cossack.*
As are you, for a youngster.
Touché.
Indeed.

Both men shifted their focus to Presley and Ezra. Whereas he'd expected Presley to make the first move, it surprised Daniel to see Ezra reach for the hem of Presley's T-shirt. With the grace of a ballet dancer, Ezra knelt and pulled the shirt over Presley's head.

When Daniel saw Presley's tits, he felt a sudden push from his balls, like he might come. He ground his teeth together, trying to hold back. *Vadim . . .*
Not to worry, Daniel. It will not happen.
It fucking can't! Not yet!
It is under control.

True to his word, Vadim's strength reinforced Daniel's control. His arousal remained high, but he expanded to allow it without ejaculating.
Thanks, big dude. Couldn't have done that on my own.
Soon, you will do this, and much more.

Even with the women about to embrace and kiss, Daniel glanced at Vadim. The implication of his remark resonated in Daniel's mind. *You're serious, aren't you?*
Yes, Dr. Daniel Hanson, I am.

When he again looked at the bed, he had another surge in his groin. Presley had opened Ezra's lingerie and had her hand on Ezra's bare tit. As he watched, she rolled Ezra's nipple between her thumb and index finger. Ezra's head lolled back, which made the thin material of her nightie fall off her shoulders. Presley leaned down and kissed Ezra's breast, and then sucked her nipple. Ezra moaned.

Jesus Christ! This is the hottest thing I've ever seen. Their arousal is nearly as intense as ours now. They will do more.

Oh, yeah! I'm ready for more.

Now comfortable that Vadim would not let him shoot off prematurely, Daniel relaxed, opened his pants, and watched.

Presley took off Ezra's top, leaving both women only in their panties. Ezra put her hand behind Presley's neck and pulled her close. When their breasts touched, Daniel's chest burned. *Vadim, what the hell is that?*

You are experiencing what the women are, Daniel. As they continue, their arousal will blend with ours, until finally we are all sharing the same heightened state.

Fuck! This is unbelievable!

This is the true path of spirit, to be one in love.

They never taught us this in Sunday school!

Perhaps it was an oversight.

Again, Daniel chuckled. *Vadim, you're a real pisser! I'll tell you sometime about the Bible Belt. Trust me, it wasn't an oversight.*

Ezra embraced Presley, and gently kissed her face. She kissed her eyelids, her nose, and her cheeks, before finally covering Presley's mouth with hers. When they kissed, Daniel could feel the sensation of Presley clutching his back, just as she had when they'd made love. He recognized her touch, and her kiss.

Vadim, can you feel that? It's Presley.

Ezra is sharing her experience with us.

What about Presley? What is she feeling?

I can feed you that, if you care to know.

I do!

With surprising finesse, Vadim shifted their perspective. Daniel felt what Presley felt, Ezra's touch and kiss. But more than that, he felt Presley's heat. He shifted in his chair, the throbbing between his legs tangible. His cock picked up the heartbeat pulsing in Presley's clit. He experienced an almost uncontrollable urge to rub against Ezra's leg.

Oh, yeah, Presley!

Enjoying yourself, Daniel?

The sound of her voice in his head caught him unaware.

You can hear us?

I heard you say my name. I thought you wanted my attention.

No, just keep doing what you're doing. This is fucking hot!

Presley and Ezra continued to kiss and caress, to lick and to suck. They fondled each other's breasts and they rolled on the bed. They touched each other everywhere except for their most sensitive places.

Then Presley got up on her knees and tugged at Ezra's panties, pulling them halfway down her thighs. Ezra finished taking them off. Then Ezra removed Presley's panties.

The two naked women knelt facing one another. Presley's eyes lit up with silver light just as Ezra's shone blue. In a simultaneous motion, their hands crossed as they reached between each other's legs. Daniel gasped aloud as fingers connected with tender, swollen flesh. The intensity of the contact also affected Vadim. Daniel heard him grunt behind him.

Hang on, Vadim. Don't come yet!

It will be soon, Daniel. If we want to finish with the women, we must stop them now!

In a blur of motion, Vadim went from the chair to the bed and grabbed Presley. He lifted her off the bed, her back pressed against his chest.

Presley kicked and squirmed, but couldn't get away from him. "Vadim, what the fuck are you doing? Put me down!"

"No, Ninotchka. We are not inclined to let you finish without us, are we, Daniel?"

"You got that right!" Daniel followed Vadim to the bed and pushed Ezra backward. "Blondie, spread your legs. You're about to get laid!"

While Daniel took off his clothes, Vadim plopped Presley down beside Ezra. "Presley Knowles, you will pleasure me as Ezra will pleasure Daniel. Open yourself for me."

Go to page 271

"Ladies first. What's your idea?"

"Do you remember what you said to me last night, about Vadim blowing you?"

"Yeah, I remember. What about it?"

"I asked him. Tell him what you said, Vadim."

"I told Presley Knowles that I am amenable, if it would please her."

"And it would please me, Daniel."

Daniel pulled Ezra in front of him, and wrapped his arms around her waist. "Maybe he should go back and visit Devon, if he's into that sort of thing. It's not my cup of tea."

"Stop using Ezra like a bulletproof vest, Daniel! What the fuck are you afraid of? I know you're not homophobic! Or are you?"

"It's all right, Ninotchka. Dr. Daniel Hanson does not want to risk being seen as less of a man than myself."

Daniel let Ezra go and walked over to the bed. "Excuse me? What did you say?"

Vadim threw the blanket off, revealing his fully erect organ. "If the women see us side by side, they will know who is more of a man."

Presley scooted off the sofa bed and went to stand next to Ezra. "Ez, I think this is about to get good. I'm going to get another chair."

"I've fucked both of them, just like you have. They already know what we've got." Daniel glared at Vadim.

"Shall we put that to the test? Presley Knowles is keen to see us both naked. I am inclined to satisfy her desires, whatever they are."

Presley came back with the rocking chair from the bedroom. "What did I miss?"

"Vadim has challenged Daniel to take off his clothes so they will be seen naked, side by side. Then we can compare their masculinity."

"All right!" Presley held up her hand for a high five. Ezra did not respond. "High five me, sister!"

"I do not know what that is, Presley."

"Smack the palm of your hand against mine. It's a sign of celebration." Presley held up her hand again. "All right!" This time, a loud clap of celebration echoed through the room.

"I hope you ladies are enjoying yourselves." Daniel had his arms crossed over his chest, his eyes again the color of dark topaz. Vadim still lay sprawled on the bed, exposed and erect.

"Not nearly as much as I'm going to. Ez, what do you want, the recliner or the rocking chair?"

"I would prefer the rocking chair, at the end of the bed, please."

"Sweetie, you've got the right idea." Presley put the rocking chair at the foot of the sofa bed. Then she pulled the recliner out of the corner and parked it beside the rocker. She ran to get the open box of Cheerios she had left beside the bed. "Ez, would you like a cup of milk? You haven't eaten anything today."

"Yes, please." Ezra had already settled into the rocking chair.

She handed the box of Cheerios to Vadim. "Here, hold this. Don't do anything until I get back." Then she disappeared into the kitchen.

Vadim stuck his hand into the box and grabbed a handful of Cheerios. He attempted to pass the box to Daniel. "Would you care for some, Daniel? They are quite flavorful."

"What a frigging circus! No, I don't want any Cheerios!"

"Presley Knowles says they are better than popcorn, especially the Honey Nut variety." He munched his handful of cereal like he was eating peanuts in a bar.

Presley came back carrying a cup. "I hope it's warm enough, Ez. I couldn't wait a whole minute for it. I didn't want to miss anything." Ezra took the cup, and Presley retrieved the cereal from Vadim. Then she plopped down on the recliner. "Why are you still dressed? C'mon, Daniel, get with the program."

"You aren't the least bit interested in what I had planned, are you?"

"For Christ's sake! I know you want to watch Ezra and me fuck. We'll get to it. But now, you're up to bat, Dr. Hanson. Lighten up, and strip!"

Daniel did not move. Ezra sipped her milk, and then handed Presley her cup. "Would you please hold this for a moment? Perhaps I can encourage Daniel to cooperate with us."

"Sure, Ez. What are you going to do?"

"Only this." Ezra opened her top and let it fall off her shoulders and onto the chair. "Presley, I suggest you do the same. Perhaps if the men can look at our breasts, it will help them get past their fears of being together."

"Ezra, you are a smart lady!" Presley handed Ezra her cup and then set the cereal on the floor. She pulled her T-shirt over her head. "So, Daniel, could you get off letting Vadim blow you while you look at our tits?"

"You are really a piece of work!"

"It's why you love me, remember? I like seeing naked men. It's hot. With you two, it'll sizzle like prime beef on the grill!"

With both women sitting in front of him topless, Daniel couldn't control his response. He tried to will himself out of getting hard, but it proved pointless. He glanced at the bed and saw Vadim lying there staring at Presley's chest, stroking himself. Then he realized he could turn this to his advantage.

"All right, here's the deal. I will strip and get on the bed with Vadim. I will let him blow me if the two of you put your hands inside your panties and masturbate while you watch."

"I can handle that, can you, Ez?"

"Indeed I can, Presley!"

"That's not all."

"Jesus, Daniel. What is this, the Camp David Accords? What else do you want?"

"I don't want to come with Vadim. I want to fuck Ezra on the bed while Vadim fucks you right beside me."

"Shit, Daniel! I've never fucked with another couple on the bed."

"First time for everything, Presley. Take it or leave it."

"It's not just up to me. Vadim and Ezra, what do you two say about this?"

"Ninotchka, I have no objection to making love beside Dr. Daniel Hanson, as long as it is you I am loving."

"Nor do I, Presley. It would be a wonderful intimacy for us to share the same bed."

"Looks like it's up to you, Presley." Daniel unbuckled his belt and unzipped his pants. "I'm calling your bluff, Ms. Knowles. Put up or shut up. What's it going to be?"

"All right, you win. We'll masturbate and then fuck. Satisfied?"

"I expect to be very satisfied in a few minutes."

Daniel took off his pants and then his shirt. "Shift your hairy ass over, Vadim, and give me some room."

Vadim looked directly at Daniel's cock. "Your organ is of a reasonable size, but mine is bigger."

"Presley never complained when I fucked her, did you, Presley?"

"Nope. You both stretched me." Presley looked from one man to the other. "Vadim, yours might be a little longer, but Daniel's is a little thicker. I'd call it a draw. What do you think, Ez?"

"I would agree, Presley. I would say both men are amply endowed, and most pleasing to the eye."

"Mmm-mmm-mmm, they are hunks, aren't they?"

Seeing Presley leer at them provoked Daniel. He dared Presley to go further. "Well, Presley, let's see your hand in your panties. If you like looking at us so much, it seems you should be playing with your clit while you drool."

As expected, Presley accepted the challenge. "You're right, Daniel." She stretched the elastic band and stuffed her hand deep inside her panties. Daniel could see her fingers working

as she rubbed her clit. "That's good! Now it's your turn, unless your cock has turned into a pussy!"

Vadim shifted to the other side of the bed. Daniel sat down
on the edge. He had had only one homosexual encounter in
his life, except for Vadim's violation the day before. When he
was fifteen, he and a friend had shared a pup tent on a camp-
ing trip. Neither of them had ever experienced oral sex, so
they'd blown each other. Daniel remembered he'd liked it,
probably more than he should have.

He swung his legs up onto the bed, and positioned himself
so he could clearly see both Ezra and Presley. Presley had a
steady rhythm going with her clit. Daniel could see her pac-
ing herself. Ezra still held her cup of milk. *Maybe you'd better explain to Ezra that she has to do what you're doing.* He
directed the thought at Presley, and then nodded toward
Ezra.

Presley heard him clearly. She immediately turned to Ezra.
"Ez, honey, he means it. You have to put your hand in your
panties and touch yourself too."

Ezra put down her cup. She looked into Daniel's eyes as
she slipped her hand inside her panties. With her free hand
she rubbed her breast. *Now you will honor your pact with
Presley, Daniel. You will allow Vadim to put his mouth on
you.*

He had stalled as long as he could. He focused on the
women, and tried to relax. "All right, Vadim, do me. Just
don't block my view."

*Dr. Daniel Hanson, when I am finished, you will be like
Devon, and wonder what my organ would feel like in your
ass.*

Not a chance in hell, Vadim! Daniel braced himself. He
didn't expect Vadim to be gentle. Daniel grunted when
Vadim's mouth covered his organ. He hadn't anticipated the
sensation of Vadim's whiskers against his skin. The bramble
bush of facial hair against his cock made him grimace.

Remembering that Presley and Ezra were watching him,

he tried to remain stoic. But Vadim made that impossible. It felt as though he would suck the liquid out of his balls. Presley's voice cut though his head like a razor. *Think you'll last long enough to fuck, Daniel?*

To his astonishment, Vadim answered. *Dr. Daniel Hanson will certainly sustain long enough to fulfill the pact. I will see to it.*

Had Daniel not been rendered speechless by Vadim's ministrations, he would have had one hell of a good laugh. The expression on Presley's face was priceless. He heard her spit back, *What the fuck, Vadim? Don't help him! He's been an asshole about this! Blow him until he comes!*

Daniel wanted to cheer when he heard Vadim's response. *Presley Knowles, I am looking forward to loving our women side by side. I will help Daniel sustain so we can share our pleasure and our climax.*

Fuck you both!

In spite of being overwhelmed by sensation, Daniel managed to shoot back, *You will!*

Except for his adolescent experiment, Daniel had no experience with men. That fact notwithstanding, he knew Vadim blew him like a pro. And those damn whiskers! Every time he moved his head, they would scrape his dick like a Brillo pad.

He knew Vadim had to be helping him hold on. No way in hell could he endure this kind of oral assault on his own. Even with his balls about to explode, he didn't come. He watched Presley and Ezra rubbing their clits, and could see they were working harder. Ezra's tits bounced like water-filled balloons as she rubbed herself. Close to being incoherent with arousal himself, he forced a clear thought from his head. *Vadim, the ladies are getting close, I can feel it!*

As can I, Daniel. It is time.

Vadim abruptly lifted his head, releasing Daniel's cock from his mouth. He zeroed in on Presley. "Ninotchka, I am ready. Come to the bed."

"Such a romantic invitation! How could I possibly refuse?"

Presley peeled off her panties and crawled onto the bed beside Vadim.

Daniel felt a surge of strength and knew Vadim fed it to him. It provided him with the control he needed to continue. "Ezra, take off your panties."

With the grace of a swan floating on a lake, she slowly approached the bed. "I would prefer you do it, Daniel."

He reached up and hooked his fingers in the elastic waistband. The sheer black panties hid nothing. But when he tugged them down her thighs and saw her golden curls, undiluted lust flooded his body.

Daniel grabbed Ezra's wrist and pulled her down beside him. After taking her panties off, he pushed Ezra backward onto the bed. "Blondie, spread your legs. You're about to get laid!"

Vadim followed suit, positioning Presley beside Ezra. "Presley Knowles, you will pleasure me as Ezra will pleasure Daniel. Open yourself for me."

Chapter Nineteen

As Vadim knelt between her legs, Presley glanced at Ezra. Daniel had her pinned to the bed, preparing to enter her. Ezra reached down and grabbed Presley's hand. Presley saw the now-familiar blue streaks on her face.

Are you all right, Ezra? Presley could tell Daniel wouldn't stop, even if Ezra wanted him to stop. He was too far gone.

My sister, I am the happiest I've ever been! Ezra squeezed her hand and sent Presley a wave of the sheer bliss that had made her cry. Presley understood. Ezra felt like she had finally come home.

At that moment, Daniel penetrated Ezra. The suddenness of his entry made Ezra gasp loudly. She still held Presley's hand and gripped it like a vice. The sensation of being filled overwhelmed Presley even before Vadim entered her. When Vadim's cock did slide inside of her, Presley groaned. He stretched her, his girth evidence of his extreme arousal.

The men shared a wavelength, as did the women. When the two couples united in physical love, the four people merged in a sensual cloud of combined sensation. Not one of them could tell where personal experience ended and shared experience began. They all swam in an Elysian pool of otherworldly rapture, a Garden of Eden of their own making.

The incredible masculinity of both men as they claimed their women rivaled that of Apollo. Vadim humped Presley with a forcefulness that should have left her helpless under him. But it didn't. Instead, she met his thrusts, and managed to lift his full body weight as she did.

She couldn't see Ezra, but she could feel her. Daniel had the throttle wide open, and thumped her without mercy. Ezra soared like an eagle as Daniel pummeled her. She had completely opened herself to him, body and soul. The exhilaration of riding the wind with him had taken Ezra to a place she had never been.

The fucking went on longer than Presley thought possible, considering how close to orgasm they had all been when they'd started. She had to let go of Ezra's hand so she could hold on to Vadim. She knew Ezra had done the same with Daniel.

When the moment came for their shared climax, the room exploded with light. It seemed to Presley that a thousand strobe lights had gone off. Instead of her orgasm making her shake and quiver, she felt quiet and light and free.

She reached for Vadim. Rather than being on top of her, he seemed to float beside her. *Where are Ezra and Daniel?*

They are here. Presley focused on the space opposite where she and Vadim had found themselves. Rather than seeing them, she felt them. She also sensed Daniel's confusion.

Vadim, what happened?

Our bodies suspended when we climaxed. We are floating in the ethers.

We have to go back! Ezra said I can't stay here, or I'll die!

You are stronger now, Ninotchka. So is Dr. Daniel Hanson. You will not die. We will go back.

I want to see Daniel.

As soon as Presley voiced her desire, she experienced movement. In the next moment, she hovered beside Daniel.

Presley?

Daniel? This is what happened to me before, when Ezra took me out. Now you know what the fuck happens!

It's good to know your foul mouth follows you wherever you go.

It's good to know you're okay.

I can't tell which way is up or down, or how to get home. Can you?

The wizard will explain it. Where's Ezra?

We are here, Presley. Ezra and Vadim appeared beside them. The sound of Ezra's calm voice reassured Presley.

Ez, what the fuck happened?

This is an unexpected occurrence. Our combined frequency reached a critical mass as we climaxed. We spontaneously suspended.

This is what happened to you and Vadim in Abilene!

It is exactly what happened to us. Except this time, we will all go back using your silver cords as tethers.

Shit, Ezra! I don't understand what a silver cord is! How the hell can I use it as a tether?

You do not have to do anything, Presley. I will take Daniel back using his cord and Vadim will take you back using yours. All you need do is relax and enjoy the ride.

Presley felt Daniel moving toward Ezra. She did the same with Vadim and then asked, *Are we ready to do this?*

Ezra directed them. *Daniel, hold on to me. Presley, you hold on to Vadim. We will be back in your living room before you know it.*

The floor seemed to suddenly solidify under Presley's feet. She had her arms around Vadim's neck. As soon as she'd oriented herself, she looked for Ezra and Daniel. She turned just in time to see the blue mist separate into two bodies and then solidify, the same way Ezra and Vadim had appeared at the laundromat the night before.

"Are we all here?" Daniel had his arm around Ezra's waist.

"There's four of us. We didn't lose anyone."

Ezra led Daniel to the sofa. "Sit down, Daniel. Allow yourself time to settle."

Presley sat down beside him. "How are you?"

"Disoriented, and dizzy."

"It will pass. When Ez took me out before, I felt motion sickness for a few minutes. That didn't happen this time."

Daniel rubbed his forehead. "I know the old joke about touching the face of God when you come, but this is ridiculous!"

Presley poked him in the side with her finger. "Hey, this'll be one to tell the boys in the locker room!"

"Yeah, right! Then I'll tell them about how blue cows fly over the moon."

"Yours are blue? Mine are silver!"

"Such wit! When we take our act on the road, you're elected to do stand-up."

"I've been told I'd be good at it, sort of like Kathy Griffin or Margaret Cho."

"What the fuck time is it anyway? We have to meet Scott at four."

Presley glanced at the clock on her desk. "It's only one-thirty. We'll make it in time. Anybody want some lunch?"

"I would love some ice cream!" Ezra already had on a pair of her new jeans and a low-cut top.

"How did you get dressed so fast?"

"Vadim is also dressed."

Presley turned to see Vadim in his jeans and white shirt, complete with cuff links. He had a mouthful of Cheerios, and had just dipped his hand into the box for more. "Damn! You guys have to teach us to do that!"

"They have to teach us how to do a lot of things. It seems like we're in kindergarten." Daniel grabbed his clothes from the floor. "I'm going to take a shower. You should probably do the same. You're the one going to the doctor's office for an exam."

Presley sniffed under her arm. "I don't stink. I smell like cherry wine and herbal soap."

"You're doing better than I am. I smell like I've been picking honeysuckle."

"I'll make us some food, and then I'll shower. I don't want to offend."

"Too damn late for that, Presley. You've made being offensive into a lifestyle." Presley threw a sofa cushion at Daniel's back as he disappeared into the bedroom.

Presley found her T-shirt and panties and put them back on. "Ez, I'm going to scramble some eggs for Vadim. Want to try some?"

Ezra crinkled her nose. "I'd rather have ice cream."

Using the same negotiation technique she had seen her friends use with their children, Presley bargained with Ezra. "Tell you what. If you try some eggs and a piece of toast, I'll stop at the store later and get you whatever flavor of ice cream you want."

"Chocolate?"

"If that's what you want, that's what I'll get."

Vadim came up behind Presley and slid his hand under her shirt. "Do I get some as well?"

"You just did, buster! In spades!" She pulled his hand away from her breast and went to the kitchen to make some eggs.

Presley scrambled a panful of eggs, enough for everyone. She made Ezra and Vadim some toast and warmed more milk. Vadim ate like a champ, going back for seconds even before Presley had eaten all of hers. Ezra picked at her eggs, but ate the toast, putting more jelly on the last bite.

"You like the grape jelly, don't you?"

"It is satisfying. I am enjoying it."

Presley had an idea. "Why don't you put some on your eggs?"

"But that's not what you did. You only put it on your bread."

"You can put it right on your eggs too, if that makes them taste better to you."

Ezra took Presley's advice. She slathered grape jelly on top of her eggs. By the time Daniel came out of the bathroom, she had already eaten half of them.

Daniel stared at Ezra's plate, now a purple and yellow mess. "What the hell is she eating?"

"Scrambled eggs and grape jelly. There's more eggs in the pan if you want some."

"Really healthy, Presley! This is her first solid food. She shouldn't be eating jelly!"

"Why the fuck not? She didn't want the eggs at all until we put jelly on them. The way she likes sweets, she won't have that hourglass figure for long."

Ezra swallowed another spoonful of eggs. "There is no concern. I will not gain weight."

"Like hell you won't! Ez, it's a fact of life here. We all gain weight if we don't have a healthy diet."

"But I am already at the ideal weight for my frequency. That is the weight I will maintain."

Vadim poured himself another cup of milk. "That is true for me as well. My weight is calibrated for my frequency. I will not become heavier."

Presley needed to get cleaned up for her doctor's appointment and got up to put her dish in the sink. "What about Daniel and me? Are our weights calibrated?"

"Your frequency is still rising. Once it stabilizes, your weight and your age will be optimized. Then you will be fully calibrated."

Daniel slowly sat down in the chair beside Ezra. Presley actually saw the color drain from his face. He looked like he might throw up. "Daniel, what is it?"

He didn't answer Presley. He spoke directly to Ezra. "What do you mean, when our weight and our age are optimized, we will be fully calibrated?"

"When your frequency stabilizes in the higher vibratory field, your weight will be set at a point of maximum fitness for your frequency. Your age will revert to a time of personal power. For you and Presley, I suspect that will be now. Then you are calibrated."

"And what is a calibration?"

"Your calibration becomes the blueprint to which your physical body regenerates. My blueprint is this body, and that is Vadim's."

"Jesus Christ!"

Ezra appeared totally calm, and Daniel still looked like he might vomit. "What is she saying, Daniel? I don't understand."

"Presley, she's saying we aren't going to age. Whatever happens when we reach this peak vibration is how we will stay."

"Holy shit!"

"Ezra, is there any way to stop this?"

"No, Daniel. It is permanent. It is what happens in the world of spirit, and higher vibration. You and Presley are simply ahead of schedule."

The enormity of Ezra's revelation hit Presley between the eyes and her knees buckled. "Ninotchka!" Vadim caught her, even though he had been sitting at the table when she'd almost fainted. Presley had not seen him move.

She leaned against Vadim's chest. "Give me a minute. I'm lightheaded."

Daniel went to the cupboard and found a bottle of brandy. "It's no damn wonder you nearly went down. This shit just doesn't seem to stop!" He poured Presley a drink. "Here, sip this. Doctor's orders."

"I need to shower. We have to leave soon."

"I don't want you in the shower alone. Vadim, go with her and make sure she doesn't fall."

Presley felt the scar on her forehead. "Christ, Daniel! I could crack my head open again and it wouldn't matter, would it?"

Daniel stared at her forehead. "At least now I understand how you healed so damn fast."

"Come, Ninotchka. We will see to your bath."

Presley pointed to the eggs left in the pan. "Ezra, make sure Daniel eats something. I don't want him fainting on the street."

"I will, Presley. He will have proper nutrition before he leaves with you."

Vadim led Presley into the bathroom. "Ninotchka, perhaps it would be better to sit in a tub of water than to stand under it."

"I need to wash my hair."

"I will help you clean your hair. Please, you must sit for a time, and let the hot water calm you before you go with Daniel."

Presley didn't argue. Vadim drew her bath. She undressed and climbed into the tub. Vadim took off his shirt, being careful to put his cufflinks on the shelf by the sink. Then he knelt by the tub. "Lean back, Ninotchka, and wet your hair. I will support you."

Vadim held her as she dunked her head in the water. When she sat back up, she pointed to the rack hanging on the shower. "The shampoo is up there. I have to skip the conditioner, it's too oily."

Vadim stood and reached for the bottle. "This is hair soap?"

"I suppose you could call it that. Squirt it on your hands and rub it into my hair."

Vadim massaged the shampoo into Presley's scalp, his strong fingers relaxing her as much as cleaning her hair. Again, he helped her to lean back. He supported her with one arm while he rinsed the suds with his other hand.

"The soap is out. Is your hair finished now?"

"It's done. Now I have to bathe."

"I will clean you."

"What? You'll wash me?"

"Unless you object to my doing so."

"I don't object, not at all. No one has ever offered to wash me before."

"I find touching your body most pleasing, even in the bath."

Presley enjoyed the pampering and appreciated the care Vadim took. When he scrubbed her back, she thought she had died and gone to heaven. That's when it really hit her. She blurted out the thought as it came into her head. "Vadim, will I die?"

He matter-of-factly answered. "No, not as you nearly did in your accident."

"What will happen?"

"When you are ready to leave, you will consciously suspend. It will be your choice."

"What about you?"

"It will be the same for me. Remember, we share your cord."

"Where will we go?"

"That, dear heart, is an open-ended question. God's house has many mansions."

"Vadim, no matter how you look at it, this is all over the top."

"It is a considerable amount of information for you to integrate, to be sure. I have been across for four hundred years, and I am just beginning to understand. Ezra knows much. We will all learn from her."

"Thank God one of us knows something."

Daniel knocked on the door. "Presley, it's three o'clock. We have to leave soon."

"I'll be out in a few minutes. Vadim, we have to finish up here. I have to get dressed." He quickly washed her legs and feet. When he cleaned between her legs, Presley sincerely regretted being so short on time. He rubbed her briskly, and she wanted more. He sensed her impulse.

"Perhaps when you return from your outing with Daniel, you will allow me to finish what we have just started?"

"As long as I don't disappear. I don't mind your making me dissolve into a puddle, as long as my body stays solid."

Vadim laughed. "You will soon learn, Presley Knowles, that the physical body is as illusory as death."

"Says you!"

Presley finished her bath, and Vadim helped her out of the

tub. He continued his pampering as he dried her with a big bath towel. She put on clean clothes, figuring jeans and a nice shirt would do. When she came out, it was three-fifteen.

Daniel and Ezra were still in the kitchen. He had an empty plate sitting in front of him. "Good, you ate something."

He smiled at Ezra. "She threatened to force feed me if I didn't eat on my own. I think she meant it."

"I did mean it, Daniel. You do not yet know all that I can do."

"That's the damn truth. Are you ready, Presley?"

"I'm ready. We'll go downstairs and grab a cab." She remembered Vadim and Ezra would be alone until they got back. "Will you guys be all right here by yourselves?"

Vadim put his arm around her shoulders. "We will be fine, Ninotchka. I will put on the television. Perhaps we will watch Pay-Per-View. Daniel explained to me how it works."

Presley shot Daniel a dirty look. "You taught him how to get Pay-Per-View? My cable bill will be through the frigging roof!"

Ezra grinned. "My sister, you need not worry about such things. Spirit will provide."

"Daniel, let's get going. I'm already going tilt. I don't need any more information right now."

"Me neither. Let's see what Scott has to tell us."

They got a cab quickly and headed uptown. Neither of them said anything for several minutes. Daniel broke the silence. "You're awfully quiet. Are you worried about this exam?"

"No. It's not that. We both know what's going on. Whatever the tests say, it's not going to change anything."

"Then tell me why you're not talking."

"Vadim told me something while I took my bath. It's so over the top, I can't wrap my mind around it."

"What could be more over the top than what we already know?"

Presley spoke softly, so the cab driver wouldn't hear. "How about that we aren't going to die?"

Daniel blurted out, "That's impossible!"

"Shhhhh!" She pointed to the cab driver, who, fortunately, was busy talking to his dispatcher. "Not according to Vadim. We'll leave here by choice, not because the Grim Reaper has come to collect us."

"Presley, this is total insanity! How the hell did all of this happen?"

"It happened because I had an accident and died. I'm one up on Harry Houdini. I did come back. You are the unlucky son of a bitch who couldn't keep his dick in his pants. If you hadn't fucked me in Abilene, you wouldn't be involved."

"I'm not sorry about that, Presley."

"Then you're crazier than I am! I fucked up your life, Daniel. I didn't mean to, but the bottom line is, I did."

"Ezra says it's my soul's choice to do this. She says it wouldn't be happening if I hadn't agreed to it, consciously or not."

"Do you believe her?"

"I'm beginning to." Daniel glanced out the window. "We're almost there. A few more blocks. His new address is close to Columbia University. I don't think I told you. He teaches a course there a few times a week, on clinical anatomy."

"He must be good."

"He is. He can also hold his own in neurology, even though it isn't his specialty."

"Then he'll be able to read the EEG?"

"Both of us can. It's interpreting the results that could get dicey."

"What do you think it will show?"

"I don't know. It's a damn good thing I can go to Scott with this. If I ask him to keep his mouth shut, he will."

The cab stopped in front of a new high-rise building with a tree-lined plaza leading to the main entrance. The building had as much glass as it did brick; the windows glinted in the sunlight. A row of small balconies jutted out from the corner, obviously designed to optimize the view of the Hudson River.

"Shit, Daniel! This is where your roommate has his office?"

"It's the right address. I guess so."

"My doctor has a basement office in an old brownstone. The carpet gets wet every time we have a bad storm. How the hell can Scott afford this?"

"He told me his practice is thriving, and that he's doing well. Looks like he wasn't kidding."

They made their way through a stylish art deco lobby. A uniformed guard behind an oversized desk stopped them. "Excuse me, may I help you?"

Daniel assumed an impressive air of authority. "Yes, thank you. I'm Dr. Daniel Hanson and this is Presley Knowles. We're here to see Dr. Scott Brewer."

"Could I see some identification, please?"

Daniel took his driver's license out of his wallet. Presley still had her passport in her purse. The guard took both IDs.

"Is that sufficient?"

The guard examined their photo IDs and then returned them. "Yes, thank you. You have to sign the guest log before entering the building. Then take the elevator to the twelfth floor. Dr. Brewer's offices are right outside the elevator."

While waiting on the elevator, Presley poked Daniel. "His offices? Jesus, Daniel, maybe you should think about being his partner!"

"I have been. Let's see how this shakes down."

When they got off the elevator on the twelfth floor, they had no trouble spotting Scott's offices. A large sign hanging beside double glass doors read DR. SCOTT BREWER AND ASSOCIATES.

"Daniel, who are his associates?"

"I don't know any of them. They're graduates from Columbia. Scott met them in the class he teaches."

"Looks like he's covered all the angles, doesn't it?"

Daniel chuckled. "I used to play poker with him. He beat

the crap out of me every time. If he hadn't graduated med school, he probably would have sold used cars."

"That's reassuring. A closet used car salesman is about to give me an EEG."

The receptionist buzzed them in. "May I help you?"

"Yes, please. Dr. Daniel Hanson to see Dr. Brewer."

"Dr. Hanson! It's good to finally meet you! Dr. Brewer has told us all about you."

"All good, I hope?"

"Absolutely! He told me to take you and Ms. Knowles to your office when you arrive."

"I don't understand. My office?"

"He has an empty office beside his that is still vacant. He says it's for his future partner. A little bird told me he hopes that will be you."

The receptionist led them down a long hallway past a series of examination rooms. The last two rooms were large offices, one across the hall from the other. The receptionist pointed to the one on the left. "That is Dr. Brewer's office." She led them into the one on the right. "This is the vacant office I told you about. The associates have offices on the other side of the floor."

"Does Dr. Brewer rent the entire floor?"

"Yes. That's why we moved. He needed more space to expand his practice. We've only been at this new location for about six weeks. Please, make yourselves comfortable. Dr Brewer will be with you in a few minutes. He's with his last scheduled patient now."

"Thank you."

Presley walked around the office, checking out the furniture. "Damn! This desk is walnut, and the chairs have leather seats." She went to the window. "Look at that! There's the river! Both his office and this one have a view of the Hudson! Fuck, this is a hard sell! He wants you here with him, Daniel!"

"No pressure, right?"

"Well, don't we have to keep all of our options open? We don't know what's going to happen with this."

"We?"

"Yes, we! The four of us are morphing into the Teenage Mutant Ninja Turtles! Whatever one of us does now affects all of us."

"We shouldn't be discussing this now. Scott will be here any minute."

Presley could sense his turmoil, so she backed off. Daniel occupied himself looking over the medical books on the bookshelf, while Presley stared at the river. Within five minutes, Scott knocked on the door.

"Dan?"

"Hey, Scott. Good to see you again." Daniel met Scott at the door, shook his hand, and then hugged him. "You've put on a little weight, buddy!"

"My wife's a good cook. She makes sure I'm well fed."

"How is Sarah?"

"Pregnant, and puking. Other than that, she's doing great."

Presley felt left out, so she cracked a joke. "She must be a special lady if she can cook when she's puking. When I'm nauseous, I don't want to look at food."

Scott came into the room, obviously checking her out. "You must be Presley Knowles. It's nice to meet you."

Scott held out his hand. Presley grasped it in a firm handshake. A jolt like an electric shock moved through her arm. Daniel felt it too. She heard him say, *Steady, Presley. Take a deep breath*.

She did as Daniel said, breathing deeply as images flew through her head: pictures of Daniel in med school, Daniel as the best man at Scott's wedding, Daniel holding Scott's first child at the christening. In spite of the machine gun slide show she'd witnessed, she managed to smile. "I guess you two have quite a history together."

"We sure do. I've known Dan since we went to med school together. Did he tell you we were roommates?"

"He told me. I think he also mentioned being the best man at your wedding? Is that right?" Presley wanted to test what she had just seen.

"Yeah, he was. Got drunk as a skunk too."

"He didn't tell me that."

"I bet he didn't! You two will have to come over for dinner. I'll show you the pictures."

"That would be lovely." Presley made a mental note to try to see some pictures later, on her own. Daniel heard her.

You don't have to snoop. I fucked the maid of honor, if that's what you want to know.

Thank you, Dr. Hanson. Now I know where to look.

Presley forced herself not to laugh when she heard Daniel audibly snort. Scott heard him too.

"What, you don't want your lady to see what a Don Juan you can be?" He turned back to Presley. "I have pictures of him at the reception I've kept to use as blackmail, if I ever need them."

Presley smiled, more at Daniel's reaction than at Scott's revelation. "Hang on to them. You never know when they might come in handy."

The instant rapport Presley had with Scott seemed to irritate Daniel, not to mention the focus of the conversation. He changed the subject. "The EEG will take at least an hour. Maybe we should get started."

"How about some background? What happened?"

Presley let Daniel tell Scott about her accident in Abilene, and the time she'd spent in the hospital there. He gave Scott her medical history, by the book. She wondered what reason he would give for this EEG. What he said startled her.

"Presley came back to New York earlier this week. She called to tell me she's had several odd neurological incidents that could best be described as perceived psychic activity, which is why I came to New York. I want to rule out the possibility that her accident might have triggered a form of temporal lobe epilepsy."

Presley flared. *What the fuck, Daniel! You know I don't have epilepsy!*

Don't contradict me, Presley! It's the best way to explain what is happening.

Scott addressed Presley directly. "Have you seen any colored lights or had any memory loss?"

Presley wanted to make a wisecrack, but a warning look from Daniel changed her mind. "No, nothing like that."

"Then what have you been experiencing?"

Presley gauged her answer carefully. "I know things that I shouldn't know, and recognize things I haven't seen before."

"We all get flashes of déjà vu. Our memory can play tricks on us sometimes."

"Not like this." Knowing full well Daniel would be pissed off, she nonetheless told Scott something that would get his attention. She had clearly read what he had on his mind.

"You received the results of the amniocentesis this morning. There is a history of spina bifida in Sarah's family and a history of Down's syndrome in yours. When you got the results this morning and found out your baby is normal and healthy, you called Sarah right away to tell her. She was so relieved she started to cry and had to put the phone down."

Scott didn't say anything. He quietly walked over to Presley and ran his index finger the length of her scar. He took a penlight out of his pocket and looked into her pupils. As he studied her eyes, he asked her a question. "Tell me something. What sex is the baby and what are we going to name it?"

With no hesitation, Presley answered. "It's your first boy. You and Sarah decided on the name this morning, after getting the test results. Instead of Scott Jr., you decided to name him Daniel, after his godfather, with the middle name Scott.

You'd planned on telling Daniel this afternoon and asking him to stand for the baby, except now I've spilled the beans."

Presley heard Daniel's "Jesus Christ" at the same time she heard Scott clear his throat. Scott took her hand and led her to the door. He paused beside Daniel. "Looks like you have yourself a witch. Let's go do the EEG."

Scott took Presley into an examination room, where the EEG machine sat beside the paper-covered table. "Sit on the table and let me take your blood sample first."

"I hate needles. Don't hurt me."

"I won't. Make a fist for me."

Presley hopped up on the table and made a fist. She closed her eyes while Scott inserted the needle. She only felt a slight pinch on her arm.

"You're pretty good at that."

"I've had lots of practice." Scott drew three vials of blood and Daniel marked them with her name and the date. "Now, we'll do the EEG. Dan, have you coached her on what to expect?"

"Not really, there hasn't been time."

"Presley, lie down and relax. This won't hurt at all. Keep your eyes closed and don't talk. Try to stay still. If you feel drowsy, go ahead and fall asleep. I'm going to wire you up now."

While Scott attached the electrodes to Presley's scalp, Daniel reinforced Scott's instructions. "Remember, Presley, Scott said don't talk. I know that alone may kill you, but see what you can do to cooperate."

What Presley answered aloud was, "I'll manage, thank you." What she spit at him in her mind was, *Fuck you!*

He shot back, *Anytime, any place, redhead. If we live forever, we'll have plenty of opportunity!*

Scott interrupted their exchange. "Are you comfortable, Presley?"

"I'm fine."

"I have a blanket if you get chilled. If you need it, I'll throw it over you."

"Thanks. I'll let you know."

Scott flipped on the machine. Presley closed her eyes and settled in. If she ended up napping through this, all the better.

"Here, Dan, have a seat. I'll sit on the stool."

"Thanks."

"So, you and Presley are an item?"

"I suppose you could say that. It's the first time I've ever followed a patient out of Kansas."

"Hell, I've been trying to get you out of Kansas for years. What's she got that I haven't got? Don't answer that!"

"I'm glad your baby is healthy. I didn't know about your family history."

"I thought maybe you were pulling a fast one on me. I wondered how the hell you got your hands on the amnio results. Knowing you, it's possible. You could have pulled some strings. But when she told me our family history and that we're naming our kid Daniel, I about shit my pants."

"Well, you sure as hell hadn't told me any of it! I nearly dropped a turd myself when she blurted it out."

"No one knows any of this except Sarah, and she's home puking as we speak. We made our final decision about the name today, just like Presley said. I wanted to tell you face to face. Better that than an e-mail or a phone call. How the hell did she know about my personal life?"

"Like I said, I need to rule out epilepsy. We'll see what the EEG shows."

"You know as well as I do epilepsy doesn't create mind readers!"

"Yeah, I know."

"Dan, you're not telling me something. I've known you too damn long not to see that. You never could bluff in a card game."

"Even if I tried to explain it, Scott, you wouldn't believe me."

Presley's voice cut through his head. *Now you fucking know how I felt! Go ahead, try to explain it to him. Let's see if he reacts like you did!*

"What's wrong, Dan? What happened?" Presley opened her eyes. She saw Daniel leaning over the EEG machine, apparently reading the graph.

"I want to check something." Scott came to look over his shoulder.

"What the hell? Let me look at that." Daniel moved aside, so Scott could see. "This is fucking impossible!"

"Yeah, I know."

"She's been in theta, had a sharp burst to gamma, returned to theta, and has now dipped to delta. She dropped right through alpha and beta, which is where she should be registering. With these readings, she shouldn't be conscious."

Daniel turned to look at Presley. "Are you conscious, Presley?"

"Of course I am! I've been listening to the two of you talk about me like I'm not in the room."

"Her brain waves didn't fluctuate from delta, even when she spoke to you."

"Keep watching."

Presley, talk to me like this.

What do you want me to say? Should I tell you how I feel like a fucking amoeba in a Petri dish lying here while the two of you study that chart?

"She just spiked to gamma again, dropped back to theta, and dipped into delta, just like before. She's going from the basement to the attic without taking the stairs. I've never seen anything like this!"

"Welcome to my world."

"Dan, what the hell is going on?"

"You said you have another machine. Get it and wire me up."

Presley raised herself up on her elbows. "Daniel, what the fuck are you doing?"

"Proving you don't have epilepsy. Get the damn machine, Scott."

Why are you doing this? He'll know you're messed up too.
Maybe I want him to know.

Scott picked up the phone. "Hello, Jennifer? Could you get the portable EEG machine with the laptop from my office? Bring it to examination room two, please."

Scott glanced at the graph. "Looks like it happened again while I was on the phone. You know what's causing this, don't you?"

"I might. We'll see if I'm right."

"Care to brief me on your diagnosis, Dr. Hanson?"

"No, Dr. Brewer, I don't. I'll let you draw your own conclusions."

Someone knocked on the door. A young woman came in with a laptop case and a smaller version of the machine Presley had attached to her. "Thank you, Jennifer. I'll take it from here."

Scott put the laptop on the counter and turned it on. While it booted, he reached into the case and pulled out what appeared to be a cap covered with small buttons, which Presley guessed were like the electrodes she had stuck directly to her head. He plugged the wires from the cap into small holes in the machine, and then plugged the machine into the laptop.

He moved the chair beside the counter. "Sit down, Dan, so I can put this on your head." Daniel sat down and let Scott hotwire him.

When Scott turned on the box, the laptop instantly started beeping and the graph scrolled across the screen. He positioned Presley's machine so he could see both EEG charts at the same time.

Daniel sat with his eyes closed and arms crossed over his chest. "What do you see, Scott?"

"With only minor fluctuations, your brain waves are the same as Presley's, theta dipping into delta."

Presley, talk to me.

What is this going to prove, Daniel?

It will prove what Ezra told us, that our frequency is changing. My guess is these instruments can't measure what's happening to us. Our brain waves are now outside the normal bell curve. Our new normal is abnormal to these machines.

Shit, how are you going to explain this to Scott?

I don't know.

"All right! Stop whatever you're doing! You've both spiked into gamma. I want to see if you both fall back into theta."

Presley remained quiet and so did Daniel. Several minutes passed. "Well, Scott? What's the verdict?"

"Have you two been fucking in a nuclear reactor? Except for that, I don't know what the hell could cause this to happen. You're both low theta again, on the edge of delta. The odds of your both having the same brain malfunction are at least a billion to one."

"At least. But there it is."

"What did you do to cause the gamma burst? I could see your expression change, the way it used to when we had an exam. Your forehead creased, like you were concentrating."

"I was talking to Presley."

"You were what?"

"Talking to Presley, and she was talking to me."

"You haven't spoken since you sat down here."

"Not out loud, but we can in our heads."

"You mean telepathically?"

"That's what I mean."

"Christ, Dan. You graduated magna cum laude, and have been an M.D. for years. You're the best doctor I know. I never thought I would hear you talking such bullshit. What the hell has happened to you? Did the redhead promise you some pussy if you did drugs with her? Is that it?"

"Dr. Daniel Hanson is not talking bullshit, and Presley Knowles does not use drugs."

Presley smelled him before she saw him. She turned her head in the direction of the familiar voice. Then she closed her eyes and whispered, "Oh, my God!"

Vadim stood by the door, and he looked pissed as hell!

Chapter Twenty

Scott grabbed for the phone. "I don't know who the hell you are or how you got in here, but I'm calling security!"

Daniel pulled the electrode cap off his head. He got to Scott before he dialed and snatched the phone from his hand. "No, Scott. He's with us."

"What the fuck do you mean, he's with you? Nobody came in with you!"

"This is Vadim, and I swear to you, he's with us."

"Dr. Daniel Hanson is telling the truth. I am with them."

"How did you get in here? Security should have stopped you."

"I entered directly. I did not encounter your security."

"You had to! You can't get into the building without ID."

"I do not have papers as yet."

"What? You're here illegally? Fucking shit, Dan, what have you gotten yourself into? This has to be about drugs! It's the only thing that makes sense!"

Presley interrupted Scott's rant. "Daniel, you'd better see this." She pointed up toward the ceiling.

"Jesus Christ!"

"I thought you'd want to know." Presley had spotted wisps of blue mist. When she looked up, she saw Ezra's cloud floating overhead.

"Scott, sit down."

"What are you going to do? Tie me up and rob me?"

"I might have to gag you, but I'm not going to rob you." Daniel forcibly pushed Scott into the chair. "Sit down! You'll thank me for this in a minute."

Daniel looked up toward the ceiling. "It's all right, Ezra. You can come in now."

The blue mist slowly spiraled down toward the floor, assuming the shape of a woman. Within a few seconds, it had congealed and Ezra stood beside Vadim, wearing her new skirt with another low-cut top they had bought yesterday.

Presley laughed. "You changed clothes. That looks really good on you!"

"I wished to impress Daniel's good friend. Hello, Scott Brewer. I am Ezra."

Daniel put his hand on Scott's shoulder. "So, Scott, are you impressed?" Scott didn't answer. "Vadim, how about some vodka? I think my buddy here could use a drink."

"I would agree, Daniel." Vadim focused on the counter beside the laptop. Silver light seemed to move from his eyes to the marble countertop, where it solidified into a bottle.

Daniel picked up the bottle of vodka. "Nice work, Vadim. You'll have to teach me how to do that." Daniel filled a paper cup with vodka and handed it to Scott. "Drink this."

Scott bolted back the vodka and passed the cup back to Daniel for more. "Are you going to tell me who the hell they are, and how you got involved with them?"

Presley pulled the electrodes off of her scalp, so she could go stand by Vadim. "It's my fault."

"Ninotchka, there is no blame. It is our destiny."

"Bullshit, Vadim! If not for me, Daniel wouldn't be in this up to his neck." Presley spoke directly to Scott. "I had a near-death experience in Abilene. When I fell asleep at the wheel, Vadim intervened and saved my life. Vadim and Ezra are ghosts, Scott. They followed me home after my accident. Daniel is the innocent bystander who happened to be on duty in the emergency room when they brought me in."

"There's a little more to it than that, Presley. Spending the week together after your accident is what sealed it."

Scott drank his second cup of vodka. "For the sake of argument, let's say for the moment that I believe you. What the hell happened to your brain waves?"

"From what Ezra has told us, our frequency is changing. Because of our connection to them, we are becoming what they are."

"Yeah, right! You're becoming ghosts."

"We are not ghosts!" Vadim's voice echoed in the small room. "Our consciousness vibrates at a different frequency than yours, but we are no less living beings! Why can you not accept that God's house has many mansions, and that we live in a different house than you do?"

Vadim strode across the room and took the vodka from Daniel. He didn't bother using a cup. He took a long swallow straight from the bottle.

Scott stood and challenged him. "If what you say is true, why aren't there more of you around? Shouldn't we be up to our assholes in dead people?"

"You are. You do not have the eyes to see."

Scott poked Vadim's chest. "You seem pretty damn solid to me. I can see you just fine."

Daniel stepped in. "Scott, I wouldn't piss him off. He can be one mean son of a bitch when he wants to be."

"It is all right, Daniel. I will answer your friend's question. You can see me because Presley Knowles has agreed to hold me. If not for her, I would not be able to manifest for any length of time."

Presley threaded her arm through Vadim's. "You can think of it as though I'm sponsoring Vadim, and Daniel is sponsoring Ezra."

"Dan, you agreed to this?"

"Come here, Ezra." Ezra had been standing quietly by the door listening. When Daniel asked for her, she came to him. "Scott wants to know if I agreed to this. Did I?"

"You agreed to hold me as Presley agreed to hold Vadim. We are now bound, one to the other. What is done cannot be undone."

Scott shook his head. "Dan, you mean this is permanent?"

"Seems so. I don't know how to undo it. Do you?"

"Your whole brain chemistry has changed."

"I expect my DNA has too. Don't know if I want to find out for sure. Coming here to see you today showed me what we're in for if we try to take it further."

Presley had to throw in her two cents on that one. "For the record, I'm not doing this again. I'm not taking any more tests and being treated like a freak."

Scott muttered, "Well, if the shoe fits . . ."

Presley turned on him. "Why the fuck is it that we can use a wireless laptop or a cell phone and no one questions it? There's no connection to anything, no wire, no plug. But they work! We watch television and we listen to the radio. Do we see the radio waves? Hell, no! But we know they exist. So why is it so frigging hard to accept that we can do the same goddamn thing?"

Daniel agreed. "She's got a point. What we're doing is like tuning the radio, changing the station inside our heads to hear a different frequency."

"You sound like you believe all of this!"

"Scott, I don't believe it. But I'm living it. I have to come to terms with what's happened. It's like an incurable disease. I have to accept it, and adjust my lifestyle to accommodate the changes. I have no choice. "

"Are you giving up medicine?"

"I don't want to. I'm a doctor. It defines who I am."

Ezra lightly touched Daniel's arm. "You are a healer. You cannot be otherwise. It is your soul's calling, just as it is mine."

Daniel kissed Ezra's hair. "Pretty lady, I hope you're right."

Presley noticed that for the first time, hearing Daniel call

Ezra "pretty lady" didn't sting. Presley could feel affection for Ezra growing inside of Daniel. Ezra glanced at her, acknowledging she felt it too. Presley saw the blue drops forming in her eyes. *Daniel, grab some tissues for Ezra. She's about to cry.*

Daniel leaned behind Scott, picked up a box of Kleenex and handed them to Ezra. "Here, Ez. Your makeup is running again."

Ezra took some and dabbed at her face just as the blue tears slipped out of her eyes.

Scott picked up the conversation. "Well, if you aren't giving up medicine, are you going back to Abilene?"

"My house and my job are there. I have to go back."

"You have a job here, if you want it."

"You would still take me in as a partner, even with all of this?" Daniel waved his arm to indicate the other three.

That didn't sit well with Presley. "Don't you mean 'even with all of them'?"

Daniel didn't back down. "I suppose I do."

Scott took the bottle from Vadim and poured himself more vodka. "I still don't know if I buy the ghost thing, but this guy makes damn good vodka. Cheers!" Scott toasted the group and belted back the booze. "The offer for the partnership still stands. That office is yours, if you want it."

Damn it, Daniel, say yes! That means you could stay in New York.

Daniel's answer disappointed Presley. "I need to think about this, Scott. I don't want my situation to disrupt your life, or your practice."

"Think you could do the Edgar Cayce thing?"

"The what?"

"Diagnose people the way Cayce did. My mother had all of his books. I read a few of them while I still lived at home. He could diagnose people while in a trance. I never bought that either, but hey, who knows?" He held up his cup, pointing to Presley. "If she can tell me the results of my baby's amnio, you sure as hell should be able to tell me if I have a cyst on my dick."

"You do, and you're worried that it's malignant. It's not. It's definitely benign. But you should still have it removed. It could block your urethra if it gets any bigger."

"Jesus Christ! I haven't even told Sarah about that. I have an appointment to have it checked next week."

Presley wanted to applaud. She refrained, only saying to Daniel, *You're the man!*

Daniel smiled as he responded, *I thought you already knew that.*

"You're talking to her again, aren't you?"

"How did you know that?"

"Your expression changes. Those creases in your forehead give it away."

"Your powers of observation always were better than mine."

"That's why I'm a better diagnostician, and a better poker player, than you are. It's a good skill to have."

"Hell, I just diagnosed a lump on your dick without even seeing it! Thank God for that! Examining your dick is the last thing I need!"

"I'm nobody's fool. I found a female urologist. If I have to have my dick handled, I want a woman to do it."

Presley felt the tension ease within Daniel as the two men relaxed back into their friendship. Obviously feeling her probing him, he glanced at her. He winked at her, acknowledging he had the situation in hand. Then he turned back to Scott. "Could we stop talking about your dick, please? There are ladies present."

Ezra giggled. "But Daniel, I am enjoying the discussion about Scott's dick. Please do not stop because I am here. And I am sure Presley Knowles does not mind. She is fond of male genitalia, as am I."

Daniel appeared to have swallowed a live goldfish before he burst out laughing. Scott had a similar expression, then grinned broadly as he said, "Christ, Dan, you have a live wire there!"

"I'm just beginning to understand how much of one she is! Ezra, you are a pistol!"

"That is a good thing, Daniel?"

"Yes, pretty lady. That is a good thing." This time, Presley rode the wave of affection carried by "pretty lady." Her eyes welled up. She could see the seeds of love in Daniel growing. He was falling in love with Ezra.

Ezra took several tissues from the box and handed them to Presley. "Here, my sister. Your eye color is starting to run as mine did."

Presley didn't catch the overflow of tears in time. Steaks of mercury-colored liquid colored her face. The fluorescent light caught the shine and Scott noticed. "Presley, I looked in your eyes. You aren't wearing any makeup. What is that?"

"Nothing." Presley quickly wiped her face and crumpled the tissue in her hand.

"To hell it isn't!" Scott took the penlight out of his pocket. The unexpected brightness of the light in her eyes made Presley blink. She pushed his arm away.

"Get that thing out of my face!"

Then she heard Daniel's voice in her head. *Turn them on, Presley. What the hell! He's seen everything else.*

Scott again tried to shine the light in her eyes, and again Presley pushed his arm away. "If you really want to know what this is, I'll show you. Just remember, you asked for it!"

Presley glanced at Vadim, who nodded his consent. *I will help you, Ninotchka. Relax, as I have taught you to do, and let me in.*

Presley took a deep breath. With surprisingly little effort, she opened herself and felt Vadim move into her. As he did, her eyes began to grow warmer. Staring directly into Scott's face, she allowed the heat in her eyes to build.

Scott backed away from her, nearly tripping on the stool. "What the fuck is that?"

"I hate to do this to you, buddy, but I really want you to get what's going on here. Look at me."

Scott turned around to look at Daniel. "Jesus Christ! They look like Christmas lights!"

"Blue is Ezra's color and silver is Vadim's. It's like Presley and I caught a virus from them. Their eyes glow the same way. When Ezra and Presley cry, their color runs."

"Fucking shit, Dan, this is huge! They really are ghosts, aren't they?"

"With all due respect to Vadim, they really are." Daniel's eyes slowly dimmed until they returned to normal. "Depending on how this goes, I may need your help with a few things. That's why I want you to know the score."

"What kind of help? I don't know if I can treat any of you. Your bodies . . ." Scott's voice trailed off.

"Our bodies what?"

"Your bodies don't seem to be human anymore. At least they've changed enough so that ordinary human physiology doesn't apply. I don't know how the hell I can help you if I can't measure what is normal."

"For one thing, Ezra has sleep apnea, a bad case of it."

Ezra interrupted. "What Daniel means is that I snore. He believes I sound like a truck driver and Presley is of the opinion it is the sound of a boxer with a broken nose."

"Ezra, what happens is that you stop breathing in your sleep every few minutes. Then you gasp for air. That's what makes you snore." Turning back to Scott, Daniel continued. "I suspect it has something to do with how she died. She had pneumonia and couldn't breathe. That's why I need you to examine her."

"You're asking me to treat a post-mortem case of obstructive sleep apnea for a ghost?"

"That's what I'm asking you to do. I need to rule out any obstruction. If it is central sleep apnea, which is what I suspect, it has deeper roots. Then we will have to find the underlying cause."

"Have you looked at her?"

"I don't have any equipment here. I couldn't."

Scott stared at the floor for several seconds before he answered. "Dan, I thought I'd seen some pretty outrageous things in my career, but this one tops them all! It's damned impossible to say no, with your being part of this. Let me call Sarah. We may be here awhile."

Scott called his wife to tell her he would be visiting for a while with Daniel, and then spoke to his receptionist to tell her he would be staying later with Dr. Hanson. After confirming that all the scheduled patients had been seen, he told her to go home.

When Scott again approached Daniel, Presley saw the shift in them from friends to doctors. "What do you think the best diagnostic approach is, Dan?"

"X-rays are the least invasive, but we probably need to do an endoscopy to really see what's going on."

"She would have to be sedated for that. Can she handle it?"

It surprised Presley to hear Ezra again interrupt. "You will not have to medicate me to examine me."

Daniel responded as a doctor to a patient. Presley recognized his bedside manner from Abilene. "Ezra, you would have to be sedated for the procedure. We need to put a small tube with a camera attached to it down your throat so we can see how you breathe when you're asleep."

"I will enter a stasis sleep. It is not necessary to make me sleep artificially. Vadim will help me to wake when the examination is over."

Scott started to say something and Daniel waved him silent. "Ezra, explain to us what you mean."

"It is possible to slow my body functions down and enter a deep sleep state, much like some animals do in the winter. I will not feel any physical sensation while in stasis. Vadim will join with me, and wake me when it is time."

Scott sounded incredulous. "Does she mean she's able to hibernate?"

"I think that's what she means." Daniel turned to Vadim. "Big dude, this is serious shit! She says you can bring her out of this. Can you?"

Vadim didn't answer. Instead his eyes began to glow, as did Ezra's. They turned to face one another, the silver and blue light creating a hazy mist between them. Presley tried to tune in to what was happening, but couldn't connect. She silently spoke to Daniel. *Do you know what they're doing?*

I have no idea.

For several seconds, no one said anything. With his eyes dimming only slightly, Vadim turned back to Daniel. "We have sufficiently joined. I can wake Ezra when it is time."

You fucking better wake her up! If anything happens to Ezra, and we can't bring her out of it, I'll send you back to wherever you came from with my bare hands!

Presley heard what Daniel had said to Vadim. She held her breath, waiting for Vadim's reaction. He seemed more amused than pissed. "Dr. Daniel Hanson, you do not trust that I will bring your lady back to you?"

Completely ignoring the light show he had just witnessed, Scott immediately picked up on the comment. "Your lady? Dan, I thought you and Presley had a thing going. You're involved with Ezra, too?"

Vadim didn't give Daniel a chance to respond. "Dr. Scott Brewer, you do not know that your friend has shared his bed with Presley Knowles and with Ezra?"

"Goddamn, Dan! You've been busy, haven't you?"

This time, Ezra jumped in. "That's how Daniel knows about my snoring. He cannot sleep when we are together."

Scott muttered, "I bet he can't!"

"If we're all finished talking about my sex life, can we get on with this?"

Daniel's exasperation tickled Presley. She couldn't help rubbing it in. *Now Scott knows! You really are a stud puppet!*

Fuck you!

Presley laughed. *Isn't that my line?*

"Would you two mind speaking up? Those of us here who are still mere mortals would like to know what the hell you're saying."

Presley happily offered Scott a recap. "I just called Daniel a stud puppet and he told me to go fuck myself. You didn't miss much!"

"Jesus Christ! I feel like the ringmaster in a frigging circus! Ezra, lie down on the table and go to sleep. Scott, get the damn endoscope. Vadim, do whatever the hell it is you need to do. And Presley, shut the fuck up! I'm going to take a piss." Daniel stormed out of the room.

Presley had to ask, "Has he always been this pissy?"

"Hell, yes! If he didn't do well on an exam, I would bunk with another friend for a few nights, or we risked having a fist fight."

"I hear you! He got into it with Vadim yesterday."

"They had a fight? I would have paid to see that."

"From what I understand, it wasn't pretty, was it, Vadim?"

"Dr. Daniel Hanson learned a lesson, to be sure. I do not take well to being attacked."

"Danny-boy sure as hell got himself into it this time! It figures his pecker got him into trouble. I always thought it might." Scott left to retrieve the endoscope.

Ezra and Vadim didn't move from where they stood. Presley realized they didn't know what to do. "Ez, you have to get on the table and go to sleep, like Daniel said."

"With his anger, I couldn't determine if he meant it."

"He did. Do you understand what they're going to do?"

"Yes. They will look inside my body to see why I snore."

"That's part of it. They really want to see why you are having breathing problems when you sleep." It occurred to Presley to ask, "Do you have any idea what could be wrong?"

"The scars from my other life are deep. While conceiving my new body, I may not have seen all the wounds. There were many to heal."

"I bet there were. Don't worry. Daniel will figure it out."

Ezra looked at the table. "It is high. How shall I get on it?"

"I jumped up, but you have a skirt on. Vadim, will you help her up?"

As easily as lifting a small child, Vadim scooped Ezra up and cradled her in his arms. Before putting her on the table, Vadim reassured Ezra. "Do not be concerned. I know what must be done." Presley sensed deep tenderness in Vadim as he kissed Ezra's forehead and then gently put her on the white paper covering the table.

"Vadim, is this dangerous? I mean, her going to sleep like this?"

His matter-of-fact tone did not cushion the impact of what he said. "When Ezra enters stasis, not only her body, but also her consciousness will sleep. She cannot wake herself. She is trusting me to bring her back."

"You mean, if you don't wake her, she will stay asleep?"

"Yes."

"For how long?"

"It is possible to remain in stasis for many years before waking. The time is unknown."

"Ez, you're sure about this? They could just give you a shot. It will make you sleep for a while. You don't have to take this risk."

Ezra took Presley's hand. "But I do, Presley. For Daniel to see, I must allow. If only my body sleeps, what is hidden will not become visible. I must step back and allow the healer in Daniel to emerge. It is the only way I will heal and he will understand."

"She again speaks in riddles, Ninotchka. Do not encourage her to do so. Allow her to sleep, and trust that I will wake her when the time comes."

Presley stepped back and allowed Vadim to stand by the table. "Take care of her, Vadim. Bring her back to us."

"I shall, Presley Knowles."

Ezra closed her eyes. Presley stayed with her as long as she could. But just like a radio station fading out in a car, Ezra's frequency disappeared. Not wanting to distract Vadim, Presley swallowed the fear that welled up in her throat.

Vadim held Ezra's hand and remained focused on her. When Daniel returned, he saw Vadim by Ezra. "Is everything all right?"

"Ezra's asleep, and Vadim is hanging on to her." Presley grabbed Daniel's arm and pulled him aside. "Daniel, whatever you do, don't mess with Vadim. Let him stand there and hold her hand, or whatever he needs to do. He's the only one that can wake her up."

Daniel nodded his understanding. When Scott wheeled in the cart with a monitor on top, Daniel went to help him. "Set it up on the other side, Scott. Let Vadim stay with her."

The two men quickly got everything set. Even with Ezra's slowed breathing because of her stasis, they could already hear her difficulties. She would intermittently gasp for air, with a sound like someone choking. Then she would snore, as she tried to breathe. "Dan, there is something seriously wrong here."

"I know. I've been listening to it for two nights. If she weren't already dead, I think she would have suffocated by now."

Scott pointed to the blanket. "Presley, cover her up. Her body temperature is falling. She feels cold."

Presley got the blanket. Before throwing it over Ezra, she put her hand on her leg. "She feels like ice!"

Again fear welled up in her throat. If not for the choking noise and intermittent snoring, Presley would have thought her a corpse. Vadim quietly said, "Ninotchka, do not worry. Ezra will come back. She has gone very deep, but I am there with her."

Presley nodded, unable to speak. The thought of losing her sister again broke her heart. She shook herself out of that thought and finished covering Ezra. She tucked the blanket around her, and then got out of the way.

Daniel and Scott had gone to the sink to wash their hands before putting on latex gloves. When they returned to Ezra, Scott deferred to Daniel. "Dan, do you want me to thread it or do you want to do it?"

"I'll do it. You watch the monitor." Daniel carefully threaded the flexible tube down Ezra's throat. Presley winced watching him do it, but Ezra didn't stir. Scott noticed it too.

"She's really out, Dan. She hasn't moved at all."

"I know she's out. I can't feel her."

"What do you mean?"

Tell him, Presley, I can't right now.

"Scott, the four of us are wired together. It's like we are plugged into each other. Ezra is unplugged right now. I can't feel her, and neither can Daniel. Vadim is the only one holding the wire."

"You're sure he's got her?

"I'm sure."

Daniel continued maneuvering the tube down her throat. "Scott, do you see anything?"

"Not yet, Dan. Everything looks normal. Keep going."

Daniel's focus was nearly as intense as Vadim's. Presley saw sweat running down Daniel's face and into his eyes. She took a handful of tissues and quietly said, "Let me get the sweat out of your eyes."

Daniel nodded, and stopped while Presley dried his face. When he resumed threading the tube, Scott directed him. "Dan, very slowly, go a little farther down."

Daniel meticulously followed Scott's instruction. Presley watched the screen as the camera moved ever so slightly. Suddenly Scott said, "Hold it, Dan. Back it up."

Presley saw the camera recede, and then Scott said, "Jesus, no wonder she can't breathe. Don't try to push the endoscope any further. Her trachea is nearly flat."

"Scott, take the camera. I need to see what you're seeing."

Scott and Daniel switched places. As Daniel watched, he

saw Ezra's trachea flatten at the point where Scott held the camera. She suddenly gasped, and forced the passage open again. Then she snored, pulling in as much air as she could in one breath.

Scott moved the camera slightly deeper. "Do you see how flat the tube gets? I've seen this in patients with advanced muscular dystrophy. It's like she has a degenerative muscular disease."

"She did, a very long time ago. Her scoliosis must have compressed her trachea. When she's awake, she has the muscle support to hold it open. When she is sleeping, she relaxes and the muscle memory takes over."

Presley had been quietly standing on the side listening. "Daniel, is that why she got pneumonia?"

"Probably. If she hadn't, she wouldn't have lived much longer with this. She would have suffocated in her sleep."

"Can you fix it?"

Scott glanced at the screen as he turned the camera. "She's going to need surgery to correct this. We may have to insert a stent to hold her throat open."

"She's not going to need surgery, or a stent." When Daniel turned around, it startled Presley to see his eyes shining the color of a Kansas sky on a clear day. "Vadim, do you have her?"

"Yes, Daniel. She is doing well."

"You know what I'm going to do?"

"Yes. It is what Ezra expected."

"You do your thing, and now I'm going to do mine." Daniel took off the tight gloves as quickly as he could and tossed them aside. He put his hand on Ezra's throat. "Presley, watch the screen and tell me when you see her throat opening. Scott has to hold the endoscope steady so he doesn't injure her."

As Presley watched the screen, she could hardly believe what she saw. The pink flesh of Ezra's throat turned blue, the same color as Daniel's eyes. Just like inflating a long balloon, the blue tube opened. "Daniel, you're doing it! Her throat is opening!"

"Is there enough room for Scott to move the camera deeper?"

"He has plenty of room."

Again, Scott glanced at the screen. "She's right. I can see where I'm going now." He continued to watch the screen as he threaded the camera deeper into Ezra's chest. "Her whole damn respiratory system is blue! What the hell are you doing, Dan?"

"I'm healing her. It's what she wanted me to do."

Presley again wiped Daniel's face. "Do you know your hand is blue?"

"Yeah, I know. And it's hot as hell! Scott, can you tell if she's open in her lungs?"

"Almost there, buddy." With the finesse of a microsurgeon, Scott navigated the tiny camera through Ezra's chest. "There they are, moving like bellows on a pipe organ. She's open, Dan!"

"Remove the endoscope, Scott. I want Vadim to wake her up." He continued to hold his hand on Ezra's throat. "Tell me when you're clear."

Scott slowly pulled the long tube out of Ezra's throat. Presley watched the extraction on the screen. "Okay, Dan, all clear. It's out."

Once Scott had fully removed the tube, Presley went to stand by Vadim. "How is she?"

"She is quiet, Ninotchka, The examination did not disturb her."

"Vadim, wake her up." Presley could see the concern on Daniel's face. But more than that, she felt it. She knew Daniel had the same fear she did, that they had lost Ezra.

In the latest of the many extraordinary moments Presley had recently witnessed, Vadim's solid body thinned until only silver vapor hung in the air. Then, the vapor moved. It hovered over Ezra's body and then disappeared into Ezra's chest.

No one said a word. The three incarnates stood in awe as they watched the inner workings of two eternal beings. When the mist emerged from Ezra's chest, it spiraled into a blue and silver braid. The braid separated, with the silver one coalescing once again into Vadim. The blue one hung suspended over Ezra, a delicate cloud of feminine haze. Then, as if it were being absorbed by a sponge, it faded into her chest.

A moment later, Ezra opened her eyes and smiled.

Chapter Twenty-One

Daniel always slept with his cell phone by the bed. He never knew when the hospital might call him for an emergency. When it rang, he automatically grabbed for it, and answered as he always did. He'd forgotten he'd told his service to pick up his calls.

"Hello. Dr. Hanson speaking."

"Hanson? This is Eric. Where the hell are you?"

Daniel sat up in bed. Ezra lay beside him, sound asleep. He muttered into the phone, "What time is it?"

"In Abilene, it's ten o'clock. In New York, that would be eleven o'clock."

"How did you know I'm in New York?" As the fog of sleep evaporated from his head, Daniel fully realized he had Dr. Richards on the line. "I didn't tell you or anyone else where I went."

"Just a hunch. I looked up the address of the Knowles woman. You're with her, aren't you?" Daniel again looked at Ezra, sleeping peacefully beside him. He smiled, realizing that she hadn't snored all night and her breathing appeared normal. "Dan, are you still there?"

"Yeah, Eric, I'm still here."

"You didn't answer me. Are you with Presley Knowles?"

"Well, I'm in her apartment, but I'm with someone else right now."

"Who the hell are you with?"

"A friend of Presley's. Her name is Ezra."

"Jesus Christ, Hanson! Are you taking Viagra?"

"Don't need it. I'm doing all right on my own."

"Excuse me, while I live vicariously for a moment! You're there with two women?"

"Yes."

"No damn wonder you left on personal leave! I figured if someone had died, you would have told me."

Daniel couldn't help himself. He burst out laughing at the irony of Eric's comment.

"What in blue blazes is so funny?"

That set Daniel off again. He tried to compose himself. No way in hell could he tell Eric the truth, so he covered with a wisecrack. "Well, old man, these two ladies have tried to kill me over the last few days, but so far, I'm still kicking."

"Are you drunk?"

"Hell, no! I'm as sober as a judge, thank you very much! Are you going to tell me why you called?"

"To find out if your sorry ass is in trouble, that's why! It's not like you to just disappear and not say a word to anyone."

"I'm all right. Some things came up I had to handle." He swallowed the laugh that bubbled up from that one.

"It sounds like it's been up for the last three days, for God's sake! Put it back in your pants, Hanson, and get your ass back to Abilene. We need you here."

That sobered Daniel like nothing else could have. "Who's covering for me?"

"I have a couple of the new residents covering. But they don't have the emergency room experience you have. Luckily, you were still here for that car accident the other day."

"Eric, my plans are up in the air, for more reasons than I can explain."

"You're a little old to be sowing your wild oats, Hanson." Daniel could hear Eric's temper rising. "There are people here who depend on you. You have responsibilities that you seem to have forgotten."

"I haven't forgotten them, Eric. Far from it."

"Then, I will ask you again. When are you coming back to Abilene?"

"I don't know, and that's the truth. There is more going on than I can talk about. I have issues here that are personal."

"Well, Hanson, you're going to have to decide what's more important to you, being a doctor or getting laid. I'm working on the schedule for next week. Are you on it or not?"

"Will you give me until tomorrow to let you know?"

"I can hold it until tomorrow morning. If I don't hear from you by then, you're not on it. Understood?"

"Perfectly. You'll hear from me by then."

"Don't disappoint me, son." Eric hung up.

Daniel closed his phone. Ezra put her hand on his arm. He hadn't realized she'd woken up. "Daniel, you are upset."

"Did you hear what just happened?"

"Yes. I heard what was said, and I also heard your heart."

"What did you hear?"

"I heard your home calling to you, and I heard the song of a healer pulling you back."

"Ezra, what the fuck am I going to do? This is an impossible situation! I'm damned if I do and damned if I don't."

"Nothing is impossible, Daniel. Spirit provides."

Daniel tried to temper his impatience. "Ezra, this is the real world. Things aren't as simple here as you seem to think they are."

"You do not understand the ways of spirit, Daniel. We are never given more than we can manage, and where there is true need, a door will open."

Right on cue, Presley knocked. "Ez, Daniel, are you guys all right? It feels like something's going on."

Daniel shouted back. "Something is. We need to talk."

Presley came in. "What's going on?"

"Where's Vadim? I want him in on this."

Presley pointed toward the bathroom. "He's been in there for a while. I think he might be having trouble. The food he's eaten finally worked its way through. This is the first time he's had to seriously go."

Daniel threw back the blankets and got out of bed. He knocked on the bathroom door. "Vadim, if you're having problems, tell me. Don't forget, I'm a doctor. I can help you if you're having a hard time."

In a strained voice, Vadim answered. "I do not need your help, Dr. Daniel Hanson! A grown man takes care of his business alone!"

"Yeah, and a Cossack shouldn't kick a gift horse in the mouth!" Daniel came back to Presley. "He needs warm water to flush his bowel. Do you have any sort of douche kit that has an enema nozzle?"

"I might. Let me check in the closet."

While Presley rummaged in the closet, Daniel put on his clothes. He could feel Ezra studying him. "What are you looking for, Ezra?"

"I am looking for the answer, Daniel. It is inside of you. I hope to help you find it."

"Good luck."

Presley came back carrying a small box. "Is this what you want?"

"That will do the trick. Now, Ms. Knowles, if you care about him as much as you say you do, take it in there, and make him use it."

"You're joking, aren't you?"

"No, I'm not. I would do it, but you heard him. He won't let me. Fill the bag with warm water, and then attach the hose and the small nozzle. You should be able to figure out the rest."

"What if he won't let me?"

"Tell him if he doesn't let you help him, I'll be in. He's

hardly in a position to argue." Daniel glanced at the door. "Presley, he's having some serious pain, and he's shielding you from it. He needs help."

"Aren't you the one who's supposed to enter the lion's den?"

"My turn's coming. This one's got your name on it."

Presley didn't bother knocking. She opened the door and walked in, slamming it shut behind her. Daniel knew she could handle Vadim.

Daniel sat down on the edge of the bed. Ezra knelt behind him and rubbed his shoulders.

"I'm glad Presley is distracted by Vadim. I have a few minutes to figure out how to tell her I'm going back to Abilene today."

"You have made your decision, Daniel?"

"Hardly. I just know I've got to go back, if for nothing else, to get my affairs in order." Daniel reached around and pulled Ezra onto his lap. "I'll have to see if I can get a flight out of New York this afternoon. You'll have to get back there the way you came."

"I am invited to accompany you?"

"You damn well better accompany me! By the way, how do you feel today? You know you didn't snore last night."

"I am very well, thank you. My throat is open and strong. I knew you could fix it." Ezra's eyes sparkled. "And you slept well, Daniel?"

"Like a baby. It's the first really good night's sleep I've had in days."

"That means I can share your bed and you can rest?"

"Oh, yes, pretty lady, you can certainly share my bed, although the vote's still out on how much rest I'll get."

"I will let you sleep, sometimes."

Daniel gently squeezed her breast. "Not too often, I hope?"

"You have to rest. I do not want you exhausting yourself loving me!"

Daniel laughed. "My dear, that's a distinct possibility."

"I want to travel with you, Daniel."

"You haven't made the papers yet, Ezra. You can't get on a plane without ID."

"I will make the papers for Vadim and myself before we leave. But we do not need them to go back to Abilene."

"We do if we intend to fly."

"Daniel, you can come with me, I do not have to go with you."

"Say that again."

"You can travel with me. If we leave from Presley's home and reenter inside your home, no one will see."

"You're serious, aren't you?"

"Yes, indeed! You are not yet strong enough to suspend and travel on your own. But you can if I am with you."

"No shit!"

"If you are talking about Vadim, he is managing with Presley's help."

Daniel wasn't sure if she meant that as a joke, or if she meant it seriously. Then she smiled. He knew she had just yanked his chain. "Ezra, this is going to be some trip. Now, we just have to tell Presley and Vadim."

While waiting on Presley and Vadim, Ezra took all her new clothes out of the closet and put them on the bed. She studied each article of clothing intently before choosing an outfit to wear. Daniel's curiosity got the best of him. "Ezra, what are you doing?"

"I had to pick the clothing I will wear to travel. Since I will only be able to take with me what is on my body, I want to make sure I can re-create all my clothes once we are at your home."

"I can't take my suitcase home?"

"No. When we suspend, only that which is attached to our bodies will go with us. We cannot transport luggage."

"But I can take my wallet and cell phone, right?" Daniel

patted his pockets to make sure he had them. "They have everything I need to take with me. Oh, yeah, and my keys. I can't get into my house without my keys."

"Whatever you carry on your body will go with you." Ezra gathered the clothes she couldn't take and returned them to the closet.

"Once we talk to Presley and Vadim, you have to make your identification. You'll need to take your ID with you."

"I will travel in my new denim trousers. They are comfortable, and they have pockets the same as yours. I will carry my papers in them."

"Before you tackle creating IDs, you and Vadim have to pick second names. You'll need to have full names on your documentation."

"We'll ask Presley for help. She is very imaginative."

"Help with what?" Presley had just come out of the bathroom.

"Help with picking last names for these two illegal aliens. How's Vadim?"

"Better. The threat of your coming in did the trick. He preferred my assistance to yours. Once we got the water in him, he had an easier time of it. You were right about flushing him out. It worked."

"I had to go to medical school to learn what my mother always knew, except she added the embellishment of a soap chip to the process."

"Didn't that burn?"

"Yes, which is why it's a good thing I went to medical school to learn the right way to do it." Presley had closed the bathroom door behind her. "Is he finished?"

"He'll be out in a minute. I made him an impromptu bidet with the hose. He's using it now."

"Any thoughts on names?"

"Actually, I do have some suggestions. I thought Ezra Ekberg, like Anita Ekberg in *La Dolce Vita* and Vadim Ivanov, like Nikolai Ivanov in the Chekhov play."

"Those aren't bad. What do you think, Ez?"

"I like the name Ezra Ekberg. And I like it when you call me Ez, the way Presley does."

"And I like the name Vadim Ivanov." Vadim had finally emerged from the bathroom. "It is a good, strong name from my time. It suits me."

"Then I'll show Ezra the samples I found and she'll create the IDs in a few minutes." Daniel braced himself for what he had to do. "Now that you're both here, we need to talk."

Vadim put his arm around Presley's waist. Daniel could see he already knew. Vadim had positioned himself to support Presley once he made his intentions known.

"Why do you look like you're about to tell me someone died? Daniel, what's going on?"

"Ezra and I are going back to Abilene today. I got a call from the hospital. They need me."

As he'd expected, Presley did not take the news well. "Mother fuck, Daniel! Just like that, you're leaving? And taking Ezra with you?" A sob erupted from deep inside Presley's chest. She pushed Vadim's arm away and ran to the living room.

Daniel went after her. He beat Vadim into the living room, without having any awareness of having gone through the door. Not stopping to think about what he had just done, he grabbed Presley's arm. "Will you let me explain, for Christ's sake?"

"What's to explain, Daniel? You're leaving. End of story, right?"

"Fucking wrong, Presley!" Daniel turned Presley around to face him. Tears streamed down her face like liquid diamonds. "You know damn well how we're connected. We will never be separated, not even if we want to be." He brushed an auburn curl back from her forehead and ran his finger down her scar. "And, I hope you know, I don't want to be."

"You don't?"

"No, I don't." Ezra and Vadim had joined them in the living room. Daniel didn't care. "Ezra and I are going back to Abilene, but I haven't made any decisions yet. My life is there. I can't just walk away from it."

Presley laid her head against Daniel's chest and sobbed. "I don't want you to go, and I don't want Ezra to go. It feels like my heart is being ripped out."

The intensity of Presley's heartache nearly brought Daniel to his knees. Vadim stepped in. "Ninotchka, Dr. Daniel Hanson will be back. He likes your pussy too much to not want more!"

Vadim's crude remark hit Presley like a glass of cold water thrown in her face. She lifted her head and stared at Vadim in utter disbelief. "What the fuck did you say?"

"Dr. Daniel Hanson wants you in his bed. He may leave now, but he will be back to get more pussy."

"How can you say that in front of Ezra? That's the rudest thing I've ever heard!"

Rather than being upset, Ezra calmly agreed. "My sister, Vadim only speaks the truth. Daniel is quite intoxicated with your heat. My loving him is not the same as when you are with him. He will certainly want to be with you many more times."

Presley took a step back and looked squarely into Daniel's eyes. "Are they right? Will you come back to be with me?"

"Do you want me to?"

"Yes, of course I do! That is, if Vadim doesn't kill you when you touch me."

"As I understand it, he's missed his chance. He can't kill me now."

"Dr. Daniel Hanson is correct. I cannot kill him. But I can take him in hand as I did before, if he should deserve it."

"I'll keep that in mind, Big Dude." Hoping to keep Presley distracted, Daniel had an idea. "Vadim, after we leave, why don't you take Presley to the karaoke bar? Does she know you sing?"

"I have not told Presley Knowles that I sing."

"Sing what?" Presley walked away from Daniel and went to Vadim.

"Songs, of course."

"C'mon, Ezra, let's go make some IDs. Let Vadim explain to Presley how he can sing."

Daniel showed Ezra the identification samples he'd found, as well as his Kansas driver's license and Presley's passport. He told her to make herself Swedish and Vadim Ukrainian. Beyond that, he had nothing more to offer her.

Ezra focused on the samples she had to use. Her whole body glowed with a blue aura as she concentrated.

With remarkable precision, she created each piece of ID, including accurate photos of her and Vadim. She went the extra mile and created green cards.

"Goddamn, Ezra, these look real!"

"They are real, Daniel."

"How did you do that?"

"I accessed the necessary information in the Akashic. Then I followed the trail back to its source. The government agencies that issue these documents now have Vadim Ivanov and Ezra Ekberg in their files. Once we had proper history, the documents manifested as you see them."

Daniel picked up their birth certificates. "So, you are thirty, and Vadim is thirty-two?" Daniel grinned. "You made Vadim younger than Presley? She'll love that!"

"It is his age. I did not choose it."

"Whatever you say, Ezra. I don't pretend to understand any of it. I'm just glad you have ID."

"Then what I have done is satisfactory?"

"It's more than that, Ez. It's perfect." As he gathered the documents from the table, Daniel heard Vadim singing. "I wonder how the hell he knows 'Kiss From A Rose'?"

Ezra and Daniel went back to the living room. Just as he had in the karaoke bar, Vadim stood in the middle of the living room, singing his heart out. Presley sat on the sofa, smiling like she'd just won the lottery.

Vadim sang the song like he'd written it, just as he had sung "Purple Rain" at the bar. When he finished, Presley applauded enthusiastically. "My God, you're good!"

"Thank you, Ninotchka. I am happy my voice pleases you."

"Presley, how did he know that song?"

"I had the Seal CD on top of the pile. I popped it in, and played 'Kiss From A Rose' for him. After listening to it one time, he sang it perfectly!"

"He did the same thing at the bar. Damned if I know how he does it, or how Ezra did this." Daniel gave Presley the documents.

"These look real!"

"That's what I said. Ezra says they are real."

"That's impossible."

"Apparently not. I hope we never have to find out, but Ezra says they are both officially documented. At least, they have the papers that say they are."

Ezra put her arm around Daniel's waist. "We are. No one can question our identity now."

"Well, then, maybe it's time to go home."

"Already?" The smile on Presley's face faded. "You haven't even had breakfast yet. I wanted to tell you both my news while we eat. "

"It's probably better if I don't eat. I don't want to throw up in my living room. Tell us your news now. What happened?"

"I got an e-mail from the *Times* this morning. They like my work, and really like the Eisenhower piece I did. They want to talk to me about a staff position writing feature articles for them."

"Considering that Eisenhower story nearly got you killed, it seems only right you should get something more than a paycheck from it. Congratulations!"

"Thanks. Vadim told me that it's karmic balance. Maybe he's right."

Ezra agreed. "It is your karmic reward for allowing your

destiny to unfold. Indications are you will be quite successful in this work."

"Thanks, Ez. Hearing that helps me know what to tell them if they make me an offer." Presley gave Ezra back her documents. Then she opened her arms for a hug. "You know, I expect you to phone home as soon as you two are in Abilene. If I don't hear you, make sure Vadim does." Presley's silver tears dripped onto her shirt.

Ezra tucked everything into her pockets and then hugged Presley tightly. "Remember, my sister, we are only a thought away."

"I'll try to remember."

"I must speak to Vadim, and explain what we are about to do so he understands."

"Will we be able to visit?"

Ezra smiled. "That's why I need to explain."

Ezra and Vadim went into the kitchen, leaving Daniel and Presley in the living room. "So, this is it?"

Daniel took her in his arms. "Presley, for God's sake, stop acting like you'll never see us again! That really is impossible!"

"Sorry. I'm not usually such a wuss. But, fuck, Daniel, the last few days haven't exactly been easy."

"I know. At least I'm leaving you in capable hands."

"You are talking about Vadim, aren't you?

"He loves you, Presley, and will go to the mat for you. Don't tell him I said this, but I like him."

"Yeah, I do too."

"I know."

"Are you going to tell Scott you're leaving?"

"He left the door open for me yesterday. He knows I'm adjusting to everything that's happened, and that I need some space to think through what I want to do. I'll call him after I've made my decision."

"It's amazing he was so cool with it. After he got over the shock of what happened, he seemed fine."

"That's why we're still friends. He's the man!"

"No, you are, remember?"

"I do." Daniel kissed Presley's forehead. "We have to go. Ezra is waiting."

"All right then. Let's do this."

Daniel and Presley went to the kitchen. Daniel nodded toward Presley, and Vadim immediately put his arms around her. Ezra threaded her arm through Daniel's. "Are you ready?"

"Ready as I'll ever be." Without another word, Ezra and Daniel disappeared into a blue cloud. The mist faded and they were gone.

Stay with Vadim and Presley in New York, continue reading
Follow Daniel and Ezra to Abilene, turn to page 330

Chapter Twenty-Two

Vadim held Presley for several minutes as she cried. Not only did the uncertainty about their future overwhelm her, but Daniel and Ezra leaving had broken her heart.

"Ninotchka, you must quiet yourself. Dr. Daniel Hanson and Ezra Ekberg will be back."

In spite of her grief, Presley had to smile. She had grown accustomed to Vadim using Daniel's full name. Hearing him use Ezra's new name for the first time somehow cheered her up.

"Vadim Ivanov, I need to blow my nose!"

She grabbed a wad of paper towels and wiped her nose. Even her mucous had turned silver. "Jesus, Vadim, what's next? Am I going to pee silver?"

"My urine is yellow. I expect yours will also remain so."

"That's a comfort." Presley dried her face, and then tossed the towels into the garbage. When she tried to get a bead on Ezra and Daniel, her head crackled with static. She couldn't hear or see anything. "Do you feel them? I can't. I'm too upset."

"They are still suspended. Ezra is helping Daniel to focus; he is disoriented. He must concentrate on his home, and then Ezra will take them there."

"Is Daniel all right?"

"Indeed he is. He now has a strong image of his house, and they are moving in that direction."

Presley again tried to calm herself so she could hear Ezra. "I still don't hear anything, Vadim. Are they in Abilene yet?"

"They are coming into form now."

Presley waited. Suddenly, as clear as a church bell, she heard Ezra's voice in her mind. *We are in Daniel's living room. All is well.*

"Vadim, did you hear?"

"I did." Vadim grinned. "You do not think I am taking Ezra Ekberg's calls?"

Presley swatted his arm. "Smart ass!"

Presley, can you hear me?

Daniel?

I made it! I'm home!

How do you feel?

Shaky, and queasy. Good thing I didn't eat. I would have lost it.

No wonder! Scotty just beamed you to Abilene.

I feel like Dr. McCoy. I signed up to practice medicine, not to have my atoms scattered across the country.

Well, it seems they all came back together. Is everything accounted for?

For the first time, Presley felt the ripple of Daniel's laughter move through her like she had felt Vadim's. *Everything you care about is back and already getting hard!*

Good to know.

By the way, remember earlier, when I chased you into the living room?

I remember.

I didn't go through the door. Ezra will have to explain that one to me.

When you find out, let me know too.

I will. Now I really am hungry. I have to see what I've got to eat here. Later.

It was as if he had hung up a phone. Daniel's voice simply

stopped. Vadim wrapped his arms around her. "You see, they are safe."

"Thank God!"

"Are you feeling better after speaking to Daniel?"

"Much."

"Then perhaps we should make the most of our time alone."

Presley could feel Vadim pressing himself into her ass. "You horny son of a gun! Aren't you hungry? We haven't eaten anything today. I'm starved!"

"The nourishment I need is not for my belly. My appetite is not for food, it is for you."

Presley turned around to face Vadim. "Well, why didn't you say so?"

"I just did, if my memory serves me."

Presley threaded her fingers through Vadim's hair. "What do you want to do?"

"Love you."

"How?"

"As I did before, when you sold yourself to me."

"You mean when I was a whore?"

"You read me well, Presley Knowles."

Presley nuzzled Vadim's neck. She could smell him, his scent always stronger when he got hot. For her, it had become the ultimate aphrodisiac. "What did whores do four hundred years ago?"

"I expect the same thing they do now. They opened their legs for men willing to pay."

Remembering Ezra's ability to manifest money, Presley teased him. "Well, then, I guess you'd better tell me what you're willing to pay for my services."

Vadim smiled. "I will pay you what you are worth." He stepped away from her and reached into the garbage. He pulled out the wad of towels she had just thrown away.

"Well, that sure as hell won't get you so much as a good grope!"

"How about these?" Vadim unfolded the towel. Inside the towel where she had dried her tears lay a small pile of glistening stones. He poured them into her hand.

"My God, Vadim!" The stones sparkled like starlight. "These are diamonds!"

"I told you I would pay what you are worth. That is only a down payment!"

"You've been watching too much television!"

"I disagree. Television is my window to your world. I must learn how to be a modern man to be with you."

Presley carefully put the stones on the table, and then put her arms around Vadim's neck. "You have to learn to function here, but I don't want you to become a modern man. I love what you are, and who you are."

Vadim held her tightly. "That is the first time you have spoken of love to me, Ninotchka."

"I thought you knew. I love you."

"The power of saying the words strengthens our bond. I also love you."

"I know you do."

Then Vadim kissed her. His hunger moved through Presley like a gust of wind. The flavor of cherry wine mixed with the taste of rich herbs, creating an ambrosial nectar of love. He picked her up and carried her to the bedroom.

Images filled Presley's mind, erotic pictures of how they'd loved in another time. She knew what he wanted. "Put me down, Vadim. I have to change clothes."

"My Ninotchka remembers!"

"You bet your Cossack ass I do! I'll be right back."

Presley disappeared into the closet. In the back, with her formal clothes, she found an ankle-length gray silk skirt. When the flared skirt shimmered silver in her hand, she whispered, "Un-fucking believable!"

She quickly stripped naked, then put on the skirt and borrowed one of Ezra's new low-cut tops. She didn't fill it out as well as Ezra did but, nonetheless, it showed ample cleavage.

When she came out of the closet, she saw Vadim had taken off his shirt but still wore his jeans. Presley said nothing to him. She propped one foot on the bed and pulled her skirt up to her knee. Vadim circled her. He sent her a picture of a wolf closing in on its mate.

Presley's heightened awareness allowed her to see Vadim's face even though he stood behind her. His eyes had become steely ball bearings, and the intensity of his stare burned into her. But he made no attempt to touch her.

Her harlot's seduction continued. She put her leg down and approached Vadim. "You don't find me pleasing, Mr. Cossack?" Trailing her hand down his chest to his waist, she stopped just shy of his erection. "You already paid me. Don't you want to collect your goods?"

When she felt an incredible rush of power, Presley knew she had him. His face hardened and his eyes narrowed. "I have never had a whoring wench that could satisfy me. You think you are better than any of them?"

"I know I am! Lift my skirt and you will see."

"I am not ready to lift your skirt! You do not tell me. I will tell you when I am ready!"

Vadim's tone should have frightened her, but it didn't. He had once again become the warrior that had taken her with him so long ago. Presley had also disappeared. His Ninotchka picked up Vadim's hand and put it on her breast.

"You do not fool me! You want the softness of a woman!" Just as Vadim flexed his fingers to feel her breast, she pushed his hand farther down. "Lift my skirt, and you will never want another."

When Presley said those words, she experienced the strongest déjà vu in her life. She knew she had said the same words to Vadim before. It was as if they no longer stood in her bedroom. They were in an inn that had ceased to exist centuries ago. It had turned to dust just as they had. In an eerie re-creation of their past, Vadim roughly pushed her down onto the bed.

"Bare yourself for me, woman!"

With fire in her heart and flames in her eyes, Presley slowly dragged her skirt up her thighs. Vadim opened his jeans. For a moment, their eyes locked. The searing heat that passed between them spoke of a lifetime past and a new life begin-ning.

Vadim practically fell on top of her. He shoved her shirt up and squeezed her breasts. Presley squirmed, trying to lodge his prick between her legs. Vadim pulled back and growled, "I have paid well. You will not hurry me!"

Never believing she could contain such arousal, or be so brave, Presley hissed back, "If you are not man enough to take me, I will find someone who is!"

She shoved at Vadim's chest with all her strength. He didn't budge.

"Have you ever studied wolves, Ninotchka? There is only one dominant male in a pack. He mates for life, and attacks any challengers for his mate."

"Is that why you attacked Daniel?"

"Yes."

Vadim blatantly claiming her both excited and enraged Presley. She shoved at him again. "No fucking man owns me!"

Before Presley could vent her rage, Vadim thrust his pelvis forward and entered her. Presley gasped, and sunk her finger-nails into Vadim's biceps. Her nails pierced his skin and a thin line of blood ran down both arms.

"You are my woman, Ninotchka! Just as I will never want another, neither will you!"

With each stroke, Vadim poured more of himself into Pres-ley. Even though part of her resisted his assault, a deeper part thrilled at being claimed by such a potent man. Presley knew she could satisfy him. She had been the only woman who ever could.

As he had four centuries before, Vadim once again claimed her. Presley knew she would go with him no matter where he went. She had before, and she would again.

Go to page 336

Daniel knew Ezra held him, even though he couldn't see her. The disorientation he'd experienced the day before enveloped him again. Although not prone to panic, he found that this situation brought him close to a full-fledged attack. *Ezra, I feel like a blind man on a rollercoaster!*

Daniel, stay calm. I have you securely. You will not get lost.

This is the kind of spatial confusion that happens to pilots. I've lost my sense of direction!

There is no direction here, except that which comes from thought.

I don't understand.

We are between your world and mine. We can go either direction. Thought directs the movement. I am holding us still until you are able to form a picture of your home. Then we will move in that direction.

You mean we could move farther out if we wanted to?

We could, and we eventually will. But you are not ready for such a journey. You must learn to walk before you can run.

Point well taken. Talking to Ezra as if it were a normal conversation calmed him and nearly made him forget he had no physical body. *Talk me through what I need to do.*

Pick a room in your house and clearly picture it in your mind. See it as though you were standing in it. I will do the rest.

Daniel picked his living room. He saw his sofa, the pictures on the wall, and the grandfather clock in the corner. The bottle of Kentucky bourbon he'd bought the day Presley left still sat on his coffee table, with a tumbler sitting beside it. He hadn't finished the last glass he'd poured. That's when he realized he wasn't imagining the room. He was actually looking at it!

Years of medical training surfaced. He didn't let his concentration waiver. He held the image even as he felt movement. He felt like a dog sticking its head out of a car window as a rush of air seemed to hit him in the face. He looked down, and saw the bourbon and glass sitting on the table in front of him.

His knees gave out. Ezra caught him as he folded like a paper doll. She lowered him to the sofa. "Take a deep breath, Daniel. The dizziness will pass in a moment."

He did as she said, fighting back the nausea that welled up in his throat. Closing his eyes, he stayed still until his inner ear stabilized. The feeling of having to retch subsided, and he started to feel better.

He heard Ezra telling Vadim and Presley they'd had a successful trip. As he opened to hear their reaction, Presley's fear for him became palpable.

Daniel spoke to Presley directly, telling her himself that he had made the trip without incident, except for some lingering queasiness. Her obvious concern for his equipment made him laugh. He reassured her nothing had been lost in transit, and that all pertinent organs were functioning properly.

He still felt queasy, but it seemed to be more hunger pains now than motion sickness. "Ez, are you hungry?"

"Do you have any ice cream?"

"I have some homemade butterscotch ice cream. A local dairy makes it. You can have some after you have some real food."

He dug in his freezer and found some bacon, egg, and cheese Hot Pocket sandwiches. After he heated them for three minutes in the microwave, he and Ezra had lunch. Once he'd eaten, his stomach settled and he really felt like he'd come home.

While Ezra ate her ice cream, he called the hospital. He couldn't tell Eric he was already back in Abilene, but he could tell him about the schedule for the next week. While Daniel waited for the nurse's station to page Dr. Richards, the answer he needed hit him. He knew what he had to do.

"Hello, Dr. Richards speaking."

"Hello, Eric."

"Hanson? I didn't expect to hear from you until tomorrow."

"I wanted to let you know, put me on the schedule for the emergency room next week. It has to be three consecutive days. Going forward, I may have to cut it to two, but for the next few weeks, I can do three. Sorry to say, you'll have to take me off the regular schedule. I can't manage doing rounds anymore."

"Why not?"

"My reasons are personal. If it's a problem holding a part-time position with the schedule I laid out, then I'll have to resign."

"You know damn well I'll put you down for the three days. It would be easier on you if I could mix them up."

"No, I've got other commitments. If you can accommodate me, I'll be able to pull my emergency room shifts. Otherwise . . ."

Eric interrupted. "You told me. You'll resign."

"I'll have no choice."

"Well, son, I don't know what the hell you've gotten yourself into, but I'll give you what you want. Does Sunday, Monday, Tuesday work next week?"

Daniel smiled and winked at Ezra. "That's perfect."

"I'll notify personnel about the schedule change. You're sure about this?"

"I'm sure."

"I hope you'll eventually tell me what the hell is going on."

"Maybe sometime. Not just yet. Oh, by the way, is the pediatric volunteer program still accepting people?"

"I'm sure they are. They can always use help with the kids."

"Presley's friend Ezra may be interested in volunteering."

"She's coming back with you?"

"Yup. Wait until you meet her. You'll see why I'm bringing her home with me."

"Goddamn, Hanson!"

"See you on Sunday."

When Daniel put down his cell phone, Ezra jumped up and hugged him, nearly knocking him over.

"Whoa, Ezra! What's that for?"

"For trusting, and for finding the answer."

"Do you think it will work?"

"Your soul spoke, and you listened. It will work."

"Will it fly with Presley and Vadim?"

Ezra grinned. "What do you think?"

"I think I want to show you my bedroom. Did you finish your ice cream?"

"Yes, and I want some more. But it will wait until after you show me your bed."

"Didn't I say bedroom?"

"Yes. But it is your bed that interests me."

"Let's go upstairs. I'll show you both. Then I have to call the bus station and get a schedule to Kansas City. My car's still at the airport."

"You do not have to take a bus!"

"Yes, I do! I can't appear out of thin air at an airport parking lot!"

"As you wish, Daniel. We will travel your way here."

Daniel took Ezra's hand and led her upstairs to his bedroom. "Ez, how adventurous are you?"

"Daniel, I want to do everything there is to do with you. I know what you did with Presley. I want to do all of that, and more."

"I saw a side of you with Vadim that you haven't shown to me. You're a strong woman, Ezra, able to hold your own in any situation. I wouldn't mind feeling some of that strength in the bedroom."

Ezra's smile made Daniel pray for Vadim's stamina. "You wish me to be a dominatrix for you?"

"You know the word?"

"I heard it in your mind, and saw the black boots you would like me to wear when I spank you."

Daniel wondered if the beads of sweat on his forehead were blue. "Can you manifest them?"

In a heartbeat, Ezra's clothing disappeared. She stood in front of him wearing thigh-high leather boots and nothing else. She held one hand up in the air. A black leather paddle materialized in her hand.

"Jesus Christ!" Daniel stood in awe, the unbelievable beauty and strength of the woman in front of him taking his breath.

"Daniel, take off your clothes."

He didn't argue. Too flustered to try the clothes trick, he stripped to the skin the old-fashioned way. His erection jutted from his groin. Ezra shamelessly stared at it and licked her lips. He tried to read what she meant to do, but she blocked him.

"You enjoy my breasts, do you not, Daniel?"

"You know I do."

Ezra slowly approached him. When she got close enough, she lightly tapped his erection with the paddle. Daniel winced. "Kiss them. Show me how much you like them."

He knew she had read his fantasy about her, that she would force him to lick her tits. He didn't care. Ezra stood still as a statue as he kissed and licked her breasts. Only when he sucked on her nipples did she begin to show her arousal.

When she put her hand on his head to stop him, it surprised him to see her wearing long black gloves. She had somehow manifested them without him seeing her do it. "You will now kneel and pleasure me with your mouth."

He had always dreamed of a stacked blonde ordering him to suck her clit. He wasted no time. He knelt and buried his face in the blonde curls. When he circled her clit with his tongue, Ezra trembled. She tasted sweet, like honeysuckle and strawberries. He lapped at her until she moaned.

The moan turned into a command. "You will stop now!"

He could tell she had come close to her climax. So had he. "Stand and bend over!"

Determined to hold on, he reached deep inside and found the place where he had connected to Vadim. If he could do what Vadim did, maybe he could stop himself from spurting when Ezra swung the paddle.

Invoking the memory of Vadim's control from the day before, he braced himself. Ezra didn't hold back. The flat leather surface hit his ass with a *CRACK*. His balls tightened, but he didn't come. She smacked him again. His ass burned almost as much as his prick. She swatted him hard and fast, at least four, maybe five more times, he couldn't be sure. The scalding heat in his groin muddled his brain.

Suddenly she stopped and pushed him forward. "Sit down on the bed!" The authority in her voice told him he'd better damn well do what she'd said to do. He sat down.

Without any prelude, she straddled him. His cock slipped into her up to his balls. With extraordinary strength, she rode him. He dug his fingers into her ass, trying to keep from falling backward onto the bed. When he realized he could reach her anus, he acted on impulse.

Before she could stop him, he pushed his index finger into her asshole. Ezra squealed, partially stood up and then slammed back down onto his lap. With her climax upon her, Daniel held her still. Her pussy clenched when her muscles contracted, squeezing his cock with incredible force.

Again invoking Vadim, he heard himself say, "I am ready now." With those words, he allowed the steaming liquid in his balls to fill Ezra's body, and the fire in his blood to ignite her soul.

Chapter Twenty-Three

"You know, you could get off your lazy ass and help me unpack some of these boxes!"

Daniel looked at her as if she was being unreasonable. "Cut me some slack, Presley! I just got here. Anyway, this is your stuff. I don't know where you want to put any of it."

"You've been here half a fucking hour already. And excuse me! The boxes in the kitchen have the dishes, which you've been using for the last six months! Daniel, it's not hard. You open a box, take out a stack of dishes and put them in the cupboard!"

"Why are you being so frigging bitchy? You've been grousing about this move since the closing. If you remember, you jumped at the chance to get a bigger place to share with Ez and me when we are in New York. When I asked you last summer, your eloquent response was 'Fuck, yes!'"

"That was before I realized how much work moving is, and before I knew that Vadim and I would have to do most of it. Oh, and did I mention that was also before I knew I'd have an article due and that we'd be moving the same week as the christening?" Presley exhaled. Actually, she huffed.

Daniel completely ignored her rant and got up to get his briefcase. "Speaking of the christening, Scott sent this home with me today." He opened the case and took out a gift bag. "Sarah had two copies made already, one for each of us."

Presley took the bag and opened it. In a simple gold frame was a photo of her holding Scott and Sarah's new son, with Daniel looking on. "I still can't believe they asked me to be Daniel Scott's godmother. I've never been anyone's godmother before."

"Well, I'm the godfather to all three of their kids. Let's hope nothing ever happens to Scott and Sarah, or we'll need more space than we have here."

The photo made Presley laugh. "Look at the expression on my face. I'm standing there holding this baby, posing for the picture, and Vadim shoots me the thought, 'Ninotchka! This is my vision! I saw you holding this child! You did not conceive with Dr. Daniel Hanson!'" She did her best to imitate Vadim.

"Hey, that's pretty good! You've been practicing."

"A little."

"Anyway, that's how I found out he thought you might have a baby with me instead of with him. Ezra says that can't happen unless we want it to happen."

Presley patted her side. "Well, I still wear my trusty patch. Ez told me I don't have to now. She says I can consciously control when I conceive, like she does. I really don't want to test it."

"Well, we've been humping like rabbits for six months, and she hasn't gotten pregnant yet. She's doing something to stop it." Daniel glanced at his watch. "Where the hell are Ezra and Vadim, anyway?" They had gone for groceries an hour before.

"They don't know the Upper West Side. They're used to being in the Village. Tune in and make sure they aren't lost."

While Daniel went in search of Vadim and Ezra, Presley dragged a box of reference books into the third bedroom, which they had converted into office space. Daniel and Presley agreed that they needed a separate space to work, Presley for her writing and Daniel for whatever paperwork he had to bring home.

Presley had discovered several months before she couldn't write in the living room. There were too many distractions. When Vadim wasn't watching television, he'd have the stereo on. And when Daniel and Ezra were there, she'd talk to them instead of working.

Writing on staff for the *New York Times Magazine*, she had more frequent deadlines. When she'd almost missed one, she'd decided she couldn't wait until they moved to have a quiet place to write. That's when she'd crammed her desk into her bedroom so she could write without interruption. Now she had a separate room for it.

They had ordered another desk for Daniel to use. He seemed comfortable with his new schedule, three days a week in Abilene, in the emergency room, and four days in New York, in his new private practice with Scott. Both the hospital and Scott gave him flexible hours, so he could manage both jobs. Scott knew his commute didn't require travel time. However, in Abilene, they still marveled at how he could manage such a strenuous schedule.

Ezra loved working as a volunteer at Memorial Hospital in Abilene. She had started out in pediatrics and now also worked with the elderly. Once they got settled in from the move, she planned to work with Daniel at Scott's office. When Daniel asked Scott about hiring Ezra as his physician's assistant, he had only one stipulation. He told Ezra she can't be in the room while any man was having his blood pressure taken.

Daniel came into the room grinning.

"So, where are they?"

"God help us, there is a Häagen-Dazs store down the street. On the way back from the market, they stopped for ice cream."

"Oh, don't begrudge her that. Just be glad she's not gaining weight because she loves ice cream."

"In Abilene, I'm lucky if I can squeeze any real food in the freezer. We must have six different flavors of ice cream in there right now."

"Daniel, I hate to break this to you, but your love of Hot Pockets doesn't make them real food!"

"Says you!"

"You should be careful with that line! You know, that's what started this whole thing."

"I remember." The last six months had been a whirlwind of change. Actually, more like a cyclone.

"I went to Kansas and joined Dorothy in Oz. Thank heavens you made the trip with me."

"Would that make Ez Glenda the good witch?"

"What does that make me, Margaret Hamilton?"

"I told you once that you were a very beautiful, very bad witch. My opinion hasn't changed. After all, bad witches give the best head." Daniel swatted her ass. "You didn't know that's why I suggested this arrangement, Elphaba?"

"You should thank Pay-Per-View for your blow jobs."

"You'll have to explain that one."

"You haven't noticed every time I'm alone with you, Vadim checks out Pay-Per-View? I can gauge how many times we fuck every month by my cable bill." Presley bent over to open the box of books she had dragged into the room.

"I think we're behind this month. How about a quickie?" Daniel ran his index finger down the crack of her ass.

Presley stood up and handed Daniel the box opener. "Here, stop thinking with your dick and make yourself useful. Open those boxes against the wall for me. The labels fell off. I have no idea what's in them."

"Yes, Mom."

Presley flipped him the bird. Daniel patted his ass and made kissing noises with his lips. She could feel his heat, and would have loved to stop for a quick one. But fucking wouldn't get the unpacking done, and she really wanted to get it done.

They call that the nesting instinct. Didn't think you had it, but I guess you do.

Stop reading me and open the damn boxes!

One by one, Daniel zipped the razor down the taped boxes

and opened them. They were mostly books and papers, but he did find a box of shoes, a box of CDs, and Presley's Elvis clock.

He pulled the statue of Elvis out of the packing peanuts. The oversized guitar had a clock imbedded in it. "What the hell do you want to do with this artistic masterpiece?"

"My Elvis clock! That goes on my desk!" Presley took it and put it beside her computer. "I want it where I can see it."

"Remember, I'm sharing this office. I can't tell you how much I want to look at that when I'm in here."

"This clock is important to me. My parents gave it to me for my birthday. I'm his namesake, after all."

"Does that explain why you're so eccentric?"

"No, I'm peculiar by choice, not because of my name. But it does explain why my upper lip occasionally twitches."

Daniel chuckled. "I should have known better than to ask."

Presley pointed to the open boxes. "Where does that stuff go?"

"Most of it stays in here. But the shoes should be in your bedroom, and I'm sure Vadim will want the CDs in the living room."

"He asked me for them this afternoon. I didn't know where they were."

"Is he still going to do his Saturday night gig at the bar on Bleecker now that we've moved?"

"He loves singing there. I hope he does. But he doesn't like the subway."

"So, we'll take a damn cab! That's no reason to stop. Has he given any more thought to auditioning for a singing job that pays him something more than free drinks?"

Presley pulled another box out from under the desk and took out some newspapers. "He's started looking at these, but hasn't auditioned for anything yet."

"*Backstage* and *Variety*. Interesting. Does he understand the jargon they use?"

"I've explained most of it. He says he'll know when it's the right vehicle for him. He's watching the ads for it."

"With the inside track he has, he'll probably find it." Daniel tossed the papers back in the box. "Let me go change clothes, and then I'll come back and help."

"Gee, wish I'd thought of that."

"You did. That's where I got the idea."

"Very funny, Dr. Hanson."

Presley went back to the living room to get the picture. She put it on her desk, where she would be sure to see it. Vadim had asked her after the christening if she wanted to have children with him. She'd answered honestly. She wasn't ready, and didn't know if she'd ever want to have a family, given their situation.

Vadim simply said, "There is time. We do not have to decide now, Ninotchka."

They certainly had time. Presley looked at the picture of Daniel Scott and thought about how he would have a normal life. He would grow up, have a family, grow old, and die. What would he say when he became older than his godparents?

Over the last months, Presley had tried to look ahead to their future. Always, she would pull back from it, as the grand expanse of all the years ahead overwhelmed her. She went to the window, looked down at the street, and wondered how many more times they would have to move.

She had been so engrossed in her own thoughts, she didn't hear Daniel come back in the room. "Presley? What are you looking at?"

"I'm watching the people walking by. Daniel, how long do you think we'll be able to stay here? I don't just mean in this apartment, I mean in New York, or in Abilene? Eventually, people will notice we aren't aging."

"We can always say we have portraits stashed in my attic."

"I'm serious. Have you thought about what we're going to do? How are we going to manage this?"

"We have time to consider our options. Don't stress about

that now. Ezra says we'll learn to travel at will, between our world and theirs. We'll have choices we don't even know about yet."

"I suppose you're right. But it still scares me." She turned around. "I could use a hug."

When Daniel raised his arms to hug her, Presley noticed he had something in his hand. "What the hell is that?"

"I found it in our bedroom." Daniel handed Presley the strap-on dildo he had given her as a Christmas gift. "Since it belongs to you, I thought I would return it. Did I miss something today?"

Presley took the not-so-subtle gift from Daniel. "You know we haven't used this yet."

"Then why was it on our bed?"

"When I unpacked it today, Ez wanted to try it on."

Daniel grinned. "Did she say why?"

"She said something about having a housewarming party this evening, with the four of us. I can't imagine where she got such an idea, can you?"

"She no doubt accessed it from the Akashic."

"No doubt. I'm sure there will be a few more entries there tonight."

"From your mouth to God's ears."

Presley smelled Vadim just before she heard him. *Ninotchka?*

I'm here, Vadim.

Could you open the door? We forgot our keys.

"Did you hear?"

"I heard. If not for the grocery bags, they could have slipped in under the door."

Presley and Daniel went to help Ezra and Vadim with the groceries. As Presley expected, they had Häagen-Dazs and Hot Pockets, neither of which had been on the list. Vadim had also made sure to get plenty of milk and dark bread. Other than that, they'd gotten everything Presley had written down.

Since it was already dinner time, they decided not to cook

and called out for Chinese. After dinner, Presley tried to rally the troops to continue unpacking. Daniel wouldn't hear of it.

"No way in hell am I going to unpack boxes tonight. I want to enjoy our new home."

"Dr. Daniel Hanson is correct, Ninotchka. We all deserve a night to be together."

Ezra also vetoed the idea. "Presley, please! Can we not just be together tonight?"

Presley knew she wouldn't win this one. "You guys have made ganging up on me an art form."

Daniel offered no apology. "It's the only way to win an argument with you. It took a few months, but we figured it out."

Presley thought she already knew what they had planned. "Ezra, I think we are the live sex act entertainment for the evening."

"It is more than that, my sister."

"What does that mean?" Presley's alarms went off. "What the hell are the three of you up to?"

Vadim stood and raised his glass. Ezra and Daniel followed suit. "The three of us dedicate this night to you, Presley Knowles. If not for you, we would not be together." They all raised their glasses and drank.

Daniel continued. "The housewarming we have in mind for tonight is actually more of a Presley warming. We want to show you, each in our own way, how much we love you."

Ezra concluded the obviously rehearsed speech. "So, my beautiful sister, we all ask that you allow us the chance to love you, together."

Presley sat dumbstruck. Her companions were proposing a gang bang. They were the gang and she was the bang. She didn't know what to say.

Vadim broke the silence. "Ninotchka, do you trust me?"

"You know I do!"

"Dr. Daniel Hanson came to me and explained his plan. I agreed that we should do it."

"You're all right with this?"

"I certainly am. The experience will serve you, and will reinforce the connection we share."

Ezra took the initiative to get the evening started. "Come. We must change our clothes."

"Change into what?"

"Something I have brought through for tonight." Ezra led Presley into her and Daniel's new bedroom. "Here, Presley, put this on. I have one, too."

Presley unfolded the red material Ezra had given her. It took a second to register what she held. "For Christ's sake, Ezra, this is a lace bustier. And it doesn't have any cups or panties!"

"Isn't it wonderful? Mine is black." Ezra had already undressed. "Your garter belt and stockings are on the chair with mine."

Sure enough, draped over the chair were two garter belts with stockings, one red and one black. The stockings had lace tops which matched the bustiers. Ezra picked up the black set.

"Of course, Daniel had nothing to do with this."

Ezra sat on the bed to pull on her stockings. "Yes, he did! He found the pictures on the Internet for me to copy. He knew exactly what he wanted us to wear."

"I bet he did!"

"Please, do change into your lingerie. It will not be nearly as pleasurable for the men if you do not."

Presley kicked off her shoes and unzipped her jeans. "When you asked me for the strap-on this afternoon, was that because of tonight?"

"Yes. I wanted to make sure I could put it on."

"You're planning on using it with me?"

"Yes. Daniel asked me to."

Presley whispered, "That son of a bitch! He planned this whole damn thing!"

"My sister, it is not just Daniel. We all want to take you over the rainbow tonight."

Presley had never been one to say no to sexual adventure, but this one gave her pause. Even with the promise of immortality, with her three life partners solely focused on her, she wondered if she would survive it.

When Presley came out of the bedroom with Ezra, both outfitted in their costumes of the day, another shock awaited her. Vadim and Daniel had stripped naked. They were on the open sofa bed. "Oh, my God! Ezra, look! Daniel is blowing Vadim!"

"It is for you, Presley. The men know you have wanted this for months. They put aside their differences and agreed this would be a gift for you."

Presley circled the bed, looking at the action from all angles. Daniel had Vadim's cock in his mouth, blowing him like he'd been doing it his whole life. Presley knew Vadim's stages of arousal. She could tell he had a healthy head of steam up.

Suddenly, she felt him pushing his excitement at her. She pushed back, still ambivalent about the focus being on her.

Open to me, Ninotchka.

And then what, Vadim?

Then, we switch places, my beautiful one.

Since that first week in Abilene, she loved it when Daniel licked her. He hadn't done so recently, and she missed it. Tentatively, she opened herself to Vadim. A rush of heat hit her, like opening a furnace door.

She heard Daniel speak to Ezra. *Ez, the strap-on is in the office. Get it and put it on.* Without a doubt, Daniel had orchestrated this whole event.

He lifted his head. Vadim's cock popped out of his mouth. "All right, Ms. Knowles. It's your turn."

Vadim rolled off the bed and took Presley's hand. Like escorting a princess to her throne, he helped her onto the bed. Daniel's eyes burned into her as he opened her legs. "I knew red would be right for you. You're fucking hot!"

Daniel buried his face between her legs. When his tongue connected with her clit, it seared her like a branding iron.

Vadim crawled back on the bed. He massaged and kissed her breasts.

While the men worked her over, Ezra emerged from the office wearing the strap-on. With her tits and dick, she looked like an exotic hermaphrodite. She stood at the end of the bed and watched for several minutes. In her hyper-aroused state, Presley couldn't stop staring at Ezra's tits. They made her even hotter. She wanted to feel them pressed against hers.

Suddenly Ezra shouted, "Enough! Leave her!"

As if they were two schoolboys being reprimanded, Vadim and Daniel both stopped. They moved to either side of Presley, and Ezra crawled onto the bed. She crept toward Presley like a stalking cat, her eyes glowing like opals.

Presley had never seen Ezra like this. She emanated power and confidence, reminiscent of a high priestess at a sacrificial altar. Presley's heart pounded. Just before Ezra touched her, Vadim pinned one of her arms to the bed and Daniel pinned the other. Then they pinned her legs between theirs so they could rub their cocks against her thighs.

There she was spread-eagled on the bed, with the two men she loved holding her down. In what resembled a pagan ritual, Ezra penetrated her.

Presley had become accustomed to seeing a kaleidoscope of colors when she made love with Vadim, but this surpassed anything she had ever seen with him alone.

She released herself into the cosmic artist's palette where everything became color and light. An extraordinary sense of being those colors engulfed her. The fire in Ezra's belly moved into hers, the union of their womanhood manifesting the goddess in each of them.

Vadim and Daniel masturbated against her thighs. She understood her consorts were paying her homage as they allowed her femininity to fuel their potency and virility.

Ezra showed no mercy, pounding the dildo into her as if it were flesh and blood. Presley knew Ezra felt each stroke, and that she would fuck until her own climax hit. Rather than resisting, Presley relaxed into the exquisite torture.

Ezra's momentum increased, and the men rubbed harder. In the moment when time stopped and identities dissolved, a blinding flash of light coated Presley's inner vision. It seemed as though she floated in a pool of love so deep and so profound it obliterated everything she had ever known as real.

Vadim, Ezra, and Daniel floated beside her, and inside her. They shared one mind, one heart, and one soul. They had gone over the rainbow, together.

Read on for a sneak peek at
PRIVATE PARTY,
Jami Alden's newest novel!

1

Julie Driscoll was, without a doubt, the most beautiful bride Chris Dennison had ever seen. Her strapless ivory gown left her arms bare, and, if he closed his eyes, he could imagine how silky her skin would feel against his fingertips. Though her veil obscured her face, he could vividly picture wide, long-lashed eyes the color of the Caribbean sea at sunrise; her small, slightly upturned nose; and full pink lips. Her breasts swelled tastefully against the bodice of her dress, though even that was enough to make his mouth dry and his palms sweat. With the wide, poofy skirt of her wedding gown nearly spanning the entire width of the aisle of San Francisco's Grace Cathedral, she reminded him of a luscious dollop of whipped cream, tempting him to lick her up with one lusty sweep of his tongue.

His chest got tight as she approached, his stomach twisting in knots as every step led her closer to the altar. She was really going to go through with this. He'd had eighteen months to mentally prepare himself, and still the realization hit him like a fist in the gut. He clenched his hands into fists, took a deep, calming breath, and willed himself not to turn tail and run from the church as fast as he possibly could. He'd made a promise, and unlike some men in his family, when he gave his word he kept it.

"Who gives this woman in marriage to this man?"

Chris watched, a sour ache building in his stomach, as her father, Grant, lifted her veil to reveal a nervous-looking smile that didn't quite reach her eyes.

"Her mother and I do," Grant replied, and Chris swallowed back the curse screaming in his brain as Julie's groom, Chris's older half brother Brian, stepped forward to take her trembling hand.

"Where in the world is he? It's time to cut the cake."

"I'm sure he'll be here any minute." Julie Driscoll Dennison attempted to soothe the frazzled wedding planner. "Why don't you have one of the ushers check the bathroom, and I'll see if he's out in the lobby."

Honestly, you'd think Brian would know better than to disappear in the middle of the reception.

"Everything okay?" Wendy, Julie's maid of honor, sidled up alongside her and asked.

"I can't find Brian. He probably needed a moment to himself."

Wendy quirked a brow. "Right . . ."

Okay, so Brian wasn't exactly the introspective type, but still, it was his wedding day. God knew Julie was all but overwhelmed by it all. "I don't suppose you've seen him."

Wendy shook her head. "Where's his brother? I thought it was the best man's job to keep tabs on the groom."

"He left right after he did his toast," Julie said. She smiled a little when she thought of Chris's toast. So practiced, so polite. So unlike him. Chris wasn't the kind of guy who worried about what people thought of him, especially not the stuffy, overly self-important crowd attending her wedding. His easygoing, casual style made him stick out in this crowd, even as he tried to fit in.

Unlike Brian, who could have been a GQ cover model, Chris's dark brown hair was always a little shaggy, his big, muscular body always looking a little too big for his clothes. But he had looked absolutely delectable in his tux, the white shirt a seductive contrast to his skin, burnished from the strong Caribbean sun. Chris had always been gorgeous in a rough around the edges kind of way, and he'd only improved in the five years since she'd seen him last.

She closed her eyes, trying not to imagine the acres of tanned muscularity he had hidden under that tux. She'd thought she'd gotten over her silly teenage crush on Chris a long time ago, and her wedding day to his half brother was no time for her to resurrect it.

She mentally slapped herself. Today was her wedding day, for goodness sake. All of her months of hard work and planning had finally come to fruition, and now was not the time to revisit her long-dead infatuation with her fabulous groom's black sheep of a younger brother.

She exited the ballroom and made her way down a hall, stopping to chat politely with guests along the way. As she neared a utility closet, a thump sounded from behind the door. Then a giggle. Then a moan.

A decidedly masculine moan.

Her stomach somewhere around her knees, Julie had an awful premonition of what she would find behind that door.

"You son of a bitch." Her voice sounded very far away, like it came from the end of a long, echoing tunnel.

She squeezed her eyes shut so tight her eyelids cramped. This could not be happening. It simply couldn't.

But there was no mistaking Brian, frozen mid-thrust as he nailed another woman against the wall, who was gaping over his shoulder at her in a way that would have been comical under other circumstances.

She spared the other woman a quick glance. Ah, of course, the lovely Vanessa, Brian's newest assistant. She had suspected Vanessa's employment had more to do with her mile-high legs and oversize chest than her secretarial skills, and she kicked herself for stupidly giving Brian the benefit of the doubt. But the last time she'd caught him cheating he'd sworn to God, on his grandmother's grave, and the title of his prized Ferrari, that it would never, ever happen again. He'd promised that the next time he would have sex would be with Julie, on their wedding night. And with their wedding plans forcefully in motion, it had been easier to believe him than to admit she was about to make the biggest mistake of her life.

"Julie, it's nothing. It doesn't mean anything." Brian fumbled with his tuxedo pants, grabbing at his cummerbund as the trousers slid back down around his ankles. Vanessa had pulled her skirt down and made a dive to retrieve her underpants. The action sent Brian stumbling backward over a mop and bucket, and he landed on his ass in the middle of Vanessa's chest.

Julie had never been sucker punched, but she imagined this was what it might feel like. A sharp hit to the middle of her lungs, a sensation of all the air leaving her lungs, leaving her gasping like a dying trout. Pain radiated through her, accompanied by the icy burn of humiliation. Still, she grasped for control, trying not to let Brian see that she was blowing apart from the inside out, into a thousand tiny fragments. Her mind worked frantically, searching for the appropriate thing to do or say in a situation like this. But there was no sweeping this under the rug with social niceties.

Taking a mop handle and shoving it somewhere extremely painful was probably not the best response, however appealing it was at the moment. "We're supposed to cut the cake now," she said stupidly.

In a daze, she made her way back to the ballroom. How could she have been so stupid? Allowing herself to be hauled to the altar like some sacrificial cow. Sweet Julie, perfect Julie, always doing the right thing for her parents, for her family, for the business. So determined to never make a fuss that she had refused to acknowledge the truth about her husband-to-be.

Barely conscious of her actions, she pushed open the door to the ballroom of the Winston hotel, the crown jewel in the

D&D luxury hotel empire. Her father, Grant Driscoll, and Brian's father, David Dennison, had acquired the property just two years ago. Within a year, it was giving the Fairmont a run for its money as *the* luxury hotel in San Francisco.

But she didn't even see the beautifully redecorated ballroom with its elaborate chandeliers and silk wall coverings that conveyed an atmosphere of old-fashioned elegance and luxury. She didn't care about the tens of thousands of dollars worth of white roses that adorned each of the seventy tables that had been set to accommodate the wedding guests. She didn't even care when she stumbled into a waiter and a glass of merlot splashed down the skirt of her custom-made Vera Wang wedding gown.

She moved through the crowd, seeing nothing but blurry flesh-colored shapes of guests as they tried to catch her hands, to kiss her cheeks and offer congratulations. Ignoring everyone, she made her way to the dais at the front of the room currently occupied by the band.

As she reached the first step, she felt a firm grip on her arm. She didn't even acknowledge Wendy as she shook off her grip.

Signaling the band to stop, she grasped the microphone and lowered it until it was at mouth level. It was then that she realized she was shaking. Not just a little tremble of the hand, but a full-body quake. She stared out into a crowd that represented a who's who of San Francisco society. Out of the corner of her eye she saw the mayor hitting on one of her cousins. Her father's business partners, city councilmembers, and wealthy financiers and their spouses stared at her expectantly.

Julie licked her lips and grasped the microphone. Her knuckles were white as she clenched the microphone in a death grip. Glancing to her right, her stomach clenched as two waiters wheeled out the five-tier chocolate raspberry with vanilla fondant icing wedding cake, and positioned it next to her.

"Can I have everyone's attention please?"

The request was totally unnecessary—everyone was staring at her in slack-jawed astonishment.

"I appreciate that you have come here to celebrate what was supposed to be the most special day of my life." A vague, outer-body sensation overtook her, enabling her to see herself as though from across the room. What would the little psycho bride say next? "Unfortunately, my special day has been ruined by the fact that my husband"—she gestured to the back of the ballroom, where Brian fought his way through the throng—"decided that his wedding reception was a perfect place to screw his new assistant."

A chorus of gasps and murmurs rippled through the crowd, snapping everything into sudden, vivid focus. Mouths gaped, eyes bulged as people craned their necks to catch a glimpse of the errant groom.

"So, while I encourage you to continue to enjoy the festivities, I'm going to call it a night." She gathered up her full skirts and had barely made it to the edge of the stage when Brian finally reached her.

"Julie, I'm sorry, please, you have to listen." Brian had combed his hair and straightened his tuxedo, and was once again the epitome of perfectly polished masculinity. Grasping her arms so tightly she knew she'd have marks, he said in a pleading voice, "I'm a sex addict. It's an illness. I can't help myself, Jules—"

She wrenched out of his grip, and a surge of rage violently snapped her out of her state of shock. It was exactly the sort of excuse Brian would come up with—one absolving him of all personal responsibility, eliciting sympathy rather than blame. Suddenly, so furious she feared her head might burst into flame, she yelled, "An addict? For an addict you sure haven't had a problem keeping your hands off me!"

Brian walked toward her determinedly, and she backed away and tried to skirt around him. "Can you blame me for trying to avoid a permanent case of frostbite?" he muttered so only she could hear. But for the crowd he said, "How can you turn away from me when I need your support?"

Every eye was riveted to the drama playing out on stage.

"Get out of my way, Brian." She had to get out of that room, away from everyone and everything that had forced her into this public humiliation.

He moved again to grab her, and she instinctively reached behind her, her fingers coming into contact with the smooth surface of the cake. Turning slightly, she grabbed the surprisingly heavy top tier. Using every ounce of strength in her body, she ground it into Brian's shocked face.

"You might want to zip up your fly," she sneered.

She straightened her shoulders, and raised her chin haughtily, as she, Julianna Devereaux Driscoll, the perfectly poised princess of the D&D hotel empire, removed her wine-stained, cake-smeared, wholly enraged self from the ballroom.